# TUNNEL UNDER THREAT

## JONATHAN CREED

PAUL PUBLISHING LTD

First published in Great Britain in 2022
by Paul Publishing

1 3 5 7 9 11 12 10 8 6 4 2

Printed in UK by
Bell and Bain Ltd, Glasgow

ISBN (Paperback) 978-1-8383331-8-8
ISBN (Large Print) 978-1-8383331-9-5

# PAUL PUBLISHING

## *Author's introduction.*

Welcome to *Tunnel under Threat*, the third book in the series. The main plot was first written while living and working in Oxford in the nineteen eighties. It was a very long thriller and despite it being finished, it never was published at the time.

Now some forty years later, I have now taken the time to rewrite it to make it 'fit' with the previous two titles already published.

I would remind the reader that this is a work of fiction and any similarity to any business or person is entirely accidental. *Lindsay's and Co Ltd*, as before, have allowed their name to be used.

## Titles by Jonathan Creed

# CHARACTER LIST

## LICD or BOTGB

| | |
|---|---|
| Chief Superintendent | |
| Ruth Sanders | New Head of LICD after CS Rose |
| Bill Sutherland | Works for LICD Husband of Jane |
| Jane Sutherland | Works for LICD Wife of Bill |
| Martin Fitzroy | Works for LICD head of IT |
| CS Rose | Head of BOTGB/LICD |
| Simon Reed | |
| aka William Dawson | Government troubleshooter |
| Gail Rose | His office assistant. |
| | Daughter of CS Rose |

## Prime Minister

| | |
|---|---|
| Margaret Thatcher | PM during building of Tunnel |

## ARI

| | |
|---|---|
| Patrick O'Conner | Hotel owner and former ARI Cell leader |
| Michael Brady | Member of ARI and follower of Joe. |
| Pat Doyle | Member of ARI |
| Seamus Kelly | Member of ARI |
| Barry Ryan | Member of ARI |
| Michael Brady | Member of ARI |
| Lenny 'smoke' | Member of ARI |
| Lorcan O'Connor | Member of ARI |
| Patrick O'Reilly | Member of ARI on trial in London |
| Mr Green | Solicitor and works with ARI |
| Colleen Kent | |
| aka"Cats Eyes" | Thief and part time driver for ARI |

## Police

| | |
|---|---|
| DS Cooper | North Highland Police based in Golspie. |
| DC Rogers | Seconded to North Highland Police. |
| DCI James Rogers | Thames Valley Police (Marlow) |
| DCI Andrews | Folkestone Police |
| PC James Black | Folkestone Crime Prevention |
| DI Rogers | Oxford CID |
| PC Cameron Gray | Oxford Police |
| | (Son of DI Gray in Golspie) |
| DI Geroge Armstrong | Exeter CID |

## *Eurotunnel characters.*

| | |
|---|---|
| Joe O'Brien | Unemployed Worker from Belfast |
| Sarah O'Brien | His wife |
| Sam Brooks | Site Manager |
| Sean Smith | Head of Personnel |
| Charles Meadows | Deputy of Personnel |
| Mary Orchard | Secretary to Sean and Charles |
| Thomas Swift | ID engraver |
| Martin Andrews | Joe's immediate boss. |
| Justin Cassy | Fuel attendant |
| Kenneth Brown | Lorry driver and manufacturer of new drug. |

## *Russians*

| | |
|---|---|
| Ivan | Russian businessman |
| Boris | Ivan's henchman and go to person. |

## *Others*

| | |
|---|---|
| Ian Mackenzie | Bomb disposal |
| Judith Mackenzie | His wife |


## ABBREVIATIONS

| | |
|---|---|
| **BOTOG** | Boot Out Terrorists from Great Britain |
| **LICD** | London International Crime Department |
| **ARI** | Armed Ready for Insurrection |
| **YEO** | Your Eyes Only |
| **TUT** | Tunnel Under Threat |

# *Prologue*

## LICD Headquarters, London

The new head of the London and International Crime Department (LICD) looked around the room. Most of her senior staff sat at the oval desk and she observed that they were all men. Well, that would have to change soon.

Chief Superintendent Ruth Sanders had risen to the current post the hard way and knew that a lot was expected of her recent appointment. A large file sat opened in front of her. It contained a review of two cases that had been solved by Bill and Jane Sutherland. She glanced at her notes, not really needing to, as she already had rehearsed what she was about to say.

"Gentlemen, if I can have your attention, please?" The low conversation that had been going on, stopped at once. "Thank you. I know that some of you will be shaken and disappointed by my appointment. I want to work with all of you, however, there will have to be some changes." A hand went up. "Yes Simon?"

"Are these changes to be limited to London or on an International wide basis?" She smiled inwardly. Trust it to be Simon to raise the international question. He had been considered to take charge of the International side of things, but that decision had been delayed following the deaths of Harvey Brown and his wife.

"For the time being, they are going to be limited to London. There is to be a full investigation around the deaths of both Harvey and his wife but until that is concluded, things will probably stay as they are."

Ruth paused and took a sip of water from the glass in front of her. "There is one matter that needs to be addressed quickly. I am talking about a replacement, on a temporary basis to start with, to cover Harvey's workload.

I have a couple of names in mind but am open to suggestions as well. Anybody at all?" She looked around the room but as she had thought, nobody would put their hand into the air. Ruth was too new for them to know much about her yet. "Well then, I would like to propose either Bill or Jane Sutherland. Does any-body have any objections?" A silence greeted her, then a hand was raised. "Yes?"

"Either of them would be good, on a temporary basis. They usually work as a team though and that might cause a bit of friction if one was promoted over the other one. Just saying, that's all."

"Good point. I'll bear that in mind."

Simon raised his hand somewhat hesitantly. "How long will the post be temporary?"

"Until the investigation into Harvey and his wife has concluded. I take it that there are no objections to them being considered then?"

"Not from me." said the lone voice at the other end of the table. "We need to have young blood at the top and they have helped solve two recent cases. I would suggest that you get a small team of two others and yourself to look into the background of both and then take the decision." Ruth smiled and nodded her approval.

"Let's have a show of hands for that suggestion, shall we?"All the hands except Simon's went up. "Then the meeting is finished. Simon, a word please." Ruth rose and, picking up her file and water, walked out of the meeting room towards her office. Simon reluctantly followed her out.

# *Chapter 1*

London, Golspie, Belfast, Dornoch.

Unaware of what was being discussed, Bill and Jane sat in sunshine overlooking the Thames sipping hot drinks that they had just bought from the van that parked outside LICD each day. The sun sparkled on the water as small boats made their way up and down the mighty river. Jane tapped Bill on the arm.

"Take a look at the boat over there, the red one moored near to HMS Belfast. It looks like the boat…"

"…Bragging Rights. Here, let me go and get a set of binoculars from the office." Bill handed his cup to Jane and walked quickly back to the office. A short while later he returned with a set of each of them. He put his to his eyes and scanned the boat's side. The name Bragging Rights stood out clearly. He put them down and took the two cups from Jane to let her see for herself. "Well, of all the places." said Jane with a smile.

"Not really that surprising, the boat was converted at Gravesend and the boatyard had to sell it to somebody else. Wonder who bought it."

"Probably some Yuppie or other. They would have loved that name." laughed Jane, putting down her glasses and reaching for her drink. "Peaceful after the last case, isn't it?"

"Be careful, isn't that what we both said just before the last case started?" said Bill with a smile. He finished his drink and crumpled the cup in his hand. Jane did the same and they both stood and went back into the office.

+

On the outskirts of Golspie, a hotel was in the final stages of a major refurbishment. Most of the main contractors had left leaving only the furniture removers. In the kitchen a chef and his small team were putting the various utensils into cupboards and under worktops. Standing just inside the main door a tall man looked on with a clipboard in his hand, ticking off the items as they came into the hotel. Two men, holding a large hand-carved oak cupboard, came slowly up the stairs and entered the hall. "Where do you want this?" The man consulted his clipboard.

"Ground floor, room opposite this one." He pointed with his hand, then moved across and held the door open for them to take it in.

"Thanks," came the comment as they manoeuvred it into place. They went out to the van to bring in the desk that was due to go into the same place.

Suddenly the phone rang on the reception desk. The man with the clipboard looked at it with a surprised look on his face. The phone hadn't been connected yet, at least that was what he had been told. Putting down his clipboard, he picked up the phone and spoke.

"Hello?"

"Hello Patrick. Now there is a voice I haven't heard for ages. How is the new hotel coming on? I understand you have gone into the accommodation business these days. I wonder if you might like to put one or two of the lads up for a few nights?" "Now look here Pat Doyle, I want nothing more to do with you or your type. I have moved on; things are very different now. How did you get this number anyhow?"

"Now, now, don't go losing your temper Patrick. You know, there are supporters of the cause all over the place. If only the UK Government knew where, then they would have kittens. I'll come up and see you sometime. I don't know when exactly, but it wouldn't hurt for you to be civil now would it?" Patrick took a deep breath

"Look Pat, things are very different now. I have moved on and run a business. A hotel business in Scotland."

"Yes, I know that, but why Scotland of all the places you could choose?"

"Business and it is a nice place to live."

"I'll take your word for that, until I see it for myself that is." The phone was put down and Patrick stood holding his phone, and then he replaced it and returned to telling the removal men where things were to go.

+

In Belfast, Pat Doyle replaced the phone and looked at his group of men that had gathered in the disused warehouse. "Well?" said Seamus "Did he agree to what you proposed? We need to fly out tonight if he did."

"No Seamus, he did not. He said he wants nothing more to do with us. We can't have that now, can we?" The men growled their disappointment at the news.

"Look Pat, that is well and good, but we need to get out of the province right now or next thing we know, we could all be arrested." said Barry with a look that could kill if the long crowbar in his hand hadn't already that is.

"I hear you, Barry. Normally I would come with you but I have a boat to unload. I'll let you have some cash. I suggest you think about leaving, in the short term anyway. I may take a journey to speak to Patrick. Face to face he may not say no so easily. Stay in touch." Pat moved over to the office safe and opened it and removed a bundle of money. Quickly he divided it up into seven even bundles and put three back into the safe. The remaining four bundles he put into separate brown envelopes and stuck them down. Then he walked out to the group of men and placed the envelopes on the table nearby before returning to the small office. The men had seen this happen many times before. The amounts would probably be the same in each envelope, it was just luck as to who had which one. Silently they picked up the envelopes and left the warehouse one at a time. The last one to leave turned and looked across at the office, where Pat now stood outside with his arms folded.

"He came through before, why not now I wonder?"

"Who knows? I'll try and find out. Good luck." Then he pulled the doors to the warehouse shut behind him.

+

In Sutherland, late that night, Patrick looked tired but satisfied. The furniture had all been placed exactly where he wanted it. Now he was in the new bar helping himself to a soda water. Normally he would have chosen a whisky, but tonight he wanted a clear head.

He had moved on from the days that Pat Doyle had talked about. He was also concerned that the UK security forces could have arranged for his phone to be tapped. He finished his drink, locked up the hotel and drove off down the drive to his flat in Dornoch. Had he known it, he would have stayed at the hotel. On the Broch within the grounds of the hotel, a lone man stood. He held a shotgun, broken for carrying, loosely in his hands. He had seen Patrick lock up and leave the hotel. He wasn't too concerned as he had already found out where Patrick lived. Smiling he left the Broch and made his way towards his car parked by the track that led to the beach.

When he got back to his flat in Dornoch that night, Patrick made a few discreet phone calls to find out what Pat Doyle had really wanted. Now satisfied that he would be able to deal with things, he retired to bed.

The car swept into the square and parked in one of the spaces that lined it. The driver switched off the engine and waited as it cooled. Bending down, he felt under the seat for the small box that contained the gun he sometimes needed. Not being able to see the flat from the car, he got out and locked the vehicle. You couldn't be too careful he thought to himself. He crossed the road and walked through the cathedral churchyard, silent and quiet, though that may change soon he thought to himself. Turning to the left, he could see the flat and the lights had just been switched off.

Good, he had the element of surprise then. He moved to the metal gate and lifted the latch and pushed it open. Unlike earlier this morning, when it had squeaked loudly, it now moved silently. Stepping inside he reached down to the ground and picked up the small can of oil he had left earlier in the day. Quickly he stepped up the small path and up the staircase to the front door. Reaching into his pocket, he removed the copy of the front door key that he had got cut the day before. He had already tried it earlier when Patrick had been at his hotel. Inserting the key, he took the oil can and as the door opened, put a small amount on each hinge. Quickly he stepped inside and closed the door behind him and went slowly along the corridor. He could see a light coming from under the door at the end of the corridor. He felt in his pocket for the gun, took it out and smiling, walked slowly towards the door. It was times like this, that he really enjoyed his job. Should he knock or just open it he wondered? The light under the door went off. That decided it, he thought. He would wait for ten minutes, then surprise the sleeping, Patrick.

Ten minutes later, he heard snoring coming from the room. He reached out and turned the handle and flung open the door. Taking in the form in the bed, he fired in quick succession three shots and then closed the door and left the flat. He had done what he had been asked to do. What happened next was up to others.

# *Chapter 2*

Dornoch, Golspie.

Patrick had spent the night in the spare room. He had heard the footsteps in the hall, had quickly put a couple of pillows under the duvet and gone to the door. Snored a few times, then quickly got into the fitted wardrobe. He had heard the door open, and the three shots fired in quick succession.

After an hour, he had got out and smiled. He hadn't touched anything but went into the other room to sleep soundly. Now having dressed and eaten breakfast he was walking towards the police station. He had decided to report the attempt on his life, if only to have the police looking for the person who had done this. Though, knowing the likely suspect who had arranged it, that person had probably already left the area. Quickly walking up the flight of steps to the police station, he pushed the door open and went inside.

An officer stood behind the desk and looked up as Patrick entered. "How can I help you sir?"

"I want to report an attempt on my life." "I see. When did this attempt happen sir?"

"Last night, after I had gone to bed. I heard the door being opened, hid and waited. Then the person fired three shots and left."

"And do you have any idea as to why or who this person might be sir?"

"No. But I haven't moved anything. The keys to the flat are here." Patrick handed a spare set over to the man. "You might like to have a look around and see if there any fingerprints or that sort of thing. Here is the address and my phone number. I have to go to work, sort it by tonight, will you?" Patrick turned and left the police station with a smile. The officer scratched his head, picked up the paper and keys and went through to his boss. This would be a waste of time he thought to himself, nobody attempted to murder anybody in Dornoch, least not as far as he knew.

+

DS Cooper parked his car in the car park of the building site. In front of him was the new hotel, not new, just refurbished to a high standard. Formerly it had been:The Grand East Sutherland Hotel, The East Sutherland Hotel and now this was to be its third incarnation. A quick look at the site board confirmed its new name.

*The New East Sutherland* Apparently so confident was the new owner, that the word hotel was not going to be put on the front. He smiled, people would always call it The Grand East Sutherland Hotel, whatever the name might be. He reached under the seat and took out the folder. Opening it, he read again the paperwork that he had received from the planning department. They had passed the plans long ago but had then spotted a new extension at the rear that hadn't been in the plans. Normally they would have gone direct to the owner, but they had history with this person. They had asked Cooper if he could join them in a site meeting. He looked at his watch; he was slightly early. He got out and locked the car. Then he walked slowly towards two portakabins that were situated near to the main building. As he got nearer to the door, he could hear raised voices coming from within. He stopped and listened.

"I need this site cleared, everything gone, by tomorrow at the latest, do you hear me?"

"You can shout all you like but the work isn't finished at the rear of the building as you added that after we had started. Why the rush anyhow?"

"Why the rush? We were supposed to be open two weeks ago. Can we clear the car park at least?"

"If I send my staff to clear the car park, then the extension will fall behind, so which do you want, the extension to fall behind or to have a clear car park for a hotel that is not open yet!" "Ok, go and finish the extension, but I warn you, no more delays."

"Fine." The door to the portakabin opened and a tall well-built man walked out, followed by Patrick who spotted Cooper right away.

"What do you want? I know you, don't I?" Cooper took his badge out of his pocket and flicked it open.

"DS Cooper, can I have a word inside please?"

"What about? Hang on, who is that arriving now?" The planning officer had arrived and was getting out of his car. He walked over to the office and smiled at Patrick.

"Planning officer Andrew Smith. Can I have a word?"

"He asked first," Patrick said pointing to DS Cooper. Cooper smiled at both of them.

"We are all together. Shall we look at the rear of this wonderful hotel? The views must be wonderful." Patrick groaned and looked at both men.

"Ok, how much is this going to cost me?"

"Let's take a look first, shall we?" said Andrew Smith. He turned towards the hotel and started to walk towards it. Sighing, Patrick looked at Cooper and started to follow the planning officer towards the back of the hotel.

An hour later the planning officer had left promising a letter and list of costs for the additional extension at the rear. Cooper was walking back to his car. Patrick stood in front of the hotel and looked thoughtfully at the policeman as he walked back to his car. It had been a pain, but they hadn't found the 'extra' places that he had arranged to have installed into the hotel at the same time as the other building works. He walked into the office and sat down at the desk. He knew that his site manager was right, a choice of a nice clear car park or finishing the extension. Well, that choice didn't apply anymore, at least not until the paperwork for the extension came through. He looked at his watch and decided that he would drive back to the flat for his lunch.

Half an hour later he pulled up outside the flat and went up the stairs to find the door wide open. Cautious now, he slowly stepped inside and made his way along the corridor.

"Anybody there?" he called out as he did so. But he didn't receive any reply. He peered around the door into the bedroom. Nobody there, he turned and walked through to the kitchen.

Nobody there either. Worried now, he moved towards his office. Pushing open the door slowly, he found a man seated at his desk. "Who the hell are you and what are you doing here?"

"DC Rodgers." He held his badge up for Patrick to see. "I am on secondment to the North Highland Police force. They told me you reported an attempt on your life. I was asked to investigate it. Interesting that you had no idea as to who it might be yet took a phone call from Northern Ireland a few days earlier." "How the hell do you know that?"

"Phone records, wonderful things, record all the calls to enable BT to charge you the right amount. All I needed to do was to ask for the records for this phone."

"So, what have you found out?"

"Phone number is Belfast. It will take BT a couple of hours to find out who the owner is. Then we can start to look at the man behind the attempt."

"But that is not who the man was."

"And just how do you know that Mr O'Conner? After you had said that you didn't see the person. You didn't see who it was did you?" He sat looking at Patrick with a pair of hard blue eyes. "No, no idea. Just wondered why you think it is connected to a phone call, a phone call that is apparently from Belfast. How quickly could one person get from Belfast to Dornoch in that time frame?"

"Phone call a few days ago, time enough to get from Belfast to Dornoch I would think. Or perhaps they asked somebody to come and do the work for them. I'd recommend that you change the lock. It is too easy to get copies cut. Go for a special type that only the keyholder can get copies from a reputable locksmith. You can ask at the police station, they'll give you a list of them. I'll catch up with you later, now I know where to find you." He rose from the chair and left the flat, leaving Patrick fuming inside.

Patrick went to the bank and asked for some change, to make a phone call to Belfast. He decided to walk down to the phone boxes by the Post Office and stepped inside. Patrick was about to dial the number when he stopped and replaced the phone. Now, the person who had arranged for his death probably thought him dead. Probably better that he didn't know that he was alive and ready for revenge.

Smiling broadly to himself, he stepped out of the phone box and made his way to the hotel on the corner of the square. Inside he ordered a coffee and sat and thought out what his next move might be. His own hotel was coming on nicely, ok the planning department was a pain, but apart from that, he was fine with how things were progressing. He wanted to get back at the man he knew was behind things, but also needed to keep his head and name clean. He was trying to stay on the right side of the law. Patrick didn't want anybody, and certainly not the police, taking an undue interest in his hotel or any of the other businesses he may have to run in the future.

Sighing, he took a piece of paper from his pocket and sketched a few words down, what he'd write to Pat Doyle when he got to the hotel. Meantime, another coffee wouldn't go amiss.

+

In Golspie police station, Cooper had just sat down at his desk when the phone rang. Sighing, he picked it up.

"DS Cooper."

"DC Rogers here sir. Just returned from looking into an attempted murder of a man in your neck of the woods. You might know him, Patrick O'Conner. BT have identified a phone call to Mr O'Conner from Northern Ireland a few days ago. I looked up his file before going to the flat. Very little to go on, but a mention of a possible connection to an attempt to destroy the Channel tunnel back in the day. I've asked the NI boys to see if they have anything on him as well. Just thought you should know, being as he is a new hotel owner on your patch, so to speak."

"Thanks Rogers, I'll write a small note to that effect. Keep me informed of any further developments will you?"

"Of course." Cooper replaced the phone thoughtfully. He flicked through the list of numbers on his personal phone book and smiled as he got to the 'L's. He dialled the number and waited for them to pick up the phone.

# *Chapter 3*

London same time.

Bill looked across at his wife as she replaced the phone and looked thoughtfully at him.

"That was Golspie police. DS Cooper, remember him?" "Yes. What does he want?"

"Patrick O'Conner, aka 'The Boss' lately new hotel owner." "And?"

"Attempt on his life, at his flat last night." "Is that right?"

"Seems to be. Left the keys with the police for them to look. A DC Rogers, on secondment to them, visited the flat, managed to find out that Patrick had received a phone call from Belfast and asked BT to find out who it is. Now Cooper wants to know if we have anything on O'Conner either official or unofficial."

"I'll need to ask Ruth, she has yet to appoint anybody to replace Harvey, so anything that he might have approved or know about, has to go through her first."

"Do you want me to come as well?"

"Not for now, start looking to see if there is anything about him on HOLMES first." He smiled at her and picked up his phone to arrange a meeting with Ruth.

Half an hour later, he was in her office seated opposite Ruth. He had heard that she had made her way to the top the hard way and didn't take fools kindly.

"Well, make it quick, I don't have all day."

"Does LICD have a file on a Mr Patrick O'Conner. Northern Irish, we believe. Currently working as a hotel owner in East Sutherland." He sat back and waited.

"Is it essential for an investigation that is ongoing?" She looked over the top of her glasses at him.

"Well, he says that he had an attempt on his life in East Sutherland. The police up there don't really want to have gangsters and such like roaming around killing people." He watched as she typed at her computer and then looked over the top of the screen at him.

"There is a file. However, it is only to be released on the authority of higher people than me. I think you had better fill in the request form asking for the file and its contents and pass that up through the usual chain of command. Give it to me, and I will get it passed to the right people. It takes time." She indicated that he could leave, and Bill rose, nodded at her and left, closing the door after him.

He quickly walked back to his desk and sat down at his computer terminal and looked up the file on Ruth. She had made her way up the ranks from the bottom. However, she tended to use people and investigations as stepping-stones to rise through the ranks. He closed the file down and walked over to Jane.

"Care for a coffee?" "You buying?"

"Yes, the nice stuff outside." She picked up her coat and reached around to switch off the computer.

"Ok, since there is no coffee shop outside, what gives?" "Ruth wants me to write up a report asking for the O'Conner file."

"So, what is wrong with that?"

"Nothing, I suppose, but I looked at her file it appears that she rises by using people and investigations. She wanted to know if this was linked to any ongoing investigation."

"We can't say it is, really, can we?" said Jane softly. "Nothing concrete, that we can use. Ok, so the North Highland Police are concerned, but until something happens, something that we can be called in about, I don't see that we can start to help them, do you?"

"Not really. Harvey would have said yes like a shot." "Remember though, Harvey is both dead and under investigation for corruption of a police officer." "Just don't want to be used, that's all."

Jane put her arm around his shoulder. "I understand that, really I do. Write up the report, hand it over to her and see what happens. She can't use it for her own ends if you put in the request formally." Bill smiled at her and laughed.

"No, I suppose she can't." He looked across the Thames and then turned to walk back up the stairs to their office.

+

Two hours later, the request was finished, and two copies had been printed as Jane had suggested when walking back from the car park. Bill neatly stapled one together and put a copy into an internal envelope addressed to Ruth while the other went into the drawer of his desk, which he then locked. Bill looked across at Jane.

"Just taking this to her office," he said. Then walked quickly over to the corner office, which looked out on two sides onto London and the other two, across the office. A secretary sat at a desk in her own little office and looked up as he approached.

"Yes?"

"Just this file for Ruth."

"I'll see that she gets it. Thank you." He turned and walked back to his desk. Well, he thought, he had done as she had recommended. Now all he had to do was wait.

Ruth leaned back in her chair and put her two hands together as though in prayer. She wanted to promote Jane, there were too few senior women officers in the force. However, the senior men would probably fight her decision. She thought back to the meeting she had and smiled as she thought of Simon and his bull in a china shop way. Switching on her computer, she quickly typed a short note that went to the top three people in LICD requesting that Bill be put on a six month trial period to replace Superintendent Parker, and then for Jane to have the next six month trial for the same post. After a year, LICD would review both and decide as to which would take the role.

The secretary knocked the door to Ruth's office and put her head around the door. She had an envelope in her hand.

"Request from DI W Sutherland for background on a Mr P O'Conner. It's marked for YEO." She put it on to the desk and left the room. Ruth stretched across the desk and took the envelope and opened it. Then leant back and read Bill's request.

# Chapter 4

## London, Marlow

Bill and Jane arrived early that morning planning to get down to the stack of paperwork they both had managed to acquire since their return from Sutherland. Bill looked down at his desk, where a white sealed envelope lay addressed to him. Curious, he sat down and slit it open. Inside was a single white piece of paper. He took it out and read it slowly.

*You will be shortly getting a promotion for six months, tread carefully during this period.*

He looked across his desk at Jane and passed it over to her.

"Found this on my desk. What do you make of it?" She took it from him and read it to herself. Then passed a piece of white paper across to him to read.

*You will be getting a promotion in six months. Tread carefully during this period.*

"It's the same note," Bill said in amazement.

"Not quite, yours says for six months, mine says in six months. See?" He compared the two of them side by side. He looked across the desk and smiled at Jane.

"Wonder when we will be told?"

"We have already it appears," Jane said. She looked up as Ruth Sanders entered their office. Bill unlocked his desk and put the two notes into the top drawer, then closed and locked it again just before she approached them.

"Bill a word in my office please." Turning, she walked towards her office. Jane tried not to smile as Bill walked behind her. Once inside the office, Ruth sat down, and Bill remained standing.

"Bill, I know you have had some successes for LICD in the last few years, which is great. Now with Harvey and his wife dead as well as the external inquiry into his dealings with known criminals, it is vital we appoint a new leader to replace him as soon as possible."

"Quite so."

"I would like you to take charge for six months. See how things go, see if you like that sort of responsibility. Any questions?"

"A couple that come to mind." "Go on."

"Any decisions I make, do I have to ask you to approve them? Also, what happens in six months' when the trial ends?" Bill stood and watched her carefully. Ruth leaned back in her chair. "Two very good questions. One, it's your department, your decisions. If you think something is too big for you to handle or need advice, then I can be consulted at any time. Two, in six months, we will look at the previous six months and decide then. In the meantime, your pay will increase to reflect the higher position, that is if you take it?" She leaned forward towards him. "LICD is in a very precarious position. If the external investigation finds anything that is currently not one hundred percent straight, then in all probability, LICD will be shut down. Do you understand me?"

"Yes. Perfectly clearly. I'll take the day to decide and get back to you as soon as I have made up my mind. It's a lot to think about. Thank you. Is there anything else?"

"Keep in contact with the police in East Sutherland; something is going on, but at present, I cannot say more than that. You can go now. Take the rest of the day off to think about things. Shut the door on the way out." She bent down and opened the drawer to the desk, indicating that the discussion was over for now.

+

Bill stood at his desk and let out a big sigh. Jane, the only other person in the office, looked across at him.

"I've to take a day off to think about a six-month promotion." "I see. And?" She folded her arms across her chest and looked up at him.

"We are to keep East Sutherland police in the loop, something big is brewing, but she hasn't told me what." Jane looked at her workload and took a file off the top and opened it.

"This looks interesting. Several people have been seen entering a workshop in Marlow, but the workshop is never open. Also, the rest of the units are all closed."

"Why is it on our watch?" asked Bill. Jane scanned the few pages and looked up.

"Apparently, the industrial unit they were seen at, is owned by the same people who also own units in Golspie and elsewhere. HOLMES had linked the two, hence the report. We could go and look, what do you think?"

"You know, we could do that, or I could go home and spend the day doing nothing at all, while knowing you are working hard here."

"But?"

"But Marlow sounds a better option, come on." He reached down and picked the file up off her desk and turned and started to walk out. Jane turned off her computer and having grabbed her coat, followed him out of the office.

In her office, Ruth had seen what had taken place, even though she hadn't heard anything. Smiling, she reached into her own desk and took out a small box which she opened and removed what lay inside. She held it in her hand and gazed at the vibrant yellow colour that it had. She read again the note that had come with it before replacing it. Reluctantly she phoned a number that she knew by heart and waited for the other person to pick up the phone.

"I've told Bill about the promotion trial that you suggested." "Did you put the file where they would find it?"

"Of course. Don't you think it is a bit risky, sending them down there?"

"Most of the stuff has been removed already. I doubt they will be quick enough to solve it. Have you shredded the ARI TUT file yet? It would be a disaster for them to get hold of a copy."

"Relax, all the files have been disposed of or shredded. They cannot connect anything to me or you. How about your loose ends?"

"I've got a couple of friends making sure that those loose ends are dealt with quietly and efficiently." The line went dead, and Ruth replaced her receiver in a thoughtful, but troubled manner.

+

Bill and Jane, having arrived a the car park, stood and wondered if they should take their own car or one of the pool cars. Bill looked across at her.

"Our own car, nobody has had time to tamper with it."

"Do you really think that anybody would?"

"Never know, remember the fire in the car park? Now get in." Jane did and Bill took the passenger seat as she started the engine.

"Right, Marlow here we come." Jane let out the clutch and the car roared out of the underground car park and into the sunshine.

+

An hour and half later, the car parked opposite the Industrial Estate, and both got out and looked around them. For a weekday, the place was surprisingly quiet. Ok, it was a bit far out from the centre, but nobody was about at all. None of the units looked open and the place had a disused air about it.

"Wonder where everybody is? Place is deserted."

"Let's find the right unit and take a look." suggested Jane. Reading the file that Bill had taken off her desk, he looked at her.

"Unit 12A." Jane quickly counted the units and laughed. "Thirteen units, so they call it 12A rather than 13, which otherwise would probably be unlettable." They walked towards the last unit and looked to see if there was a number on it anywhere. Not finding one, they moved on to the adjoining one and found it marked 'Unit 2'. Both looked at each other and ran towards the other end of the block. A black wooden door was positioned alongside the lattice steel shutter that was currently down and padlocked. Bill peered through the shutter to see a glass fronted office. Jane reached into her bag and took out a small, but powerful torch.

"Here, put this as close to the glass as you can get it." She passed him the torch and he could just make out the machinery of a printing firm. A written notice was stuck to the glass.'*This is Unit 12, go through the door on the right to get to Unit 12A above us.*" Bill turned off the torch and moved back from the shutter.

"In there is a notice telling people that it is next door." Jane moved to the smaller wooden door and tried the handle. It turned and the door opened noiselessly outwards. Looking puzzled at Bill, she moved forwards and looked inside. A long unlit corridor stretched in front of her with noticeboards all along one side. She looked at Bill, who shrugged his shoulders.

He found a half brick and wedged the door open, then both walked inside and down the corridor. At the far end, there were two doors. Trying both, one was locked and the other opened. Choosing the unlocked one, they walked up some stairs and turned left along another long corridor towards a door at the end.

"We must be over the other units, at the back of them." said Bill.

"I figured that out Bill."Reaching the door, Jane knocked on the door first, then with no answer, turned the handle and moved into the office with Bill following right behind her.

+

In the room, monitors were attached to the wall on the left, all were on and showed different views of the outside of the units and the two corridors they had just walked down.

A bank of machines was underneath the monitors, two switched off and one with a red light, indicating it was on. On the adjoining wall there was a row of two drawer filing cabinets with a mirror positioned above them. The wall opposite the monitors contained a large picture of the Thames at Marlow while the wall on the right of the door contained a row of clothes hooks. In the centre of the room a large partner desk sat and two swivel chairs, old editor style, one on each side.

What couldn't be missed though was the body hanging on the coat hooks, with the arms outstretched and two nails in each wrist holding the body in place. Both stood and said nothing at first, then they quickly backed out of the room and left the unit for the car park.

Once outside, they stood and looked at each other and took a big gulp of air. Bill looked at the row of units and then walked to the end where he reckoned the room had been. Only a wall was there. No windows, nothing to show what was upstairs. Jane was on her phone, calling LICD and waiting to be put through. Bill touched her arm and took the phone from her and switched it off.

"What are you doing? We need to report this, get a team here and…"

"…the first thing we will be asked is what are we doing down here? I am supposed to be on a day off. I know we would love to find out what is going on up there, but is it really linked to our case file? The fact that we had a tenuous link of the unit to one in Scotland has been broken with that scene upstairs. Somebody has beaten us to finding out what is going on. Let's close the door and leave it as we found it. What do you say?"

"Nice idea, but just stop a minute, we may be on video. There were cameras everywhere, at least that was what the monitors showed. Let's phone it in, after you have spoken to Ruth. Be realistic, you didn't really need a full day to think about it, did you?" She tugged at his arm and smiled.

"Suppose not." Sighing he tapped the number of Ruth's direct number and waited for her to pick it up.

"Ruth Sanders here, how can I help you, Bill?"

"I'll take the offer and we are at Marlow. Been a bit of a murder down here, a possible, if weak link to East Sutherland. Think we should see if we can learn anything of interest."

"Marlow you say?" "Yes, Marlow."

"If you get time, try the restaurant *The Meat and Two Veg*. I have heard good reports about it. Remember Bill, you have a lot of responsibility now you are a leader. Use it well. I'll contact the local police and fill them in for you then." She hung up and Bill turned to Jane.

"We can stay and find out what is what." His mobile phone rang, and Bill answered it. He listened for a few minutes then switched it off. "We are to stay put till a forensic team comes and make sure nobody else gets into Unit 12A."

"So let's lock it and wait." said Jane and walked towards the car to get a padlock from the boot.

Ever since they had discovered the unit in Golspie, they had been keeping a strong padlock and key in the car.

It wasn't too long before a series of police cars, followed by a white van swept into the Industrial Estate and came to a halt just in front of them. A policeman got out and reached inside the back seat to remove his headgear. Jane nudged Bill.

"Wonder how long before he goes away, once he knows LICD are here?"The man approached them both.

"DI Sutherland?" he asked looking at them both. "I'm DCI James Rogers. I am here to take charge, thanks for what you have found and done, but I'll take over from here on in." He started to move away and Bill coughed loudly, stopping him in his tracks.

"Maybe you haven't heard, we are from LICD. If you want to check this, then contact Ruth Sanders of LICD. I can give you her direct number." He watched the colour drain from the face of Rogers. "If you want to stay and assist, that will be fine with us, but we take priority. If LICD find nothing to connect this with any case of theirs, then we will of course hand it back to you. Ok?"

"Have no choice then do I. Better call you sir and you can call me James I suppose."

"We could do that, or you can just call me Bill and my wife here, Jane and we will call you James. Now let's allow the forensic team to do their stuff shall we?" Bill smiled and James smiled back at them both.

"That's me told I guess."As he finished speaking, a long black van swept up beside them. He nodded at it"our forensic team." After introductions, they all walked to the door to unit 12A and Jane unlocked the padlock. Then the team suitably dressed, started to carry out their painstaking work.

+

Six hours later Bill and Jane, now dressed in protective clothing and holding solid torches, returned to Unit 12A. This time they walked quickly down the corridors and instead of going up the stairs to the office, they walked through the now open, other door and down a flight of stairs to a large area underground, by the look of the rough cut walls.

The forensic team had broken the lock on the door and one person had checked the place out before they had been called in. A string of temporary lights was hung on hooks that stretched out across the rough cut roof. Large metal supports held long lengths of timber to support the roof and presumably, the car park above as well. The floor was concrete and had been polished to a glass like finish. Along one side of the room, which was about six metres by ten metres, were three desks of laboratory equipment, with flasks and pipes and electric cables running between the various bits of apparatus. Large cables for electricity ran the length of the room, ending in large red five pin plugs. Bill turned to James.

"Any chance we can get some proper lights on down here. They must have used a generator of some kind."

"A big one too, judging by the size of those plugs," added Jane. "Probably kept on a lorry round the back of the unit somewhere."

"I'll go and see then." replied James and left the two of them in the torchlit room.

"What do you think this was being used for Jane?" Bill watched as she went a bit nearer to the equipment that was before them. She took one of the flasks and held it closer to her torch.

"I don't think it was drugs, take a look at this flask." She held the flask towards Bill. "I've seen something like this before somewhere, can't think where though." Bill took the flask from her and held his own torch at it. Just then the string of lights came on, emitting a low, but far better light than the torches. Both sighed and switched their torches off. Now able to see more of the room's contents, a long counter ran at right angles to the desks of laboratory equipment and in a corner of the room there was a large oven. It's door closed. Bill moved over to the oven and removing his glove, he put his knuckle against the door and withdrew it quickly. He felt in his pocket for a new glove and put it back on. Jane had watched all of this and now laughed.

"Hot?"

"Very, which makes me wonder how, given the electrics were not on." He switched on his torch and peered around the back of the oven. "Ah!" he said in a satisfied voice.

"What?"

"A cable goes through a wall, to where I have no idea. Bet it is linked to one of the other units we saw. We need to find out the owners of all the units, see if any are in the same name as this one." James reappeared beside them and smiled.

"There is a generator at the back of the unit, under a tarp, cable neatly coiled up with the matching plug like the one we saw in here. Connected and switched on. I see we have light. Hello, what's that oven used for?"

"Good question. Don't touch it, it is very hot. We think it may be connected to one of the other units, as the other electric is connected to the generator." said Bill. Jane poked him in his side. "Look at the desks." Bill turned and saw lights had come on and a faint hum from somewhere started up. Liquid started to bubble in the flasks. Jane turned to James. "Go and switch the generator off. Until we know what this is, I think we should resort to our own means of lighting this place up." James nodded and ran up the stairs. A few minutes later the lights went out and the equipment stopped bubbling. Bill and Jane left the room and went back up into the daylight. Once outside they stood and looked again at the front of the building.

"You wouldn't think that from here such a place existed, would you?" said Bill.

"No, and yet nobody noticed the workmen digging it out?" "Probably all done at night. Place would be deserted by then, nobody to ask questions or the like."

"Suppose so. Wonder what it was for though. No sign of the usual things for drugs."

"We'll let the team find out and report back to us." said Bill with a shrug of his shoulders. Just then one of the forensic team came up to them.

"There is something you need to see; in the upstairs office I mean." He turned and led them back towards the unit and up to the office.

"You finished in here?" asked Jane.

"Totally. What we found are two files. They are on the desk, but they were in a locked safe, behind the wall of the cabinets." He turned and left them. Bill went over to the desk and sat down and opened the first file. Jane followed him and picked up the other one. Looking around She found another chair and sat down to read it. Silence descended as they read the first few pages and then looked at each other. Bill spoke first.

"If this is to be believed, it is going to cause a fair bit of disturbance across the various security departments. We will need to take these back and read them right through. What's in your file Jane?"

"Connections between LICD and the new rising Russian Mafia. Bit worrying really. I agree with you, we need to read these through. Bill, I think I have remembered where I saw what was in the flask. It looked like…" She stopped as Bill shook his head at her. James had come into the office and looked around.

"What did you think it looked like Jane?" he asked. "Something I may have seen in London. I will need to have a really good think." She replied with a smile. "Anything we can do for you?" Jane asked as she shut the file on her lap.

"Just to let you know we have sorted the lighting and turned off the apparatus downstairs. Haven't switched off the kiln yet, as we have still to find out where it is connected to. Trying to find who the other units belong to, so they can open them for us. In the meantime, one other bit of news. The body was killed somewhere else a few days ago apparently. Then it was brought here and nailed up. Whoever owns or runs this office, it was a warning to them."

"You don't think it was the person who ran this then?"

"No, if that had been the case, why bother to nail them up in the office? Any staff would have fled if they found their boss like that. No this is most likely one of his staff. A warning to him or her."

"Anything of interest in the filing cabinets?" asked Bill.

"Take a look. They seem to be full of invoices and other documents that any business would use in a day-to-day manner. If it's ok with you, I need to go back. Can you lock up the premises?" "Sure." said Jane with a smile. "Scribble directions to the police offices. I assume you want us to drop the keys off."

"Of course." James did so, then turned and left them. Bill stood up and went over to the filing cabinet and opened one at random. He took out a suspension file and opened it, then replaced it and took another one and did the same. Bill closed the drawer and looked at the row of cabinets and smiled grimly at them.

"What's the matter?" asked Jane.

"Very clever. Very clever indeed. All rubbish. Look at any file in any cabinet." She went and opened one and took out a file. Then opening the file, she read the first page and looked up at Bill.

"All about other businesses in different parts of the UK. So maybe there is a connection?"

"Look at the dates on the paperwork." She did and looked puzzled at him.

"Ok, it's a few years old."

"How many years exactly?" She looked down at the file again. "Fifty years, give or take a few."

"How many businesses do you know that keep records that long, in a regular office I mean."

"I get your point. We'll need to have this gone through in a really thorough fashion."

"What is interesting, is that the two files I pulled out had two different businesses on the paperwork, but as you say, we need to get this bagged up and taken back to LICD to really check it out. We'll seal the place up and leave a person to keep an eye on…"

Jane interrupted him. "Bill, the video recorders, they may have filmed the person bringing in the body."

"Ok, let's get the video tapes and paperwork bagged and sent to London." He glanced at his watch and groaned. "It's too late for a meal at the restaurant that Ruth recommended. How about we find somewhere on the way back and head home. We can make an early start in the morning." He looked across at the row of cabinets and turned back to Jane. "We need to get some more staff working on this with us. We could take James on board, working down here."

"Good thinking. I'll go and see how far the forensic team have got downstairs." She left the room and Bill looked down again at the file in front of him. He put it into an evidence bag and did the same with Jane's file. Then holding them tightly, Bill left the office to its secrets and past.

Downstairs the forensic team were packing up. The room had revealed no fingerprints, but as one of the team had remarked, in a laboratory everybody would have been wearing gloves. Jane arranged for the various equipment and the files to be taken to LICD overnight then went outside to wait for Bill. She kept an eye on the door to the unit, so was surprised when Bill appeared from around the back of the units.

"Thought you were still inside."

"No, think I may have figured out where the electric feed for the oven is." He led her over to the shutter in front of the printers. "Right, take a look with your torch at the wall of the printers." He watched as she shone her torch through the gaps and onto the wall.

"It's a nice North Highland Scottish calendar. So what?" "And the year on the calendar is?"

"Oh! 1985. Nobody keeps a calendar up that old. The year before, maybe, but not seven years old."

"I think it is a front for where the electric is taken from. We'll ask the electric board where the bills are sent to when we get back to the office." They turned off their torches and went back to the car and waited for the forensic team to finish up.

# *Chapter 5*

## London next day

Jane awoke with a start. Glancing to her left, she saw that Bill was already up. She glanced at the clock and groaned loudly, 4am. She wanted to go back to sleep. Getting out of bed, she grabbed a dressing gown and went through to the office they had created in the flat.

"Morning." he said brightly, aware she had come into the room. "Do you know what time it is?"

"Of course, I couldn't sleep, so came to see if I can find any connections between the files."

"Do you need me?" she asked yawning.

"Not if you are as tired as all that. Go back to bed." "If you are sure?"

"Positive. Now go back to bed before you get cold." Smiling, she bent forward and kissed the back of his neck before leaving the room. Bill bent forward and carried on reading.

+

Three hours later, Jane, now showered, dressed and having eaten, felt a whole lot better. The file that Bill had read was lying on the sideboard. He nodded his head towards it.

"Makes for interesting reading. The ARI and Russia are connected in ways that we never knew of. It keeps referring to an operation called TUT. I'll see if LICD have any info on that when we get in."

+

When they arrived at LICD that morning, Bill found a file on his desk with a YEO sticker on the front and a note in Ruth's handwriting.

*Only for you both to read, no notes and hand it back to me once you both have read it.*

Taking a paperknife, he slit the top of the envelope and took out a file marked PATRICK O'CONNER. He looked across at Jane and waved the file in the air at her.

"Looks like I have some serious reading to do. I'll be in one of the silence rooms. Fetch me if you need me for any reason." Once in the room, he removed the file and started to read it.

FOR LEVEL 5 AND ABOVE ON A YOUR EYES-ONLY BASIS ONCE READ, RETURN TO DEPARTMENT FILE

DO NOT TAKE NOTES OR PHOTOS.

Mark O'Conner aka Patrick O'Conner
aka 'The Boss'
Key Dates
1959 (Approx.) Born
1968 Saw father killed in revenge attack 1969
     Joined 'The Youth of Ireland' junior wing
     of ARI.
1980 We think he joined the main ARI 1980 August
     Killed first person, no proof though.
1984 Promoted to run a branch of ARI following
     death of its leader, (A suspicious death)
1984 In Autumn, ~~Believed to have~~ now
     known to have connections to Brighton
     Hotel Bombing. Known after as Patrick
     O'Conner.
1986 Wanted in connection with bombing of
     Europa Hotel.
1987 Leaves NI for Ireland and then we think
     to England.
1988 Vanishes off the radar. 1988-1990?
1990 First appears in Oxford in connection
     with drug supplies to students.
1990-1992?

 Born of a good family, kept his head down and
studied at school, then in 1968 saw his father
killed in front of him at his home. This made
him join the ARI and he quickly made a name for
himself as potential leader material.
 In 1980 following a brief training week in
the South, we think he became one of their
fastest runners and in time, a killer. Careful
always to clear up after any killing, we and
the Northern Irish police have never had any
evidence to hold him. The nearest we got to
anything tangible on him was that he might have
been seen with Patrick Ryan in Brighton the
night before the hotel blow up. After this, is
known as Patrick. In 1986 the Europa hotel was
attacked; people spoke of a man matching his
description going into the hotel ten minutes

before the bomb went off and five minutes before the radio warning was given.

He made an escape by crossing the border to Ireland and then by boat, but where to? He vanished off the radar for quite some time, but from late 1989 the drug supply in Oxford seemed to increase. It could be that he diversified. At that time a person called 'The Boss' kept coming up in conversations with known dealers around Oxford. The previous head of supply was found dead. We think, but are not sure, he likes to collect good antiques and paintings of renowned quality.

No idea as to his actual base, has no record, officially, in NI, England, Scotland or Wales.

European Connections:

It is thought he is known for connections to criminals In Europe.

A very rich, clever and thoughtful man, who is highly dangerous.

Anybody knowing anything about his movements during the gaps in the above is asked to contact ~~DCI Harvey Parker~~ at LICD. (Ruth Sanders)

Bill put the file down on the table and stood up and rubbed the back of his neck. Such a small amount of information.

Nothing at all about his Scottish ventures.

He picked up the file and, leaving the room, took it to Jane. "Slim pickings. We know a lot more than is in there. Take a read of it, it will not take you that long." He watched as she went into the room he had just left.

+

Half an hour later, he looked up at Jane as she angrily tossed it onto his desk.

"That is not everything by a long shot. No mention of our last report with connections to Oxford and the drug scene then. No mention of Scotland. Somebody is hiding things about him. It smells and it smells bad Bill."

"I agree, it is not a complete file. Maybe though, we don't need to let anybody else know that for now, do we?"

"Suppose not. It appears that the files and lab equipment have arrived. They are all downstairs in the evidence room. They are a bit in the way and can arrange for them to be taken somewhere else?"

"Ok, let's take a look downstairs." He rose and they walked across the office, having first put the file into the top drawer of his desk and locked it.

+

Once they were down in the evidence room, they realised why the items from Marlow were in the way. The filing cabinets and all the benches and equipment had been transported to LICD. Sighing, Bill picked up a phone and dialled a number.

"Bill Sutherland here. I need a large room to put a lot of evidence in. The same size as the board room would be ideal." He put his hand over the mouthpiece and looked at Jane. "Trying to get a room for this, so we can then work undisturbed.

"Hello, yes I am still here. Room 531. Exactly what we need. Ok, thanks." He hung up and smiled.

"Room..."

"Thirty-one, level five. I heard your side of things. Now all we need is to get it all up there from down here."

"Ah." said Bill rubbing his chin. "I'd not thought of that. Still, the lifts will help."

"Lifts are out of action for today, servicing going on." said a voice from further in the room.

"Ok. Can we leave it here until tomorrow then?" said Bill exasperated.

"Suppose so, that is assuming a new load doesn't arrive today. But with the lifts out of action that is unlikely," said the lady in charge of the evidence room with a sniff.

+

Once back in the office, both Jane and Bill got a coffee and stood looking out of the windows overlooking the Thames snaking below them. Tower Bridge to their right had no raised bridge today. Jane turned to Bill.

"Do you think the file is smaller because of Harvey's connection, or is there somebody else in LICD that we need to find out about?"

"Probably both. We'll have to wait and see what turns up." He finished his coffee and tossed the empty cup into a nearby bin. "Come on, time to go back to work." Jane followed him back to their desks.

+

Ruth had watched them both go and read the file. She picked up the phone and dialled the number.

"Just an update. Both have read the file." "The full one? For goodness sake Ruth."

"No, not the full one, the basic single sheet one. Do you think I am a fool?"

"No of course not. Just want to make sure of the facts. So, who has the full file then, you?"

"No, I handed it to Harvey, he said he would get rid of it. When the house was emptied there was no sign of it, so presume he did as he said he would."

"That's good." He hung up and Ruth replaced her phone.

# *Chapter 6*

Golspie next day.

Patrick sat in his office in the New East Sutherland hotel writing a short note to Pat Doyle. Pat, needed to really understand that he had moved on from those days. Ok, he had run close to the wind sometimes since then, but he wanted to leave that sort of thing behind him and move on.

+

Outside the hotel, on the top of the nearby broch, a man stood with a pair of binoculars peering at the hotel front door. On the grass beside him lay a rifle. He waited patiently; he had been told that the man he thought he had killed might be still alive. Now he just wanted to be certain one way or another.

+

One of the last of the few builders still working on site, knocked on the open door of the office and peered around it.

"Sorry to bother you, one of my men has seen a man on the broch. Do you want him to see what he is up to?"

"No, I'll deal with it myself." Patrick rose and went to the window of the office, then as he was about to look out, the glass shattered above him. Ducking down quickly, Patrick moved out of the office and ran along the hall to the winding stairs, taking them two at a time. He reached the top floor and entered a new bedroom.

Patrick moved to the window and peered through it. On the top of the broch a man lay on the ground, holding binoculars and a shotgun. Patrick moved back from the window and stood thinking. Could it be the same person who had tried to kill him the other day? Whoever the person was, Patrick, needed him gone and quickly.

He retraced his steps down the staircase to the ground floor. This time he went through the kitchen and down into the basement, where some of the unofficial building work had taken place.

Three tunnels ran from under the hotel. One led to the beach, another, north towards Brora coming out below the lay-by. The last one, by far the longest, went south ending up near the farm just north of the castle. He opened the door to the one that went north and took one of the two guns that hung there. Then with a scowl on his face, Patrick started to walk down the tunnel.

+

Outside, the man carried on looking through the binoculars towards the window of the office. He could see the glass had broken, but not see if he had managed to hit the man. Now he swept the binoculars across the whole of the frontage of the hotel. If he was patient, then either he would see an ambulance turn up, or else somebody would come charging out the front door, all guns blazing, so to speak. He picked up the gun and checked he had reloaded it, before carefully placing it down on the grass beside him. He glanced up and down the road that ran alongside, but there was no traffic. He could wait.

+

Patrick was about half-way along the tunnel. He had reached the curve, where the door to the basement vanished from sight and the door out to the lay-by appeared some distance in front of him. Picking up the pace, he continued on his way.

Opposite the hotel, a van pulled into the lay-by and opened its side hatch. A good location for selling food he had found, especially since the building renovations had commenced. He pottered about getting the various items out for his customers, failing to notice the man with the gun lying on top of the Broch who was facing the hotel.

Patrick reached the doorway and unlocked it with the key that was hanging on a hook nearby, before replacing it. Then cautiously, in case anybody was in the lay-by, he pushed the door open and peered around. Good, nobody parked there to see him. He quickly stepped out and shut the door behind him. Glancing at his watch, he noticed it had been an hour since he had been shot at. Would the man still be waiting there, he thought to himself. He looked towards the broch and saw the back of the man lying looking at the hotel. Smiling he set off down through the gorse towards the assassin.

+

In the hotel, the builder had gone in search of Patrick to say that all the work was now finished. Not finding him, he put the set of keys he had been given on to the desk and made his way out of the front door. It was really bad luck that he was wearing similar clothes to Patrick and that he and Patrick were about the same height and build. On the broch, the man, seeing a person open the front door, picked up the rifle, peered down the sights and pulled the trigger. Without bothering to look back, he quickly started to move down the path to the track leading to the hotel grounds and its car park.

Patrick, his head bent down as he quickly picked up his pace, had not seen the man take aim and fire, but he heard the sound and looked up. The man was no longer there. Cursing, Patrick now ran down into the driveway to the hotel. A blue estate car shot down the road and out onto the main road. Patrick stepped back out of its way and looked on as a dust cloud rose from its back wheels. Realising he had just missed his opportunity, he turned and looked towards the hotel. For the first time, he could see that the front door was open, and a body was spread across the top two steps. Patrick ran to the front door. A quick check of the pulse made him realise that the man was dead. He stepped over the body and, careful not to touch anything, moved to the office and picked up the phone to call the police.

Ten minutes later, the police had arrived and had put tape around the area. Patrick had left the office and moved to the bar area, where DI Cooper was now standing opposite him, watching Patrick pour a drink from the bar.

"Are you sure you don't want one officer?"

"Quite sure thank you. You say you have been shot at, yet it is not you that is lying dead on the steps is it? So, who is that man?" "The shooter? Sorry, but I don't have a clue. The man on the front steps is one of my builders. Look at the office to the left of the steps as you enter, the window is in pieces, that is where I was standing when he shot me, attempted to shoot me, the first time."

"And where exactly were you, when he shot your builder?" Cooper asked quietly. Patrick stopped for a minute. If he said he was outside, he would be asked how did he get there? If he said he was inside, how did he hear the shots? He looked at the policeman.

"Think I was at the rear of the hotel, clearing the last of building rubble out of the kitchen."

"I see, I just wanted to make sure everything is clear and correct, for the record, you understand?"

"Yes, yes, of course," Patrick nodded furiously.

"Then you will not mind if I take a look at the kitchen area, will you?"

"No, not at all." Patrick tried to recall if the door to the basement had been shut or left open, but the policeman had already started to walk in the right direction. Putting down his drink, Patrick followed him towards the kitchen. Once inside, he took a quick glance at the shelves that concealed the door. Nothing had been left open.

He turned back to Cooper and watched as the policeman made his way slowly around the steel worktops and out of the side door.

Once outside, Cooper turned to the right and saw at once the front door about five hundred yards from him. He went back inside and looked at Patrick.

"I can see how you would hear somebody cry out from in here if you were by this door. Please can you show me where you stood when the man was shot?"

"Well, as I don't know exactly when he was shot, as I said, I was probably out the back. Turn to the left and you will see the pile of rubble." Cooper did as he had been told. Sure enough a pile of rubble of wood, plaster cement and such like were piled up about four feet tall.

"Messy for you in the long term."

"Mm, I'll be moving it soon, just needed the kitchen clear ready for cleaning before we start to load the shelves and units." "Right then, I'll be off for now, don't leave Sutherland and do look after yourself and the hotel." Cooper left the kitchen and walked around the hotel outside. Forensics were starting to pack up, the leader moved over to Cooper.

"We know the gunman used a rifle, we are going to look at the broch next, could be he dropped things up there. The trajectory indicates that from the direction of where the gun was fired."

"Right, send me your report as soon as you can, eh?" Cooper turned and made his way over to his car and drove off towards Golspie. He would phone Bill or Jane and give them the update he thought to himself as he drove down the road.

+

Patrick stood in the kitchen and looked at the secret door behind the shelves to the tunnels. Lucky, he had closed it. He went over and locked it, just to make sure the hotel was secure. Then, he closed the kitchen door to the side of the hotel, before walking through the hotel, switching off lights as he did so. Reaching the front door, he paused and looked down at the steps where a rough chalk outline showed where the builder had died. A van nearby was being packed up. Conscious that he was exposed to any would-be killer, he pulled the door closed and locked it. Then Patrick went down the steps and over to his car.

+

In a new car park in Golspie, the blue car driver sat and got his breath back. Across the back seat, under a groundsheet, lay the shotgun. Now convinced that he done what was required of him, he got out of the car and walked back towards the Post Office where he had seen a phone box. He could call the person who had wanted Patrick killed from there.

Twenty minutes later, he replaced the phone and looked out across the road at the bowling green. Sometimes he wondered what sort of life he would have had if he hadn't taken the choices that he had earlier in his life. A lady tapped the glass and glared at him. Smiling, he pushed the door open and stepped out into the evening night. She stepped inside and closed the door after her. Walking back to his car, he replayed, in his head, the conversation that he had just had. Now it seemed that he had to drive to Folkestone for his next assignment.

# Chapter 7

## Moscow, Russia

The door to the office swung open and his new secretary put her head around the door.

"Sorry to disturb you sir. There is a message on my answer machine that I think you should hear." She held the door open as Ivan rose from his desk and walked over to her. Brushing past her without a word, he sat down and pushed the replay button on the machine.

"Ivan, this is a very old friend with a piece of advice. A business is opening in the north of Scotland. A nice hotel, a really nice hotel. Maybe, just maybe, you should take a holiday, hmm? You have made some enemies over here and it would be best if you, how to say this, disappeared for a while." The phone line went dead, and he pressed the delete button and looked anxiously across at his secretary.

"Get me the next flight to either Aberdeen or Inverness. It can be private or public but I must be on the next flight." He walked quickly out of the room and down the stairs to his car. Outside the driver was standing having a cigar, not expecting to see his boss for a while, so he was taken aback when he appeared. "Get in the car, I am going to the Dacha to pack." He got in the back and the driver flung the remains of his cigar over the wall and got in and drove off in the direction of the Dacha.

+

Two hours later Ivan had packed - well his staff had packed all he needed for a few weeks away. Ivan had left the Dacha behind him as his driver drove him the airport. He knew of only one hotel that fitted the description he had been given. He also guessed who was likely to be behind it too. His contacts had found out a lot about Patrick in the past but been unable to find anything as to the whereabouts of Ivan's previous secretary, who had just upped and left without a word.

+

In the woods that surrounded the Dacha two men rose from the open ditch and looked at the building in front of them. They said nothing to each other, as the plan had been discussed and rehearsed long before they had set out to carry out their orders. Now they approached the two entrances, one to each, and placed the sticks of explosive at the base of the doors. The man at the front pressed the doorbell and stepped back into the night. He pressed the remote-controlled detonator as the door opened. Seconds later the door at the rear exploded as well.

With both exits now well on fire, there was no escape for the few remaining staff in the building. After ten minutes his associate reappeared and together, they ran across the clearing and into the Dacha, which was now alight. With their flameproof clothing on and a small tank of air on their back, it was not a big problem to check the rooms and make sure that everyone had died. Now satisfied, they tossed a few hand grenades into some of the inner rooms that had yet to catch fire and ran from the building to the sounds of explosions ringing in their ears.

+

That night on Russian news, a report described how an accident with a frying pan and some spilt vodka had destroyed one of the best examples of a Dacha that had survived The Great Patriotic War. It was hoped that it would be rebuilt at some point. The two men looked at one another, laughed and drank some more vodka before switching off the television in the corner of the flat they were holed up in. One looked at his companion and smiled cruelly.

"Think it is time that Ivan is told what has happened to his precious Dacha?" The other man nodded his approval and picked up the telephone and pressed the button that would connect him.

+

The car swept up to the airport departure doors and came to a stop. In the back of the car, its phone was ringing. Ivan picked it up carefully, for as far as he was aware, only a very select few knew his car phone number.

"Hello? Who is this?"

"Ivan, we have heard some bad news. We have just learnt that a large Dacha has gone up in flames, something about a frying pan and vodka. I do hope it wasn't yours." The voice stopped and the phone went dead. Ivan looked at it and replaced the phone in its cradle. He got out of the car and took the suitcase from his driver.

"Everything alright sir?" the driver asked nervously. With his boss, anything could cause him to lash out with his tongue, or worse, his fist.

"Not really sure, check the Dacha on your way back to the office, will you?" Then he turned and walked into the airport terminal building. The driver sighed, he knew that going to the Dacha was not on his way back to the office, but he would do as he had been asked. He got in and started the engine.

Two hours later he pulled up in the dark woods and put the headlights on full. The burnt out remains of the building were picked out in the beam of the headlights. Leaving the engine on, he got out and walked carefully over to where the front door had been. Bending down, he took a plastic bag out of his coat pocket and swept some of the residue into it. Then did the same at a few points around the building. He turned back to the car and got in and drove off towards, not the office, but a set of laboratories that his boss funded generously.

Regardless of the time of day, he knew would get the answers to the questions he had. They would tell him what substance had been used to start the fire. It certainly was not a frying pan and vodka, he thought to himself with a grim look on his face as he drove.

+

On the plane Ivan sat and read the magazine that had been put on his seat. After a quick scan through it, he put it on the adjoining seat and, having already put his seat belt on, put his head back and closed his eyes. He had every confidence in his employees and was sure that it would not be his Dacha that had gone up in smoke.

He had asked his secretary to book a room at the hotel in Scotland. When asked which one, he had told her to find out. It was a new one, how many did she think there were that would have just opened in the north of Scotland?

+

Four hours later the plane touched down at Heathrow airport and after half an hour the few people on board had left the plane. Ivan was the last person to get off it. Once in the airport, he quickly made his way to the gate for the next flight to Aberdeen.

He had been told on the flight that he had twenty minutes to get to the right gate or he faced a seven hour wait for the next flight. Getting to the gate eventually, Ivan found he was the last one to board the flight. Smiling at the attendant, he found his seat and sat down next to a man with a briefcase stowed under the seat in front of him. The attendant went through the preflight checks and announcements, as the plane taxied out onto the runway.

# Chapter 8

## Golspie, St Petersburg.

Patrick drove his car quickly into the car park in front of the hotel. He had overslept and now it was nearly midday. All signs of the builder's materials and vans had now gone. The only remaining vehicles and workforce on site were busy laying tarmac in front of the main doors. A sloping ramp wound down to the car park. Disabled access. Not a requirement, but it had helped the planning to go through.

Patrick got out of the car leaving the car keys in the ignition. He walked over to the men working on the tarmac. He informed them that they could move his car when they got to that part of the car park. He went to the front door and let himself in. The chalk outline had been washed away with the rain overnight.

He entered and switched on the lights which illuminated the hall and the staircase at the end. Pleased with the overall effect he walked down the building switching on lights and making slight changes to the bits of furniture here and there. He reached the kitchen and was surprised to see the other door, to the outside, wide open.

Cautiously he moved forward and looked left and right, then moved across to the open door. He peered round it and came face to face with Ivan.

"What are you doing here? Don't say you were passing by. More to the point, who are you and what do you want? We are not open yet."The Russian laughed and put out his cigar. Then he slowly ticked off his fingers one by one.

"I am here to see this wonderful hotel. No, I was not passing by. I am a," he paused to think"a friend that you knew from way back. What do I want? A room of course. You will be opening soon though I think? Am I right? Oh, my name? Ivan, you can call me Ivan. I have a terrible memory." He leaned in close to Patrick. "Ivan the Terrible, hmm, what do you think to that?"

Patrick leaned back and looked at the Russian. "Do I know you? I think I recognise your voice."

"You may have heard about me before. So, are you open yet and can I have a room please?"

"We are not open yet but will be tomorrow. As you will have seen, the car park is still being finished. I'll get you a brochure and prices." Patrick left the man and went back inside to the office. Once he had picked up the leaflets he turned to be confronted by Ivan, who had followed him into the hotel.

"Very nice, very nice indeed. Any bookings yet?"

"No, not yet." Patrick watched nervously as the man calling himself Ivan, flicked through the brochure and price list.

"I'll take the rooms at the top of the hotel. Both." He slowly produced a bundle of notes and tossed it over to Patrick. "Take the bill out of that, then put the rest into your safe. I'll be staying for at least two weeks, maybe longer. If the money starts to run out, let me know." Ivan turned and walked up the stairway to the top floor and Patrick heard the door open and shut.

He sat down, not quite sure what to make of the last twenty minutes. At least he had his first paying customer. Patrick returned to the office and put the money into the safe. He would sort the paperwork later. He had a hotel to open and staff to greet.

+

In his room which overlooked the broch remains, Ivan had phoned his office. Despite the hour, somebody would be there. Eventually the phone was answered.

"Hello?"

"Where have you been? I expect this number to be answered as soon as it rings. Understand? Good. What is the position regarding my Dacha?"

"Not too good sir. The place has been burnt to the ground. The police had been informed."

"Fool! We don't need to involve the police at this stage." said Ivor with some anger in his voice.

"If you will let me finish sir. The Police were called by somebody else. They didn't hear it from this office." His secretary paused and wondered what he would want her to do now that she knew.

"Ok, so keep the police sweet and they can find out who did this. When you do find out, phone me on this number day or night. I'll come and," he paused,"talk to them in the lower office." He hung up and went through to the large en-suite and had a shower to try and clear his head and make sense of what was really going on.

+

In a flat on the outskirts of St Petersburg two men sat drinking vodka. They had done as requested, namely burn the Dacha and tell the police. The payment had already been transferred to their Swiss bank account and now they were enjoying some relaxing before their next job. A phone rang in the flat and they both looked at one another. As far as they were aware, nobody knew they were even in Russia. Their normal base was the Netherlands.

If they needed help, they could ask for two people they knew in Oxford that ran an antique shop.

"Don't answer that." "Why not?"

"Nobody is supposed to know where we are. So just don't answer it." He stood up and finishing his glass of vodka took the glass to the sink to wash it. The phone kept ringing. The other man looked at it and then at his associate.

"Just pick it up and say nothing then." Suiting the action to the word, he picked it up and held the receiver slightly away from his ear. The other man walked over to listen as well.

"I know where you are holed up. I have another job for you. Here is the offer, four men and double your usual rate if they are killed without the police knowing how. They are based in the UK. Phone this number if you want the job by 9.00am tomorrow. Oh, don't think I don't know what you did in Moscow, any double cross and the authorities will hear of just who was responsible for that fire. No deaths reported though, strange that, don't you think?" Then the phone went dead as the caller hung up. The two men looked at one another and said nothing. They swiftly gathered their few belongings together and cleaned up the flat. Within the hour they had settled the bill and were driving towards the airport in the hired car.

Later that night a fire took hold in a first floor flat in St Petersburg. Two bodies were found in one of the flats, of Dutch origin, if the police were to be believed.

# Chapter 9

## LICD Headquarters, London

Bill picked his way through the many items that filled room 531. As arranged, all the items from Marlow Unit 12A had been transferred and now resided in the largest office at the top of the building. It had been arranged in the same manner as they had found it in the Unit. Tape on the floor marked out where walls, doors and the like would have been sited. He moved to the filing cabinets that had lined one of the walls of the upstairs office. Pulling open one of the drawers he found it empty. He moved to another cabinet and did the same thing. It too was empty. He tried all the drawers; all were empty of the paperwork. Bill sat down on the desk and looked across the room as Jane walked in.

"The paperwork has gone. The stuff in the drawers I mean. All gone."

"What, the stuff that was years old? All of it?" "All of it."

"Have you asked the forensic department if they have kept it for some tests?"

"No, not yet. I'll go and do that and ask if they have kept anything else back." He left the room and Jane went and pulled a few of the drawers open, empty as Bill had described. She looked at the room and went over to the rack of video recorders and pressed a few to eject any tapes. Nothing came out. So the tapes had gone as well, she thought to herself as she waited for Bill to return.

+

In the underground car park, a man in a smart suit was on the phone.

"I've taken the files and video tapes."

"I hope you stored them safely somewhere?" "Yes, I stored them…"

"…don't tell me. If LICD can't get them, that is all I need to know. I'll be in touch when I next need your services."

"You did say, this was the last time I needed to help you. It's getting harder and riskier to do the sort of things you want. Security has been stepped up."

"Just remind me, how much you owe the casino? Did I say that this was the last time? Well, I hate to disappoint you, but that is not going to be the case." He hung up and the phone line went dead. The man in the suit cursed loudly and then walked slowly back to his desk.

+

Bill approached Ruth's office and looked at her secretary. "Is she in?" He nodded at the office door.

"No, gone to Oxford. I'll just check her diary." She flicked a large black diary on the desk and then looked up at Bill. "Due back around three this afternoon. Has a meeting in Oxford regarding a new drug that is being handed around the students?" Bill looked down at her.

"Did she say or leave anything for me?"

"Afraid not sir. Do you want to make an appointment? She will be in all day tomorrow morning. She is meeting the DCC between 10 and 11 but is free all the rest of the morning. Shall I put you down for 9.00am?" She looked at Bill enquiringly.

"Make it 8.00am if she is in then." The secretary flicked the pages forward and carefully wrote Bill at 8.00am for the following day. "Thank you." He turned and left, making his way down to the forensic department.

He pushed the door open, as a man brushed past him clutching some files. Bill made his way into the office and sat down at an empty desk. He waited patiently as the Head of Forensics finished talking on the phone. Replacing the receiver, she turned to Bill and nodded at him.

"Ten minutes I can give you. Outside, now." She picked up a file and led Bill up a flight of stairs at the opposite end of the office. They walked along the corridor and she pushed open the fire door and stepped out onto the metal platform at the top of the stairs.

Waving the file at Bill, she looked out across London's skyline. "We are supposed to be stopping terrorism and other criminals. I do wonder sometimes if we are helping them, rather than hindering them. Right, to business. The items you wanted brought back from Marlow. Well, there didn't seem any point in the filing cabinets being brought here, they were all empty when my team moved them to the room upstairs. We wondered why you would ask for empty cabinets to be moved from Marlow." She looked at Bill and he said nothing, he was stunned.

He knew that they had been full of files, well the drawers he had tried and opened had been. What was going on he wondered to himself. Then looked across at her.

"They had files in them at Marlow, I didn't check all the drawers, but the few I did open had files of businesses going back fifty years or so. There would be a lot of paperwork. How long did it take your team to take them out of Unit 12A and pack them and bring them here?" For the first time she looked a bit flustered.

"It's like this, we are working flat out with a small team, everyone wants our services at a moment's notice. We finished working in the office and moved to the lab down in the basement. I oversaw the work that was going on down there because with the flasks and their contents they needed to be handled very carefully. We don't know what is in them for now. So, I said that we could use a firm that we use from time to time. I showed them where the office was, told their leader I wanted all the contents taken out and transported up to LICD. As I say, we have used them in the past with no problems."

"How long was the office empty before they arrived?" "Twenty minutes tops. They are based in the industrial estate in Marlow. A quick phone call and they said they would leave at once." Bill tapped the top of his lip with a pencil and wondered how it would be possible for a firm to empty that number of drawers of their contents in that short a space of time.

"Ok, can you get me the address and contact number of this firm. Meanwhile I'll go and take another look at unit 12A." Bill turned and left her office and headed back to Jane.

Jane looked up as Bill walked in. He looked furious. She waited for him to compose himself and then spoke.

"No files downstairs then?"

"No, a firm that they use, packed everything up and drove here with it. Also, the office was left unlocked and unoccupied for twenty minutes. Not anywhere near enough time to empty all the filing cabinets before this firm came and took them away." He looked at Jane. "Come on, we are going back to Marlow. I want to check out the other units." Bill and Jane returned to their office, first to make a quick phone call arranging to be able to collect the keys to the other units as well as Unit 12A from the Police Station in Marlow.

In an office in LICD, hunched over a rack of machines the man with a suit sat. He had been listening intently on a set of headphones and writing down what was heard. Putting down his headphones, he picked up the phone and dialled an internal number.

"We are in danger of being discovered. Bill has found out that the cabinets didn't have the paperwork moved to LICD. They are going back there as we speak. We need to get the other units emptied asap.

+

In a room used as an office in Marlow, the phone rang, and a large thick set man picked it up.

"Yes?"

"Get the other units empty of anything that is not related to their businesses."

"And how long do we have to do that?"

"Hour and twenty minutes." The man in Marlow laughed at hearing that.

"You're joking right? It would take my team a week to clear the units, all of them that is. Why the rush?"

"LICD have worked out that the files in the cabinets didn't go from Marlow to London. Bill and Jane are driving down as we speak. I don't want them to find anything that would link Marlow to this office, understand?"

"Then leave this to us. We can soon make sure they don't have access to units 1-12." With that he hung up. In his office in Marlow, he sat for a few minutes, then picked up the phone and spoke to one of his men. "I want you to go and get twelve strong padlocks, all different. Then go and replace the ones on Units one to twelve on the industrial estate. Use the locksmith that we have used on the odd occasion, not our regular one. Oh, I need this done in the next forty minutes or I'll be after you."

He replaced the phone and smiled. Then he dialled a number in Europe to speak to the person who was really pulling the strings…

…In an office in Europe the phone rang but went unanswered.

+

Bill and Jane had got hold of some tools. Bill had insisted that they went prepared for anything. In the boot of the car a selection of various tools, bolt cutters and other bits and pieces were crammed into a box that filled most of the boot. On the back seat sat a scanner and a desktop computer and monitor as well as an external hard drive. It had taken them the best part of an hour to get the permissions and equipment before they had managed at last to set off towards Marlow.

# Chapter 10

Marlow two hours later.

Doing as they had been told, the two men had purchased strong padlocks and were now busy switching the existing padlocks on the first twelve units. They had just finished unit 12 as Bill and Jane drove into the industrial estate. The two men moved out of sight in the hope they would hear something.

Jane got out from the car, while Bill took a key that he had collected from Marlow Police, having been assured that they were all keyed alike for ease of gaining access. He moved across to Unit 13 and put the key in the padlock and smiled as it turned easily.

"Seems to be ok. The key opened the padlock with no bother at all."

Jane pushed past Bill and walked up the flight of stairs to the office. Once inside, she took a quick look around, but apart from the bloodstains on the wall and floor, the room was empty. Satisfied, she turned and followed Bill down to the underground room. Pushing open the door, he peered around the room and then closed the door.

"Nothing inside. So, units one to twelve are next." Jane turned and led the way up the stairs and out into the fresh air. Bill carefully relocked the padlock and moved down to the adjoining unit.

"Why start at unit 12 Bill?"

"If you had to move a load of rock and earth, would you cart it down to Unit 1. I think this may be worth a visit first. We can work back down to Unit 1." He put the key into the lock and tried to turn the key. "Funny, they said back at the Police Station that all the padlocks were keyed alike."

"Here give it to me." Jane took the key from Bill and tried to get it to turn in the padlock but also failed to do so. Bill left her and walked back to the car and moved it closer to the Unit.

From the boot of the car, he took out a portable angle grinder and moved up to the padlock.

"We'll soon be inside. Stand back." The tool spun into action and true to his word, a few minutes later the smell of hot metal and a broken padlock lay in two bits on the ground.

Jane took the metal grilled shutter and pushed it up out of the way. Behind it was a large glass door. Bill reached behind her and gave it a push. It opened slowly and noiselessly. Jane went back to the car and got out the torch that each team member was given. Flicking it on, she let the beam flash around the room. As she did so, Bill caught sight of a bank of light switches and flicked them on. Lights flickered on and lit up the whole unit. Jane moved across to one of the four desks and ran her gloved finger across the blotting pad. A line was clearly visible where her finger had been.

"Dusty." she remarked out loud. She looked around to see where Bill was. He had climbed up onto a raised area and was trying to move a hessian bag. "How did you get up there?" she asked in amusement.

"On the first desk, then put my foot on the piece of wood carefully sticking out." He pointed in the general direction, and she saw where he meant. She picked her way carefully across and climbed up alongside to join him. Wiping down her trousers, she looked at where Bill stood. Around thirty or so hessian bags were piled singly across the floor, but towards the walls they were piled in twos and threes. Jane reached into her pocket and took out a sharp knife. With a quick swipe the bag opened, and earth spilled onto the floor.

"Guess we now know where the soil was put." grinned Bill at her. Jane had bent down and was putting her arm into the bag and pulled out a small phial of clear liquid. Bill took an evidence bag from his jacket and held it open for her to drop the phial into. Once she had done that, he sealed the bag and they both let out a sigh. "How did you know where to look, Jane asked Bill with a frown.

"I reasoned the soil would be too heavy for just storing in such an unlikely place, most people would dump it just inside the door, not so far to go. But this team had to put sacks up on that raised area. I was suspicious, that was all. I think the phial will need to be analysed at Porton Down." They did a careful count of the number of sacks and then made their way back to ground level. They stood listening as the wind rattling the panes of glass set into the roof. They took a last look around and Bill smiled as he pointed to the calendar.

"No modern printing equipment. It is all very old, not new." He said as he wandered around the old dusty machinery. He came upon a roll top desk and pulled the roller up, revealing a neatly equipped desk. Notepaper, fountain pen, empty bottle of ink, dried up, and a few gummed envelopes. He reached in and took a piece of the notepaper and looked at the heading. Then he placed it in an evidence bag and walked over to join Jane, who was waiting at the door to the unit.

"What have you found?" having watched him bag the notepaper.

"Old notepaper. Headed notepaper at that." He indicated to Jane to switch out the light and drop the security screen. He looked at her and smiled. "We don't have a new padlock."

"Just leave it and phone the local police to come and put a new one on it," Jane suggested before walking to the car and putting the two evidence bags in the boot and locking it. "Unit 11 then?" She moved in front of it and tried the key, but as before nothing happened. "This is too much of a coincidence, don't you think Bill? Bill, are you listening to me?" He had his torch out and was peering through the screen. Nothing seemed to be in the unit, well nothing that he could see anyhow.

"Let's call them now. They can bring some new security and we can wait and access the units then." Suiting the action to the word, he took out his phone and pressed the right number.

+

The two men peered around the wall of Unit 12A to see the backs of both Bill and Jane standing outside Unit 11. Moving back out of sight, they walked along the side of the unit and around the back to the rear of Unit 11. Once there they found a small metal door that was shut but remained unlocked. Pulling the door open, both men entered and walked up the flight of rough wooden stairs that led to another mezzanine floor. Beneath them were hundreds of plastic sacks, most filled with either soil or rocks. Some had a coloured plastic tie around the neck of the sack, concealing much more unpleasant things in them. The pair of them lay down and found the small holes in the ply that they had previously made. Then they just waited to see what would unfold.

+

At the front of the units Bill and Jane just waited. After a few minutes a police van swept into the Industrial Estate and stopped just in front of them. A smiling James Rogers got out and walked up to the front of the unit.

"We'll soon have this open for you." he said taking a large pair of bolt cutters off a nearby constable. "What do you expect to find in here?" he asked as the cutters made short work of breaking the padlock.

"Not too sure, but the people who made the basement in Unit 12A must have put the soil somewhere nearby." reasoned Bill.

"You might be right. After you." James pushed the metal roller up and reached inside to put a light switch on, nothing happened. "I'll take a look around the back, see if the electric has been tampered with." Leaving Bill and Jane at the front, he disappeared around the back of the units. Jane flashed her torch around the room. Bags stretched across the floor, as far as she could see. Each bag had been tied with mostly white plastic ties, about one in ten had orange ties and a small select few, she counted six, had red ties. Suddenly the lights went on and she turned her torch off. Stepping inside, she could see that unlike the adjoining unit, this one didn't have an inner door. Small vans and cars could have reversed up and into the unit. Always assuming the bags of, whatever was in them, had not been there. Bill had walked across the top of the bags and was trying to open one with an orange plastic tie. He tried to lift it off the lower level of bags and couldn't shift it.

"Come and give us a hand." he called out to James, who was making his way slowly from the back to the front of the mass of bags. Like Bill he too was walking across the bags that covered the floor of the unit. Getting to Bill at last, he struggled to stay upright. The two men bent down, and both lifted the bag clear of the others, only to have to put it down again.

"That is some weight. Like a ton of rock." James remarked. The two men bent down and lifted it and moved it slowly across the sea of plastic bags. After about half an hour they reached Jane, who had been watching this with an amused face. "Right then, let's see just what is in this heavy bag." Suiting the action to the word, he cut the tie and the bag sprang open. Inside was, what appeared to be on first sight, a dust. The two policemen looked at one another and laughed.

Upstairs the other two men watched and said nothing. They were anxious to see if the Police did the same with the red ties. If they did, then the whole operation would be stopped. Ten minutes later the sound of the shutter being pulled down reverberated around the unit and both men in their hiding place breathed a sigh of relief.

# Chapter 11

## Golspie, Inverness and Marlow

Ivan sat on his bed wondering how he could get Patrick to help on his side of the drug distribution. He remembered Patrick from some years earlier, but it was obvious that Patrick had forgotten who Ivan was. Never one to let the grass grow under his feet, Ivan got up and grabbed his keys and walking cane that he had picked up at the airport and left the room. He had contacts in the ARI who would make Patrick see sense and join Ivan in his small scheme.

+

At Inverness airport, the flight from Belfast had just landed and a short slim man, was clearing security. Once Pat Doyle had gone through into the main concourse, he looked around to see where the lockers were. Seeing the sign indicating them, Pat made his way towards them and removed a key from his pocket. Locker 240E was the one he was looking for. Finding it, Pat looked around him to make sure nobody was nearby. Reaching inside, he found the two items he expected and a piece of paper with an address on. Quickly he read and memorised the address then screwed the paper up and pushed it into his pocket. The other two items he placed in the inside pockets of his jacket, which was resting between the handles of the small bag he had brought with him. He didn't plan on this being a long break.

He left the airport and made his way to the bus stop and waited for the express bus to Inverness to arrive.

+

In a suburb of Oxford two men pushed the door open to a shop with the sign above the door reading *Patrick Reily Jewellery*. As the bell sounded, Patrick looked up at the two men.

"Can I help you?" He wasn't too concerned, as all sorts of people visited his shop, some to have items to sell, others to have rings adjusted. It was when one of the two men turned the sign from open to closed and stood with his back to the door that Patrick started to worry.

"Patrick Reily?"

"Yes, that is me."

"We have a message to deliver." "And?"

"This is the end." Two shots in quick succession killed Patrick outright. The man bent down and tied up his shoelace, then nodded at the other man by the door before replacing the .22 revolver into his pocket and they both left, dropping the catch and being careful to wipe down the door handle before pulling it closed after them. One looked at the other and smiled cruelly.

"One down, now just the rest of them to find."

"So quick and quiet. No fuss, just a neat end tied up." said the other as they walked down to the car and got in to drive towards Wales and ferries to Ireland.

+

Pat Doyle got off the bus and made his way across to the railway station. He had seen it as the coach approached the bus station. Once on the platform he looked up at the screens showing the next trains leaving and arriving. He saw that the next train was due in five minutes. Pat walked to the booking office where a few people stood patiently waiting for their turn. He glanced at his watch impatiently. Finally, it was his turn.

"Return to Golspie. Going today, not too sure when I will return."

"One month return to Golspie, would that be alright?"

"Yes, that is fine. Please hurry I want to catch the next train." He watched the man process the ticket and tap in the amount. Seeing how much it was, Pat placed enough to cover it on his side and slid it over, the ticket coming to him at the same time. "Keep the change." He picked up the ticket and ran towards the platform. A guard was slamming doors closed and saw Pat approaching, so he held a door open, and Pat climbed on board. With a loud whistle the train moved slowly off towards the far north.

+

About three hours later the train approached Dunrobin Station and Pat pressed the button to stop the train. Alighting on to the small platform, he walked swiftly down to the road and looking both to his left and right, Pat saw that the hotel was about a mile away. He crossed over the road and walked along towards the hotel.

The sun was shining and there was a cool breeze blowing in from the North Sea. He had to admire Patrick and his new business as it was a grand looking place. He felt sure that he and Patrick could agree on the need for him to come back to Belfast. Or at the very least, a donation to the ARI would be welcome. He strode onwards towards his destination.

+

In the hotel, Patrick had watched anxiously as Ivan came down the ornate stairway and walked towards the front door. Without saying a word, the man flung open the door and left the hotel. The door slammed shut on the sprung hinge and Patrick gave a sigh of relief.

Now perhaps he could get on with the business of running a high-class hotel. Patrick bent down to carry on with doing the financial books.

Pat Doyle walked quickly up the three marble stairs and pushed the door open; he peered around the door and gave a shout.

"Anybody at home?" In the office Patrick gave a small shudder as he recognised that voice. Putting down the pen, he rose and went through to the reception desk. Standing in front of him was Pat Doyle.

"May your troubles be less, your blessings more, and nothing but happiness walk through your door. It's grand to see you, Patrick. How are you?"

"Pat Doyle what are you doing here?"

"Didn't I say I would look you up? I wanted to see the place for myself."

"Take a look around, only one suite is in use right now. The top floor. Go anywhere else you want to; I have bookwork to do." With that Patrick left Pat and returned to his office.

Whistling an Irish tune, Pat walked to the bar and poured himself a drink, then taking it with him, he set off to tour the hotel. He liked what he saw. Tastefully decorated and filled with good quality pieces of furniture Pat guessed that this would have set Patrick back a pound or two. He went outside and walked across to the broch and after climbing to the top, sat down on the grass and finished his drink. The location of the hotel was stunning, he would give him that, but why not help the ARI when he was asked? He stretched out and carefully placed the empty glass on the grass beside him before closing his eyes…

…Three hours later he awoke as the sun was going down and he quickly got up and walked back to the hotel. As he arrived at the door, a large man pushed him to one side and strode up the steps and into the hotel. Pat looked at the back of the man and followed him into the hotel.

+

In Marlow Bill and Jane had entered Unit 10 and this one seemed empty. A quick walk around didn't produce anything out of the ordinary, so the shutter was pulled down and they moved on to Unit 9. Once the padlock had been cut and the shutter pushed up, Bill and Jane stepped forward and pushed open the glass door that was situated behind the shutter. Bill moved back quickly, nearly knocking Jane over.

"Don't go in Jane. The stench is awful." Jane stepped back and one of the two policemen stepped up to the door and pushed it slightly with his foot. Like Bill, he stepped back smartly.

"He's right. There is something nasty in there. We'll phone for a forensics team to come down, they are better equipped than we are for dealing with anything that nasty." Bill nodded his approval and he and Jane stepped a bit away out of hearing and the smell.

"Bodies?" asked Jane with a shudder.

"I don't know, it didn't smell like that. We'll just have to wait and see."

"We could open up the remaining units while we wait?" "Good thinking." Bill walked over to the policemen and after a quick discussion, they moved to Unit 7 because given the proximity of Unit 8, they decided to leave that one alone. Inside the unit were large plastic containers. Most were empty with a sticker half removed. X… rd was all that remained. Some still seemed to have a bit of liquid still at the bottom. Jane moved to undo the lid, but one of the policemen touched her on the arm. "I wouldn't do that; you don't know what is in them. Best leave it to the experts." Jane looked across at Bill and he nodded. She stepped back and wandered through to the small kitchen and WC at the rear of the unit. She reached into her pocket and took out an evidence bag and carefully turned it inside out. Jane put her hand into it and picked up a small jar filled with blue tablets. Turning it back as it should be, the jar was now in the bag, without any fingerprints being added to those already there. She sealed the bag and wrote the place and time and date and returned to Bill. He noticed it at once and raised his eyebrows.

"What do you have there?"

"Found it in the kitchen. I have not touched it. Think we should get Porton Down to look?"

"Think that might be a good idea. The forensics team will be here in about an hour. We'll crack on with opening the other units then, shall we?"

After an hour, all the units had been opened apart from Unit 8. Units 1 to five had just been businesses, but it appeared as though they had just closed and no one returned. Orders were laying waiting to be processed in each of the five businesses. Jane looked at Bill as they came out of the last unit.

"Something not quite right. Why are all the units not in use? Those last five are as if their owners had just left. I mean orders that are waiting to be filled, lying there."

"Stop right there Jane. Something you said - orders waiting to be filled. Come on". He turned and went back into the unit. Jane shrugged her shoulders and followed Bill inside. He was waving an order form at her. "See this, take a look at the date." Bill passed it to her. Taking it from him, she moved under the lights and read the date. June 19th, 1988.

"But that is four years ago. So, this unit stopped doing whatever it did, four years ago?"

"Yes. But now look at the order, what it is for." Jane read on down to the order itself.

"Four hundred diamond (Industrial standard) cutter heads. For delivery by 12th November 1988. Payment in two parts. Half on acceptance of the order and half on delivery at **Eurotunnel Folkestone Works gate entrance 3**."

"Bill, does this order for diamonds mean that is the reason for all this?" She waved her hand at the units.

"Not diamonds, diamond cutter heads. Those sorts of diamonds are the ones used for cutting rocks and such like. Maybe that was what the rocks were for, testing them before delivery."

"Ok, I get that Bill, but how would you test the cutter head in a small, relatively small, unit like these?" Bill scratched the back of his head and then smiled and looked at Jane.

"Come with me." He ran across to Unit 12A and flung open the door and stepped inside. Then he opened the door to the basement. Switching on the lights over the stairs he looked to both side and grinned.

"What is it Bill?"

"Look at the sides, covered with plywood. Now why bother to do that on a roughly made staircase and in a basement that has been dug out after the building was put up. Come on, help me take this sheet of ply off here." He reached and tried to pull the sheet away from the side. Jane looked on bemused and then went back to the car and returned with a crowbar.

"That better?" she asked with a grin. He took it from her and prised it into the small crack at the bottom of the sheet of ply and it bowed then split into two pieces. He passed the crowbar back to Jane along with the smaller bit of ply. Jane looked at the wall he had exposed. It was cut in a circular manner. By now Bill had removed the other piece and they could see that it curved at the top and bottom. "They used a small machine to cut the stairwell out. That did two things, made it easy for them and tested the cutter heads. Genius," Jane said with a smile.

"Them or me?" asked Bill.

"Both of you. What gave you the idea?"

"Two things, the rocks in the bags, all very small and even. The cutters, where would you get something like that tested? The size of the Eurotunnel boring machines would have been huge. Far too large to bring here to test. They would have to test the cutters before they were fitted. Hence the rocks and the basement." He wiped the dust off his hands and went back outside. Jane stood looking at the wall, then went down to the basement and looked around her. This room appeared square, but she wondered if that was also cut out by machine. Then she turned and joined Bill outside.

+

In the bar of The New East Sutherland, Ivan sat nursing a vodka and across the table from him Pat Doyle sat holding a glass of whisky. He swished it around the glass and took a sip.

"Not bad, not as good as Irish, but not bad at all. How is the vodka?"

"Not bad." The two men both sat looking at their drinks. Having barged past Pat on the way in, Ivan had been told in no uncertain manner that people didn't do that to guests. Patrick had come and suggested they both have a drink and settle their differences over the table. Having done so, they now sat drinking and looking at each other. Both men didn't really want the other man to know what they were really doing in East Sutherland.

## Chapter 12

## Marlow, Belfast & Golspie

Bill and Jane had stayed overnight in Marlow. The initial findings from the forensics team were to be announced today. They sat at the rear of the briefing room and waited for DCI James Rogers to start the briefing. The noise died down as he entered the room.

"Right, pay attention everybody. The initial findings from the forensics department are as follows." He looked at the papers in his hand

"One, all the firms bar one, that had offices and businesses on that estate were either taken over or closed after a Russian business bought them all. The exception was a firm that made industrial cutters. They appear to have disappeared without trace."

"Two. The lab under Unit 12A is making a new and potentially very addictive drug. All we know now is that the base element is a weed found in Scotland somewhere, not a drug called weed, but some sort of weed plant. We need to find this and get samples to Porton Down asap. They, whoever they are, seemed to have made around a ton of this drug. At least that appears to be the case from the empty containers we have found." He took a sip of water from the glass in front of him.

"Three. The rocks found in bags were of the same type as was used to create the basement under Unit 12A."

"Four. Unit nine, the smell has been traced to certain bags as well as the drains. Apparently, there was an attempt to dispose of five or six bodies in the drain, but it then got blocked so they then used black bin bags. It also had been used in the past for storing the drug. Traces of it were found on the floor of the unit. Any questions so far?" He nodded as Bill raised a hand.

"Yes?"

"This weed, do we have a name for it or not?" Bill watched Rogers flick back through his notes.

"Yes. It is called sheepsbane - why, do you know where it is found?"

"Sutherland, mostly east Sutherland."

"Very helpful Bill." He turned his attention back to the whole room. "So, I want the unit split into three groups."

"Group one to look at the Russian connection, who is it, or who are they? Find out and get back to me."

"Group two to try and track the firm that made the industrial cutters.

"Group three to start trying to get a handle on this new drug, how long has it been in production? Have supplies hit the streets? Who knows about it and where did it originate from? Use our usual people out there. So, get out and sort it fast." He stepped down off the raised podium and walked to Bill and Jane.

"Ok, you are in charge, I get that. Can you do anything at the LICD end at the same time. Also see if there is anybody growing this," he paused to think, "Sheepsbane on an industrial scale and if so, whereabouts?"

"Do you have contacts in east Sutherland? Please can you use them?"

Jane nodded and looked at Bill hopefully.

"We have contacts within the east Sutherland police, so we will get in touch and keep you informed if we learn anything new." said Bill. Rogers nodded and left them so he could return to the others.

"Well, that is interesting. Notice there was no mention of either ARI or anything else Irish. Come on, we'll go back to LICD." Bill turned and left the office walking towards the main door of the police station. After a few minutes, Jane followed him out of the building.

+

Two men drove off the ferry at Rosslare and followed the signposts marked 'The North' and M11. Knowing they were heading to Belfast, they didn't need to stop and ask directions. They planned to stop on the other side of Dublin and go off the main roads to cross the border at a less well protected point. They had contacts that they had already spoken to and had a place to stay already arranged.

+

The following morning the two men were up early and on the A4 heading towards Belfast. The driver looked across at the other man.

"Do you have the address?"

"Sure. 1 Devon Road Belfast." Reaching into the glove compartment he removed a map and a .22 revolver and then checked to see if it was fully loaded. Smiling he looked at his companion. "Just get us there, I'll take care of Pat." He patted the gun with a smirk. They drove onwards.

An hour later the car pulled up in Devon Road and parked outside number 3. Looking up and down the road, the gunman got out and walked quickly to Number 1 and rang the doorbell. Inside the bell sounded through the house, but nobody was there to hear it. He pressed it again and looked up and down the road, but nobody was around. Swearing lightly under his breath, he used the gun to break the glass of the front door and reach in and turned the lock to let himself in. Once inside, he carefully avoided the broken glass and pulling on a pair of gloves moved further into the house. Ten minutes later he knew the house was empty. The only thing of interest that he had seen was a scribbled address in East Sutherland, a hotel, that Pat had written down on a pad of paper beside the phone in his office upstairs.

The gunman tore the paper with the address off the pad and retraced his steps down to the front door. He bent down and picked up the larger fragments of glass and dropped them in the rubbish bin in the street outside the house. Then he strolled back to the car and got in.

"Not in. Looks as though he may be in Scotland at a hotel called New East Sutherland."

"Nothing for it, but to go to the next one on the list. Who is it?" He watched as his associate removed the paper from inside his jacket pocket and looked at it.

"Seumas Kelly."

"Him? Ah well if you say so. The address is?"

"16 Sutherland Avenue. Just around the corner, isn't it?" "Walking distance, but we'll take the car anyhow." He pulled out and drove down the street and turned left at the bottom before taking a right and pulling up outside 16 Sutherland Avenue. "Give me the gun, I'll do it this time." He took the gun and got out of the car and walked quickly up the drive to the large bungalow that stood before him. As he did so, the front door opened, and he looked up as Seumas appeared in the doorway. He noticed that he had his head turned inwards as though he was talking to somebody inside. Taking quick aim, the gunman fired a single shot at the heart and saw the body collapse on the steps. He turned and walked quickly back to the car and got in. The car pulled away quickly, narrowly missing hitting a car coming down the opposite way.

In the bungalow Seumas started to move and rubbed his chest. Good job he had been wearing his protective body armour. Still hurt though. He went back inside and locked and bolted the door behind him. Then went through to the kitchen and took down a bottle of whiskey and a glass and poured a large one for himself. He took it through into his study and sat down at his desk to draw up a list of possible people that might have arranged this.

The car pulled up outside a phone box and the driver looked at his companion.

"Give the man a call, tell him that we have two dead, and one is in east Sutherland some hotel or other."

"Ok." He got out of the car and went and made the phone call. A few minutes later, back in the car, he looked at the driver. "We are to carry on as arranged, but to do it at night. Not so much chance of anybody being around to see us then apparently."

"Well, that is true, but it may be more difficult to park with people not at work and we may have to walk further to and from the targets." He glanced in his mirror and pulled out and drove to an address that they had been given as a safe house.

+

Seumas phoned Barry first to see if he was alive and in. He heard the phone ring and then it got picked up.

"Hello?"

"Barry, are you ok?" "Sure. Why do you ask?"

"Meet me, no get hold of the rest of the group and meet me in the usual place in an hour." He replaced the phone and went and got his gun and some ammunition. Then having loaded the gun and put the safety catch on, he left the house, but not before setting the alarm and cameras. He walked to the meeting place. He had a score to settle and to see if it was just him or were others being targeted as well?

+

Barry had phoned Pat Doyle and being unable to contact him, crossed him off the list in front of him and phoned Lorcan and Gray, both of whom were in and agreed to meet as arranged. As an afterthought he phoned Patrick O'Reilly in Oxford but got no response. Barry looked at his watch and frowned. The shop would be open now, it wasn't lunch time after all. He put a question mark beside Patrick and then left to go to the meeting place.

When he arrived Seumas, Lorcan and Gray were already there. "Well, Seumas, why the meeting? Something in the wind?" "No Barry, I was targeted today, fortunately I was wearing body

armour, hurt like hell but still here. I wanted to make sure that nobody else was being targeted. I tried to get hold of Pat Doyle but couldn't get a reply."

"I tried phoning Patrick O'Reilly in Oxford, yes I know that he isn't over here, just wondered. The shop would be open now, yet no answer to the phone. Couldn't get hold of Pat Doyle either. So potentially, we could have two dead and one attempt on you Seumas."

"Somebody out to kill the group then?" said Lorcan with a growl.

"Looks that way." said Seumas. "Who do we know that knows all our addresses and wants us out of the way?"

"Lots of people want us dead, but they wouldn't know all the addresses. Patrick O'Conner and the guy in Oxford we did a job for a few years ago." said Barry with a frown.

"Can't be Patrick, he is running a hotel up in Scotland, at least that is what Pat Doyle told me a couple of days ago. He said he didn't want anything more to do with us. Wanted to keep clean and not be linked to anything dodgy. Dodgy, I ask you, nothing we did was dodgy was it?" Gray smiled at the others and for the first time at the meeting they all laughed. Then Barry looked at them all.

"Think we had better make ourselves scarce, take a few days away from the houses. Go south for a few days maybe?" They nodded their agreement and the meeting broke up. All of them had bags for emergency stashed in different locations. All they had to do was get to them and leave Belfast.

+

In the New East Sutherland, Patrick put the phone down and lit a cigar, things were going along just fine. He walked out of the office and down to the bar. He had to get rid of the Russian first though. Pat Doyle, that was a bit of luck him coming here, though he would have to be careful. He wanted to remain as clean as the driven snow if he was to make the hotel a success. In the bar, Ivan was pouring himself a first vodka of the day. He looked up as Patrick entered the bar and took the vodka from him.

"Bar isn't open yet. We need to talk. Come with me, outside." He poured the vodka down the sink and turned and walked to the kitchen and out through the side door. Ivan looked on in amazement and then got up and followed Patrick outside.

"So, what is it you want to talk about?" he asked Patrick.

"I don't want you staying here. You can pack your bags and go and find somewhere else. I remember where I met you before and know what you want, a base in the north Highlands to distribute your drugs from. Well, I don't want anything to do with you or that kind of business. Understand?" He bent down and picked something from the ground in front of him. He rose and brandished the piece of metal bar in the face of the Russian. Ivan smiled and took the bar and bent it in a U in front of Patrick. He poked him in the stomach.

"Now you listen to me. I hear what you say but, and it is a big one, I have enough information on your background that would get you locked up for years. Information that has cost me a lot of money and time to find out. Ok, I would leave the hotel, but could cause you a lot of trouble, planning etc. I doubt you have planning for all the 'changes' that you have made. Well, have you? Thought not. Listen, I know that you think I am not the right sort of customer for your new business. I can slip into the background; you wouldn't know that I was even there. All I want is for you to hold some," he paused, "stock for me for a short while, not to sell, not to distribute, just to hold. I would pay you well. You could use my Dacha from time to time, well you could once the improvements are made. Come on, what do you say to that?" He looked at Patrick and smiled. Patrick knew that if such a file existed, then the Russian was probably right.

"Alright, I hear what you are saying. First though, I want to see some evidence of this file that you say you have before I decide. In the next two days. If you can't produce it, then you leave and have nothing to do with me, fair enough?"

"Ok, I hear you. Now let me have a vodka before hours and I'll arrange for you to get sight of some of the file. Will that satisfy you?" He looked at Patrick and smiled at him. Patrick nodded in agreement, and they went back into the hotel.

# Chapter 13

## LICD Headquarters,London

Jane sat back in her chair and sighed. For all the computers and information at their fingertips LICD didn't seem to have a large file on Patrick O'Conner. Bill had said to concentrate on him as he was based in East Sutherland and that was where Sheepsbane came from so was bound to be involved somehow. Bill entered the office with a coffee in each hand. He placed one on her desk and sat down opposite her at his desk.

"Got anywhere?" he asked, before taking a sip of coffee. "Too hot." He put it down and switched on his computer.

"Nowhere fast. I am really surprised that LICD or the Met don't have much on Patrick. We know the connections between him, and Amsterdam exist. It's as though somebody in LICD has been and deleted most of the information that we need off the records."

"You know, you might have thought of something Jane. Where is that folder on the link between Russian Mafia and LICD? We read it at Marlow, now what's happened to it?" Bill drummed his fingers on his desk as he tried to recall what he had done with it. Jane sipped her coffee and then gulped.

"Bill."

"Yes Jane?"

"I remember I had been reading the file and I put it down on the desk in Unit 12A when we had first found the basement lab. It's probably upstairs in the room with all the other items that were brought back from Marlow. Come on." Jane rose from her desk and made for the door. Bill sighed and followed her out of the office, forgetting to switch off his computer.

+

A man, seeing them leave the office, made his way over to Bill's desk and sat down and seeing the computer on, he smiled and tapped in a code. Minutes later he was typing away putting a designed piece of computer code that would enable the people he had to do this for to know exactly what Bill was doing. Five minutes later, he left the desk and went over to the fire exit and ran up the stairs to the room that Bill and Jane were heading to. He had been told that a file in there needed to be removed as soon as possible. Although first a phone call was needed.

As Bill arrived at the room, his mobile phone rang. He put a hand on Jane to stop her going into the room. He listened to the message on his phone. Sighing, he turned it off and looked at Jane.

"Something has come up. We need to go back to the office and speak to Ruth apparently. Like right away. Come on, this is not going anywhere." Jane sighed and followed Bill over to the lifts. As they entered the lift, the man was opening the door an office and peering round it carefully. Seeing Jane and Bill going into the lift, he smiled and made his way over to the room and let himself in using Bill's access code. He put on a pair of disposable gloves and opened the door and stepped inside. Switching on the lights, he made his way quickly over to the desk that had been placed in the reconstruction of the lab and opened the drawers. The file wasn't there. Shutting the drawers, he looked around the other furniture, only the lab benches were in the room. He moved across the brown tape on the floor, signifying the stairs to the office. Ah, the filing cabinets, he may have more luck there. He opened the first one, nothing in it. Then the second one and again found nothing in it. Slamming the drawer shut, he stood and thought - where would the file have been stored when everything had been moved?

+

Bill and Jane went over to their desks and looked across the office in the direction of Ruth's office. Her secretary was at her own desk, so Bill made his way over to her.

"Got a message that Ruth wanted to see us both." "Urgently." added Jane, who had joined Bill at his side.

"Not from me, I don't know anything about any message for you Bill. Or for you Jane. Ruth is out of the office now. Do you want me to leave a message for her?" She picked up her pen and pad and looked expectantly at them both.

"No. Sorry, yes do that. Just ask if she has spoken to anybody else about us or the case we are working on." They turned and went back to their desks. Jane looked at Bill.

"Upstairs again. I think somebody doesn't want us to find anything out about Mr O'Conner." Bill nodded and they walked quickly out of the office and over to the lift. For once it was ready on their floor and stepping inside Jane pressed the button to the right floor and the doors closed on them.

+

The man had now looked in all the drawers of the filing cabinets. Having found nothing like a file, he had moved over to some boxes that lay half hidden behind the lab benches. Pulling one box out, he tore the tape off the top of the box and opened the flap. He reached inside and was about to take the first file out, when he became aware of the door to the office being opened. Quickly he pushed the open box back under the bench and grabbing a nearby dust sheet, put himself beside the box, wrapping the sheet over himself. Hopefully he would remain hidden till whoever it was had left the office.

Bill sighed as they entered the room. Jane followed him in and tapped him on the shoulder.

"What?"

"Shush. I think somebody has been in here. The lights were off, we didn't go into the room before, now they are on. Maybe the person is still here." she whispered in Bill's ear. He nodded and they split up, Bill going through to the lab and Jane started to explore the office. After a few minutes, they met again by the door. Bill nodded towards the Lab. Then he jerked his finger at the door indicating that they should go outside. Once outside, he tapped in his code and locked the door.

"That will hold whoever is in there. Did you see anything odd Jane?"

"Nope. You?"

"Something possibly, a box was sticking out from under one of the lab benches."

"And?"

"I don't recall seeing it before. It may have been there before, but I didn't see it if it was. Now that I've locked the door, we can go and ask security to see who has accessed the door in the last twenty-four hours. Come on." He led the way over to the stairs and started to run down them. Sighing, Jane followed him.

+

The box moved further into the room and the man climbed up from under the bench. He tossed the dust sheet into one of the cabinet drawers and picked up the box and stuck it under his arm. Making his way swiftly over to the door, he turned the handle, but it remained locked. He put down the box, took out a small device, held it to the lock and with a click, the door unlocked. Smiling he walked out and relocked door, then made his way down to the office and went and sat at his desk to see what Bill or Jane would do next. He picked up the phone ready to dial a number and then remembered that the file was still somewhere in the room upstairs.

+

Bill knocked on the door of security and went in. The room was a mass of computers and monitors, with black leads running across the floor in all directions. Sitting behind a desk in the middle of the room was Martin Fitzroy, head of security, who looked up as Bill entered.

"What can I do for you Bill?"

"Can you find out for me who has accessed the room with the property from Unit 12A in Marlow."

"Room number and level?"

"Room thirty one, level five." Bill watched as the man tapped the details into the machine.

"Well?"

"You and just you. Something odd though." "What?"

"Well according to this, you have just left the room, having unlocked it from the inside. You got your card with you?" Martin asked.

"Right here." Bill produced it and handed it over."

"I'll issue you with a new one for now. I'll send you the code on an internal link."

"And what about the access to the room? Who do you think it is?" asked Bill.

"Not sure, I'll go and look at the lock. Sophisticated little devils but they do have a means of listing all the devices or cards that are used to access or leave the room." He nodded at Bill indicating the meeting was over. Outside Jane had just got there.

Slightly out of breath and bent over getting her breath back, she looked at Bill.

"Well?"

"I'll fill you in over a coffee outside. Come on."

+

Martin Fitzroy had arrived at the door to room thirty-one, level five. On his instructions, tape had been placed across the doorframe and he had been careful to make sure that nobody else had been in the room since Bill had seen him. Bowing down to remove the tape, he ripped it from the frame and put his access card close to the lock. It clicked open and he sighed with relief. Wedging the door open, he reached inside and put another wooden wedge on the inside. Now he could remove the lock without the door moving into the room.

He set to work with his tools and half an hour later a new lock had been fitted. This one though, unlike its predecessor, could only be opened with two special keys, a lock that would be rendered useless if any other key or copy tried to open the door. Checking that both keys worked, he removed the wedge on the inside and pulled the door closed with a satisfying 'click' before returning to his office. Once there, he sent an electronic note to Bill's computer. This would have been quite safe, but for the line of code that had been placed on Bill's computer.

+

The insider had returned to room thirty on the fifth floor, only to discover Martin busy changing the lock. He retreated to his own desk and switched on his computer. He saw the new code being sent to Bill, so smiling he left his desk on the fourth floor and made his way upstairs to the fifth floor. Walking quickly, he approached the nearest fire alarm button.

Bill and Jane had been about to leave their office, when at that moment the fire alarm sounded. Bill and Jane looked at each other and joined the rest of the staff making their way down the staircase to outside. On the fifth floor, in a cupboard off the corridor a door opened slowly, and a head peered out. He had heard the footsteps going past, just after he had smashed the glass of the fire alarm. Quickly he made his way over to room thirty-one and tapped the new code he had learnt from hacking into Bill's computer. He placed a small pocket size device against the lock and the door swung open and he stepped inside.

+

Halfway down the stairs, Bill stopped at a corner and let others go by. Jane looked at him puzzled.

"Come on Bill."

"You go on ahead, I am going back to room thirty-one. I think it may be a coincidence that the alarm went off just as we were about to return to the room."

"What if it is the real thing, Bill?"

"I'll get out. Now on you go." He watched her join the stragglers going down the stairs and ran quickly back up to the fifth floor. He poked his head around the fire exit door and saw that room thirty-one had its door open. Quickly, but quietly, Bill ran across and pushed the door open wider. Inside the room a man was bent over a desk with a box beside him and a pile of paper on the other side of him. He appeared to be looking at each paper, one bit at a time. Bill looked around the room for some sort of weapon, but the only thing that he saw was, appropriately enough, a fire extinguisher. He picked it up and approached the back of the man.

"Who are you and what are you doing in here?" Bill asked. The man whirled around and seeing Bill, pushed him to one side and ran from the room, clutching the box to his chest. Still holding the fire extinguisher, Bill tore after him out of the room and along the corridor towards the lifts. At the lift door the man was pressing the button for the ground floor. He jabbed it again and again, while keeping an eye on Bill who was now strolling along the corridor.

"Give me the box," Bill said as he approached the man but stayed just out of his reach."

"No chance." Came the reply as he jabbed the button for the umpteenth time.

"Clever, aren't you?"

"I like to think so." he replied.

"But not quite clever enough. The fire alarm, once pressed, the lifts stop working." Bill said with a smile. The man looked at Bill and then at the lift indicator above the doors. Sure, enough there was no indication as to which floor it was at. With a curse, he threw the box at Bill and pushed past him, running for the fire exit. Bill left the box and papers and tore after him. He didn't plan to let him escape a second time. The man entered the fire escape and started running down it. Bill got to the door just in time to see the man on the landing below. He ran after him, jumping two stairs at a time, but somehow the man kept a floor ahead of him. Bill knew that if the man got to the ground floor and outside, he would have no chance of catching him.

Suddenly he was conscious that the other man couldn't be heard running. Bill stopped and listened to see if he could hear any breathing. Bill approached the door to floor three, only to have it flung open into his face. Then Bill saw the man, who had been behind the door, charge out and down the stairs. Bill tried to follow, but had to sit down, his hands to his head, where he could feel a bump starting to rise where the door had hit it. Sighing, he sat still and after a few minutes turned and walked slowly back to room thirty-one on the fifth floor. As he did so, the alarm stopped ringing and voices could be heard down the stairwell.

"It's a false alarm."

"That alarm is always going off."

"I think somebody pressed it wanting to go and have a fag break."

"Nobody would do that, would they?"The voices got fainter as he got further away from them. Bill opened the door to floor five and walked down towards the lifts. He picked up the box and put the scattered paperwork into the box before going back to room thirty. Once inside Bill made his way over to the desk and put the remaining paperwork in the box and carried it down to his desk. He would get security to check who had access to the new code. As far as he was aware, only the security officer and himself, but somebody else obviously knew, or they couldn't have got into the room.

# Chapter 14

## Marlow, Golspie, Oxford & Moscow

The following day, in a detached house with a triple garage on the outskirts of Marlow, an agitated meeting was going on. Two men and a woman sat on chairs around a table on which was a phone and three notepads and ten bags of blue crystals.

"So, to recap, the factory has been seized, the office has been seized and the police have opened the remaining units at the industrial estate, that is right, isn't it?" She nodded across at one of the two men. He coughed and looked at the other two.

"Unfortunately, yes. That is about the size of it. Fortunately most of the stock and a lot of the essential equipment had been removed before the police found the lab. We have most of the paperwork, thanks to a quick phone call from Justin, thank you Justin for that tip off. It was just a case of getting more bodies on the ground and we formed a chain to get the files and paperwork out before the police came.

When can we move the stock from the garage, please? My wife is due back in two days and always parks in the garage. She would have kittens if she saw the stock and couldn't get the car inside."

"Well Kenneth, once we have found new premises, we can move the stock. Have you seen anywhere suitable yet?" asked Justin.

"Not yet. I have put word out that we need a new unit, a large one."

"Boys, I think we are missing the point here. Our friend from Eastern Europe will not be too pleased if he hears how much stock has gone into the police hands. It's taken three years to get it onto the streets. It is as addictive as we expected. Justin, how many bodies did we have to dispose of at the unit?"

"Twenty in total. Five down the drains and the other fifteen in the black bags. With the chemicals that we used, there would not be a lot for the police to identify who they were. Sad but a fact of life, that when you start to develop a new drug." He stopped and looked at the others. "What? What is it?"

"Justin, there are a few, let's say, problems with the first and second batches. It is addictive, as we were told to make it so, but if the user has more than five doses a day, then they start to up the dose to more than five and die within forty-eight hours. As we are targeting a wider market than usual, anybody who needs to work longer hours, less sleep and feel less exhausted, that is a huge market. After all the USA were the among the first to try it out. But they did stop when side effects started to appear."

"So, what are you saying, we stop until it is safer?"

"No, what I am saying is that we relocate, away from Marlow, somewhere else completely. I'll have a talk with our man in Europe, see what he wants us to do. Meantime Kenneth, I want you to widen your search of premises to across the UK. Justin, be sure a tell the users to not exceed taking more than five times a day as stock is limited. I'll talk to our man and I'll move the stock to a safer place than in your garage Kenneth. Anything else?"

"LICD." muttered Justin. "What about them?"

"They are a smart bunch. They have already opened the units, despite us arranging for the padlocks to be changed from the ones that the police used."

"We have contacts within LICD so don't worry on that score. Now are we finished? Good." She stood up and watched as Justin left the house. She turned to Kenneth and smiled. "Come and help me load the stock into the Landrover will you? After I've moved this lot, I must get back to work."

+

About two hours later, the Russian heard his phone ring. He reached into his pocket and taking it out, answered it.

"Yes?"

"There is a problem. The end users, if they have more than five doses a day, they start to go mad and die within forty-eight hours. Also, LICD have found the units…"

"…Yes, I already am dealing with LICD. Get a new lab set up, anywhere in the south. It doesn't have to be Marlow. Do you need money to do that?"

"A bit of cash is always useful. Post to me as usual." The phone went dead, he fingered his beard and left the hotel to walk into Golspie.

+

In Oxford an old lady walked up to the door of *Patrick Reilly's Jewellery* and peered in through the door. It had been closed for three days now and she wanted to collect her ring that he had said needed to be made smaller. It all seemed quite normal. Still, it wasn't good enough, she thought to herself as she walked back to her flat. Once inside, and having made a cup of tea, she decided to phone her neighbour, as she worked for the police and might know what to do.

Half an hour later a police car drove up to the shop and two policemen got out and one shone a torch through the glass.

Nodding to his colleague, they broke the glass on the door and reached inside and turned the latch. Opening the door, the smell hit them at once. One of them phoned it in while the other stepped slowly inside and looked over the counter. He could see a body lying there, so he left the shop and stood outside waiting for the rest of the team to arrive.

+

In Golspie, Ivan had purchased a large yellow padded bag from the local post office and having gone to the seat outside, put a bundle of cash into the bag and sealed it. Then he arranged for it to be sent parcel post to an address in Oxford. Once done, he left the small post office and walked down the main road towards the bank on the opposite side of the street. He needed to arrange for a safe deposit box to be started in Golspie.

Patrick had seen Ivan leave the hotel from his office. He quickly rose and left the office to go and search Ivan's rooms. Grabbing the hotel house keys, he made his way up the stairs to the two rooms that Ivan used. Opening the first, he could see at once that it remained unused. He relocked it and moved to the other one. Once inside, he carried out a quick search of the room. Smiling at what he found, he left it in place and left the room and relocked the door.

As Ivan walked back into the hotel, Patrick stepped out from the office and stopped him going any further.

"Do you have the file yet?" said Patrick.

"Not yet. You said you would give me twenty-four hours. I have put things in motion though."

"Do you want anything else, or is it purely about the drugs?"

"Why Patrick, what do you take me for? I am a businessman like you. What else could interest me over in Scotland?" He looked at Patrick, but Patrick said nothing and returned to his office, slamming the door closed after him. Ivan looked at the office door and then went to his room. Once inside he checked the hiding place where he had put the item, it was still there. So, what was Patrick so wound up about he wondered. Sitting down, he tried his phone, no signal. Cursing under his breath, he went back down and outside.

He made his way to the broch and climbed to the top, where there was a strong signal and nobody nearby. He tapped out the number for his office and waited. After a few minutes the phone was answered by his secretary.

"You at the office?"

"Where else would I be at this time of day?" she replied. "Good. Good, I want you to look in the office archives and see if there is a file on," he paused for a few minutes,"pendent locks, or anything to do with them. Ring me on this number in the next half an hour." He pressed the button to end the call and stretched out on the grassy hill.

+

In the office in Moscow, his secretary was busy looking through the index that was kept of all the files in the office. She thought she had found the file, but on opening it, found there was nothing inside. She took another look on the side and front but failed to notice that on the back of the box file was, in very small writing, a simple word 'Amber' nothing else. Putting it back on the shelf, she decided to look under Pendent on the computer, but that didn't do the job either. Sighing, she looked at the clock and noted that almost half an hour had gone. She picked up the phone and rang her boss back.

+

Ivan awoke with his phone ringing in his pocket. Cursing, he reached inside and took it out. Looking at the screen, he saw it was his secretary and answered it.

"Found it?"

"No, nothing at all sir. There is a file box, but nothing in it at all. Do you want me to carry on looking?"

"No, don't bother." He hung up without another word and thought back to the last time he had seen the file. He recalled that he had asked his old secretary to shred it. When he had left the office, the shredder had been going he recalled. Obviously, the file had gone then, pity, but there you are.

Ivan stood up and walked back to the hotel, failing to notice that on the embankment opposite, a man with a set of binoculars had taken a keen interest in him.

# *Chapter 15*

London, Marlow, Belfast

Bill dumped the box and paperwork on his desk. Jane looked across at him.

"That it?"

"Part of it, I don't think all the paperwork that was in the filing cabinets would have fitted into this one box. It's in a bit of a muddle as it was thrown at me, and he had already put a pile to one side in room thirty-one." Sighing, he took the first piece of paper off the top and looked at it. He started to put it down, then noticed the date was 1988. Quickly he flicked through some of the other papers on the top, all were mixed up, but all had 1988 mentioned. He put his hand further down into the box and took about a third of the paper out and placed it on his desk. Then he took another piece out from the box. This one was dated 1978. Bill groaned. "This is going to take me ages to sort."

"Not if we both do it. Go and put it in the car, we'll take a meal in tonight and then afterwards we'll sort it into some sort of order. Agreed?" said Jane with a smile.

"Agreed." Bill put the paperwork back into the box, opened his drawer and took out a dozen or so empty files, which he added to the top of the box. Then, picking up the box and files, he made his way down to the car park below the offices.

+

Later that evening, having eaten, Bill and Jane started to sort the paperwork. It soon became obvious that there were three separate files, but all mixed up. An hour of rough sorting resulted in three different piles on the table in front of them.

Bill got up and went and poured them both a glass of wine, before coming back to start again. He passed one of the glasses to Jane.

"We've made a start. Let's begin with the 1988 ones first, shall we?" said Jane.

"Ok, but why that one?"

"It's the largest pile." She pulled it towards them and took the first piece off the top. "Date order, if they have a date on them that is." Bill took half the pile and moved to the coffee table to give Jane more room to spread the paperwork. Even though it looked as though they would be working long into the night, Bill started doing the same on the coffee table. The sooner they finished, the sooner they may learn exactly was going on.

+

In another house in London a man was about to phone his contact in Russia. Picking up the phone, he dialled the number and waited for the person on the other end to pick the phone up. He knew this number was always manned. Not relishing this call, he had to say how he didn't have the box or the paperwork, despite the money being written off against his gambling debts.

+

In Marlow a team of police were busy pouring over paperwork that had been recovered from some of the units. They had discovered that four of the units appeared to have received an offer to buy the business or the unit outright. A company that had appeared to be based in London, had on further investigations, been a front for four other companies that were linked to a firm based in Panama. Once that had been discovered, a few of the team had thrown their hands in the air with disgust. In a corner office a woman remained bent over her desk and it appeared whatever she was doing, she was doing it intently. Nobody had noticed her late arrival that afternoon, nor taken any interest in her nice new Landrover sitting outside.

Outside Unit 12A Kenneth looked up and down the road that led to the units. Nobody about. The blue and white police tape was attached to a series of metal poles that had been hammered into the tarmac. They surrounded the whole front of all the units. He ducked under the flapping tape and made his way to the back of the units. More tape was here too, but he ignored it and moved to the rear of Unit 11. Putting on some gloves, he tried to pull open the rear door, surprisingly it opened easily. Glancing up and down for one last check, he moved into the unit. Now the bags had been taken away, the smell inside, although not as strong as before, still lingered.

Obviously, the police hadn't yet looked at the drains, he thought to himself with a smile. Then he moved to the small kitchen at the rear of the unit. Now empty, he climbed onto the worktop that ran along one wall and standing up, pushed the ceiling tile up and to the right. He put his hand into the gap and felt to the left, good, the packet was still there. Catching hold of it, he withdrew it and placed it on the worktop, before putting the ceiling tile back in place. Then he jumped down and put the packet into his inside pocket. Taking cloth that he had brought with him, he produced a bottle of bleach and started to wipe down all the surfaces he had touched or stepped on before leaving the unit and closing the door after him.

Kenneth made his way over to his car and drove off out of the industrial estate as a police car drove past him going in the opposite direction.

+

Later that evening, in Belfast, two men left the house where they had been staying and drove back to Seumas Kelly's house. It was dark and no sign of any lights on in the house as they drove past the entrance. Parking nearby, the two men got out together and walked up the drive. Both men had dressed in black and wore black balaclavas as well. Only their eyes could be seen, that and the .22 revolver in the hands of the one leading them towards the front door. As they approached, the external lights came on. The revolver coughed twice, and the night went dark again. Splitting up, one went to the back door and the other approached the front door and knocked before stepping back and to one side.

Inside the house, Seumas was standing under the stairs watching the two men approach the house. His external lights may have been shot out, but the cameras that were positioned in the trees and on the wall running around the parameters, were seeing everything he needed to know. Smiling, he reached for his shotgun and crawled along the floor of the hall and up the stairs. Outside the two men were getting impatient waiting. The front door was getting knocked for the third time, when Seumas had opened a window overlooking the rear of the house and taken aim and shot the gunman standing there. With a scream, he dropped to the ground clutching his knee. Seumas, smiling, quietly closed the window and moved to the front of the house, to look out onto the drive. On hearing his partner scream, the gunman at the front of the house had ran around to him at the back. Seeing him on the floor, holding his knee in agony, he knew that Seumas was in the house. Swearing loudly, he bent down and picked up his partner.

"Shut up. Seumas is the only man who can do that from inside. Now come on, I'll take you to that tame doctor we use." Bent double, he carried the man down the drive and out to the car. Opening the rear door, he put his partner into the car and shutting the door, ran back up to the house. Taking careful aim, he fired at two of the tyres of the black BMW that was outside the garage. Then ran back to their car and drove off at speed.

"Not so fast, this knee." He glanced at the man on the back seat, who had now gone white in the face. Driving faster, he crossed two red lights and swung out of the city towards the countryside. He knew the way, having been there on a few occasions in the past.

+

In Golspie, Ivan was busy trying to get hold of his contact in London to check that the two files had been removed from the industrial units. The same ones that Bill and Jane were now looking trying to figure them out.

+

At Golspie police station, the phone rang on DS Cooper's desk. Groaning as he had been about to finish his shift for the day, he picked up the phone.

"DS Cooper. Highland Police Force."

"DS Cooper, it is DCI James Rogers of Marlow Police. Sorry to bother you, but I need anything you may have on any Russian Mafia and anything at all on Sheepsbane, a toxic weed that grows up in those parts I understand?"

"Russian Mafia? Sheepsbane? What is going on down there? I can get the files out of storage tomorrow and I'll dig up some information on Sheepsbane as well if you really need it. Who put you on to me?"

"Bill Sutherland did. Said you were the man to go to."

"Ha! I might have guessed. Ok, give me your number and I'll fax down what I know tomorrow." He scribbled the number of the fax and replaced the phone.

+

In an antique shop in Oxford, two men knocked on the door and pushed it open. Glad to be home after such a long trip away, they went through to the back and nodded their approval at the meal that lay in front of them. A woman got up and saying nothing, took the hot plates from the oven and put on the table. Then she picked up the Oxford Mail and pointed to the headline.

**Jewellery owner killed in shop.** Nothing taken says police. We are appealing for anybody who saw what happened five days ago. More details on page three.

She nodded at the two men and pointed at the headline.

"I hope you don't think it was us?" said one of the men with a laugh. "We were out of the country, attending to some business." The other man kicked him under the table, and they continued to eat their meal in silence." She left the paper and went out to the shop at the front of the building. With a location as good as this, she kept the shop open later than most other shops. A woman entered the shop and indicated that she wanted to see the picture hanging on the back wall of the shop. Smiling, the lady behind the counter moved forward and beckoned her behind the counter for a closer look. Business was going to be good this year, she thought to herself, as she started to explain how she had come by it.

+

Bill looked at Jane and smiled.

"Well, that is everything we have in chronological order I think." The piles of paperwork were now merged into two piles. One was an old firm's finances, going back years. The other was much more interesting. It described a meeting of ARI (The Army ready for Insurrection), at least that was what one of the bits of paper had said it was called. A team of six to eight people had planned to blow up the channel tunnel. However, it appeared that the leaders had ruled such a risky plan not to go ahead.

The details of the plan, up to the point of being ruled out, were sketchy to say the least. What really caught their attention was the mention of a contact in both Oxford and Exeter. Somewhere that had not been on the radar of LICD.

"Who to tell at LICD though? Said Jane if there is in an insider and we know there is, from the attempt to take this box, who is it and how far up the ladder do they go? We are going to have to really be very careful over this case Bill. Now I don't know about you, but I am ready for my bed." She glanced at her watch and gave a groan. "Three o'clock in the morning." Then she rose and left the room, smiling as she passed Bill, who it appeared, was already fast asleep with his head resting on his hands at the table.

# *Chapter 16*

## Golspie, London, Marlow

The following morning, Ivan sat at the desk in his room. Unless he got the file today, he would have no hold over Patrick. He got up and helped himself to another whisky from the decanter on the table. Although he preferred vodka, he was starting to get a taste for this Scottish drink, Whisky. Sipping the glass, he went back to the desk and started to make a list of people and phone numbers that he could get hold of in a hurry.

+

On the fourth floor of LICD, Ivan's contact was desperately trying to locate a file that he knew LICD had on Patrick O'Conner. The one that was accessible on the system was a very brief one, the same one that Bill had been shown. However, he, like Bill, didn't believe that was all that LICD had on Mr O'Conner, so he was trying to dig a little bit deeper but also trying not to be caught by Martin Fitzroy, the security officer. He knew that all the computers were linked to the security office as well as the IT dept. This was his third and final attempt to try and open a file, that he thought, may contain what he wanted. Beside the computer was a pad of paper on which were lots of names and words, all crossed out. His previous two attempts had drawn a blank. Now he sat drumming his fingers on the desk as he tried to think what password would have been used by Harvey. He had been surprised to find that the work files that Harvey had used were still on the system. Now after two attempts he guessed why. Nobody knew the password to open them and delete the folders. He knew that unless he got the file to his Russian contact, his life would not be worth anything at all.

+

Bill and Jane had arranged for a meeting with Ruth. Her secretary had said that afternoon was the earliest that she could see them both.

Also, that morning, Martin Fitzroy had asked Bill to meet him outside of the offices. Wondering what about, Bill had gone to the car park and now waited for him to turn up. He glanced at his watch for the third time and looked up as Martin Fitzroy turned the corner and came over to him.

"So why the meeting out here?" asked Bill.

"I have found out that somebody has access to our systems. You have had a bug put on your computer. Anything you type on it, or anything sent or received can be seen by this other party. I've changed the code again on Room 31." He passed Bill a piece of paper. "Don't write it down, once you remember it, destroy this paper. I am trying to see who is behind this, but they are very clever. I think they may be after Harvey's files so I have left the empty folders on the system for now. It looks as though there is something of interest that Harvey knew about. What, I have no idea. For now, I have downloaded the information that was on the files to these three floppy disks. Look after them, it is the only set there is. Don't use the computers at LICD, use your own at home, assuming you have your own that is?" Bill nodded and took the floppy disks from Martin as he did so.

"Right then, I'll go back in. Remember what I have said." He turned to leave, then turned back towards Bill. "Keep an eye on Ruth as well, she might not be as wonderful as some people think." With that, Martin left Bill holding the disks. He looked at the paper he had been given, remembered the code and then walked over to the car and put the paper and disk in the boot. He locked it and walked back to his office. Now he was aware of a possible, no definite, infiltrator to LICD, he would keep his eyes open for anybody who he thought was acting in a suspicious manner.

+

Upstairs on the fourth floor, the man had tapped in his third and last attempt at getting access to the files. He carefully checked the set of names that he had typed in, just to make sure of no spelling errors and hit the return key. A few seconds later the screen appeared with the message scrolling across it. THIRD ATTEMPT FAILED. YOU HAVE BEEN LOCKED OUT. THIRD ATTEMPT FAILED...

Banging the desk with his fist in frustration, he looked around to see if anybody else had heard him. But nobody else was in the room. He had checked when he came in but had been so engrossed that he wouldn't have noticed anybody else enter, even if they had done so. Switching off the computer, he stretched his arms and legs and stood up and walked around the room, trying to think of what to say to the Russian. Whatever he said, the consequences would not be pleasant he thought.

He decided to do some real work, so he switched on the computer again, only to find a new message scrolling across his screen. THIS COMPUTER HAS BEEN UNLINKED FROM NETWORK. THIS COMPUTER HAS BEEN UNLINKED FROM THE NETWORK...

He gazed in horror at this new message. What did this mean? Was it a network-wide fault or more personal to him? Quickly he ran over to another machine and typed in his entry code and hit the return button. The same message came up on the screen. Sighing with relief he thought it must be a network problem. He decided to go and get some refreshment while it was sorted. He left the office and went downstairs to the canteen.

+

Martin Fitzroy gazed at the bank of cctv screens and smiled as he saw the message on the computer on the fourth floor resulted in a switching off of that computer. Just as he had hoped, this would now give him time to get up there and see what hidden codes lay inside its hard drive. He had suspected the person who used that computer but could not prove it yet. Now, maybe, he would be able to do so.

Leaving his office and locking it securely, he made his way to the IT department and procured an identical computer, then made his way to the office on the fourth floor. On arriving, he looked up and down the corridor before entering and locking the door. It was the work of a few minutes to change the computers over and reconnect the leads. Then picking up the computer, he returned to the IT department and explained what he wanted them to do.

+

Bill got back to his desk and scribbled a note, outlining what he had been told and slid it across the desk to Jane. She read it, tore it into small pieces and dropped them in the bin.

That evening at their home Bill and Jane took the floppy disks and once loaded, opened the files that Harvey had kept.

+

In Golspie at the New East Sutherland, Ivan was furious. He had heard from his informer in LICD, learning that he didn't have access to the files that Ivan believed Harvey had. Having said to Patrick that he would produce the files that day. He was fast looking like losing any chance of using the hotel to store, and one day, sell the stock of his latest drug from. He had found out that a lot of stock was now in the hands of both Marlow police and LICD. What stock had been saved, was being stored at a location he didn't know about. It seemed to him that his grip on his businesses were being eroded. Replacing the phone, he looked at the list of names and numbers on the pad in front and decided to dial the first number, an Oxford number of a shop he thought would be happy to help him.

"*Oxford's Historical Antique emporium.* How can I help you?"

"I need to speak to one of the two boys. Now."

"I'm sorry, both are out now. Give them a call back around an hour from now." The phone was replaced, and Ivan looked at it in disbelief before carefully replacing it and deciding to go outside for a walk and to kill an hour or so.

+

Patrick had noticed Ivan leaving the hotel and decided to take the opportunity to make a call to Oxford.

In *Reilly's Jewellery shop* a phone rang. The two policeman who were keeping an eye on the shop, following the owner's death, looked at one another.

"Don't answer it, it may go to the answer machine." Muttered one under his breath to his colleague.

"And if it doesn't?"

"The place is closed, so it wouldn't make any difference then, would it?"

"Suppose not."They both looked at the phone as the answer machine gave its message.*'I am unable to take your call right now as I am busy with a customer, please leave your name and phone number and I'll get right back to you. Speak after you hear the tone. Beep…*

"Pat, its Patrick, Patrick O'Connor, I wouldn't be phoning you, but I need you to get in touch with a couple of the lads. Seumas and one other, say Lenny, he'll know the right people for what I want you to arrange. Get back to me as soon as possible, if not faster. You know the number, probably have it in your…" BEEP. Tantalisingly, the caller was cut off mid-sentence. The two men looked at one another.

"We need to let the governor know about this; it sounds important."

"Ok and the first thing he'll say is 'what was the telephone number?' so if we find that first, it might help things along, don't you think?"

"Probably you are right. I'll have a look under the counter, you look in his office at the back."The two of them then started looking for any kind of notebook or phone pad. A few minutes later the one in the office gave a shout.

"Found it. Come on through, I think this may lead to something bigger if we look for some other information to take with us, it may lead to us getting up the ladder of promotion."

His colleague joined him and looked down at the phone pad where a few names had been listed in no particular order as far as he could see, but the letters of ARI did make him stop and think.

ARI Cell.
Leader Patrick O'Connor, always the boss? Second Seumas Kelly.
Barry Ryan Pat Doyle

Lorcan O'Conner (no relation) Jane/Eva ? Money? Scotland?
~~Dutchman Klaas Van Miere~~ Killed

"What does ARI mean?"

"Who knows? The names sound Irish and there is a mention of Scotland too. Think this is enough to give the governor yet?"

"It would be, except for the missing phone numbers."

"We'll carry on looking then." The two men left the pad where it was and carried on searching.

It was three hours later, having found only the number for a hotel in Ireland, that the two policemen took the notepad and locked up the shop, leaving a young constable on duty outside for the night. Once back at the police station in St Aldates, they left a note for their superior along with the notepad. Then, having finished their shift for the day, one went home to sleep, his colleague went and started to pack for his three-week holiday in the north of Scotland. Somewhere he had suddenly had an urge to visit.

+

In Marlow that evening, the team that had been tasked with finding all they could about the new drug had a breakthrough. A specialist Army lab near Exeter had been helping them to identify the various ingredients that made up the drug. The phone rang on James Rogers desk, and he picked it up quickly.

"DCI Rogers speaking."

"Good evening, sorry to phone you so late. It's Lympstone here. We have managed to separate the ingredients from the sample of the drug you sent."

"Go on."

"Well, the main ingredient is Sheepsbane, found in East Sutherland and some of the isles. Curious plant. You wouldn't want to let it touch your skin, yet if it is refined and taken as a tablet it doesn't do much to you, other than keep you awake. However, adding the two other main ingredients does result in two effects. Firstly, the person taking it can work for hours without needing sleep and their sense of awareness and connection is much sharper. The US army trialled something similar in Vietnam but ceased using it once the side effects became known. Second, if the person takes more than five doses a day, then they can soon get very real hallucinations, think that they are invincible and so on. Also they need to take more and more of the drug and that leads them to quickly going mad and reckless. If they didn't kill themselves by being reckless, the increase of doses would kill them in two or three days at the most."

"What are the other two ingredients?" asked Rogers.

"That's where it gets interesting. One is called XV3rd, and the other is a refined drug used by the USA between 1950 and 1953. When the effects became more widely known they stopped using it. It made soldiers think that they could charge straight at somebody else who might be firing at them and that the bullets wouldn't hurt them."

"And where does XV3rd come from?"

"Russia. See what I mean about it becoming interesting. Two of the ingredients, one from each of the two countries that were at loggerheads for years." Rogers took a moment to digest this information.

"Anything else?" he asked the lady. "The boxes that it is supplied in." "What about them?"

"The firm went out of business a few years ago. Late 1980s. The only place that we have seen these boxes before was at one of the sites of the Eurotunnel workings."

"Interesting. Anything else?"

"Not now, I'll write it all up and fax it to you. Do you want a hard copy as well, if so, I'll post one out to you?"

"Thank you, do that please. You have been very helpful." Rogers replaced the phone and leant back in his chair. Eurotunnel works, USA and Russia? He would forward the information to LICD, it sounded more their sort of area of expertise he thought.

# Chapter 17

## Moscow, Golspie, London and Marlow

Ivan expected his staff to work the long hours that he put in. In return he paid them well and let them have long holidays. His secretary had been working well into the night on a regular basis and really needed a break. The phone beside her was off the hook. Ivan had been phoning constantly with lots of different requests that normally she would have delegated to other members of his staff. Ivan, though, had been insistent that only she was to do the work. Hence the phone being off the hook for a couple of hours.

His latest request, demand more like, had been to get a new supply of XV3rd and ship it out to the UK as soon as possible. That was all very well, she thought to herself, but he hadn't supplied an address of either where to source the wretched stuff or where to send it. Placing another box file on top of the rising pile beside her desk, the top one toppled over, taking all the other box files with it. Cursing, she got up and started to put them into some sort of order. It was while she was doing this that the underside of one of the boxes caught her attention. A piece of paper had been sellotaped to the bottom with one word. *AMBER* written on it. Frowning, she finished sorting the remaining box files and put them back on the shelves, turning down the last one on its side to know where she had got to. Then she picked the file with the word Amber stuck to it, walked through to Ivan's office and typed that into his computer. After a few minutes a file appeared on the screen.

`Project Amber. See Dacha.` Excited, she quickly typed in Dacha, project Amber and pressed at once the computer started to fill the screen with pages of information, most of which was unreadable. Then across the bottom of the screen came a sentence that she didn't really want to see.

`...FILE IS TIME CRITICAL. ONCE PRINTED FILE WILL BE REMOVED FROM MEMORY. PRIMARY PARTY WILL RECEIVE NOTIFICATION. FILE IS TIME CRITICAL...`

She ran over to the printer and switched it on, within a few minutes the printer started to print reams of paperwork. Sighing, she left it running and returned to her office. XV3rd would have to take priority for now.

+

In Sutherland though, Ivan was not really concerned with what was going on in Moscow. He had a bigger problem; time had run out for producing the file on Patrick and Ivan knew that now he had no lever to use against him. Sighing, he packed his few items together and went down to see Patrick in the office. It wasn't often that he had to admit defeat, but this was one of those occasions.

+

At Moscow airport, a flight from Heathrow had just landed. On board were two policemen, in plain clothes, from Marlow, tasked by Rogers to find out what they could about the Russian side of things. A long conversation with a very helpful member of LICD had resulted in learning an awful lot about Ivan and his connections. Once out of the airport, they collected the hire car that had been arranged for them and set off for a Dacha address they had been told about.

+

At LICD, the man sat back in his chair. He knew that Ivan would be after him and probably end up killing him as well. So, tipping off the two Marlow cops may keep Ivan off his back, for a while at least. He tapped the keyboard of his computer to check the next flights to New Zealand. Then he got up and locked the door to his office. He pulled out the bottom drawer of the filing cabinet and removed a large file. Smiling, he looked the front of it and weighed it in his hands. By a stroke of good fortune, he had found the door to Room 531 open last night and had a good look around. This file had been in one of the two drawer filing cabinets pushed against the wall, with the drawers towards the wall. He had moved four of them to get to the drawers and had been rewarded by finding this file. He weighed it in his hand and wondered who would be best to receive it?

+

Bill and Jane had overslept that morning, having spent the last few nights looking for answers into the paperwork they had recovered. Now they rushed along to the rearranged meeting with Ruth Sanders, hoping they wouldn't be too late and might learn something more about what was going on. Bill knocked on Sanders' door.

"Come in," a voice said from inside. Pushing open the door, Bill let Jane go in first. Ruth was sat at her desk, a desk that, apart from a single ring folder and a fountain pen, was completely empty. "Shut the door please Bill." He did so and they both stood in front of her.

"Please sit down, this may take a while." Ruth pointed at the three chairs in front of her desk.

"Somebody else coming?" asked Jane.

"Maybe." replied Ruth touching her two hands together as if in prayer. "It depends on how things progress. So, I'll tell you what I know, and you can tell me what you knew and maybe we can start to solve this case?" She leaned back into her chair.

"Late last night, we got information sent to us from Marlow that the three main ingredients of the drug found in the units in Marlow are," she ticked them off on her fingers one by one. "Sheepsbane, XV3rd and an ingredient found in the USA, manufactured and used between 1950 and 1953. Our American cousins are a bit reluctant to let us know exactly what it is and where it is stocked or sold at present. The PM is having a conversation with the President as we speak. This 'special relationship' that is made so much of these days. In addition to this, the bags it is supplied in came from a firm that went out of business in the late 1980s and the only place where they have been found before is in Folkstone at the Eurotunnel works.

Now from Oxford, we have learnt that a list of Irish names has been found in an investigation of a shooting in a shop in a suburb of Oxford. This list has a name you will know of; Mr Patrick O'Connor. It lists him as the leader of this cell."

"IRA?" asked Bill.

"No Bill, not IRA but ARI. Not too sure what it stands for, it has been one that has kept under the radar so far. No claims of any bombings or such like. The A, we think, stands for Armed. As to the R and I, that is under review."

"Splinter group off the IRA?" asked Jane looking at Bill with a stare.

"Don't think so, as I said no claims of bombs etc. So please get yourselves back to Sutherland and investigate Patrick O'Conner, keep him under surveillance and don't be afraid to let him get rattled. One other thing. We have learnt that there has been a killing and an attempt on members of the ARI in Belfast. In broad daylight apparently. One of the two men attacked was wearing body armour, stunned, but not killed." She looked at the pair of them.

"So, if I am right here, we have links to Sutherland, Marlow and Russia as well as Northern Ireland?" said Bill.

"Correct. I also have instigated a search on HOLMES for any information about Patrick and Eurotunnel to see if there is a link somewhere. If there is, we can bring him in for questioning. Now, what have you both learnt?"

"We have an incomplete file on various businesses going back more than seven years," Bill said. Now we would like to expand the team and see if there is a connection to the units where the files were being stored." Bill said.

"We spent most of last night sorting out the paperwork into some sort of order. We would like to carry on today if that is ok with you?"

"Good idea, go back home and carry on sorting the rest out. Make a list of any connections and let me know asap. You can go now."They both rose and left her office. Once back at their desks, Jane looked at Bill.

"You didn't mention the ARI and that we now knew what it really means." she said.

"Yes,The Army Ready for Insurrection. Come on, let's return to the flat." Bill said with a smile.

+

Ruth picked up her phone and dialled a number. After a few minutes she left a message on the answer phone.

"Ruth here. Told Bill and Jane to concentrate on Patrick, claimed I didn't know anything about the ARI or the drugs. Keep me posted going forwards."

+

The car drove up to the ruins of the Dacha and stopped. Leaving the headlights shinning onto the ruins, the two policemen got out and walked over to the ruined remains. One took out his camera and took a few photos of the remains before moving in a bit closer. His companion put on some disposable gloves and made his way through the ruins to where the kitchen would have been. Using his hand to clear an area in front of the remains of the oven, he took out a sharp knife and cut a large square in the floor covering. He put the knife away and bent down and pulled the cut piece up off the floor. Underneath was a wooden trap door. He took a careful look around, before pulling the trapdoor upwards. It revealed a set of stone steps going down under the building. His companion joined him and shone his torch down the steps.

"After you." He smiled as the other man went down first. At the foot of the stairs the torch beam picked out on one wall a large, thin and tall chest. It was locked with three padlocks. Again, a photo was taken. The two of them didn't move anything but shining the torch around the room saw that in one corner of the room were a pile of plastic sacks. They moved over and pulled one onto its side.

Stencilled on the side of the bag were XV3rd Not for Human use. The camera clicked again, then the two men heaved one of the sacks across to the steps and up to the car. Carefully placing it in the boot of the car, one of them returned and put things as they had found them. Then they got into their car and drove off.

Two hours later the car swung into the drive of the British Embassy and parked at the entrance. A screen was placed around the car, while the bag of XV3rd was removed and carried into the embassy for sending in the diplomatic bag to London next day. They would fly home that evening.

+

Kenneth stretched his arms and stood up. He had been looking at newspapers and copies of Exchange and Mart to see if he could find any industrial units for them to restart production. He had ringed two adverts. One was a large industrial unit in Oxford. The other was in Exeter. While Oxford looked a better location, he thought he had heard somewhere that Oxford had been no go for some reason or other. He looked again at the advert. Not really Oxford, Eynsham. A short way out from Oxford and very cheap for the size of the unit. He got up from his desk and went out to his car. Once inside, he turned on the radio and having glanced at his road atlas, set off from Marlow towards Oxford. He thought it better to look before reporting back.

+

DCI Rogers looked at his watch as his computer flashed a message across the screen. Smiling he reached behind it and turned it off and then left the office to head for home. His two men had been and found what they needed and were now heading back to London. He had been staying at the office in case anything had happened, and he was needed to sort things out. Now though, he could go home to his bed.

+

Ivan's secretary had gathered the paperwork from the printer, neatly put it in a ring binder and then placed it on his desk. Down in the IT part of the building sat a woman, who she knew, liked her. Maybe she could adjust the computer to appear as if nothing had happened. She left the office and went to the lift and pressed the button to take her to the IT department.

+

Patrick looked up at Ivan as he appeared and filled the office door frame.

"Yes?"

"I'm checking out so can you give me the money I left you please?"

"Just a minute, you said you had a file on me, you would produce it in two days and now you are checking out? Where is the file then?"

"I couldn't get it in the time."

"Right then, let me get your bill ready." Patrick reached into the safe and took out the bundle of money and then typed an invoice on the computer. He counted out the cost of the stay in front of Ivan and passed the remaining money back to him. "Do you want to count it?" Patrick asked.

"No. I know where you are if you had short-changed me. One last thing, can you run me to the railway station?"

"Dunrobin or Golspie?"

"Golspie."

"Ok, let me lock up first," said Patrick as Ivan picked up his case and left the building.

## Chapter 18

### Ireland, Golspie, Eynsham, London, Moscow

The gunman looked at his partner lying across the back seat. Having got him to the doctor they had used before, he had managed to get him fixed up, but said it was unlikely he would walk without the support of a stick or cane in the future. After that, they had spent two days staying in safe houses and one night in the car. Now they were parked outside a railway station that would take them to Dublin and then south to Wexford. From there they would get to Rosslare and a boat back to Fishguard. They would leave the car in the garage of a supporter; he would dispose of it weeks later.

"Not done exactly what we were asked to do, have we," he said from the back seat.

"No, can't see that they will be too happy about that. Still, we know that Patrick O'Reilly is dead. It was just unlucky that we didn't get Seumas."

"That still leaves Lenny, Pat, Barry and Lorcan running around and now knowing that somebody is wanting them dead."

"Maybe not. Two attempts, one of which was in Oxford, they might just treat it as a revenge of something they had done in the past. You had better get up, our train goes in a few minutes, and it will take a bit longer with your knee like it is." He helped him up from the back seat and out onto the road. Having shut the car doors, the two men set off towards the station. The key left in the ignition.

+

Pat Doyle looked out from his room at the New East Sutherland and thought of his friends back in Belfast. He hoped that they had taken his advice and gone to ground. On his desk lay his gun and beside it the ammunition for it. He picked it up and stroked it, as another person might stroke a pet. Smiling, he put it in the jacket pocket and the ammunition for it in the other one, Satisfied, he took a last look around the room and picked up his case and walked down the spiralling staircase to speak to Patrick.

He was surprised to find that the front door was shut and locked. He made his way to the empty open plan kitchen and wandered through it into the pantry adjoining it. A door to the outside was closed as well. Pat tried it. It was also locked. Now starting to worry, he returned to the front of the hotel and picked up a leaflet showing the various floors and the fire exits. Over the course of the next ten minutes, Pat found they were all either locked or in some cases padlocked. He returned to hall and sat down. It was like being in a gilded cage, but still a prison.

He looked up as the front door opened and Patrick walked in. "Pat, I'd forgotten you were in the building. Sorry about that.

Come and have a drink in the bar for old times' sake." He walked off in the direction of the bar and Pat rose and followed him, his hand firmly on the gun in his pocket.

At the bar, Patrick moved behind it and left Pat on the customer's side.

"So, what can I get you Pat? A nice 21-year-old Bushmills?" He reached up to fetch the bottle but felt the prod of a gun into his side.

"Don't even think about moving to get a drink. Turn around slowly and go and sit down over there." Pat pointed with the gun in the direction of the tables that were pushed up near the wall. Patrick did as he was told and moved over to the tables. Pulling a couple of chairs out, he sat down and watched Pat do the same. Pat kept his gun levelled at Patrick.

"Pat why the gun? I am not going anywhere, look around you, I have a business to run."

"Shut up and listen. The ARI needs you and the support that you bring as well. This is a very nice place. It is perfect for the hiding of people as and when needed. A room on the top floor, access to the fire escape to avoid having to check in and out. It's perfect I tell you. I had a good look around, when you locked me in by accident, as I said before, a nice place. Now what do you have to say to that?"

Patrick had kept his hands on the heavy table and while listening had held on to the edge of it. Now with a roar, he stood and lifted and pushed it straight at Pat, trapping him against a wall. Bending down, he picked up the gun that had dropped to the floor and waved it in the face of Pat.

"Now you listen to me. I stopped being part of the cell of ARI after Folkestone. I needed a new start, this is it. You, my old friend, have outstayed your welcome. Now I strongly recommend that you go back to your friends and tell them I am not having anything to do with you again. Do you understand that but in case you don't, I can use this gun to remind you more permanently?" He pushed the gun barrel up against Pat's cheek and waited for a reply.

"Now Patrick, how long have we known each other? Ten or fifteen years. You have always been there for us. Why not now? I get that you want to be a businessman, but nobody will take any notice up here of an occasional Irish or Northern Irish guest, hmm?" He looked at Patrick with a defiant look in his eyes.

"Get up, you obviously didn't get my message the first time. We are going outside for a little walk. You in front, me behind you. Leave your case, you will not be needing it for this short trip." Keeping the gun pointed all the time at Pat, the two men walked slowly down the hall and outside into the car park.

"Walk towards that broch and when you get there, walk to the north side and then walk into it." Pat looked at Patrick, who kept the gun pointing in his direction.

"Then what?"

"Get there first. Now start walking." The two men moved off in the direction of the broch.

+

Cooper sat at his desk. The request for him to see if there was a Russian Mafia connection had made him smile, that was the easy bit. He had gone and looked up the past two cases that had involved LICD and then faxed it down to Oxford and LICD. Though he had wondered why LICD hadn't got their own copy. The sheepsbane, that was a bit more difficult. He had found a book called 'The Natural Material for Dying.' He had read it through and found it was more about dying wool for spinning than anything else. He had been about to replace it when a piece of paper fell out of it. Bending down to pick it up, he noticed that it had some writing on it.

*Sheepsbane can be found in parts of the north Highlands. A very good colour of blue can be achieved using this weed. However, the weed is deadly to touch and will result in death within a few hours. Always use gloves and when finished, dispose of weed carefully as its toxins still can remain in the liquid. It doesn't appear to transfer the deadly part to the...* Here, frustratingly, the paper was torn and the remainder of the writing missing. Cooper took the paper over to the photocopier and made a few copies. Then he faxed one to Oxford, Marlow and LICD. The LICD one he marked for the attention of Bill and Jane. Then Cooper walked out of the office and up to the main library in Golspie. He wanted to see if they had any photos of this toxic plant.

An hour later he had found what he was looking for. A large photo in a book entitled '*Toxic weeds and how to deal with them*'. He borrowed it and took it back to the station with the intention of photocopying it. As he passed his desk, the phone rang and he picked it up, putting the book down on his desk as he did so.

"DS Cooper, Highland Police. How can I help you?"

"Cooper, it's Bill and Jane here. We may need to come up to your neck of the woods in a few days. Can you arrange for us to stay locally somewhere please?"

"Sure, it will be good to see you both again. New East Sutherland is about to reopen. The one where the Grand East Sutherland was. I'll slip along and book you a room."

"Make sure it overlooks the broch, will you? All the best." Cooper replaced the phone and after photocopying the page in the book, he walked out to his car, clutching one of the photocopies he had made. For somewhere in the back of his memory, he could recall sheepsbane being mentioned in the case where he had first met Bill and Jane. That was at the hotel. Though then it had been known as *The Grand East Sutherland Hotel*. He turned off the A9 into the car park and saw two men walking across it towards the broch. One looked as though he was holding a gun. Cooper accelerated across the car park and braked hard just a few feet from in front of the two men. He got out and produced his warrant card, flipping it open at the two men. "Stop right there. Police DS Cooper. Both of you, put your hands above your heads. You," pointing to Patrick, "drop whatever it is you are holding. Now!" Patrick and Pat did as they were told. Patrick dropped the gun on the ground.

"Now kick that gun over here." Patrick did so. Still keeping an eye on the two men, Cooper bent down and retrieved the gun. He placed it in the car, which he had left with the door open. "Right, now let's go back to the hotel. Nice and slowly." He spoke into his radio as they all did so. "I need backup at the *New East Sutherland*. Now!" As they approached the open door, he indicated they should stay outside. "Sit down on the steps the two of you."

"Look DS Cooper, I can explain," said Patrick, but the look from both Pat and Cooper made him stop talking. Five minutes later the requested back up turned up and they were taken to Golspie police station for questioning.

Cooper stayed for a look around the hotel. He hoped to find something that would explain why Patrick would risk all he had in something so obviously criminal. A young PC had stayed behind to help and make sure Cooper did everything as per the book. As they both entered the hotel, the first thing that Cooper noticed was the small bag belonging to Pat in the hallway. He nodded at the bag.

"Remind me before we go, that needs to be taken back to the police station."They moved on into the office of the hotel, but apart from a few telephones number that Patrick had written down, there was not much else to see. Cooper copied the numbers into his notebook and moved out and towards the bar and kitchen areas. After an hour of exploring the hotel, it was apparent to both of the policemen that nothing of any interest was in the hotel, other than the phone numbers and the case. Cooper had found a series of keys hanging in the office, each one marked and had taken the ones for the front door. Once they had retrieved the case and locked up, they returned to Golspie to question the two men.

+

Kenneth swung the car into a layby and got out and stretched his legs. He was just on the outskirts of Eynsham and wanted to get a bit of air after driving over from Marlow. A road traffic accident had resulted in him driving miles out of his way and now it was getting late, probably too late for visiting a warehouse in normal circumstances, but this was anything but normal. He removed the piece of paper with the directions on it from his back pocket and read them again. Then he walked around the car and opened the passenger door and took out the road atlas that he had brought with him. He traced the road to the industrial estate and smiled. A five-minute drive on this road, turn left and then right and he was at his destination. He got back into the car, threw the atlas onto the seat beside him and pulled out of the lay-by onto the road.

In his haste to get to the warehouse, he hadn't bothered to glance in his mirror. Had he done so, he would have seen the large lorry thundering up the road towards him. Now the lorry had carried the remains of his car, now in two pieces, further on up the road before coming to a halt. The driver of the lorry sat for a few minutes, badly shaken by what had happened. He decided to get down and walk back to the lay-by, where there was a phone to report any breakdowns. Sighing, he picked up the phone.

+

In London, Bill pushed their dining room table back against the wall, while Jane went and got a set of small tables they had and placed them on either side of the main table. Then they returned to carry on sorting the larger of the three piles of paperwork into date order.

An hour later they stood and looked at their hard work. On the table there were now two piles. One in date order the other had no dates but had lots of references to the group calling itself ARI and mention of a plot to attack the channel tunnel being built between Folkstone and Sangatte in France. The date-ordered one, mentioned the purchase of the units in Marlow and the use of the trial of the mini boring machine to carve out the basement laboratory. It described in

93

some detail how money would be transferred from Russia to the UK and how to start to work on manufacturing a new addictive drug. What it failed to mention was who was behind it and the identity of the people working in Marlow. Jane looked at Bill and half smiled.

"So, we have the background to the units and to an idea to blow up the channel tunnel."

"An idea that was vetoed by those higher up in ARI it appears." added Bill and poured them both a cup of tea.

"Agreed." said Jane"But is it still worth keeping an eye on the units then?"

"Doubt it. The people behind this." he nodded at the paperwork,"are just as likely to start up again somewhere else. Wonder how Cooper is getting on in tracking down a supply of sheepsbane?"

"Finding it, that might be easy. Finding a large quantity of it, that is probably harder to do." She finished her drink and put the mug in the dishwasher before returning to the table with a two-hole punch. "Bill, let's get this filed in the correct order and then we can start to relax." He nodded his agreement and they started doing just that.

+

At LICD, Ivan's contact had placed a large folder into a Jiffy bag and stapled it closed. Then he had written the address on the outside and walked down the stairs and out of the building. He intended to post it at a Post Office, rather than using the internal mail room. Better that nobody knew what he had found out. A copy of the file was also stored on a floppy disk, which he had in his top jacket pocket. Once at the Post Office, he decided to send it the most secure way and arranged to do so. The man behind the counter slid a small self-adhesive label across to him and asked him to put the sender's address on it. Without thinking he scribbled his own address and slide it back to him. Then having stuck the right stamps on and the address label on the reverse. The man placed it in a green bag and told him how much he had to pay. He paid and left the Post Office and walked back to the car-park. He still had to collect his ticket to New Zealand but had arranged to do that the next day. Feeling smug, he drove out from the car park and on towards his flat.

+

In Ivan's office, his secretary had managed to convince the IT lady it might be worth her while to attempt to remove her name from Ivan's personal computer. She was standing at Ivan's desk with the cover off and bits and pieces were all over the desk. She had changed the hard drive and was in the process of reassembling it when Ivan

94

arrived. He had watched the woman from the door to the office and then walked up and tapped her on the back.

"What the hell do you think you are playing at?" he roared at her.

"Sorry sir, your computer has a small problem, a possible hack, and I have sorted it and am just putting it back together for you," she lied.

"Hm, well get on with it as fast as you can. I need to work. How much longer will you be?" Ivan looked at his watch and adjusted it to reflect Moscow time.

"Twenty minutes sir. Twenty five at the outside."

"You have twenty minutes, so make them count." Ivan turned and left her to get on with the job in hand. The IT engineer, sweating a bit, bent down and returned to her task in hand.

+

Half an hour later Ivan's office had returned to normal. Ivan, sitting down, switched on his computer and clicked on the messaging service he paid for. A few messages came through. Then he heard the fax machine in the outer office whirl into action. A few minutes later his secretary walked in with some faxes in her hands.

"A few faxes. Two were junk, the others were one from LICD, one from Marlow and one from Tain." She placed the five on his desk. "I've put the junk ones at the bottom of the pile. The shredder needs emptying, so I will do that, then if you want them shredded..." She left the room and Ivan looked at the fax from his contact at LICD.

*Unable to access file/s on the LICD computers. Have been found out and left LICD. Don't bother trying to find me, have gone far away.*

He re-read it and placed it on the desk. Then he read the one from Marlow.

*As you might now know, Units 1-12A have been opened by the police. Have started to look for new premises. K is driving further afield from Marlow. Have you sourced a new supply of XV3rd yet? Police have most of it now. Also have reports of people overdosing and dying. What do you want us to do about this? We are also out of sheepsbane. You promised us a new supply three weeks ago. With users demanding us for more supplies, we don't want to lose them at this stage.*

He placed it on top of the other fax and picked up the third one.

*You said to keep an eye on NES, have seen owner and another man both appeared to be picked up by the local police. You want to take over the hotel? It is an easy lock to break.. Need a replacement weapon though.*

Ivan smiled at the third fax and stood and walked through to his secretary. He placed the fax on her desk.

"Get him a new gun. Tell him not to go near the hotel but keep Patrick under surveillance." He turned and left her to do as he asked.

# Chapter 19

## Marlow, London, Oxford

She drove her car into the industrial estate. As hoped, the place was deserted apart from a bit of blue and white police tape flapping in the breeze. She drove around to the back of the units and switched the engine off. Her reasoning was that if anybody did happen to drive by, they wouldn't see any cars around and most likely would turn and leave.

She reached into the back seat and took the bag that was lying there, then left the car and walked along the back of the units to the rear of Unit 12. Looking up and down she failed to see anybody. Pleased with herself, she opened her bag and took out a roll of small highly specialized tools. Approaching the lock, she squirted some liquid into it and then moved away. A flash and a lot of smoke came from where the lock was. Now there was a small hole in its place. She placed her hand through the hole and reached across to turn the handle. The door opened slightly towards her. Sighing with relief, she picked up the tools and her bag and moved inside.

Once inside Unit 12 she moved around the dusty printing equipment and towards the small kitchen area. The range of cabinets above and below the worktop didn't interest her. She moved to the one under the sink and opened the door. As she had hoped, the police had removed all the usual items found there. Bending down, she reached in with a small screwdriver and turned the water off. Then tying a handkerchief around her nose, unscrewed the sink drain from the waste pipe. Two screws at the rear of the sink, hardly noticeable, were also undone and the whole sink could now be removed. Struggling, she lifted it up and out and placed it on the floor beside the unit. The smell coming from the open drain was not good, but ignoring that, she reached through and pressed a small brick that had been behind the sink. A section of the wall swung inwards leaving a hole big enough to climb into.

She returned to the car for her torch and some rags before going back into Unit 12. This time she moved quickly across to the sink and climbed in, legs going in first into the dark hole that was in front of her. She squeezed the rest of her body into the dark space and switched the torch on. Now able to see that much clearer, she shuffled along the sloping passage that went down and around to a much larger room. Once inside, she quickly checked to see if anybody else had followed her, but nobody had.

Swiftly, she moved over to the wall of metal cabinets, some now rusty with age, and repeated her lock destroying trick. Once opened, she removed the small gold coloured bars that lay inside and shut the door. Stuffing them into her bag, she retraced her steps and squeezed her way back out under the kitchen counter and into Unit 12. Swiftly working, she put the sink back as she had found it and just placed the wastepipe under it. From a glance it appeared to be connected, but if anybody tried to use it, well they would get wet feet. Smiling, she left the unit and went to the boot of her car.

Carefully she put her bag and the bars of metal inside and picked up the new lock she had purchased earlier that morning. Twenty minutes later a nice new lock, with her now holding the keys, had replaced and filled in the hole in the door. Looking up and down, again, just to make sure nobody was around, she locked it and went back to her car to drive off, pleased with her morning's work. The only thing that she had failed to do was to sweep up the sawdust and shavings from fitting the new lock and repaint the new wood.

+

DCI James Rogers was feeling pleased with the way things were moving. He had heard that his two men were now back in the UK and probably driving to Marlow at this moment. In the meantime, he had to drive to London to do two things. One to speak to Ruth Sanders and the other to collect a bag of XV3rd from the British Embassy, who, while being helpful, didn't want the bag on their premises for any longer than was required. His radio phone crackled into life.

"DCI Rogers speaking."

"Just to update you on a development or two. Your two men are back in Marlow. Secondly a PC doing the rounds at the units on the industrial estate has reported some sawdust and wood shavings at one of the rear doors to one of the units. Since they were supposed to be sealed and unused, we are sending a patrol to check it out more fully."

"Fine, keep me posted if anything else turns up." He turned off the radio phone and continued driving towards London, little knowing what was about to happen next.

+

Jane and Bill had got to LICD early that morning as they had a meeting arranged with Ruth Sanders and didn't want to be late. The file that they had pieced together had the potential to send a high-ranking person within LICD to prison for a very long time. Both Bill and Jane could hardly believe that the person would risk their job in return for working for the Russian Mafia. They had discussed the findings with each other for some time last night and eventually had decided to meet and inform Ruth of what they had found. They had taken a copy and put that in their safe deposit box at their local bank. On the outside they had written 'ONLY TO BE OPENED BY EITHER OF ACCOUNT HOLDERS OR ON BOTH OF US DYING TOGETHER.' Now taking each other's hand and a deep breath, they went into Ruth's office.

An hour later they reappeared and walked towards their desks. Ruth had been as unbelieving as they had been, but when shown the file and the names linked to it, had been convinced. She had told them to take a trip to Golspie, best that way to avoid being around LICD when the news broke later that morning.

Once Bill and Jane had left her office, Ruth picked up the phone and dialled a well-known number.

"Hello, just to let you know that Bill and Jane have uncovered the file that incriminates a person in LICD. I'll try and head them off on a wild goose chase, but remember, they are a very clever team."

+

Half an hour later at their home, there was a red card on the mat saying,'*We tried to deliver an item of mail today, you were not in, so have taken it to the address below:- The Post Office, Main St, Embankment Building two, The Embankment, London. Please bring some id with you of the address the item is addressed to.*'

Jane and Bill packed their two cases and then went to collect the item of mail. Once outside the Post Office, they both looked at the large packet and then at each other. The address on the back of the packet, was they noticed, the home address of the person they had spoken about to Ruth that morning. Why would the person send a packet to Bill and Jane they wondered? Putting it on the back seat they drove along the road and north towards Golspie.

They were just clearing the inner ring road when Jane's phone went off. She dug into her bag and finding it, answered it.

"Jane Sutherland."

"Where are you at the moment?"

"Just clearing the North Circular about to go onto the A1. Why what is up?"

"Have just heard from Oxford police, so can you go that way before heading north. It may be to your advantage." Jane looked across at Bill.

"Need to go to Oxford." She shrugged her shoulders by way of an apology.

"From here! Ok, you'll need to direct me though, once we are on the A1." he replied. Jane reached behind Bill and grabbed the road atlas,"

"Hello? You still there Jane?" crackled her phone. Grabbing it with her other hand, she put it to her ear.

"Yes, we are on the A1 so give us some time to get over there, we'll have to take a bit of detour. I'll phone you back later." She switched off her phone and looked at Bill. "Oxford then."

"Just give me the directions from here on in." She smiled and looked down at the road atlas now on her lap.

"Head off towards Hemel Hempstead and then to Aylesbury and over and down to Oxford. That is the main road and quickest from here."

Two hours later they pulled up outside Oxford police station and having parked, went inside. A policeman moved forward as they entered.

"DCIs Jane and Bill Sutherland by any chance? I'm PC Cameron Gray. You know of my father, DI Gray, Golspie?" He watched as the connection was made and Jane and Bill smiled at the policeman.

"Yes of course, we can see the likeness now, can't we Bill? How is your father?"

"He took early retirement, but still shows a keen interest in the police up there. I moved away - it was the same set of questions each night. Anyway, that is not why you are here. A lorry hit a car that pulled out in front of it yesterday and normally that would be sad but dealt with. The victim is a person who has been given a flag on HOLMES. When his details were being typed in, it flashed up and a connection to Marlow and to LICD was made. A Kenneth Brown. Here is the record for you." He passed them a large manilla brown envelope. "Quite a past. I've got to go, but nice meeting you. Where are you heading next?"

"Northwards to Scotland."

"Say hello to dad if you get that far north that is." He smiled and left them holding the envelope. They looked at each other, nodded and went back outside to their car. Bill started the engine and drove out and towards the roads heading north. Jane slid her finger along the gummed flap and took out a sheet of paper about the man known as Kenneth Brown. It made for interesting reading.

*He was born in southwest Scotland in 1957, his family had moved to Northern Ireland when he was aged three, grew up in West Belfast before being apprenticed to a firm of metal dealers. Learnt to drive and weld metal also obtained a licence to drive HGV lorries of all sizes. Worked in Northern Ireland till age 31 he upped and left to work in Folkestone on the Channel tunnel workings.*

<u>*Theory and hearsay.*</u>
*Heard to be working in Marlow for a firm that produced industrial diamond cutter heads. Tracing owners of firm has been elusive. Other sightings have been reported of a similar man selling some sort of drugs on the streets in and around Marlow and Oxford. No police record as of date of this report. XX/XX/1992.*

Jane finished reading to Bill and sat taking it all in. Here was somebody who was linked to Northern Ireland, had a Scottish connection and may have dealt with drugs in Marlow. And now he was dead. She banged the dashboard with frustration. Bill looked across at her bemused.

"What's wrong?"

"He might have been a useful person to talk to, with the links to Scotland, Northern Ireland and drugs."

"And now he is dead. We can't bring him back to life to question him, so let's acknowledge what we know and move on. Care to take over driving in half an hour or so?" Jane nodded and they drove on into the evening.

+

Now back at her house in Marlow, the lady had put the two bars away in her safe and was on the phone trying to get hold of her contact in Oxford, still unaware that he had been shot in his shop.

+

Jane pulled the car into the hotel car park and got out and stretched her legs. Bill did the same and looked across at the hotel entrance.

"Hope they have a room for us tonight."

"Bound to at this time of year." So, saying, she took her case out of the boot before removing the packet they had collected early that morning. Bill picked up the file they had collected from Oxford and his case, then they walked over to the entrance and into the hotel.

After a nice meal that night, the pair of them sat down and opened the file and stared at the attached paper on the front.

*Bill and Jane.*

*By the time you get this, I will have long gone. It would take too long to explain my reasons for working for Ivan. However, here is a file that might help you, I've put it together from interviews and information gained from LICD as well as some presumed text, that I added to fill the gaps.*

*Do with it what you will, it might be useful in bringing those to justice. Though from a contact I used to have, it appears that somebody else is going about killing them one by one. Don't try and trace me.*

*All the best to both of you. You make a good team, too good! Simon Reed*

*PS Don't trust your immediate supervisor with too much information.*

Jane opened the file and stared at the first page. Then she started to read it, passing a sheet at a time to Bill as she did so.

```
ARI TUT Files. Final Copy.
Originally four copies: UKPM/FPF/EPF/OPF
From interviews, tape recordings and other files
located in:- Folkestone, Oxford, Exeter and London.
```

This is now the only copy now stored at
LICD's Secure Data Centre.

```
Joe O'Brien             Unemployed worker in Belfast
Sarah O'Brien           His wife.

Eurotunnel Company
Sam Brooks              Site Manager
Sean Smith              Head of Personal at Tunnel Site
Charles Meadows         His deputy
Mary Orchard            Secretary to Sean Smith
Thomas Swift            Identity Disc engraver
Martin Andrew           Joe's boss.
Justin Cassy            Fuel attendant
Kenneth Brown           Lorry Driver

Security services.
Simon Reed/
William Dawson          Government trouble-shooter
Gail Rose               His office assistant
Margaret Thatcher       UK Prime Minister
Ian MacKenzie           Bomb Disposal Expert
Judith MacKenzie        His wife
```

| DCI Andrews | Folkstone CID |
| PC James Black | Folkstone Crime Prevention |
| CS Rose | Head of LICD |
| DI Rodgers | Oxford CID |
| DI George Armstrong | Exeter CID |

| Terrorists | |
| Patrick O'Conner | ARI Cell Leader aka The Boss |
| Colleen Kent. | Bank Robber and Driver of ARI. |
| Michael Brady. | ARI member |
| Lenny 'smoke' | ARI Hit man. |
| Patrick O'Reilly | ARI on trial in London. |
| Pat Doyle | ARI member |
| Seumas Kelly | ARI member |
| Barry Ryan | ARI member |
| Lorcan O'Connor | ARI member |
| Mr. Green | ARI Solicitor |

# 1.28

## 1988

Joe O'Brien looked at his wife Sarah across the breakfast table. He had just opened a letter from the consortium that were building the euro-tunnel and they wanted him to go for an interview.

Silently he passed the letter over to her and she put down the paper and read the letter.

He knew that she would not want him to go but knew that they needed the money. It was at least a reply. Much more than some of the firms he had written to.

"Well?"

"Well, I think that you ought to think about it long and hard before you decide what to do. I know that it is an offer for an interview but do not rush into things."

"All right, but if I went what would you do?"

"Keep going I guess." She smiled and leaned over the table and kissed him, then rose and handed him back the letter. "It is your decision, I guess. I'm off to do the dishes." Joe sat there turning the letter over in his hands and, wondering if he should go or not, he decided to go for walk around the block and maybe by then he would have made up his mind.

"I'm going out for a walk to think it over, I shall not be long."

"Ok, can you get some stamps for me if you go past the Post Office."

Joe got his coat and walked out of the front door. Could he manage to go all that way and keep the house going? And Sarah, what did she plan on doing? He would rather that she came with him, but the letter had said that wives or girlfriends could not accompany them. He knew it would be a wrench as they had only been married one and a half years. Joe walked around the streets not really thinking where he was walking or where he was going.

After about two hours he had decided to go and try for the job. He walked back to his home to find Sarah was sitting on the sofa knitting and looked up as he walked in.

"Well?"

"I am going to try for the job. I think it is unlikely that I'll get it." "I thought you would, so packed a suitcase and found out that a flight that goes tonight. I suggest you try and get to that interview as soon as possible." Joe leaned over and kissed her. "You're one in a million. Now where is that number?" Half an hour later, he had arranged an interview in three days' time. He would fly down to London; they would reimburse him his costs. Things were moving so fast he was finding it difficult to think. Joe looked over to Sarah. If he got the job then he may have to start work at once. "Sarah, If I get the job…" his voice tailed off. "I know, you will have start at once, now go for it. We need the money to clear some of the debts we have run up."

"What will you do?"

"I'll survive. I used to type; I'll see if I can take that up again." "Well, that would make me feel a lot better when I am over there. I'll phone you when I get there and on a regular basis." Sarah took his hand.

"Save our money, one phone call a week is enough." "If you say so."

"I do, now let's get you on that plane." Sarah walked over to the phone and arranged a taxi to take Joe to the airport.

Two hours later they were saying their good-byes, and the taxi was outside waiting. As they had already decided that Sarah would not come to the airport. Joe turned to Sarah.

"Well, this is it. I don't know when we'll see each other again, but Sarah, do write as soon as I give you an address."

"You know I will. Mind you write to me, I have put some notepaper and envelopes in the suitcase along with some stamps so there is no excuse."

"Goodbye Sarah." He leaned over and kissed her fondly. "Goodbye Joe." She turned and walked back into the house, as he got into the taxi which pulled away from the house and towards the airport.

Joe stood around the lounge of the airport. There was no going back now, his plane was called, and he made his way over to the gateway that led to the aircraft.

Once in his seat he turned his head and looked up and down the aircraft. There didn't seem to be many passengers on the plane, which would mean that it would be a quiet flight. The plane started its engines and then after the usual warning of not smoking and fastening of seatbelts as well as the safety talk, the plane started to roll forward and slowly built up the speed along the runway, then before he knew it the plane was up and away heading for London.

## 2.28

Joe stepped off the plane from Belfast on to the concourse of one of the passages leading to customs at London's Heathrow Airport.

All around him thousands of people were either coming or going on holidays. Noise and television monitors blared out information at him like some nightmare scene from a film.

The departure lists were changing with their repetitive clacking of the boards. Joe made his way over to the luggage collection point. It took him about twenty-five minutes before his case appeared. Stepping forward, hr took the case and left. Brady carried on following Joe as he had been told.

Ten minutes later Joe was outside looking for a taxi that would take him to London so that he could get a train to Folkestone.

Having found a taxi,he climbed in to be taken towards London. Brady took another taxi and in best film fashion, told the driver to"follow that cab".

On arriving at St Pancras, Joe made his way over to the information centre on the platform. He had noticed a sign saying"book-a-bed-ahead"The lady behind the counter informed him that he could book a bed in the next town he was visiting. At this Joe brightened considerably, so he booked a room at a small guest house on the outskirts of Folkestone not too far from the workings of the channel tunnel.

Brady following him, meanwhile purchased a first-class ticket and walked off to the right platform to await the train. He was most anxious that Joe didn't catch sight of him. He had been told to follow Joe and report where he was going to stay.

He stood and waited behind one of the columns of the station. Had anyone bothered to look, they would have seen a man reading a magazine, but closer inspection of the man would have revealed that his shoes had dried red clay on the uppers and the sides as if he had walked around a building site, which was exactly what Brady had been doing before this assignment.

He had received a phone call in Ireland to get on the plane and follow Joe to England and find out where he was going to stay. If this Mr. O'Brien was any use to them then that would be a bonus. He knew that there was always the wife to threaten. It never surprised him how easily a man would give in if his wife was threatened. This was why they tended to go for married men rather than single men as no blackmail pressure could be applied to them as a rule.

. The train pulled into the station and Joe picked up his suitcase and boarded it. The table was full of used plastic coffee cups and empty crisp packets that had been wedged down the back of the seats. Joe sat back and thought to himself 'This is really it; I have come this far; nothing can go wrong now can it?'

Meanwhile in the first-class carriage Brady was settling himself in to his seat. He knew that few people travelled first class and it was extremely unlikely he would be disturbed. He sat down and looked at the case that had been delivered into his hands just before the train arrived.

He had been and still was in the ARI for years. While he worked in the building industry, few people knew that his specialty was following people without them knowing. He did run a small back up team of his own. Even the ARI didn't know about. It was this that had enabled him to get the small case on the table in front of him. He got up and made his way to the toilet.

Once inside, he placed the small case on the toilet seat. Opening the box, inside he found a minute bug and receiver so now all he had to do was get the bug onto Joe in some way. Having tested it to see that it was working, he looked in the case to see what else had been packed. Lying on the top were bundles of used money. Three thousand five hundred pounds in used notes for more expenses. Under this there was a change of clothes and a small set of makeup.

Brady quickly changed the clothes and then set about folding up the clothes he had been wearing and put them back into the case. Next Brady took the small make up box, years ago he had been a make-up artist for an amateur theatre group but now he used it for more devious purposes. First there were cheek pads to place in his mouth, next he took a make-up pencil and darkened his eyebrows, and a crafted thin silver hair beard and moustache came next. A wig of silver and light brown hair was pulled on with a working in of greasepaint between his head and the wig. Unless anyone knew where to look the join was impossible to see.

Brady looked into the railway mirror and was satisfied with the result. He took out the handkerchief - now for the real touches a small box marked"trappings", but it made all the difference between what the police might look for and what they got. Keys, wallet, watch, loose change all went on his person. Last of all the money. Brady repacked the packet with the old clothes and packed up the box again. All that was left to do was to stretch a thin film of brown rubber all over the case and change its appearance. Now ready, Brady pulled up the blinds and left the WC to return to his seat. Once there he took out the magazine he had purchased before leaving London.

Around an hour later the train was pulling into Folkestone. Brady looked up and down the corridor as he picked up the case and the packet. As soon as the train pulled into the station and had stopped, he leapt from the train and made his way over to the lockers. Putting some money into the slot he turned the handle and then placed both the briefcase and case inside, before slamming the door closed and took the key out and placed it in a previously stamped addressed envelope which he posted in the letter box outside the station.

He spotted Joe asking a taxi to take him to the place where he was staying. Brady moved closer and he heard Joe say the name of the place"The Last Resort".

Brady had decided to enlist some known help. He would need it in getting the radio transmitter into the coat of Mr. O'Brien. At the foot of the road that led to the station he spotted a blue Mazda car parked on double yellow lines outside the nearby church. He thought he recognized the lady driver, so he walked around and tapped the window on her right. She jumped and looked to him, then wound down the window.

A very independent woman in her own right, no man would ever take the lead role in any relationship with her. She was wearing a light blue suit and a matching cravat and round her neck hung a small gold pendent in the form of a cat, the cats' eyes were small diamonds. It was a lucky charm, her ability to be able to creep on anyone and either knock them out or kill them earned her the well-deserved name" The Cat".

"I see that I had to find you as usual," Michael grumbled to her. "And I'm here parked and risking a ticket while we are talking.

Now get in the car." Brady walked around to the passenger side and got in.

"Well do you have the information we need," She asked Brady "Yes, but the job will have to be done in the early morning" "How early?" she asked suspiciously

"Five in the morning" he replied.

"Fine, now want do you want to do for the rest of the evening?" "Dinner and a little late-night shopping for both of us," replied

Brady, yawning as he finished speaking. "Anywhere in mind?" she asked him. "No, but you must know somewhere." "I do as it happens."

"Well, where is it?" He let his question hang in the air like a cloud. For some reason she hesitated, then she decided to tell him. It had been her plan to just take him there, but now something made her change her mind.

"The Fishy Plaice." She replied.

"The Fishy Plaice'," it is," Brady repeated. Starting the engine, the car pulled away towards Folkestone. She turned to him.

"I'm Colleen Kent and I know who you are." She drove on and in due course they pulled up in the centre of Folkestone and parked outside The Fishy Plaice. Colleen turned to Brady.

"Are you glad you came?"

"Did I have a choice?" They both picked the seafood special and waited for it to be cooked and served.


An hour later, Brady and Colleen had finished their food and two empty plates were in front of them.

"Where are you staying tonight?"

"Have to look for somewhere nearby. Joe is staying at The Last Resort. I wondered about staying there too," Brady said.

"Probably not the best idea. Too big a chance that he might have seen you at St Pancras and wonder why you are staying at the same place as him. You can stay the night in my house if you want, but no funny business." She looked at him and wondered what sort of man he really was underneath that exterior.

"Well in that case I'll accept." He indicated to a passing waiter that they were ready for the bill which he paid in cash. Colleen looked at him. Justifiable expenses Brady explained.

+

Joe had told the landlady of '*The Last Resort*' that he only required the room for the one night. She explained that the season was coming to an end, but since he was paying cash, she would stay open. She showed him his room and after she left, he opened the cupboard door and found an old suit hanging there. He placed his own behind it and stretched out on the bed. He made a mental note to clean his shoes in the morning then he packed himself off to bed.

Downstairs the landlady was talking to a friend that had called in.

"Why on earth did you take him in?"

"Well, the taxi driver said this was the first place he thought of when he asked him where to stay for the night. Besides it is the end of the season, and the extra money will be useful."

"True, but you know nothing about him, do you?" "So?"

"All I am saying is that you could be storing up trouble for yourself."

"He is most likely looking for work on the tunnel."

"Then I do hope so for your sake. I really do." She took a sip of tea and looked at her friend.

The next morning Joe was up and about very early. He had slept very well and now, refreshed and dressed he walked down to the dining room and in to have breakfast. Having found out which room Joe was in, Brady stood in the garden, his binoculars fixed on Joe's room. As the light went out in Joe's bedroom, Brady ran up the ladder that he had propped against the outside wall and climbed in through the open window. Inside he made his way over to the wardrobe in the corner and opened it, where he found a suit, Assuming the suit to be Joe's, he dropped the bug into the top pocket and arranged a handkerchief on top of it so that should Joe want to take the handkerchief out, it wouldn't disturb the bug.

Then hearing footsteps approaching, he closed the wardrobe door leaving the same way as he entered.

Brady ran over to Colleen, who had her car parked with the engine ticking over. He climbed in beside her and she looked at him.

`Well, what are you waiting for, we need to get out of here," he said with a snarl. She put the car in gear and let out the clutch and pushed the accelerator down hard as the tyres squealed against the road.

"Brady what range does that device have?" "Fifteen miles, over that, it tends to be a bit faint."

`That is sufficient, but what if he goes underground?" she asked.

"Then I guess we have a problem." "No, we try a different way."

After breakfast and having left his room, Joe walked down to the landlady.

"Thanks for the food and the bed, here are the keys. By the way there was a suit in my wardrobe before I unpacked."

"Thanks, I will see that it is moved."

"Ok, now can you phone for a taxi for me please?" "Of course."

+

The taxi dropped Joe of outside the tunnel works and he stood there with his suitcase on the ground in sheer awe of the size of the surface works, never mind the tunnel itself which snaked its way under the tunnel crisscrossing in two places. He had studied the details in the guest house as there had been a leaflet on it in the main reception area. A man dressed in mud splattered overalls walked towards him. Joe looked across.

"Hello, my name is Joe O'Brian. I have an appointment to see a Mr. S. Bryan."

"He is up there." He gestured with his hand towards the Portacabins that were stacked two high and along a straight section of the site. Joe gulped, this is what he was afraid of - he had feared heights for most of his life and now he had to go up two flights of portacabins and only on a rickety ladder. He started to walk towards them, when a large friendly man came put of one of the cabins on the top floor. He waved and started to climb down. Joe walked up to him.

"Mr. Bryan?"

"Yes, but call me Sean, everyone else does, Mr?" "O'Brian. Joe O'Brian."

"Well, let's go and talk in my office." He led the way over to one of the ground floor cabins and opened the door. "Come on in." Inside there was a small office with a woman typing away on a word processor. "That's Mary, she is my secretary, she also knows everything there is to know about this area of the site. Anything you need ask her. Now about this job, here is the contract and the list of likely equipment you will drive. Think you are capable of it?" Sean passed Joe a piece of paper with the terms of the job and when Joe saw the type of money, he would be getting he whistled.

"I'll have a good try, Sean."

"Good, now how soon can you start?"

"Well, I have to fix up somewhere to live, but then anytime." "Let Mary do that; you go and change and get an I.D. cut over in the I.D. hut there." He pointed out the hut on a large plan of the site that ran the length of one wall. "Oh, and Joe."

"Yes, Sean?"

"Here you will work so hard that you will want to sleep as soon as you are off shift."

"Thanks for warning me." Joe smiled as Sean left the office. "He's right you know; you will feel terrible when you have finished each day." said Mary with a smile. "Thanks!"

"That's alright, now do you know where to go next?"

"I think so." He picked up the suitcase and left the office. Outside the office Joe made his way over to the I.D. office and knocked on the door, the hut was a very basic hut, with black paint on the outside. A man's voice called out from the inside to enter, Joe ducked his head and entered.

+

Brady and Colleen had been listening intently to the receiving device but having not heard anything ever since they got back to Colleen's house. Brady turned to her and removed the headset.

"You know it is funny that he hasn't gone out yet."

"Well perhaps we should go to the site and have a scout around?"

"Alright, let's go."

Half an hour later they were gloomily surveying the site from the top of the observation tower of the exhibition centre. "I can't see any sign of him."

"Did you expect to?"

"Yes, those are the site offices."They both looked up and down the large site which had machines moving across it like toys on some large giants play pit.

"I think we have to get down there somehow," said Colleen. "And just how do you propose to do that?"

"I have just figured out a way." "Tell me."

"Back at the flat, which reminds me that you still haven't found anywhere to stay have you?" she added with a concerned look.

"Not yet."

"Then you had better stay with me until this is over, but no funny business."

"That's alright, I'll pay my way."

"Yes you will. Now let's get going." They walked back down, then drove off towards her flat.

+

"Well Joe, this is your ID disc, don't go anywhere without it. You wear it all the time, understand?"

"Sure."

"That is hard work out there but this isn't though, for once you have done the first thousand discs the rest is easy."

"By the way, what's your name?"

"Thomas Swift, Thomas is sufficient though. If you ever want to talk, then just pop in for a chat."

"Thanks,I'll remember that."Joe turned and left the hut. He had to get to the changing room before starting work that morning.

# 3.28

Joe walked across the site to one of the many portakabins where men could be seen moving in and out. He walked in and a hush fell across the room. Joe looked around and told the assembled crowd what he was looking for. They told him where to go and he left with one of the men who had been there for some time. Having changed, he went and signed in.

In the office Joe found out he was driving a JCB around the site. This didn't worry him as he had driven one many years ago. All over the site there were lots of JCB and larger excavators, while bumping around the site were large trucks with huge tyres. Joe made his way over to his JCB and started up. The man who had shown him where to come got into this own JCB in front and started the engine up. He had told Joe, when they walked over, to follow him to the end of the site where his work would start properly.

The site, being so being large, took a while to get Joes machine down there, however once there he found that time passed as he shovelled the loose rock into the waiting large lorries that stood patiently waiting for him to fill them. All too soon the day had finished and Joe was able to drive back to the diesel depot and park for the night. Then he walked over to Sean's office to retrieve his suitcase, where he had left it earlier.

+

Brady followed Colleen into her flat.

"We need to sort out the money side of things. I only want to stay as a paying guest. I thought a deposit of one thousand pounds and fifty pounds a week." He watched her as she smiled back at him.

"it's a deal."

"I thought it might be." Brady smiled at her.

"You'll want a key." She walked over to the desk and took one out of the drawer. "Don't lose it."

"Would I?"

"You might. Now go and do something useful like getting some groceries from the shop down the street."

"Ok, I'll do that." Brady turned and left the flat, softly closing the door after him.

Colleen decided to take the opportunity to clean up the room that he would have. She busied herself tidying up bits and pieces that scattered around the room. These were souvenirs from her travels. The china sphinx from Egypt, the three matching paperweights from Scotland next to them stood a small gold enamel box and on the wall an old gold mirror that she had bought at an antique fair, which was set off against the blue coloured wallpaper with gold flecks in it. Not one bit was owned by anyone else. She would not give this up lightly. She valued her independence too highly for that.

Brady arrived back laden with a box of groceries, which he put on the work surface.

"Well, there is the deposit of the flat to deal with, don't go away." He left her and walked through to his room and opened the small case that she had placed on his bed. He took out a bundle of money and closed the case again and slid it under the bed. As he walked back into the living room Colleen was getting a drink for herself. She looked up as he entered the room.

"What kind of drink do you want?"

"Irish Whiskey, Bushmills if you have it, please."

"I have some here somewhere." She rummaged at the back of the cupboard, before pulling out a bottle. "Well, what shall we drink to?"

"The success of the operation." The glasses clinked and they both sat down in the quiet flat.

"Brady?"

"What?"

"Just try that receiver again, will you?" "Ok, but can you get the dinner then."

"It's a deal." She left him crouched over the receiver, listening in intently.

Half an hour later after a nice dinner, she was taking her turn at listening, and Brady was loading the dishwasher when she called out to him.

"I've got something on the transmitter." Brady ran over and took the headset from her, to listen in intently. He heard:"I still say it isn't mine, it was in the jacket pocket when we were checking the pockets."

"So, what do we do with it?"

"I don't know, perhaps we should take it to the police. It seems very new and as we are unsure as to what it is, they may be able to tell us."

"Look, doesn't your lad know a bit about electronics?"

"A little, why?"

"Well, why not let him have a look at it first, then if he thinks we ought to, we'll hand it in."

"Fine, now you call us when he has decided."

"Ok, I'll try and get round there in the next hour." The conversion died and there was the sound of a door slamming, then quiet.

"Colleen?" said Brady "What?"

"Have you got a map of Folkestone?" "Somewhere, why?"

"I'll tell you as we drive, I'll bring the receiver, meet me outside in the car."

+

Joe having collected his case, looked across to Mary Orchard who was seated at her desk in a sweatshirt on which was proclaimed *Tunnellers do it underground.* She looked up as Joe entered the room.

"I found you somewhere to stay for a while until you find your feet that is."

"Great, where is it?" "With me."

"What!"

"Staying with me and my mother to be exact. She runs a small boarding house. It supplements her income."

"Are you sure that it will be alright?"

"I have already phoned and told her that you are coming. Now you have finished I'll pack up here." She closed the computer and put a cover on it. "Dust gets everywhere" she explained. Then they both walked out to her car that was parked by the portacabins. She unlocked the central locking device and Joe got in. Things were going along nicely – a new job and he had board and lodgings already. He leaned back and fell fast asleep. The next thing he knew was the car had stopped and he was being woken by Mary. "This is it. You go on in and sign in, I'll go and park the car." An older lady stood at the top of the steps and Joe ran up the steps towards her.

"Mrs. Orchard?"

"That's right, Mr. O'Brian. Now come and sign the register. Mary has vouched for you already." Joe looked around the walls and noticed the paintings that hung on them. It would be much later he was to discover that they were the genuine article. The bedroom had a nice thick red carpet and a huge double bed. He unpacked and went and washed, then collapsed on the bed and slept the sleep of the just.

+

"Brady, have you heard anything yet?" They had driven all around Folkestone but had been unable to track the transmitter down to its source. Now they were back at Colleen's flat eating the dinner that she had cooked earlier. Brady had been listening to the receiver.

"No, but I have only listened five times tonight."

"Well, I suggest that you try once more then give up and go to bed."

"Give up! You can go to bed; I'll keep on trying." Brady turned his attention back to the receiver and almost at once heard voices. He turned the volume up and pulled a pad toward him to write down what they said.

"...Do you have any idea where it might have come from?" "No, we were rather wondering what it was and hoping that you could tell us."

"I can tell you it's a transmitter, of what range I don't yet know, but that I can find out."

"And how long will that take?"

"No idea, look leave it with me and I'll get back to you as soon as possible. I share a shed with a friend who is interested in this sort of thing. He lives in Wood Cottage Lane. You can come over and collect it when we know more about it."

"What number?"

"Two hundred and five."

"Ok, we'll wait for you to contact us."

"Goodbye." Brady stopped listening and went and knocked on Colleen's bedroom door.

"Colleen, we must go back out. I now know where it will be tonight - and wear old clothes."

"Brady, I'm not called the 'cat' for nothing."

"Of course not, now I need a map of Folkestone and you driving me."

"It'll be in the car where you left it." "Ok, I'll go and get it."

"The car keys are on the shelf by the front door. I'll be there in a few minutes, and Brady?"

"Yes?"

"I suggest you change yourself." Brady went and changed and a few minutes later she joined him at the car.

"Do you know where to go then?" she asked him. "Yes. So, let's get there and I'll be able to get it back."

"Don't you think that if you steal it back that they, whoever they are, will become suspicious and call the police?"

"Maybe, but over something as small as this? On the other hand, when they see how new this one is, they might decide to do that..."

"That's true. Brady don't get into trouble tonight, will you?" "Why?"

"Because you said we had to keep a low profile, and that would hardly be keeping a low profile, would it?"

"No, now let's go."The car drove off and after a few minutes arrived in Wood Cottage Lane. "Turn the car around in case we have to get away quickly."

Colleen turned the car and faced it back towards the main road. Then Brady got out and started to walk down the road peering at the house numbers hoping to find one to know which way they numbered. Eventually he found one and then could work out where number two hundred and five was. In the front garden of the adjoining house stood two large fir trees and it was here that he hid himself while listening for the signal that would start to transmit any time now. It started to spot with rain, large drops falling faster. Brady clutched the receiver to his chest and thought to himself it was never like this in the films.

Colleen appeared carrying a small rolled up mac. She handed it to him silently and he gratefully put it on. A few minutes later a small group of three men in a car drove up the road and pulled into the kerb. They got out and the next-door garden suddenly lit up as the front door was opened and the three men were welcomed inside. A few minutes later the receiver crackled into life, and it was obvious that the transmitter was very close, as Brady had to turn down the volume.

"Well, it is some sort of listening device." "But it is so small."

"They are getting smaller and smaller these days." "But who uses them?"

"All sorts of people."

"So, are you going to see what it is tonight?" Brady waited with bated breath to see what the answer would be.

"No, I need to confirm what type it is first. Look leave it with me, and I'll look it up and maybe tomorrow I'll have a better understanding of it."

"So, we'll leave it to you then?"

"Ok, I'll be in touch." Brady turned off the receiver and turned contented to Colleen.

"Let's get going, I have some phone calls to make before we come back here."

"Thanks Brady. Look, am I going to get some sleep tonight?" "Of course you are, just not right now, come on." As they walked back Brady noticed a small house for sale, just right for a hideaway he thought to himself, so he made a mental note of the estate agents. He had also noticed on the map that a footpath appeared to run along the bottom of the gardens. That might be helpful for getting to the shed. Now all he needed was a suitable diversion. Perhaps he could come up with something in the next few hours.

Brady had sat by the phone for the better part of three hours assembling his plan for a diversion. The only thing remaining to do was to tell Colleen about what he planned as she might not like it.

Colleen had gone and slept as soon as she had arrived back but said to knock if he needed her. Now he awoke her again and outlined the plan to her. He had contacted"Lenny Smoke" and one other to come and cause the appearance of a fire in the front of the house. In the commotion, he would get over the fence at the back. She had to have the car ready with the engine running, for once things started, they would need to move fast.

Once he had the transmitter then they would have to get back to the flat as quickly as possible and get to bed.

The rain swept across the street almost horizontal to the road. Brady looked at Colleen and smiled, he had already seen that the two others were already st the house.

"This is it then,just be ready when I come with the transmitter."

"I will be. Now don't worry it will be fine."Then Brady slipped away into the night leaving her in the car. After a few minutes his plan swung into action and shortly there was total chaos. Meanwhile Brady had climbed over the fence and was now crouching low to avoid being seen by anyone entering or leaving the shed. Suddenly the door to the shed flew open and a man shot out and up the path muttering something under his breath, leaving the shed door unlocked and slightly ajar. Brady quickly ran to the door and went in. He saw the transmitter lying on the workbench. He quickly changed it for a small cell battery that he had bought for this purpose as it was about the same size and weight, and he just hoped that it would look similar until the morning.

Glancing around the shed there were lots of boxes full of spare parts, with each box having a different code written on it. Suddenly he was aware that the door handle was turning slowly. With no place to hide, he quickly looked for a weapon. He picked up the long-handled screwdriver before hiding behind the shed door. The door opened, he waited quietly, then as the person entered, he brought the screwdriver down hard on the neck of the intruder, the person slumped to the floor and Brady gasped for it was Colleen. Now what was she doing there? he asked himself.

He needed to get her to the car. Swinging her over his shoulder he left the shed and carried her to where he had climbed over the fence. In the distance Brady could already hear sirens approaching the scene, Colleen had started to come round.

"What happened?"

"I'll tell you later, we need to get out of here."

He helped her over the fence then climbed over himself. They both ran down the lane and out to the road. A police car was parked a few cars down from theirs and the blue flashing lights lit up the houses with regular monotony. Brady knew that one of his two contacts would have had his rifle trained on the streetlamps. As soon as Brady appeared he started firing at the lamps, one by one taking them out. Under the noise of both the gun and the darkness they both made their way back to the car and drove off, neither of them noticing an unmarked police car which followed at a discreet distance. Making fast time they were soon back at her house and once indoors, sighed with relief and both looked at each other. He passed her the small receiver.

"Look after that, we don't want it going anywhere else after all the trouble we have gone to getting it back."A loud knocking on the door made them look at one another with alarm.

"Now what?" Brady started to walk towards the door when Colleen called out.

"Brady the chain, put the chain up before you unlock the door."

"Ok" Brady opened the door slightly and there stood a police officer.

"Can I come in sir?"

"Well, it is rather late, can it wait until the morning?" "Not really sir."

"Alright." Brady undid the chain and let the policeman into the house. "What is this all about then?"

"You have just been seen speeding through Folkstone. Straight from a property that had a device detonated in its front garden."

"That's unusual isn't it officer?"

"Yes, unless there was some other purpose for the visit." "What might that be officer?"

"When we talked to the owner about this he claims he was in his shed. However, he is very reluctant to let us see his shed and he doesn't think that anything was stolen, but you can't tell can you sir?"

`No, I don't suppose you can, but tell me why you have come here to see me?"

"One of the neighbours thought she saw you getting into a car not unlike the one parked outside now."

"Perhaps she was mistaken."

"Perhaps, but I don't think so do you sir? You see I followed you from there to here just now and it was hard to keep up with you at times."

He let the sentence hang in the air. "So, I must ask both of you to come down to the station now for some further questioning."

"Are we being charged officer?" asked Colleen. "No, just helping the police with their enquiries."

"Right, then I'll go and change, it won't take long" and she walked off to the bedroom. Brady had a look of amazement across his face until he remembered that he had given her the bug just after they had got in. He assumed that she was now hiding it somewhere safe.

+

Two hours later they were both down at the police station and the policeman was seated in front of Brady looking at him in the eye he sighed.

"Let's just run through your story again shall we sir?"

"it's not a story I've told you, how many times, so why once more?"

"Well, I am not satisfied yet and I will be happy to hear it again and again until I am satisfied."

"Look, I was in bed, remembered I hadn't locked the car and got dressed and went and locked it. It is that simple, really it is."

"I wish it was, I really do."

Brady turned and looked at his solicitor Mr. Green, who had already said to stick to the one story unless they produced evidence to the contrary. So far Brady had held up well, they had been talking for four hours none stop and he hadn't changed his story once. Suddenly the policeman rose and looking like the cat who has found a bowl of cream, he walked round to Brady.

"Take your trainers off." "What?"

"You heard. Now as we have a cast of footprints in the garden, I want to see if the trainer matches it."

Brady thought if he refused, he would look as though he was guilty. If he said they could have them, then it would match the pattern, either way he was lost. He glanced at Mr. Green who looked at the officer.

"Sir, if you have the cast of the footprint, bring them here and my client will see if they match. If not then, as he hasn't been charged and you have now questioned him for four hours without any breaks, release him forthwith."

Brady looked at Green as though he were mad before realising that the policeman might be bluffing. The officer looked hard at them both, then turned and left the room, slamming the door closed after him. A new officer took his place.

"Do you want a fag or water?" the officer asked him.

"No to the fag, but some water would be nice." As soon as he had left the room, Brady bent forward as if to speak to Mr. Green, but he shook his head from side to side indicating that he shouldn't speak. A few minutes later the first officer returned without anything in his hands. Mr. Green rose to his feet and looked at the policeman.

"Well, it looks as though you were bluffing, now let my client go."

"We will when we are good and ready sir."

"Then I would like to talk to my client without the monitors and microphones being on."

"Monitors and microphones? You have a good imagination sir."

"Officer, I have been in this game long enough to know the rules, if no monitors and microphones why drag us past three empty rooms?" The second policeman arrived with the water and smiled at Brady.

"Your water." He set it down in front of Brady.

"Thank you." Brady went to raise it to his lips, but Mr. Green intercepted him and offered the glass to his lips. The two policemen looked angrily at Green, and both went out of the room slamming the door after them. "You know they really hate us." said Brady.

"And yet you are surprised at this." "Not really I suppose."

"You know that they will keep up the pressure until you give in?"

"I know that, but what else can I do?"

"Hang in there until either you reach breaking point, or I get you out of here." One of the policemen came back into the room and looked at them both.

"Right, this is where we get serious. Michael Brady, I am charging you with theft from a garden shed. You don't have to say anything, but anything you do say could be given in evidence. Now come with me."

"I'm not guilty." cried out Brady.

"They all say that." said the officer with a smile at the other policeman.

Brady knew that if any officer saw the tattoo on his back, it would be easy to check any records with the Metropolitan Police in London.

"Officer my client has been under arrest for over four hours now and you haven't produced any evidence to back up my client's arrest." said Green with a frown.

"Tough, you see we can hold him for up to three days, without charge, should we have the need."

"Then I need to call somebody."

"There are two phone boxes by the railway station."

"Thank you, officer." He turned to Brady. "I'll be back. Keep quiet and say nothing until I get back."

Then he left the police station and made his way over in the direction of the railway station.

## 4.28

Joe was fast asleep dreaming of Sarah safely by his side. Turning over he became conscious that there was someone banging on his bedroom door and shouting.

"Get up and get moving, it's ten past eight." Joe leaned over and looked at the alarm clock on the bedside table to check. He swung himself out of bed calling out at the same time.

"Ok, I'm awake now thank you." Joe went and quickly got ready. Then he made his way downstairs to breakfast. Mary and her mother were both busying themselves in the kitchen preparing his breakfast. Mary looked up as he entered.

"Do you want us to prepare a lunch for you as well?"

"Yes please, I'd appreciate that." He sat down and Mrs. Orchard brought over his breakfast and placed it front of him. "What time am I due at the site?"

"About three quarters of an hour, I should think." He spluttered as Mary said this.

"What time is it now?"

"Half past eight, but don't worry Mary will get you there on time."

"I'm sure that she will Mrs. Orchard, and thanks for the breakfast."

"Oh, That's alright, all part of the service." She smiled as she picked up his plate. "At least you like your food, and that's good."

"Come on Joe we need to be going."

"Alright, I'm coming." They both flew out through the front door and got into Mary's car. He had hardly finished doing up his seatbelt, when Mary had the engine going and was putting her into first gear and driving towards the site at breathtaking speed.

Five minutes later they arrived at the site and the car swung into its allotted place outside the offices.

"Do you know where I am working to-day?" "Not yet, but it will be on the board." "What?"

"The board, it shows where everyone is supposed to be on the site at any given moment!"

"Where is it situated, this board?"

"In the room adjoining the 'hangman's room'" "Is that the real name, if so, why?""

"Oh, it's just a name given to a room where all the suits are hung up high. It being a man's room they've called it the hangman's room, as the suits are suspended like hung men." She led him to the board and for a few minutes Joe just gaped at it like so many before him had done.

"But how do you find time to keep it up to date?"

"We don't, well not in the daily sense. It's like this, most people work in the same area on the same job for a long stretch it may be a week or a month or a quarter, but if they are on the same job, then we don't need to change the board that often, see?"

"So, what do I do?"

"If we look at the board, see you were on a JCB in 16. Find that reference and then the dates above. So that's what you will be on this week and all next week by the look of things. Now you must go and sign on. Over in that shed there. Nest to the ID hut. She opened the door and pointed it out to Joe across the yard.

Once Joe signed in, he made his way back to where he had left the JCB the night before. Climbing on board, he took a glance at the fuel indicator which it now showed almost empty. Joe decided to fill it up with fuel first. After about a short wait he moved up to the head of the queue.

"Hello, I'm Mike O'Hara, what's your name then?" "Joseph O'Brian, but I'm known as Joe."

"Then you can call me Mike."

"Thanks, now when is the best time to come and refuel?" "About half seven tonight. By then the shifts will have changed and all the lorries have refuelled and returned to work." "Thanks." Mike waved him off and Joe drove the JCB forward and towards the area that he had been working yesterday, though he found it had been transformed. A lot of earth had been scooped up into piles and then he realised that with twenty four hours working, other teams would have done this while he slept. He carried on doing what he done yesterday, lifting the soil onto the large dump trucks that kept coming like a working conveyor belt.

At one thirty he flashed his headlights at the next lorry and switched off his engine. Joe had decided that he would have his lunch now.

He watched as the nearest lorry driver, and all the others working nearby, did the same.

Once all the engines had been turned off a stillness filled the air. It was true in the distance you could, if you strained your hearing, hear other lorries. Here though it was quiet and peaceful. The driver walked up to Joe and sat alongside him.

"I usually share if there is anyone around me at lunch time. Do you want to do that?"

"Why not? I'm Joe, only started yesterday."

"Mine's Kenneth, do call me Ken. I saw that you were working this section when I looked at the board this morning."

"You know we are changing the landscape forever, aren't we?" "True but look what we are now replacing it with. It is the largest and most complex piece of engineering ever undertaken for the private sector." Both men sat in silence, Joe was thinking of the size of the operation. What he was seeing was only a fraction of what the combined sites and tunnel would be eventually.

"It's huge. I can't get my head around the size of this part, never mind the whole thing." said Joe after a long pause while they both were eating.

"You ought to go up to the exhibition, it would give you some idea of the site and they have a model railway showing the whole thing. Well, time to get back to the grindstone." Ken shook out his empty lunch box and rose and walked back to his lorry. Within seconds, loads of starlings and blackbirds swooped down and cleared the crumbs. Joe did the same, then he too climbed into his cab and both engines started almost together, and they continued their work into the late afternoon.

+

DCI Andrews stood in front of Brady and shook him violently, and Brady collapsed on the cold tiled office floor shivering with the cold.

"You're Michael Brady, a cell leader of the ARI aren't you?" "No." cried Brady from the floor. For three long hours this had been going on. He was on the point of giving in but all that kept him going was the fact that the longer he stalled the better chance of them being doubtful if he was the Brady that they were looking for.

The other policeman looked on as his superior continued the barrage of words with Brady and he said nothing as he knew that the treatment he was inflicting was bad but not yet bad enough to intervene. His superior caught his eye and stopped for a few minutes.

"Well, what are you looking at?"

"You seem to be," he paused, "a little excessive."

"Do you know why? Let me tell you why. Ten years ago, I had a brother, he was younger than me and when he left school, as there wasn't much choice of where to work, he decided to go and join the Army. Well, I pleaded with him not to join them, but he was adamant about it, so he joined up and went through the basic training, but as we were not at war, where to send him? His first tour of duty he was sent to Germany, and he came back full of tales and saying how he had heard that there was an ARI cell forming in Germany and it's their job to break the moral of the soldiers over there. He claimed to have information about it, so volunteered to go undercover to Belfast.

For a couple of weeks everything was fine. Then somebody told the ARI that he was UK Army. The ARI set an ambush and he died horribly after they had finished with him. He told the Army that someone had referred to his chief attacker as Brady, so I bided my time and knew one day I might be lucky, and here I am. When London gets down here everything will have to be done by the book. Until then he is a mine and that might help both us and stop someone else from dying."

"Ok, I understand all of that, but is it right to bring yourself down to his level?"

"His level? I don't come anywhere near his level, his level is the scum, filth, the sort who think nothing of blowing up ordinary people without warning."

"I understand, but are you sure that it is him?"

"I'm ninety percent sure and that's enough for me." "Yes, but..."

"No buts, this is him." He kicked him again. "So now what do we do?"

"Take this member of ARI back to his cell."

"You haven't produced any evidence." said Brady clutching his chest. Blood dripped from his nose onto the tiled floor.

"No, but you are being very helpful in helping us with our enquiries. Now let's get him out of here." Brady knew that once he was out of there and into the corridor that this would be his one and only chance of escape. Once in the corridor he pulled at the officer's arm and the officer taken by surprise, he did what anyone would have done, let go instinctively. Brady needed no second invitation, he flew along the corridor, and found that there was a door at the top of four steps. Bounding up two at a time he pushed against the door and all he got for his pains was a bruised shoulder to add to his other bruises. The second policeman caught hold of him and grinned.

"If you had tried in a month's time you would have been lucky, but unfortunately the doors have not been changed yet. Now are you going to come quietly, or do I have to cuff you?"

"I'll come quietly. No point in trying to escape now is there?" "There wasn't the first time." The officer led him to his cell and swung open the door. The cell was about eight-foot square, and an iron bed was bolted to the floor with a mattress on it.

"A real home from home."

"Why do you say that? Have you been in one before then? When and where?"

"Questions, questions, don't you lot ever give up? Now just lock me in and I'll go to sleep." The policeman did just that and then walked back to Andrews, who had returned to his office.

"What sort of man is that?"

"You ask me that? You who wanted to restrain me from carrying on from hitting him. What sort of man he is?"

"Yes."

"Right now, he'll be thinking up all sorts of ways to try and escape. While we have to think up all the means at our disposal of keeping him here."

"So shall I contact London?"

"Yes and ask for everything they might have on him to be faxed down to us. His height, aliases, habits, friends, hobbies the places he frequents including the continent. Got it?"

"Yes Sir." He turned and left the room. Andrews had only told the young officer half the story. Andrews recalled how his brother, Neil, had also been an agent acting for the police in Belfast. The Army had told his brother to take his wife and two children with him to make it more realistic. He had had reservations about the trip, but London were adamant it would be better cover.

Doing what he was asked of him, they all had moved to Belfast. Then two weeks later there had been a ring on the front door, he had gone and answered it, three gunmen had entered the house. One held a gun to his head as the other two pumped bullets into his furniture before doing the same to his wife and children. The gunmen told Neil to get out of Belfast otherwise he might get the same or worse treatment. He didn't move for a couple of hours but realised that he had to continue because to give in would mean that his wife and children had given their lives unnecessarily.

He thought he knew who they were and was sorry when two of the three gunmen were caught by others rather than himself. Then Neil had been transferred back to London, but just as he was within a hair's breadth of getting hold of Brady, Neil was relocated in Oxford. He had asked his brother, Andrews, in

Folkestone to keep an eye out for Brady. Then Neil had quietly returned to Northern Ireland, determined to track Brady down and kill him. Instead, somebody tipped off the ARI and he died. Where he was buried, nobody knew.

Now after three very quiet years Brady had turned up on his patch and he wasn't going to let him go lightly. Why was he here in Folkestone though? He knew that Brady was wanted on both sides of the Irish sea, so what would have made him take such an enormous risk? Perhaps the answers would come later. He really hoped so.

Andrews turned and sat at his desk, dealing with paperwork for a few hours, which seemed to him that was all the force was concerned with these days. Suddenly the young officer burst through his door and placed a fax on his desk.

"Well, what's the meaning of this interruption?"

"It appears that the Met are very surprised that we have managed to hold on to him. They have a large file and are sending down by car along with one of their top men. He is supposed to take over the questioning and he is due this afternoon."

"NO, no I'm dammed if I'll let the Met take over what might be the biggest thing that has happened in Folkestone. We have questioned him for five hours and what good did it do? I'll tell you, it achieved nothing, not one bloody thing did we learn."

He picked up the phone and asked for his secretary to get the Chief of the Metropolitan Force. "And I want to speak to him to-day, not in two days' time, do you hear?" Slamming the phone down, he swung to his young officer. "How would you get the information we wanted out of this man?"

"I'd get about six men to shadow him night and day and watch every move he made to see where in Folkestone he went."

"Then what?"

"Well, he has to make contact with someone sometime, doesn't he?"

"True, but that wouldn't be the number one person we want to contact."

"Then we shadow both."

"Now we have twelve men on overtime and it's only a possibility that they may lead us to him or her."

"So?"

"We do have a budget to keep to, and this could cost a lot of money." Andrews paused and a thought occurred to him. If the Met wanted to get involved, then perhaps they could share the expenses. The phone rang on his desk, and he reached out and answered it.

"Andrews here."

"Ah, Inspector I understand that you wanted to talk to me?" "Yes sir, I want to request that the Met do not interfere with the way that we run things in Folkestone. We do have our own ways of doing things." He paused and waited for the answer.

"Yes, well I can't see why we would want to interfere in how you run things in Folkestone, it's just this one man we need to take over from you. Look, we are sending somebody down to bring him back to London."

"No!"

"Pardon?"

"No sir, you are not taking this off our patch, share it if you like but do not take it away from here."

"And do you think you have all the resources to find his helpers and why he is over here?"

"No, that's why I suggested a joint operation."

"Are you aware that this might be a matter of national security? The PM wants to stamp out the ARI out of Britain. It falls to me to do as she wants."

"You are sending somebody down here?"

"Sort of, I am bringing somebody down with me. I'll fill you in with most of the details when I get there. By the way Brady will probably ask for his lawyer, but for heaven's sake keep him away from him."

"But he has seen his lawyer."

"Give me his name and I'll run it through the computer." "Mr. Green of '*Green, Black & Brown*'."

"And you believed it?"

"It was on the card, I had them checked out, they are a genuine firm based in Dover."

"Then he has probably just used the firm as a cover."

"We had a woman with Brady, but we couldn't hold her, so she was released."

"What!"

"Well, we had no reason to hold her here."

"If she was with him, then you can hold them for three days. So go and get her back. I'll see you in about two hours." He hung up.

Andrews looked up, surprised to still see his young officer there.

"Ok, don't stand there looking at me son, go and get that Kent woman we had this morning and bring her back in."

"But she went off with Mr. Green sir."

"Dammit, we'll just have to try and find both of them." "We could see if she went back home."

"We could, but I doubt that she will return there. We may as well be seen to do something." He swung his chair around and looked out the window. Andrews heard the door close and then he swung back to face his desk again. Sighing, he picked up the phone and told his secretary to get the men together for a quick conference. He got up and walked over to the window and lifted the blind and looked out onto the courtyard of cars and rose beds that lay beyond them.

Why did Brady have to come to Folkestone? He wondered about asking that young man to be his nearest foot soldier, his bag man as it were. Andrews knew that he couldn't stand up to the running around that might soon be needed, he was getting older and slower.

There was a crash of glass and an object landed in his office. Transfixed he looked at it as it smouldered, then dived for cover under his desk. Seconds later a flash of flame shot out and the furniture started to catch fire. He wasted no time in grabbing the fire extinguisher and aiming it towards the fire. Alarms were ringing in the offices and in the distance, he could hear a fire engine coming to the station.

Two hours later, the last of the evidence had been bagged and taken away for the forensics department to examine at their leisure. He was already in a bad mood and his temper got worse on learning that the visitors from the Met were waiting for him and had been for half an hour. He made his way through the remains of his office out into the corridor and on to meet them. Out in the 'public', as it was known, they both sat waiting.

"Inspector Andrews."

"This is DC Bill Reed from a new department that is being planned. It's to be called LICD or London International Crime Department. He is to be known as" he lowered his voice. "William Dawson. I am Chief Superintendent Rose. Hope to have control of LICD, but that depends on results, or so the PM says."

"DCI Andrews, sorry that I kept you, but there was a small disturbance just before you came."

"What kind of disturbance?"

"Nothing much. Now tell me is it Michael Brady, I presume that you have already seen him in the cells?"

"I am almost sure that it is him, but he is remaining silent now. If he is innocent then he would be pleading his innocence, wouldn't he?" said Andrews.

"I don't know, I mean if you are not one hundred percent sure, who am I to tell you what to think."

"Take a look at his file, I have it here." He passed it over to Andrews."

"Does it prove anything?"

"Come and see." The same young officer he had seen before burst in clutching a piece of paper.

"Sir, Brady's lawyer has returned with some sort of legal paper and twenty-three thousand pounds for bail bond for Brady. So we had no alternative but to let him go."

"What!" He turned to CS Rose but before he had chance to say anything his secretary burst in on them.

"Have you forgotten about your meeting with the men?"

"I'll coming right now." He turned to the chief. "You could come and fill us all in on the details and his background."

"Fine, I assume you have a photocopier on site?"

"Yes, I'll arrange for it to be in the room." He led the way to the conference room. A short while later they were all stood in front of the assembled men. Andrews outlined what had happened so far but omitted to tell them who Rose was. He asked for the windows to be opened and then he stepped forward to the edge of the stage.

"Finally, I want you to listen to Chief Superintendent Rose. Take notes if you must. For this is promising to be the start of a big operation. Now pay attention." He stepped back and Rose moved forward and a hush fell across the room.

"You have heard what Inspector Andrews had to say, and who I am. What Andrews didn't explain is what I am doing in your neck of the woods so to speak. Well, let me start by saying that you were good to capture an ARI member by the name of Michael Brady. He had an accomplice, and she was brought in as well. This was good news when we heard of this," He looked at Andrews before continuing. "We came down to interrogate both. We have been trying to catch him for years now and what do we find on arriving here? Both have now been released. While you had no reason to hold her, Brady was released by somebody paying a large bail bond. Once that happened, Brady could leave."

A murmur went around the room. "Yes, I know that you are upset, but we have some ideas as to where to start looking for them. A list has been drawn up and you will be given a sheet each at the end of this meeting. The woman is called Colleen Kent but we don't have a photo of her. Please assume that the name is an alias. Both must be caught as quickly as possible; we are being assisted by the Army tomorrow. Now are there any questions?" He waited and was not too disappointed that only one hand went up near the back. "Yes?"

"Sir, if we catch him what do we charge him with?" "How about terrorism for starters?"

"If he is ARI then why is he here in Folkestone?"asked Andrews. "I'm surprised by you Andrews. What is the most likely target that could embarrass Her Majesty's Government?"

"You mean the tunnel? Security is tighter than the Bank of England."

"That maybe what you think, but the reality is a little different. The wire fencing runs for miles and is not that closely guarded. There may be the odd notice attached to it. Bet that being a private firm, they are bound to be out there as regular as clockwork. Anyone could get into the grounds and once inside..." He left the sentence unfinished. The men in the room murmured their assent at this remark. Ever since the first post had been hammered into the ground, they had feared the worst and had been told by the people in charge that it couldn't happen. They had constantly been told by Andrews to ignore that and prepare for the worst, now it looked like happening. Andrews glanced across to Rose with a piercing look in his eyes.

"Have you thought that as we haven't heard from the ARI yet, we may be jumping the gun a bit?"

"True, but let's concentrate on getting Brady if we are to avoid trouble of any kind. Now all of you let's get to it."The men stood as one and made for the photocopier where a pile of sheets awaited their collection. Andrews, Rose, and Reed left to go to Andrew's new office, where he told his secretary not to arrange for any calls for the next two days.

"You think it will only take a few days Inspector?" "Yes, why not Mr. Reed?

"By now Brady will be miles away and heading back to Northern Ireland but he will not be going by the usual channels so it's no good looking for the ports, airports and railway stations. The places we must look for are places like old disused airdromes from the last war, are there any around here?"

"A few, I'll get one of my men to find out the exact number." "Any outside a ten-mile radius, we look at, any inside we can ignore," Rose instructed, then turned and looked at the map of Folkestone on the wall of Andrews' new office. "How many hotels, bed and breakfast and guest houses would you say there are in Folkestone,Andrews?" Rose asked.

"Well, I'd say at a guess." he paused and thought, it was difficult to put a figure on it. "I couldn't hazard a guess sir."

"No, neither could I and we haven't added in Hythe, Dover and Deal."

"No sir."

"Still, look on the bright side, I assume there is some good news?" Andrews thought for a moment, then explained to the chief about the tip off and the fire in Wood Cottage Lane. He finished his explanation and looked at Rose.

"Well, you seem to have been well informed, yet you let her go. You do know that it is likely she was his driver?"

"His driver, but why would he need a driver and a woman driver at that?"

"He can't drive as far as we know. While she is deadly. Her speciality is unarmed combat and theft without discovering she has been into a place, hence her nickname. 'The Cat'. She can drive and turn a car around faster than anyone else I know. Now I think that we should be going to Wood Cottage Lane, I'll read the file as we go."

+

Five minutes later they were driving towards the house where the trouble had been last night. Swinging the car into Firs Lane he drove on towards Wood Cottage Lane and pulled up by the house. The pair of them got out and walked up the drive. The front door opened, and a lady stood there.

"Yes, can I help you?"

"I'm Inspector Andrews and this is the new head of LICD Chief Superintendent Rose. Could we come in please?"

"Well, I haven't got round to clearing up yet, so if you will forgive the mess."

"Of course, and we quite understand." He glanced at his superior.

"Yes, we will not keep you long, we want to catch the people responsible for this."

"You would be better off to go to the shed, that's where my husband is. He thinks that something funny is going on. Follow me." Leading the way, the three men followed her down the garden path and out to the shed at the bottom of the garden. She knocked on the door and then opened it for the two policemen.

The shed was in a shambles, but what was of more concern was the body slumped across the main workbench face down with a wrench on the bench beside him. From the look of him, he wouldn't get up ever again. His right hand was clenched as a fist. Andrews took all this in and then turned in time to catch the lady as she fainted.

"We'll get back to the house and phone from there. Now give me a hand helping her get back to the house." They carried her up to the house and Andrews phoned the station from there.

Shortly, three police cars were outside the house and the forensics team had taken over the shed. The doctor, who had certified the man's death, came into the front room with a small silver disc in his hand. They had taken over the house to use as a base for the moment and the woman had gone off to the local hospital to be treated for shock.

"This was in his hand, but it's only a battery. I can't think why he grabbed that to defend himself."

"Neither can I, perhaps there is some other reason for grabbing it that will come up in time."

"it's going to take ages to go through all of his stuff, we need an electronics expert to look through everything in there."

"We do have someone, leave it with me and I'll try and arrange for them to come over." said Andrews.

"Well Andrews, what do you propose to do now?" asked Rose with a weary look on his face.

"What I just said, then have a read in more detail in your file on Brady and Kent."

"Do you mind if I stay here for bit?" said DC Reed.

"No, be my guest, but you don't mind if I leave you? You will need to find your own way back."

"No of course not."

"Right, then I'll be off." Andrews left the house and walked over to one of the police cars. "Come on, we're going back to the station."

+

Joe ached all over, he had been working solidly, apart from his lunch time break. Now he needed a long rest. He glanced at his watch. He still had another half an hour. Then again, if he was to fill up with diesel in readiness for the next shift, he could start to make tracks towards the fuel shed. Joe had driven halfway there before he noticed that the temperature gauge was almost at the top of the range.

He turned his engine off before, flashing his lights at the next lorry in the queue. The driver switched off his engine and climbed down and ran over to join him.

"What's the matter?"

"The temperature gauge is showing top."

`Well, I'd go and report it and get someone to have a look at it."

"That's alright, but I only started yesterday."

"Don't worry, look, why don't you lock up the JCB and come back with me and I'll drive you over where to go."

"Will I lose any money through this?"

"No, more than likely that you will be sent home early. Why not take advantage of the fact?" Joe grinned.

"Why not indeed."

"Go and collect your stuff and climb on up."

"But it's huge!" exclaimed Joe, as he climbed into the cab.

"I know and there is a bunk behind you." He indicated by waving his thumb behind him. Then the lorry took off driving towards the Portakabin offices. They soon pulled up at the relevant offices and Joe climbed down, and the driver threw down his coat and sandwich box. Joe waved and watched the lorry set off to the diesel depot. He entered the office and reported where the machine had broken down. He was told he would have to show the mechanic where it was exactly it had been left. He waited for a few minutes and then the mechanic walked in.

"You Joe?"

"Yes."

"Where is the JCB then? Go and get your stuff and let's go and sort its problems. I have a van full of spare parts. There is not much that I can't fix out on the site."

The van drove across the site, bouncing the two men up and down inside. Pulling up alongside his JCB, the mechanic got out and looked under the bonnet. Ten minutes later, he looked at Joe and smiled.

"Easy as falling off a log. It will take me around thirty minutes to sort this. You wait in the cab. I'll let you know when I am done.

An hour or so later, Joe was driving his now repaired JCB across to be refuelled. He made his way over to Sean Bryan's office. Mary was inside waiting for him.

"Sorry I'm late. The JCB broke down and…" She put her hand up to stop him mid-sentence.

"Listen, let's go home and get you some food and rest. You can tell me as we drive there."

"Fine." They went out to the car and once inside he found that he just nodded off. The next thing he knew was that Mary was waking him up telling him that they were home.

"This happens a lot until people are used to the work." "And when will that be?"

"Give it a couple of days."

"I'll just about cope then." He walked into the B & B with her then started to climb the stairs to his room. "I'll be down later." He shouted back as he climbed upstairs and promptly fell fast asleep. Downstairs Mary was talking to her mother.

"Why are the good ones married?" "You love him don't you Mary?"

"Yes, and I'm afraid that something will happen."

"I'd not let it go that far love. Look love, face it, he is married, and he comes from Belfast, don't you think that's asking for trouble?"

"No, not really. You know we check them out first, and he was clean as a whistle." Mary turned and left the room. She must come to terms with this, otherwise she would go mad with distraction. She went out into the garden and the scent of the roses hung heavily on the night air. She would tell her mother her decision in the morning.

# 5.28

Inspector Andrews was not a happy man, there were more than a few things wrong with the world that evening.

First he had phoned his wife to let her know that he couldn't say when he would be home. This was easy compared to having to rearrange offices following the attack. London had to be informed and finally, though perhaps it should have been first, Brady, Kent and Green still hadn't been located. To cap it all off nicely, the Army would be assisting them.

An hour later Andrews looked up from his desk as an officer knocked on the office door.

"Come in."

"Your new office is now ready sir." Andrews smiled for the first time that evening.

"Lead the way then." The pair of them walked down the long corridor and across the car park to a set of Portakabins which had been located there. He opened the door to the office and Andrew looked inside. He had been expecting a rough and ready desk and a couple of easy chairs at best. However, there was the left-handed desk, a nice print of a tiger on the wall, along with a normal, not digital, clock hanging on the wall. Beside the desk two filing cabinets stood one on each side. His only criticism would have been that there was only a wooden chair at his desk. Tomorrow he would see about getting a swivel chair, for some reason he always thought better in one of those. He was pleased with the finished result, as his grandmother used to say, "every cloud has a silver lining." There was a short tap on the door and a worried looking Chief Superintendent Rose peered around it. "I've got bad news and really bad news."

"Ok, give it to me in that order." "Brady and Kent have disappeared." "But we knew that."

"There is no trace of them in London or Belfast." "What! I mean if that's bad what can be worse?"

"it's starting to look as though they, I mean ARI, have been able to infiltrate the tunnel workings."

"No, please don't say that. What makes you say that?"

"Well, we aren't one hundred percent sure yet, but the chances that a contact is already in place we would place at better than sixty percent."

"Is it possible, but I mean what about the security?"

"What indeed? Look at this advert, it appeared in the main Belfast newspapers and is still being produced there." Rose pulled the advert out of his pocket and showed it to Andrews. "I assume that the new applicants are all being checked before being starting to work." But even as he finished asking, he felt that they were probably not.

"It appears not, the company do not dig too deep if you will pardon the pun. With the time schedule being so tight, the contractors can't afford any delays. Remember, it is a private contract, it's not as if HMG are paying for it." said Rose with a chuckle. "It could be a lot worse, protests and such like. There is nothing for it, but to ask the contractors for a list of their staff, names, addresses, the whole lot. Once we have those details we may be able to find our infiltrators."

"Ok, but let's keep this quiet if we can. You know what the human rights lot will make of this if they ever find out."

"Can't be helped, not if you want the job done properly." "I know that but just think of the scale of the problem."

"I have. Let's get down to details." Both men drew up chairs and sat down.

Andrews went to the filing cabinet and without a word, passed a file with the known ARI supporters currently in the UK. Rose took it and ran his eyes down the page of names.

"Well Andrews we had better get that list of all the names of the employees working on the tunnel project. We'll see if any of the names or addresses match with this." He tapped the file. "Got a photocopier anywhere handy?"

"Not too sure. Let me have it back, I'll get a couple of copies done and sent over to you. I think they are putting you on site somewhere, but not sure where exactly yet."Andrews stood up and went to the door and called down the corridor. "Anybody know where Chief Superintendent Rose's office is going to be?" A voice from the other end of the corridor shouted back to him. "Going directly above yours tomorrow, a first floor of additional Portakabins is being delivered."Andrews went back to his desk. "I'll get one of my men to obtain a list tomorrow from the site manager."

"Who is he?" said Rose. "Sam Brooks."

"Good, we'll get hold of him first thing in the morning. Now we need extra police drafted in and we need to notify all the other regions in England and Wales."

"Do we draw up posters or alert the media?" asked Andrews. "No, they may be seen by Brady and Kent and if they are still in the country then 1 don't want them going into hiding again." said Rose with a frown.

"Let's try and keep the details to as few people as possible need to know and all that. What do you think?"

"I agree. I suggest we meet back here the day after tomorrow, since it is unlikely that I will t be able to use my office while the ones above are being installed." said Andrews. The two men stood up and Rose left the office. Andrews sat for a few minutes, then he too got up and followed Rose out of the office.

+

Michael Brady was feeling and looking cold, damp, and miserable. Although Green had managed to release both, he knew that the three of them were now on the run from the police force of Great Britain.

With probably everyone looking for them across the country, they needed a place to hole up for at least a month. This would give them a chance to change their dress and style. Meanwhile Green had left them promising to return. Colleen looked across at him from the end of the park bench where they were sitting and hiding. For hadn't they been taught that the most obvious place to hide was under the noses of the police, as most forces would cast their nets on a wider area than where they were hiding.

"I think we should have stayed in last night don't you." said Colleen.

"Yes in hindsight. Though we didn't really have any choice." "We? You didn't leave me any choice," retorted Colleen angrily. "Alright, but at least they didn't find the bug."

"How do you know that?"

"Well, if they had discovered it, then PC Grey would never been allowed to bail us out, would he?" replied Brady. "At least nobody was killed, or we would have our cover well and truly blown." "But our cover has been blown and I don't think that the ones in Belfast will be happy do you?" replied Colleen.

"True, but it is not our problem, at least not yet." "Care for a stroll around the park?"

"Why not?"They both rose and started walking along the path and over towards a row of shops. If anybody had seen them they would have seemed just another couple. "Colleen, I've been thinking, do you remember that house that was for sale near the house where the transmitter was taken?"

"No, I can't say I do. Why is it important?"

"I was thinking we could base ourselves there and nobody would disturb us at all."

"You mean get Mr. Green to find out who is selling it and put in an offer?"

"Yes. Look out there's a policeman coming."They throw their arms around each other, and he walked past without noticing them.

"I still can't understand it, I was released without charge and a large bail was raised against you. Look let's go and hire a car and get out of here." said Colleen.

"Don't you think that roadblocks will in place already?" "Are the police really that good?"

"All right you win, let's go."They walked on but then Colleen felt a hand descend onto her shoulder, she jumped and turned around. Standing there was Green.

"You need to be more careful;I overheard your last conversation. Anybody else standing nearby would have as well. Colleen I may have your answer."

"What do you mean by that?"

"I mean Colleen, that I have a car that is ready for you both, which is parked on Radnor Park Avenue. A red coloured Rover214. R registration, very dirty so it will not be noticed. The road tax is paid in full for twelve months. In the glove box in front of the passenger seat is the map with directions on how to get your new passports and new identities when you reach your new destination, which are marked on the map as well. Any questions?"

"Yes, what happens to my flat?"

"Well Colleen, that is a matter between you and ARI Belfast."

"What are we supposed to do we do for money? I had money at the flat."

"There is a small amount to get you started in the boot of the car. Used five pound notes."

"One thing though." Said Brady." Can you look into making an offer on a house, the one near to…?"

"I heard you both Brady. I'll get on to doing that when I get back to my office. Now both of you, don't go anywhere else, other than the place on the map. Understand?"

"Yes." replied Brady and Colleen.

"Right, then you had better get along. And do take care of the car. It can't be taken to a garage, at least not for six or seven weeks." Green turned and walked off in the opposite direction. "Come on then Brady, it is not that far away."

Once they found the car, Brady went and retrieved the money out of the boot. He smiled at Green's idea of "small amount".

Brady got in beside Colleen and put on his seatbelt. He reached forward and opened the glovebox and removed the map. A revolver lay there as well. Brady started to read the note which said to make their way to Southern Ireland. He glanced at Colleen. She gunned the engine, and it took off down Radnor Park Avenue towards Radnor Park Road. At the roundabout she swung into Cheriton Road and then she drove the car around the small side streets with Brady looking more and more confused. Colleen pulled up and parked near Middelburg Square, only a mile from the centre of Folkestone. Brady looked at her in amazement.

"What are you doing here, I mean, in case you had forgotten we are supposed to be heading to southern Ireland."

"I think we should change cars and get something less conspicuous than this car."

"Fine, what do you have in mind?" "A Metro."

"And just where do we get the Metro, for we can't hire one or buy it so what did you have in mind?" asked Brady with a frown. "Bee-Hive Henry. He lives close by." She said with a grim smile." "It's true he has one, but why would he sell us his?"

"Not sell it, swop it for this one. Phone him and arrange a meeting at the amusement park, oh and tell him to book us a place on the night trawler."

"But." Brady started then stopped. "What?" asked Colleen.

"It doesn't matter."

"The Night trawler is that what is bothering you?" Asked Colleen with a frown.

"Yes, I mean it goes to Europe."

"So that's the last place we will be looked for. As for the amusement park at this time of year it will be unused with lots of tarpaulins to hide under should we need to. Don't you think that it would be the last place anyone will look in Folkestone for us."

+

The following day, Inspector Andrews sat at his desk amid the empty coffee cups that littered it. On the wall of the office a map of Folkestone had now been pinned and on it had been drawn four-inch squares which were being slowly filled in as each area was checked. The centre of the map was the police station.

So far, they hadn't reached the amusement park. A knock on the door interrupted Andrew's thought and he glanced up at the young officer he had seconded who peered around the door. "Well?"

"We think we have found the car sir." "Where was it?"

"Middelburg Square."

"Let's get moving, and we may yet pick them up." "Where from sir?"

"Take a look at the map, it's not that far from Central Station, they may be leaving by rail. Get all the cars to make for the station and ask them not to go in with sirens wailing and lights flashing."

The young officer turned and left the room, Andrews looked again at the map. Trying to think if he had to avoid being caught, he would have struck out west or east, but they had doubled back and ended in the centre, why? Maybe if he could fathom out their reasoning he would be halfway to catching them.

He picked up the phone and got hold of Chief Superintendent Rose and quickly filled him in on what had happened, saying he would be in touch once he knew more.

"'Did you manage to obtain the list of workers on the site yet?" asked Rose.

"Sort of."

"What do you mean, sort of?"

"The site manager agrees in principle but refuses to let us see them."

"Maybe I should see if we can get our trouble-shooter down here? Or I can phone the PM and see what she has to say." "You'll phone me back?" asked Andrews.

"As soon as I have a decision, yes."

The last thing Andrews wanted right now was the PM flapping around, with tight security that always went with her. While he waited, he cleared the desk of the empty cups. The phone suddenly rang on his desk, and he grabbed it quickly. Chief Superintendent Rose was on the other end.

"Well?"

"We have the rest of this week to find them. If not, then the trouble-shooter comes in." Andrews looked over at the other phone as it rang.

"Just hold the line please, I have another caller."

"Andrews here. Yes, I have pen and paper." His hand raced across the paper and his eyes widened as it did. "Right, I have all that." He replaced the phone.

"Trouble?" asked Rose.

"Not really, we have one ARI suspect living in one of the disused wagons. The only reason we discovered this was because it was on a stretch of track that wasn't connected to the tracks any longer, and there were two railway sleepers to stop anything coming and coupling it up. We are holding him for possible links to ARI."

"What's his name, I'll run a check through the computer." "Henry. Better known as Bee-Hive Henry."

"Why Bee-Hive?" asked Rose.

"He used to use a small explosive that was hexagon at the base a bit like a bee-hive, the pointed bit was pushed into whatever he wanted demolished. The effect was very little noise, but a lot of structural damage. He had joined the regular Army and after five years and a lot of training in handling explosives, left and disappeared. He has been off the radar since. The Brighton Bombing had all the hallmarks of his explosives though." said Andrews.

"Don't tell the PM that or wild horses wouldn't keep her away." said Rose down the phone.

"I must go and get the details; I'll fax them to you later." "Fine, but phone to tell me first, Ok?"

"Ok, whatever you say." Andrews hung the phone up and went out to the car park and drove off towards Central Station and the sidings. He knew he was in the right place with all the police cars all over the place. Andrews swung open his car door as it cruised to a stop and leaving the door wide open tore across to the nearest officer. "Well, where is he?"

"Over here in the van." He followed the officer towards a police van parked on a piece of rough grass near the railway wagon. Andrews stuck his head around the door of the van and saw a man dressed in a dirty pair of trainers and dark brown corduroy trousers while on top he had a sweatshirt emblazoned with the legend"Ireland's Freedom is Paramount"

"Welcome to British Justice."Andrews turned to the officer. "Has he been cautioned?"

"Yes sir."

"Yes sir." mimicked the man.

"Oh, one who talks - that makes a change." said Andrews.

"I'm not saying nothing. Pig." He spate both defiantly and with a degree of accurateness because his phlegm hit Andrews on his jacket. Andrews said nothing. Then he turned to the young officer.

"Can you get my bag from the car please?"

"Right away Sir." He scurried away and at once Andrews turned and kicked the man in the groin. The man collapsed and because he had handcuffs on couldn't do anything. He looked with a mixture of anger and defiance at Andrews.

"I am not saying nothing." he spluttered.

"Oh, I think you will, maybe not yet, but you will eventually. You see I might decide to keep that up until you tell me what I want to know. Since I don't have much time at my disposal it may be advisable to let me have the answers sooner rather than later."

"They would kill me if I did that."

"Well, you aren't going to be in much of a state if you don't are you? Think about it." Andrews kicked him on his side and then left him lying there and walked over to the railway waggon. Two officers stood on guard outside the sliding door. He swung the door back and glanced inside. A sleeping bag lay on one side and a small hurricane lamp lay nearby, stacked on the opposite side was a large pile of tinned food. A few large plastic water bottles lined the side. It looked as though whoever set this up expected him to stay a long time. Andrews pulled his head out and looked at the two officers. "Nobody is to go into this waggon except the forensics team. Understand?"

"Yes sir." He walked back to the police van and looked inside at Bee-hive Henry who was now lying on the floor.

"Feeling like talking yet?" "That depends on you lot."

"Why on earth should it depend on us?" asked Andrews in amazement.

"You give me protection and a new identity. I'll tell you lots." "Yes you most likely would, however at the moment I am only interested in one or two people."

"Off the record? Like whom?" Henry asked. "Well for starters who set you up with all this?"

"I really don't know. I was told to come here, and a van would be ready for me, then I was to await a call from them."

"Who are?"

"They didn't give any names. They are the sort that you don't ask who they are. The money hits the account once the job is done though, so they do play fair in that regard."

"Alright, who do you think they are?"

"ARI, most likely, well, that's who I would put my money on."

"Right, now when do they come here?"

"They don't, but they might go elsewhere." Andrews climbed into the van and grabbed him by the neck and pulled him upright.

"Now I strongly advise you to think carefully before you answer the next question." The man nodded as he couldn't speak. "Right, where exactly would you look tonight for them Folkestone or Ireland?"

There was a pause and then the man laughed. "Neither of those, try Europe. Yes I'd try Europe." "Europe?"

"Well why not? There are plenty of ways of getting across to Europe. Hovercraft, small boat, hydrofoil, or the tunnel, though that isn't finished yet is it?"

"Where in Europe?"

"Anywhere, there are contacts all over the place. it's not worth contacting Interpol for that reason."

"Well, for the moment, we'll charge you with terrorism and smoke bombing a house in Folkestone."

`But I haven't smoke bombed any house."

"If you say so." He turned to an officer that had come up behind him. "Take him away and book him for terrorism and bombing a house."

"But I haven't bombed any house."

"You have a problem with that?" "You don't believe me do you?"

"No, but then put yourself in my shoes, would you believe me if I told you that tale?"

"I suppose not." Andrews leapt down out of the van and slammed the doors closed on him.

Andrews walked back to his car wondering why use a van on the sidings and who was behind this plan, for although he had already felt it was the ARI, he now felt that it might be someone or a larger organisation was pulling the strings and if they weren't careful it could soon get out of hand. He made a mental note to phone Rose on his return to bring him up to speed on this new development.

As Andrews drove back to Folkestone police station, he felt that at the back of his mind there was something not quite right about this man. He tried to recall what it was but couldn't remember what.

+

Mary had told her mother that she would be sensible over Joe. She would just try and make his stay as comfortable as possible.

The next morning Joe awoke with the light streaming into his bedroom. He got out of bed trying to remember what had happened last night, then he recalled that he had been so tired he had gone to bed early and failed to pull the curtains.

He glanced at the alarm clock on the bedside table and noticed it was six in the morning. He got himself ready for the day ahead, then went downstairs and let himself out of the front door.

Outside he felt the fresh air blowing gently on his face. He decided to walk around the block and as he walked, he felt more refreshed than he had done in a long time. He strode down the road where on the grass verges there was a heavy dew, but there was very little noise from any traffic. It was like on a Sunday.

He recalled how once when he was young, he had risen early like this and had crept out into the new day, the air heavy with the scent of the new blossom of spring. He had wandered for hours, not having a watch, and had not noticed the time slip by. When he did get home the whole street was out looking for him. He had been out for about five hours and, as he recalled it even now, a smile crossed his face. He turned and slowly walked back the way he had come, but he wondered how far it was to the site? He would ask either Mary or her mother when he got in. All too soon he was back.

"Nice walk?" asked Mary. "Yes, how far is it to the site?"

"Much too far to walk each day if that's what you are thinking." "Ok. By the way, where is the phone box? You did say that there was one handy to here."

'That's right, it's under the stairs. It takes tens, twenty and fifty pence pieces. Have you got plenty of change?"

"Yes thank you." Straight after breakfast, Joe left the room and phoned Sarah, but there was nobody there, so he hung up and scooped up the change and went back into the kitchen. "Did you get through?" Mary's mother asked.

`No, I'll try again tonight. Any chance of a second cuppa? he asked cheekily.

"Go back through, I'll bring it to you." said Mary with a smile.

+

In Andrews' office, he was having a conversation with Rose. Having arrived early, Andrews had been surprised to see Rose standing in Andrews' office now that the additional floor of offices had been installed.

"I think that by now our new prisoner has had all night to think of what to say, I contacted our friends in Europe as you suggested, but they haven't seen either of them. So, what do we do now? Time is running out; I assume you have restarted the search in Folkestone?" said Rose.

"Yes, we started again last night." "What next?"

"Let's start interrogating 'Beehive' Henry again, around the clock if need be, until he breaks." Rose followed Andrews down the cells. They seemed remarkably quiet. Andrews unlocked the cell door and looked in. The quietness was now explained as they could see the body revolving on the light bulb flex, first one way then the other. Both men stood looking at one another. Then Andrews stepped back and called along the corridor. "Sergeant!"

"Yes sir?"

"Take a look in there a minute will you?"Andrews held the cell door back and the Sergeant looked in before running back up the corridor. He returned almost at once but looking a good deal whiter in the face.

"What do you want to know sir?" "Who was the last person in there?"

"Why the new Sergeant that you sent about two hours ago I think."

"Well now, you go and find him and bring him to me when you have."The sergeant hurried off and Andrews turned to Rose. "As far as I am aware there is no new Sergeant in this station." "What!" said Rose.

"I think he was killed to make us think it was suicide, and to stop him telling us anything, no other reason."

"Now what do we do then? I mean, he was the only person we had found connected to this affair."

"Carry on looking for Kent and Brady."

"Ok, but we may have to inform the PM first. I'll set up a call as soon as possible. In the meantime, perhaps you can contact the adjoining forces, alert them to who we are searching for." Andrews didn't relish the thought of the next ten minutes. They walked up

144

out of the cells and as they passed two policemen, Andrews informed them that they needed to call the Police doctor and once he had finished, to take the body down and take it for a post-mortem. He was to be given the results as soon as they were known.

He opened his office door to see that it was a complete and utter wreck, his desk was overturned, and papers were everywhere, files had been scattered like confetti. He gaped for a minute and then picked up his chair and sat down to think, why?

Noticing a breeze and realising the window was open, he left the chair and walked out of the office closing the door slowly after him. Andrews left the building and went outside to examine his window. There were only two rooms without bars at ground level, the other one was his old office. His first thoughts were how unlucky he had been, but then a more suspicious thought crossed his mind, suppose this office had been picked out for this reason? Then this could only mean someone was informing the ARI from inside the force.

Returning to the cells, he saw that Rose was watching the two officers bag the body in readiness to take it to the hospital. He looked up as Andrews came in.

"I think you had better come with me upstairs." said Andrews grimly.

"Why, something up?"

"You could say that." Rose followed Andrews up to his office and when Andrews had opened the door Rose gasped. He also was quick to realise the significance of the fact that there were no bars at the window.

"Anything missing?"

"Too early to tell yet, but I'm willing to bet the Brady and Kent files are missing."

"You are probably right, now where is your phone?" asked Rose.

"Over there, but shouldn't the room be dusted for fingerprints first?"

"Well alright, but they probably have been careful and worn gloves which wouldn't leave prints. Let's go to my office." Once in his office, the two men sat down. "Well, I had better phone her and fill her in on what is going on down here and I fancy that she will not like it one bit." grumbled Rose.

"Still, we have to tell her sometime."

"Switch on the loudspeaker part of the phone and stay here. It will save time having to explain it to you later." Rose dialled the Prime Minister's number. He was told to wait as she was in a meeting. "Get her out of the meeting. Tell her this is a matter of National Security."

"That's what they all say, still I'll see what she says, who shall I say is calling?"

"Chief Superintendent Rose of LICD formerly of the MET." "Just hold the line Superintendent." There was a long pause then the PM came on the phone.

"This had better be important Rose."

"There has been a bit of a development down here." "And?"

"We think that ARI have managed to infiltrate the tunnel. A small remote cell of just a few members. DCI Andrews is also listening on conference call. A man was arrested last night, but this morning he was found hanging in his cell."

"What had he said?" she asked.

"Nothing, we left him overnight and then planned to start serious questioning today. But somebody has been in and killed him. Then hung him to make it look like a suicide. This could be a larger problem than we think." Rose paused and, in the silence, you could almost hear the PM's brain working.

"You want DCI Reed down there? Is that what this call is for? I said you could have him next week. He has gathered a small team now. Team of three if I recall. I'll talk to them and see if they can get to you earlier. That is the best I can do for now." the PM said. Andrews leaned into the phone and spoke up so she could hear him.

"DCI Andrews speaking Prime Minister. That's not all. My office was broken into and ransacked, however it's one of only two offices that have no bars at the windows, which seem strongly significant. I feel that we might have an informer down here." "That is a serious accusation, Andrews. Yes, I can quite see why you want William down there. I'll see that he gets down to Folkestone as soon as is possible." She hung up and Andrews turned to Rose.

"Well, what do you think of that?"

"Sounds alright and it also sounds as if she isn't coming down." "Fine, now I'll leave you and go and sort out my office." Andrews started towards the door. "And I'll see if anything else has cropped up from our trawl through Folkestone."

Andrews walked to the main desk and asked the Sergeant if he had found the 'new Sergeant' yet, if not could he see if anybody remembered the face. If anybody could, then get the police artist to draw a likeness and circulate it to London, Europe, Folkestone and Belfast.

He walked out into the sunlight and around to take another look at his windows. Unlike some offices there was no soil outside the window, only concrete.

It wasn't like this in the books, he thought to himself. The windows would need to be fixed with bars. He looked in through the broken window, already the forensics team were hard at work.

"Found anything yet?"

"Some fingerprints on the phones that aren't yours sir."

"Tell me when the room is free, and I can start to make sense of the files."

"We are almost finished now, so if you give us another thirty or so minutes you can have it back."

"Half an hour then." Andrews walked on around to the front deep in thought.

+

Sheltering from the rain in the ghost train tent were Brady and Kent.

"It's so cold Brady. I wish I was back in my home."

"Where the police would be waiting to catch you. Give me the phone, I'll slip out and give Bee-hive Henry a call."

He ducked out from under the canvas and made his way to a phone box that was a few hundred yards from the fairground. He put some coins into the slot and dialled the number. He could hear a ringing tone, but after leaving it for a few minutes with nobody answering, he hung up. The coins dropped down into the small box and he scooped them up and put them back in his pocket. Looking up and down the esplanade, he didn't see any police, so left the phone box and made his way back the fairground. He stopped and moved in amongst other rides when he saw a policeman standing right by the ghost train. Brady peered out from time to time, and eventually the policeman moved on and Brady was able to return to Colleen.

"Where on earth have you been?" she asked him.

"A policeman was stood outside this ride. I had to wait till he moved away."

"Does he know we are hiding here?"

"No, I don't think so. I wonder what's happened to him?" "Who?"

"'Bee-Hive Henry' who else?" "Why isn't he coming then?"

"I phoned the number, and he wasn't there, so..." but Colleen interrupted him.

"You mean he doesn't know we are here?"

"Well, yes."

"Then let's get the hell out of here and make for Europe, we must make an urgent contact with the night trawler." They crept out from under the tent and made their way along Marine Parade. Ahead of them lay the Harbour railway station. "Colleen, what if we got a train ticket from the Harbour station?" "Well, we could buy the tickets there, but I was thinking more of stealing one of those cars and driving off towards Dover and there we could take the Hovercraft to Europe. Once we are in Europe there are no end of contacts that both of us know. Hopefully the police will be most likely looking for transport from Britain to Belfast not to Europe."

"If we can get back to the main railway station. I have a locker there with some bits and pieces that could change the way we look now. Ok, I don't have the key, but that will not be a problem. Now what about that nice red Metro over there?" Brady pointed that was parked across the road from them.

"Let's go then." It took only a few minutes to break in and start the engine. Then after collecting Brady 's box of make-up bits and pieces, they drove off, heading towards Dover.

## 6.28

Joe found that he was using the same machine in the same area. He hitched a lift on one of the lorries to where it was parked. The lorry driver didn't seem to want to talk, so Joe just sat there in the silence. Then just before he got out the driver turned to him.

"You're new, so let me just say this. There are some men on this site who will do awful things to a man, if you don't do what they want. If you are married or have family, then I suggest you leave the site today. That's all I am saying."

"Well, thank you very much. it's true I do have a wife, but I really need the work."

"Don't say I didn't warn you."

"I'll take care and thanks for the warning." Joe jumped down and waved goodbye as the lorry pulled away leaving a trail of dust. He turned around and walked off in the direction of his machine but he was so intent in his thoughts, that he didn't see or hear the two men who were following him. Just as he reached the machine, they both appeared on each side of him.

"You there, stop a minute, we want to chat."

"Maybe some other time, I'm a little busy right now." "Now."

"Perhaps you didn't you hear me? Not now." Joe made as if to climb into the cab, but one of the men grabbed him and threw him to the ground, where he lay winded. Joe glanced around and saw that nobody was within shouting distance. "So, what do you want?"

"We have a little task for you. If you do as we ask, then no harm will come to you or your family. However, if you decide that you should tell the police, the site manager, or anyone else..." He left the sentence unfinished.

"Ok, I get the picture, so what am I to do?"

"When you start work in the tunnel, we'll give you a small extra piece to put in the tunnel itself."

"What sort of something?"

"It's better you don't know, the less you know the less you can tell."

"it's a bomb isn't it?"

"Is it? You are already asking too many questions for my liking." "You can't be serious. Why would you kill loads of innocent people. I will not be a party to this."

"I think you will. Don't you have a good-looking wife in Belfast? All I will say is that we have close contacts in Belfast."

"You wouldn't."

"Maybe we would, maybe we wouldn't. Do you want to spend the rest of your life wondering if you and your family are safe?" "Look be reasonable, I only started a few days ago, it is very unlikely that I will be working down there any day soon." "True, but with our good connections I think you could safely say that you will eventually." "So how do I find you?" "You don't, we find you."

"But I haven't seen you so far."

"That's because we didn't need to see you." With that they turned and disappeared amongst the Portakabins. Joe got up and rested his body against one of the wheels of his machine. He stood there shaking and thinking over all he had heard. Maybe he should get in touch with Sarah as soon as possible. Then he thought to himself, if they had sought out him in such a short space of time, they would probably have already kept an eye on Sarah. He climbed up into the cab and started the engine and drove over to his sector.

+

Andrew's office door was knocked and then it was flung open, and a tall man came striding into the room. He didn't wear any sort of uniform and he carried a file under his arm. Producing an ID card, he placed it and the file on to Andrew's desk and stepped back.

"DCI Reed, LICD trouble-shooter. Let me explain what I can do down here. I have total freedom to go anywhere and ask whoever I see fit to do so. The only person I answer to is the PM. I have read this from cover to cover and now am aware of what has happened so far." He ticked off his fingers as he spoke. "One, you capture an ARI man and woman and then they are allowed to go."

"Two,you capture another ARI man,before you can interrogate him, he is killed."

"Three, your office is bombed and wrecked".

"Four, files appear to have been stolen from the office. Now perhaps you could tell me what is likely to happen next?" Andrew sat stunned by how quickly and how much information Reed already had learnt.

"How do you know all of this?" he asked Reed.

"By adopting the same techniques that the ARI do." "Such as?"

"Hacking communications, listening to officers talking in the canteen and of course if you saw lots of men on the streets looking in every shop, house and flat you would know that something is up."

"Oh."

"Yes, oh. Nobody challenged me when I arrived. I find that security is lousy. Since I am to take charge, there will have to be some sort of changes."

"Such as?"

"One, stop using this phone for contacting the outside world or anyone outside this office. At least until it has been checked for any listening devices."

"Two, I want all the reports to be written only once and placed on my desk. I would rather have one badly written and spelt single report, than to receive a correctly spelt one with the draft put in the bin or shredder. Even some shredded material can be put back together as the USA learnt to its cost in Vietnam."

"Three, you only liaise directly with me, no-one else."

"Four, three-quarters of your men are to be pulled off the street and arrange for just the remaining quarter to be on a house-to-house search of Dover. Send the rest to Hythe and Deal. Also contact your opposite numbers in Calais and Boulogne. See if they can start a house-to-house search over there. Inform them that more information will follow shortly. I will contact Belfast to arrange the same there. Now I need the following in my office. Fax machine, computers both personal and a link to the main police one and three phones including a direct link to London and the PM. I'll need all the files on the ARI suspects. Once I have drawn up a short list, then we will call on each one separately. So, by doing that we raise least suspicion. Any questions?"

"Yes, one. Who is going to foot the bill in the end for all of this?"

"HMG. Anything else?"

"Yes. You do you know that Chief Superintendent Rose of the LICD is down here already and helping with this. Don't you think he will be feeling snubbed?"

"No, I didn't know he was here. Yes, it's very likely he will be snubbed. Look at it this way, has he managed to find those two?"

"No."

"So, he can't complain then can he?" "No, I suppose not."

"Then let's get going." He picked up the file and turned and left the room.

Andrews rubbed his forehead and seemed to be in a daze. If this was the speed that Reed worked at, then he would be exhausted by the end of the morning, never mind the end of the day. He rose to start getting Reed's list of items together. He thought of giving the job of obtaining the Calais and Boulogne opposite numbers to Rose, then thought better of it until he had asked Reed. He knew that he would blow his top if he went to Rose first. He opened his office door and almost collided with Rose who looked very red in the face.

"Did you know Reed had arrived?"

"Yes, he has just left my office. Is this important Rose?"

"I think so. He has got a lot of gall. Do you know that he has taken complete charge of this case and you are second to him, I am to be elbowed out until he lets me know if he can fit me in. It seems to be that you are in with him. So, you can stay on the case."

"Call it luck, if I make a mistake, then heaven help me." "That's true." Rose paused for a moment. "Look, since I am not needed down here, I'll return to London, but if you need me, then phone me on this number, there is someone there night or day. I'm not saying that anything will happen, but should it, then here is where to reach me. Remember I do have the PM's ear, so to speak."

"Thanks. I'll see you out then."

"Sure, but this isn't over yet, not by a long chalk." They both left and walked down the corridor. Once Rose had left the building, Andrews thought he would walk along to Reed's office to see what he had to say. He arrived at the door and knocked sharply. "Come in." Andrews entered and took in the office. Like most people Reed had made a few changes to the room, as it gives it a stamp of individuality. He looked up at Andrews from his desk.

"You have spoken with Rose then?" "Yes, he is returning to LICD."

"Good. Now do you know the name of the site manager of the tunnel project.?"

"it's a Mr. Brooks, do want me to introduce him to you?"

"No thanks. I prefer to go in unannounced then nobody is prepared for me. Now have you called your men off yet?"

"Not yet."

"Get on with it then."Andrews turned and stormed out of the office, slamming the door after him.

+

At the site workings, Sean Smith sat at his desk while in front of him was a man who was supposed to be from the government. Though at present Sean, had doubts.

"So how can I help you Mr. Reed?"

"I need to see all the records of the Irish workmen on the site. We are conducting a survey into the numbers coming to work here, to obtain the correct information we need to see all of the sites in Britain." He shrugged his shoulders as if to say, 'what a waste of time, but someone has to do it.' He smiled, but Smith wasn't fooled for one minute.

"Do you have any identity card on you?" Sean asked pleasantly. "Of course, I should have given it to you earlier, here take it. There is a phone number on the reverse of the card." Simon settled down in the chair to wait for the outcome but he knew that if the number was phoned, a person at the other end would confirm his story. Sean replaced the phone and looked at Reed in the chair opposite him.

"It appears that you are who you say you are." "Thanks, now can we get on?"

"Sure, but you will have to look at each card on the index, that could take a long time and although you can stay as long as you want, I do have better things to do. My secretary will be only too pleased to help you, now if you don't mind." He rose to go. "One more thing, don't start to cause trouble down here, I have enough problems keeping scheduling, without the Government butting in." Reed ignored that remark and Sean left the room.

Reed glanced over to the far wall where a copy of the site work plan hung and on closer inspection he realised that this could be a quick way of getting all the Irish together. Just look for the Irish sounding names. He turned as the secretary entered the room.

"I understand that you want some help?"

"Yes, I need all the Irish workmen's files, but Mr. Smith said that they weren't filed under nationality, so we have to look up each one."

"That's what he said?" "Yes, why?"

"Well, I was asked to file them that way only last month by the head of TML himself."

"How odd." Reed thought for minute then turned to the board again. Does this represent everyone you have employed?"

"Good heavens no. Only the ones currently working on the site. The others might be on holiday or off sick. Why do you ask?"

"I was just wondering."

"I colour coded the files for ease of reference, the Irish are yellow and green." She moved over to one of the three four drawer filing cabinets and started to pull files from them.

"Can I do anything?"

"You could start at the other end near the Zs if you like." He took off his jacket and draped it over the back of the chair, then he started with the bottom drawer.

An hour later they had pulled out all the files and had them listed alphabetically in front of them, Mary had found some boxes and Simon was busy transferring the files into them.

`Why do you want all these files, is it because you want the ARI connection?" Mary asked. She could see that her statement had shaken him badly. Now she pressed on her advantage. "How many times do you think that the ARI will try and get into the site, once - twice, three times?"

"I don't know, and yes you are half right, but I would be obliged if you could keep quiet about it."

"But what is your job, clearly you are Government, but not what you told Sean."

"True, but it is better that you don't know, believe me." "There is one thing." said Mary biting her lip. "We have an

Irishman staying at our house, but he's only just arrived, and he is straight as an arrow, I know he is."

"You might think that, but if he has pressure placed on him then he might break, but why tell me, I'd have found out eventually?"

"You wouldn't have. You see since he has only just joined us his file would not have been in these drawers."

`Go on." he said looking at her in amazement. "Just how many others are there like that?"

"None."

"Ok. You did right thing to inform me. Now let's get this lot loaded into a car." He picked up a box of the files. "Tell me, why is he staying with you?"

"Well, my mother runs a B&B." "Your mother!"

"And what's wrong with my mother?" "Nothing, nothing at all." He sighed.

"Look, it is nearly finishing time. I'll drive home, you can follow. I assume you have a car?"

"Not yet. I came down by train."

"Then you had better come with me. She went inside and packed up her desk and covered her PC. Then she picked up a box of the files and looked at Simon. "Do you have somewhere to stay for the night?" He shook his head. "Then come home with me."

Mary led the way out to her car and Simon followed, both carrying boxes of the files. After a couple of trips, she shut and locked the door to the office. Then both got in and drove off to the B&B.

Once at her home he got out of his car and went and opened the car door for Mary. "Thank you for bringing me here."

At the top of the steps her mother watched this without saying anything. She could see that he was smartly dressed and had money. She hadn't any idea as to why he was here. She would have to wait until Mary filled her in. Mary saw her mother and bounded on up the drive to greet her. She turned as Bill came up to them.

"Mr. Reed this is my mother, mother, this is Mr. Reed." "At least you look smart both in looks and brains." "Mother!"

"Mary, you know I always speak my mind - it is far easier in the long run. Don't you agree Mr. Reed?"

"Absolutely, now could I come in and ask you some questions please?"

"Of course, come into the living room." He followed her in and closed the door after him.


"Now Mrs. Orchard, what can you tell me about Joe O'Brian?"

"He arrived only a couple of days ago and Mary brought him here as he had only just started. I feel that if Mary can vouch for the men in this house that's ok by me."

"Fine, now is he a reliable type or a quiet type?"

"Quiet, clean and tidy. He has phoned his wife once from here but without any success. Does that answer all of your questions?" "One more, do you have some sort of book for them to sign in?"

"Yes, I'll get it." She left the room and Reed took the opportunity to glance around taking in the detail. She returned clutching a black covered visitors' book.

"I take it they all sign in, all your guests I mean?" Brady asked her.

"All of them. I run a tight ship here. Do you have somewhere to stay tonight?"

"Not yet, Mary did say though…"

"Then you can add your details to the book." she said with a smile. "I'll go and get your keys." Mrs. Orchard shortly returned holding two keys with a fob marked 12. "I hope you have a nice night's sleep. Your room is the one on the third floor. Up the stairs and turn left at the top."

+

Colleen and Brady sat in the car they had stolen. Now that they were on the outskirts of Dover, it was obvious that the Metro had to go, but neither of them knew the town that well.

"What now Brady?"

"I don't know, just don't bug me, ok? I am trying to think." Brady sat pondering what to do. While they had slipped out of Folkestone undetected, they hadn't yet got across the channel. Then there was the disposal of the Metro to be taken where nobody would look for it or find it for some time. Putting his hand in the car door pocket he found a map and looking at it saw that they could walk straight down to the railway station, then catch a train for the Western Docks. "Look, here's what I've decided to do…" Colleen cut him off in mid-sentence.

"Hang on, I'm the one who gave up her flat and therefore don't I get a say in this?"

"Of course, but you asked me what to do next."

"I know about going to Europe, but I am having second thoughts." Said Colleen, not looking at Brady.

"Why?"

"Well, I feel that it would be better if we split up and went our two separate ways. Then the police forces would have to split their limited resources."

"But that's crazy. A single person stands out, a couple can be husband and wife, lovers, joggers anything. Why the chances of discovery of one are far higher than of two. Anyhow what will you do for money?"

"I'll manage." There was a knock on the car window and a policeman stood there. Brady wound down the window.

"How can I help you officer?" "This your car sir?"

"Yes, well that is I have borrowed it."

"Just that it's on double yellow lines and if you don't move it, I'll have to book you."

"Thanks, I'll move it now officer." He wound up the window and started the engine.

"You handled that well." Colleen said as he drove off towards the station. After a short while he pulled in and parked in the farthest corner of the car park. They both got out and walked back to the Station. Brady turned to Colleen at the steps.

"I guess this where we part. I'm sorry that I made a mess of your life, contact this number if you need anything urgently. I must be off now. Where are you planning on staying?"

"I haven't decided yet."She smiled and then she walked briskly up the steps and into the booking hall. She watched as Brady obtained his ticket at another booth before going out onto the platform. She looked after him wistfully, perhaps he had been right, but she felt that he was a harbinger of trouble. Her plan was to head for the south west via London. She planned to stay at Exeter on the assumption that nobody would be looking for her down there.

"Next." She broke from her dreams and looked at the woman behind the grill.

"I would like a National Rover ticket please." "Do you have a recent photo of yourself?"

`Yes, here are the two copies and the form." sliding them under the grill. Once she had the pass, she could alter her looks slightly.

`That will be six thousand, five hundred pounds please." Said the ticket lady. Colleen slide her gold credit card across.

"I'll need to phone for that amount. Wait here please." She watched as the woman phoned. For a moment she wondered if the police kept tabs on that sort of thing, then smiled to herself. Far too many transactions to single out one or two. The woman returned and pushed her card and the plastic National Rover Ticket across to her.

"You can use this across the whole of the UK, as well as on the ferries linking the Islands with the rest of the UK. Thank you, madam, is there anything else you want?"

"Yes, how much is it from here to Folkestone to Oxford?" "When were you planning on going?"

"A Tuesday."

"Then it would be twenty-five pounds and seventy five pence." "I'll have one, and I'll pay by cash." She slid the money under the grill and in return obtained the Folkestone Oxford ticket. Now she had what she wanted, and if anyone started to look for her they wouldn't know where to go. Obviously, they would check Folkestone and Oxford first, but the whole country was at her disposal. She had to do a few essential things first though. New clothes, new wheels and see if she could contact"Smoke" for any information on them being on the run. She left the station and walked to the public phones just outside.

She phoned"Lenny Smoke but the phone remained unanswered. Frustrated, she looked out another number and dialled that instead. "Come on," she muttered to herself.

"Speedy Pie Company, can we help you to get one to you tonight?"

"I need a cold quick pie. Delivery to Folkestone tonight, it would be delightful." Putting a stress on the 'D' to indicate that she was in Dover.

"That you C?"

"Yes, I need some cash tonight as well." "How much?"

"Ten k's"

"That's a lot to get at short notice. Maybe I'll see you at James's funeral at six pm."

"Fine." She hung up. Now she had to get back to Folkestone and find the cemetery of St James Church. Colleen decided to get directions from the information centre. Once having done that she would catch a train to Folkestone.

Two hours later she was pacing around the parameter of the cemetery. She was furious with Brady for causing her to lose the flat. If she was to make a fresh start she desperately needed money, passport and a new identity. The first and last would not be large problems. It was the passport that might be, she thought that somewhere she had read that they were changing the design of them.

She walked back to the main entrance and went inside. As she walked further in the gloom deepened and it began to get on her nerves. As she leaned back against a tombstone a deep throaty chuckle came from behind her, making her jump.

"Took your time, didn't you?" "Is that you Lenny?"

"Who else is going to sit around in a dark cemetery at this time of night?"

"Did you bring the money and the car?"The code of Pie had indicated to him that she wanted some wheels.

"Yes."

"Well, what type did you get?"

"I thought you would want something fast." "So?"

"An XJ 6 Jaguar sits out there with the money in the boot. Here is a remote-control device for opening the car doors and starting the engine from a distance. I have filled the tank with petrol and that should keep you on the road for a couple of hundred miles at least. Don't try and run it at full speed until you have done at least twelve thousand on the clock. Anything else?"

"No, that's marvellous." She turned to go.

"You haven't seen the papers, have you?" She turned back. "No, should I have?"

'Well, let's say that the pictures of you and Brady are on every paper in the country. There is a reward too."

"How much?" "Fifty K's." "That much!"

"Yes, and I have put a new passport in the car, but it does need a new photo and stamp. I am sure you know where to go for those." He paused. "This is a phone number where you can get help, but what I have done now cancels what I owed you before ok?"

"Ok."

"Good-bye then."

"Good-bye." But he had already merged into the background. "Damn," Colleen muttered softly; she knew that she had a lot going for her, but the police had been very quick. Far too quick for her liking and she would like to have to called on"Beehive" Henry tonight and see what he had to say. She walked out to the car and started the engine, then got in and drove off.

+

The next morning found Andrews sitting in his room arranging to get most of the men off the streets. Once they had returned, they were to refuel and be ready to go anywhere any time.

He finished the last of the phone calls and thought about Simon, the trouble-shooter - troublemaker more like it, he thought to himself. Pulling a pile of reports towards him he started to go through them quickly and methodically.

An hour later there was a knock on his door and Simon Reed stood there.

"Come on in and draw up a chair."

"Thanks. Do you know that having spoken to Bryan, Brooks, Miss Orchard and Mrs. Orchard not one of them knows of any regular Irishmen behaving in a suspicious manner? Now don't you think that is odd? I mean I feel that someone should know something."

"I got nowhere when I saw Brooks either. I've got my men coming off the streets. Do you have any good news?"

"Only that I have all the Irish files from the site. Currently they are at Mrs. Orchards B & B. I need to get access to a car, then I can go and get them."

"We'll take mine for now." Andrews grabbed his keys off the desk and they both went out to his car. An hour later the files were being unloaded at the police station.

"Where do we start?" asked Andrews, looking at the two boxes of files.

"Get somebody in to help sort them in date order, date of starting work. Some sort of spreadsheet would be the best solution."

"Who to trust though?"

"Any one of your good officers will do. Meanwhile I'll check the two offices to see if there are any hidden listening devices. I have known them be installed in other places."

Twenty minutes later Andrews returned with another officer, Reed was sitting starting to look at the first file. He tapped his fingers on it.

"Let's get this information onto a spreadsheet and once that is done, it will be easy to sort out in whatever order we want."

+

By the end of the day the spreadsheet was almost finished. Simon had had to give way to calling in more than just one officer to help load the files onto a spreadsheet. With four of them entering details it had speeded up the work a lot. Now Andrews was busy putting the four files together into one large file. Simon got up from the desk and nodded at the other two officers.

"You can go now, thanks for helping. Do keep this work to yourselves."They left the office without saying a word. Andrews looked up at a knock on the door as they had asked not to be disturbed unless either of them called. A policeman stuck his head round the door and looked them.

"Sorry to interrupt, but Chief Superintendent Rose is waiting to see you."

"Tell him we'll be about half an hour."

"Right sir."The head disappeared and the door closed after it. "Come on let's clear up, I don't want anyone else knowing what we have been up to." said Andrews.

They set to with a will and after about half an hour the room looked back to normal. The only thing out of place was the overflowing bin containing all the used coffee cups. Bill told Andrews to get a sack for the rubbish since he didn't want anyone coming and going through it in a fine manner.

+

"Where shall we put the files now?" asked Andrews.

`In the metal filing cabinets, then lock them." Both men set to and soon had the files and the floppy disc with the spreadsheet on, stored safely and securely in the filing cabinets. Then they walked along to Rose's office.

"Come in."They both entered and stood about five feet from his desk.

"Found out anything new Simon?" he asked as they stood there.

"I'll say what I need to, to the PM. For your information, not a lot yet, but working on it. I'll tell you more if I am allowed to," Reed replied.

"So, what have you been doing then?"

An hour later Bill finished and looked at Rose waiting for him to speak. `

"The problem is that the time limit seems to have been somewhat shortened."

"Why is that sir?" asked Andrews.

"The PM has been on the phone to me and strongly suggests that we bring in the SAS to help. I have pointed out that nothing has happened yet. By that I mean we haven't received any threats. I don't think that we are going to need anyone anyway." Said Rose.

"Why not?" asked Simon quietly.

"Because I intend to double the guard around the fence." snarled Rose angrily.

"What if they have already infiltrated the works?" asked Andrews

"Unlikely though that is, we can check the files." Said Simon. Andrews looked at Simon and said nothing.

"And If you double the numbers the ARI would soon realise that we were on to them." Simon added helpfully.

"What do you suggest then?"

"We call on the workers who were recruited first and go for getting the most information out of them."

"Anything else?"

"Yes, I intend to join the site as a workman, nobody will know me down here."

"That is a good idea, set it up will you Andrews?" He turned to Simon. "You can leave now Reed." Once he had gone, he turned to Andrews again.

"Do you know I haven't been talked to like that since I was a junior officer, but the PM has the most respect in him so we must grin and bear it I suppose." He waved a dismissal hand. Andrews left the room and closed the door quietly after him. It was only once he was walking along the corridor that he realised they had learnt nothing about what Rose had been doing. The whole thing had been one sided. He opened his office door to find his office ransacked. The desks drawers were open and, on the floor, the filing cabinets both lay on their sides with dents near the keyhole. A map of the tunnel workings had been torn down and taken. He realised that they must have struck while they were at the meeting.

"It looks worse than it really is." Said Simon as he looked around Andrews office. "They must have been here while we were with Rose. It doesn't look as though they have got the files though. That is something to be thankful for."

"Agreed. We'd better make a start clearing up the room first. They appear to have taken the map of the workings."

"So, they have. We'll have to get another one." The two me started to put the office back to rights.

"Bill, I've been thinking. We need to add somebody we can trust into our small group. I have a person in mind."

"Who is it?"

"A PC Black, we were at college together. He was a year ahead of me," said Andrews.

"If you can vouch for him, then by all means." "What cover will you use for calling on the men?" "Crime prevention I thought."

"Well, that happens to be his job. Everyone will need to be better than perfect if you are to not be rumbled." said Andrews

Half an hour later they were all filled in on what to do to make sure that all crime prevention officers knew what to do. Reed was going under cover name of PC Smythe. He had already left and was going in the company of one of the ordinary officers. This was usual practice with one officer working down each side of the street. They would have to wait and see how much new information they gathered.

## 7.28

William Dawson had spent most of the day checking the houses on the list. In most cases people had been only too happy to help the police. This had whittled down their list to just three and of those, only one was out. William had decided at that point to call it a day and go back to the station and see if there was any more information from either London or anywhere else in the country. He called over to the other officer that he was going back to the station and to come and drive him back.

"As you say sir. There is one address that we shall almost be passing on the way, could we?" He left the question unfinished. "Ok." said William tiredly. "but that will have to really be the last one."

"Fine." Both men got into the car and drove off towards the home of Patrick O'Shane. The house was in darkness and they both looked at each other.

"Doesn't look as though anybody is in, does it?"

"Well, there is only one way to find out." William heaved himself out of the car and walked up the drive. The other officer followed. William rang the front doorbell but apart from a dog barking somewhere inside, the house was silent. "I don't like the look of this. Look you go back to the car and radio for backup and forensics, while I try and get in."

"But what makes you think that something is wrong sir?" "Dog barking,dark house. Ok,let me look around the back first."

William walked around the side of the house and climbing over the side gate, found that it was bolted on the inside. Unbolting it, he walked on. He soon arrived at the back door. Inside was a large golden retriever with its front paws up against the glass. He could see through the gloom that the kitchen door was closed, and the dishes were piled high waiting to be cleaned. William called out to the other officer to join him.

"Yes sir?"

"I'm going in, there is a dog which has not had any food for some time I would guess by the condition it's in." He looked around and saw a half brick lying on the ground near a garden shed. As he bent to pick it up he noticed the garden shed window was broken. Coming from which was an awful stench. Using the brick, William broke the back door glass and opened the door. At once the dog bounded out.

Bill slowly approached the kitchen door. He felt all over it then as soon as he tried to open it he realised that something was behind it. He closed it again. Possibly a booby trap - now that could be nasty, he thought to himself.

In the garden the other officer had drifted over to the shed and having had a whiff of the smell, had been sick in the rose beds.

What was the smell? It reminded the officer of something, but he couldn't place what exactly.

He went and found William who was looking white in the face.

`What's the matter sir?"

"I think that the place may be booby trapped. Look, let's call in the experts." He phoned the station and after giving his message was told that Chief Superintendent Rose wanted to speak to him. "Put him on the phone."

"How are you getting on?"

"Like a house on fire. Do come and join us, we have a house with a suspected booby trap."

"Really William? This is Folkestone, not Belfast."

"As you like, but don't complain when the bomb squad have to come back a second time."

"Alright, I'll see you later." Rose replaced his receiver. Bill turned to the young officer.

"Married?" "Yes, why?"

"Then I suggest you avoid this area like the plague for the next two hours."

"But sir."

"No buts, I am going to try and gain access to the house again. If the ARI have run true to form then someone will have seen us go into the house and come out again and that will not have pleased them one little bit. They might just blow the lot up out of spite. Then that would make it difficult to recognise the body, assuming that there is a body that is."

"But the body is in the shed sir. I mean the smell."

"I did notice that, but I doubt it is where the body is." "So where do you think it is then sir?"

"In the house. That's why I need to get back inside." Bill left the officer and walked over to the adjoining house. It was a semi-detached and with a bit of luck and a well-stocked tool kit, he could be in there sooner than most people. He returned to the car and removed his small, but essential, briefcase.

He soon had the confidence of the neighbour and was upstairs in the roof in no time.

His plan had been to knock a hole through the wall that separated the two houses. However once in the roof he found that there was no wall between the two properties. Now that he had a bit more time, he didn't plan on wasting it. William carefully made his way across to the trapdoor and bent down. It was hinged upwards. He opened his briefcase and after removing a hammer, brought the hammer down on it hard, near the hinges.

The trapdoor fell onto the floor below. He waited for a few minutes. If anyone had been in the house, with that noise they would have come running.

William threw down his briefcase, then lowered himself from the trapdoor and fell the last two feet. He picked up the briefcase and removed a gun. He took off the safety catch and walked forward with his back to the wall, kicking in the bedroom doors one by one. Typically it was the last one which hit the jackpot.

He pushed the door open with his foot. Patrick O'Shane was lying there quite dead and naked. Quickly Bill searched each of the other rooms and found that there was nothing in any of them. It looked as though the house had been cleaned of everything but the body upstairs. Why? he wondered to himself. He retraced his steps and took a closer look at the body. This time he noticed the hands had been removed at the wrists and a single shot was in the middle of the forehead. He glanced at the knees and saw that they had been shot also. Just under the armpit of Patrick he suddenly spotted a scrap of paper.

Stuffing it into his pocket he then ran down the stairs with his briefcase in one hand and the gun in the other. Bill stopped dead at the bottom of the stairs. He could now clearly see the bomb that was placed against the kitchen door.

He moved towards it and found that it was ticking. He opened his briefcase and took out a set of small screwdrivers and some cutters. He had only seen one like this on a training exercise. Unscrewing the six small screws that held a plate in place he investigated the workings of the bomb. The fuse was attached to a tube, of what appeared to be acid. It was bubbling nicely.

From what William recalled in training, once the acid had burnt the bottom of the tube, the fuse would ignite, and the bomb would go off. With no timer to speak of, the nasty part was not knowing how much time you had left to defuse it. Blue and green wires were wired to the bomb, one at each end. Holding his breath he leaned in and cut the end of one and the ticking stopped. Quickly he cut the other wire and then extracted the remains of the tube. Then keeping it level he reached into his open briefcase and placed it in a special padded envelope that would keep it safe until he got it to a lab. He then placed the phial in the briefcase, before locking it and leaving the house by the front door. Putting down the case, he noticed the bomb squad had arrived with the rest of the police in support. William walked over to Rose.

"Why all the rush?" asked Rose with a frown.

"There was one bomb in there which I think I have defused but there may be others.

"Anybody we know?" asked Rose.

"Nobody I recognised. A bigger question is that I went in and came out without being killed. I doubt that is going to please our friends at all, assuming that somebody is watching, that is."

"No, I don't suppose it will." He turned and waved the bomb squad in. They started to walk up to the back of the house, but before William could stop them, they entered the house. Suddenly there was an enormous explosion. The shock of the explosion made the front of the house fall to the ground. Leaving it as though somebody had cut off the front with a sharp knife. It stood like that for a few minutes before more of the house came crashing to the ground, leaving the adjoining house nearly a detached property.

William and Rose found themselves on the ground with debris falling all around them. A few minutes later William looked up all that was remaining was the inside of the house. He picked himself up and walked over to the rubble. A few men in the bomb squad lay on the back garden coughing, but glad to be alive. Some of their colleagues were not so lucky. The ambulance crew, that had come with the bomb squad and other police officers started to take the bodies from the wreckage. It wasn't fair thought William to himself.

"Pity we didn't see the body." said Rose.

"But…"William stopped in mid-sentence. How did Rose know there was a body? He hadn't told him, and he was certain that the young officer couldn't have. He would have to ask him later.

"So, what did you see in there?"

"What? Not that much, I mean I was only in the kitchen after all."

"Look William, I wasn't born yesterday. So, tell me what you saw."

"Dirty dishes."

"Listen to me, I know that you saw something in there and somehow, you got in there."

"If you know so much, why ask the questions?"

"Because I don't know everything." snapped Rose. Then he turned and walked off. William stayed and looked at the pile of rubble. This had been someone's home once. The fire brigade was hosing down the few remaining fires that had sprung up. He wondered if the ARI had seen him leave or if there had been another bomb which he hadn't seen. The one thing that did worry him though, was how did Rose know so much more than he was telling? He would have to find out later. He filed the thought away for some future moment. He watched as Rose stood looking at him for a few minutes. William walked over to Rose.

"Something the matter?"

"Yes, that hole up there." He pointed it out. "It looks like a trap door entrance to the roof. But most of those usually have a pair of hinges and flap down. This one doesn't seem to have any flap at all. Now I wonder why? I might go and get the binoculars to have a closer look."

"Probably caused by the blast of the explosion." said Bill, trying not to smile.

"Doubt it, the force would have probably thrown the trapdoor upwards." Rose turned and walked back to his car. Bill watched him go and wondered if anything would be found from his earlier visit. He decided to go and get the young officer and go back to the office. He walked towards the shed in the rear of the garden, becoming all too aware of the smell as he approached it. Bill found a body on the ground with a sheet draped over it. Bending down, he removed part of the sheet and found the young officer he had spoken to lying there. He replaced the sheet and glanced up at the back of the house as one of the bomb squad came out of the remains of the house. "How come he is dead? I left him in the garden."

"We found his body in the kitchen, a tin of dog food clenched in his hand. Probably gone to get the dog some food."

"Anybody looked inside this shed yet?" Bill asked. The man shook his head. Bill looked at the door and then decided against going in. Better leave it to the experts he thought to himself with a sigh and made his way back to his car and drove off.

At the front garden, a PC walked towards Rose's car. Rose wound the window down.

"Yes, what is it?"

"Sir, we have found something in the ruins. Can you spare a minute please?"

"Lead on then." They walked over to the rubble and Rose found himself looking down onto the remains of the naked body of Patrick O'Shane. "OK, let's get a lot more men up here, I want all of this sifted through in case anything else is here. Do it slowly and thoroughly." Rose walked away and wondered what sort of people these people were. This was Folkestone not Belfast nor London. Shrugging his shoulders with a sigh, he returned to the car and asked for the body to be taken to the mortuary. Then he drove off towards the police station.

Rose swung his car on to the allotted parking space and walked into the main reception area.

"Any calls for me are to be routed through to my office as soon as possible"

"Yes sir!"

"Good." He walked on and into his office, but somehow it looked a bit different. Then he saw why. Behind his desk sat William.

"Took your time, didn't you?"

"What, what the hell are you doing here?" "Decided to give you another chance."

"I am so grateful. What do think I am some schoolboy? You have a bloody nerve coming here and saying that. I ought to." replied Rose angrily.

"Don't say anything to me. Nor do you tell me what to do or not to do. Start to grasp that important fact and we might get along."

"I just wish I could, but I find it difficult to take orders from someone who isn't one of us. Besides you don't take me into your confidence."

"While that might be true, I treat you like all the rest of the men." said Rose.

"Well, if I can't work on those terms what do we do?"

"I phone this number." He tapped a number quickly out and spoke to someone at the other end then he handed it to Rose. "It's all yours." He watched with some amusement.

"I can hold." Rose said, then he turned to William and said in a soft voice. "It's the Prime Minister."

"I know."William smiled at the way that people always treated the PM with reverence. Rose seemed to be getting some sort of rocket. He watched him replace the phone as if a dream.

"Why didn't you say who you worked for?"

"Couldn't I'm afraid. National Security and all that sort of thing."

"I see, now how can I help?"

"Go and find out whose body it is lying in the rubble and oh it's no good looking for fingerprints."

"Why not?"

"You'll see." He waved him away and dialled a local number.

"Hello, who is this?"

"SR, listen I need some information and fast."

"I've told you not to phone me here. What do you want to know?"

"Who planted the bombs at O'Shane's house and why were his hands cut off?"

"Didn't know he was dead. Give me two days and I'll find out." "You've just two hours." Rose replaced the phone. Then he picked it up and phoned through to London - he would be up later and to have his flat ready for him. First though, he returned to the bombed house, there was something not quite right that niggled him.

William also decided to drive back and looked at what was left of the house and parked behind Rose. Then he walked up and around the back. The shed stood there silhouetted against the spotlights of the fire engines. He routed around till he found what he was looking for. A long iron bar to force the shed lock. A fireman came up to him.

"What do you think you are doing?" "Breaking in, I am a policeman."

"Right sir. Look we have much better equipment to break in so let me go and get it." He ran off and returned quickly. "Now let me." He quickly broke the lock. The door swung back, and a stench flowed out. "What on earth?"

"That's what I am here to find out." "Need a hand?"

"That would be nice." He looked across the floor and over near the window was a wheelbarrow of rotting compost. So that was it, he had pushed a door down for a barrow of compost. He turned his head as he heard the fireman speak to him.

"Do you mind if I get this out of here and onto his compost heap?"

"No of course not." He couldn't remember there being a compost heap in the garden though.

William looked around the shed; if he was Patrick where would he hide something? If he knew he might die that is. There were loads of boxes and he might hide it in any of them. What about the box of odds and ends? Every shed had one. He made his way towards the shelves at the back and took down the first box.

"Sorry to interrupt, but there is no compost heap anywhere," said the fireman

"What!"

"No trace of one," repeated the fireman with a shrug of his shoulders.

"How odd, why have wheelbarrow full of compost in a shed if you don't garden."

"No idea sir."

"Ok, so where would you hide a wheelbarrow?" "In a garden shed I guess. Why sir?"

"Have you seen what is missing?" "No."

"You a gardener by chance?" "Yes sir."

"Well look around." "No garden tools sir."

"Exactly! Where would somebody get a wheelbarrow around here and more importantly, how would they get it back here if they bought it?"

"I'd get it delivered, but as you say, why buy one when there are no tools. It doesn't make sense. Now if you will excuse me, please?" The fireman bent his head and left Bill in the shed. Bill stood looking at the shelves of boxes and then went out to find a nearby policeman.

"Hi there. DCI Reed from LICD. Please can you find out if anybody has reported a stolen wheelbarrow in the last fortnight. Around here I mean. And can you see if we can get some decent lighting in here."The policeman nodded and left Bill by the shed.

Half an hour later, Reed found what he was looking for. He smiled as he held it in his hand. A small bug. It reminded him of the one reported stolen from the house some three days ago near the works. While he had been going through the contents of the wheelbarrow, he had found two booklets protected in a plastic bag. These he had carefully removed along with the small bug and had placed them all in the boot of his car, before getting in and driving off towards London. With a bit of luck he could make it in two hours.

As he drove, William let his mind run over the things that stood out so far in this investigation. His mind went back to Mary Orchard and the quick way that she had perceived what he did for a living. Perhaps he had better question Joe O'Brian and visit her again.

Maybe, once London had seen the booklets, he might show them to her. He drove knowing that the roadworks for the M20, which was still being built between Ashford and Maidstone, didn't help matters a lot.

He tapped the steering wheel and edged slowly forward. He cleared Maidstone after thirty-five minutes. Then he put the car into top gear and pulled away onwards towards London. He had tuned in the radio while he had crawled along the dual carriageway. Radio Two wasn't the one he usually listened to, but for traffic updates it was the best. He suddenly became alert as a news flash was given.

"Tonight, a masked woman robbed one of the main banks in Folkestone. We are now going over to our man on the spot, Robert Keane, can you hear me?"

"Yes, I can hear you. The situation is that tonight just as the staff were about to close the bank the woman rushed in with a sawn-off shotgun and held up the bank, before making her gateway in a blue Fiat. The police are most anxious to trace the whereabouts of either the car or the woman. If anyone has any information, they should call Folkestone…"William snapped the radio off to think. Was it too much of a coincidence that tonight of all the nights there was a bank robbery? The Folkestone police would have been very thin on the ground. And yet it could be a coincidence.

Something niggled at the back of his mind. An hour later he was home and in his flat. He owned the whole building but had divided it into three flats and he lived in the ground floor one. There was a shared basement for freezers and the like, but for now he was just interested in listening to his messages on his answer phone. He made his way over to his desk and sat down. Then he drew a pad of paper towards him and turned on the machine. One was from the bank manager asking him to visit him soon. The other was a mystery lady. He paid close attention to her message.

"Hello Reed, or may I call you William? You see I know an awful lot about you, but what do you know about me? Very little indeed, I shouldn't wonder. I want to help you. I was in a blue Fiat. But now I have changed all that for something a lot better. So fast that it could out race any car you own. You have been busy - Folkestone, London. Where now Scotland Yard? I have you in my sight both night and day. Look around and you'll see me." The phone went dead, and he whirled round half expecting to see her standing there. He made a few phone calls and then went to bed.

+

The next day he awoke bright and early and drove to New Scotland Yard. Most people see the entrance in Victoria Street, few know of the other three secret underground entrances. He had telephoned last night and asked for his secretary to arrange a meeting of BOTOG. This wonderful acronym stood for 'BOOT OUT TERRORISTS OF GREAT BRITAIN' He didn't favour it for it worked on the 'NIMBY' not in my back yard principle.

Sighing, he sat down at his desk to clear a pile of paperwork before going down to his boss. He needed to update him on what he had done since he had been placed on secondment to Folkestone.

Then they both walked along to the meeting of BOTOG. He had requested some information and when his secretary turned up with the documents, he would know some of the answers to the gaps. She stood just inside the meeting room and handed a package to Reed.

"This is what you wanted.'Beehive Henry' is not on our list." She left the room.

"Who is this 'Beehive" that was mentioned?" asked the MP representing the Government.

"Someone we trained in the Army, then he left to join the ARI but anyhow we did have him."

"Did? What the devil do mean by that?"

"We had captured him and then someone managed to get into the police station and killed him by hanging."

"How did they get into the police station?"

"Dressed as a Sergeant apparently. Easy isn't it." He turned and looked at his boss. "I must go and brief others now."

"Yes of course." William left the room and leaving his superior to deal with the rest of BOTOG, he made his way to the secure office and gathered his team together. Quickly he explained that they needed to be working in conjunction with Folkestone police and to cast their LICD net as wide across the UK as would be needed. As Bill brought the meeting to a close, the door was knocked and his superior put his head round.

"A word Bill, in my office." The door closed and Bill looked at his small group.

"You know your areas of expertise, now go and get on with it. We need the group of ARI caught or the biggest construction project for years might not get finished." He left the office and walked along to his boss.

"PM wants this wrapped up within a few days. Also wants it kept on the QT."

'That's kind of difficult as I have limited means and must not tell anyone outside of LICD and her what we think."

"I know it's difficult but do your best. She wants to see you ASAP, so go and see her in Downing Street and then return to Folkestone. Did you hear about the robbery?"

"Yes, I am sure it is connected. I think she left a message on my answer phone." He gave the tape of his answer phone to his boss. "I want to get this analysed please."

"We might have a break on that." He tapped a folder in his hands and opened it.

"What exactly?" asked Reed

"The new car that she talks about. It could be the new XJ6 Jaguar. Jaguar have been helpful and sent over all the details to us, here look." Alloy wheels, cruise controls, infra-red remote control locking and self-starting, smooth ride even at speed, but only colour for now is red."

"Do we have any number plates for this toy?" asked William hopefully.

"No, but a man was seen driving one in Dover last night." "That doesn't mean a lot sir, and you know it."

"Not usually, but what if I told you that only four so far have been sold. One in London, one in Edinburgh, one in Exeter and one in..."

"...Dover?"

"Correctly guessed. It was supposed to be in the garage of the owner, but the local dealer had asked to keep it for a week to display to other customers. The customer agreed, now it is stolen. What do you know that we don't?"

"Nothing yet, but if I see a red Jaguar XJ6 I'll take a good look at the driver." William smiled and after leaving the office, drove over to Downing Street. Driving his car through the gates, he wondered if she had really had them put them in to try and compete with the Queen. He was expected and once he had briefed the Prime Minister, he quickly walked down the staircase and out to his car.

"Folkestone, here we come." William said, not aware that he had spoken out loud. He put down his foot and accelerated out of Downing Street and turned right. As he drove out through London, he pushed the start button for the car's tape recorder and sat back to listen to some classical music.

Instead, it started to play *Seven Brides for Seven Brothers*, before being interrupted by the woman's voice. He knew that the voice wasn't supposed to be there, so he turned off the tape and pulled in at the next lay-by, where he listened to it from the start.

"Hello Bill, how did your visit to the Prime Minister go? Did she tell you to go back to Folkestone? All this running around must be very tiring for you. You could have phoned from Folkestone, but then you don't trust phones as they may be bugged? Well, I mustn't hold you up, even if you are going off on a wild goose chase. Oh,by the way I have changed from a fast car to something a little more popular and more difficult to spot. It was useful to get away from Dover though. Goodbye Bill."The tape went dead then the music from Seven Brides for Seven Brothers started again. Angrily he snapped the tape off and rewound it, before putting it in his pocket. He swung the car out and around back towards London. Half an hour later he was running up the stairs two at a time to the LICD technology office. He crashed through the doors and looked around the office. The young officer in charge looked up as he burst through the doors. William ran over to his desk and placed the two cassettes on the table.

"Can you identify the voice from the tapes?" "Given time."

"Well, that is something we are short of. It is concerning the tunnel. I just need to see if there is a match with anyone who we know is in or connected to ARI."

"Knowing that will make the job a lot easier." He walked over to a small machine which was connected to the mainframe computer. He placed the cassette in the machine and switched it on. Then tapped in a sequence of letters and numbers and watched as the mainframe whirled first one way then the other and in the meantime the tape slowly was examined inch by inch. He turned and looked at William.

"You know this is going to take about ten to fifteen minutes, why don't you get something to drink? I know that I could do with a drink myself and I am sure that you could do with something by the look of you."

"Ok, where is the canteen these days?"

"Still on the fifth floor." He looked at William quizzically.

"I work in the field more than in the office." He left the room thinking that the only time the cassette could have been placed was when he was in with the PM. Unless it had been placed before on the assumption that he was going to Downing Street, which would mean that someone inside would have to be helping the ARI.

William walked up to the canteen and had something to eat. He then purchased a coffee and returned to the recording office. He walked through the doors and was stopped dead in his tracks.

"Not another step or you join him." He indicated the prone body of the young officer on the floor who was outstretched as if he was trying to grasp the computer. Blood was already congealing around the body.

"Ok, but how come nobody came running?" asked William. "Silencer. It lives up to its name."

"Oh."

"Is this what you are looking for?" William looked at the man where in his right hand were two cassettes. He looked at the cassettes and then at the man as if judging the distance.

"it's not worth dying for, believe me."

"Oh, I believe you. Do you want his coffee?" "What?"

"His coffee, it seems a pity to waste it." "Ok, but no funny business, understand."

"Perfectly." William started walking towards the man and then when he was about three feet away, he threw the coffee in the man's face and leapt to his right. The man screamed as the hot coffee hit his face and his gun went off. William ducked down and crawled on the floor towards the desk. Bullets flew in every direction. He made it to his desk and suddenly the room went quiet. He put his hands on the edge of the desk to pull himself up, but a crushing weight was pushed down on them. William screamed.

"Shut it. Now keep your hands on the desk and make your way around the desk and sit down. I know it's wet, but you shouldn't have thrown the coffee at me." William sat down and looked at the gunman.

"Well?"

"I said shut it." The gunman brought the gun up against William's kneecap, and he could feel the coldness of the gun through the material. "Now just before I pull the trigger, I want you to think of being hit by an express train and living to tell the tale afterwards. I want you to think of the worst pain you have felt and then double it, I want you to imagine that you can't run anywhere in future. Now having received that bullet I shall continue until they are all used up. Do you understand?"

"Yes."

"Good." He pulled the trigger back and William braced himself for the impact. The gunman pulled the trigger, but nothing happened at all. William looked at the gunman, he knew that this was the worst kind of torture. "Well, well, you are good but that is no different to what I have been told about you." William said nothing at first then he saw the gunman slowly load two bullets into the gun. The trouble was he couldn't see which were the empty chambers and which were the full ones. "I'll keep on firing until a bullet comes out and you will feel pain, unless..." He stopped in mid-sentence.

"Unless what?"

"Unless you tell me what you know so far."

"I have nothing to say except this. Eventually you must leave and that might prove a little difficult if you continue to shoot policemen. The whole of the force will be down on you watching all the ports, and airports and other coastline points of entry. Go ahead and pull the trigger, someone else will take my place because there are thousands waiting to take my place to get rid of scum like you. You wouldn't even kill in the open, it must be done at night or with bombs that kill innocent civilians. Presumably you will say the ends justify the means, but whoever said that was a fool. In the end you and your kind will be destroyed, not yet perhaps but eventually and then all those deaths will have been in vain. Who do you think you are - Lionheart leading the people of Belfast on a crusade? Grow up, it's all over, look at the news the people are conditioned to the deaths on the streets."

"Do go on, I'm fascinated by all this."

"We have all the up-to-date lists of all your members so I ask you is it all worth it? Are you one of those people who throw their lives away on behalf of an out-of-date cause? We know that the money comes from America and the weapons from the Middle East. What we don't know isn't worth knowing believe me." William risked a glance around the room, why wasn't anyone coming? he wondered.

"So where do you fit in to this great plan"William continued"or are you just going to be a menial all the time. I mean, do tell me what it's like, do you do it for kicks or what?"

"The cause is paramount. We take risks that you wouldn't take in a million years. But you will feel that one day."

"This we, is it a royal we or are there more than one of you?" "There is more than one..." He stopped realising that he had been tricked. "Shut up and let me think."

"You are difficult, first I must talk, now I must keep quiet. Which is it to be?"

"Look, I told you once, now shut up and keep quiet; if you want agro you can have some." He yanked William to his feet by his hair and William kicked the gunman in the groin. The gunman fell to the floor and William finished the job by a well-aimed kick in the man's kidneys. In the process the gun fell from the man's hand and lay on the floor. William reached across and grabbed it. He glanced around the room. Over on the far side lay a bicycle carrier.

In it he found there were the usual bits and pieces in the bag that any cyclist will carry, including some rope and a padlock and chain. He tied up the man and looked around the room again and saw the cassettes were on the desk where the man had placed them. Bill picked them up and walked over to the nearest computer monitor, satisfied that nobody would disturb him. William sat down and noted that the screen was now flashing the message...

ARI TUT File:- 22/03/1989 Final Draft Four copies only: UKPM/ FPC/LICD/MET.

Code Eight. He typed in his own code added that he needed a copy and then set the printer going, he could read this at his leisure later tonight. The computers whirled one way and then the other, then the printer started spewing out a mountain of paperwork. Ten minutes later, Bill picked up the last sheet and banded it together. He retrieved the cassettes and stuffed those into his back pocket. He got as far as the door, then it opened to reveal a constable and his superior officer.

"What is going on here? Who are you? How did you get in?" "Look, I can't stop, but that man over there is the one who you ought to be questioning. If you need me leave me a message on my pager." Bill waved his goodbye and left the room.

The two men stood there taking in the implications of what he had said, then made their way over to the prisoner. When they saw their fellow officer on the floor dead, they knew that there were no limits to which they would go to get information out of this prisoner.

"So, this is what you have been up to is it? You and I are going to have a nice one to one chat." said the constable loudly.

"We'll get even yet."

"I can wait," replied the constable as he dragged his prisoner up off the floor and down the corridor to the floor below, William's boss followed the constable down the stairs.

William, who had been hiding in a nearby cupboard, took the opportunity to ran across and back into the room. He had very little time. He planned to give the young man a new name and then William would have yet another identity to draw on, which would make things difficult for people in Folkestone to say the least. Replacing the i.d.card on the dead man's person, William made sure that the computer screen was now clear before leaving the office. The constable returned just a few seconds after he had left. William ran down to his car and got in, there was a faint whiff of perfume and as he reached across to load the cassette in he found that there was already one in the machine. He switched it on, but there was no message only Seven Brides for Seven Brothers. He pulled the two cassettes from out of his pocket and put them on the glove shelf. Then he heard a motorbike start up behind him and he looked in his mirror to see a woman ride out of the car park. He turned on the ignition and swung the car around the car park and followed her.

She seemed to be heading towards the M40 and he knew that he had enough fuel to get to Oxford but after that who knows? But there was a garage on the outskirts of Oxford where he could refuel, so William followed her.

## 8.28

At the tunnel site works, Joe was coming to the end of his shift and he flashed his lights at the oncoming lorry to indicate that he was going off shift, but instead of just stopping and waiting for the replacement driver, two men stopped the lorry in front of him and got out. Joe had already climbed out of the safety of his cab, and now a look of horror crossed his face as he realised that it was the two men that had spoken to him that morning. He moved back away from one of the men, only to bump into the other one.

"What's the hurry Joe?" "Going somewhere?"

"We wouldn't want to stop you."

"I doubt that very much." replied Joe. He started to push his way towards the first of the two men. He was surprised as they let him past and climb back into the cab of his machine.

"Joe."

"I'm not listening to you."

"I think that you will, you see it concerns your job."

"What about it?"

"Here, take a look." They passed up to him a large brown envelope. He took it and ripped it open. The paper inside told him to report for duty on the tunnel face tomorrow. He would be working with one of the six machines that were digging the tunnels. He would also get a very large pay rise. He glanced from the paper to the two men and back. He could see that they were trying not to indicate that they knew what was in the paper, but it was no use, the glint in their eyes proved that they knew already.

"So, what does it say?"

"I think that you know already, and my answer is that I am not prepared to plant a bomb in the tunnel. Now that is the end of the matter as far as I am concerned."

"You deaf or something, what does it say?"

"I think that you already know the contents and you have my answer. Now please let me pass." Joe tried to pass the two men, but he might has well have tried to move a ton weight by himself.

"How much do you love your wife?" "Pardon?"

"You heard, now answer the question then we'll tell you." "Alright, a lot. Now answer my question."

"We have contacts in Belfast, they can and do strike at any time. We can simply just ask that they follow your wife and..." He paused.

"And what?"

"We'll leave that to your imagination. While you do so, remember this, we can arrange to maim a person to the extent that they will beg to be killed. Now we'll be off, but we can appear just like that." He snapped his fingers and they walked back to the lorry.

"You really don't have any choice Joe, so go do it." They climbed back into the lorry and drove away.

Joe wondered if it would be better to go home and give up this job. But if he did that it wouldn't look good on his job record that he gave in as soon as he started. What was he to do? He stood there racking his brains.

"You alright, only you look a little pale." Joe looked up to see that Kenneth Brown was stood looking up at him.

"Yes, I'm fine, I think I have been working too much, I haven't got used to the long hours yet." He gave a weak grin.

"Well, if that is it, I would see the doc if I were you when I get off my shift. Ah well, back to the grindstone. Though I have to say that at least we are working out in the open and not in the tunnels. Poor devils."

"Poor devils? They get good money, don't they?"

"Oh I am not saying the money isn't good but think of not seeing the sun for ages and the heat of working down there. No you wouldn't catch me down there for all the money in the world." He walked back to his lorry and climbed aboard, then sounding his horn drove off. Joe climbed back into his cab and pushed the window of his cab back up and drove back towards the site office.

He was beginning to wish that he hadn't been so successful in getting the job now he had the ARI to contend with. Perhaps he could say that he suffered from claustrophobia, or should he ignore it and hope that they were bluffing? Or he could choose the option of doing what they wanted, but if he did that then he would be blackmailed for the rest of his life. Should he resist and see his wife harmed?

Of course, if he had been single then there would have been no choice, but he guessed correctly that had he not been married, he would never have been approached. What he did would affect his wife as well, perhaps a phone call to her?

The trouble was that if he made the correct decision and made a stand then the cost would be high. He recalled a poem that he had been told to read some years ago.

First they came for the Communists
And I did not speak out
Because I was not a Communist
Then they came for the Socialists
And I did not speak out
Because I was not a Socialist
Then they came for the trade unionists
And I did not speak out
Because I was not a trade unionist
Then they came for the Jews
And I did not speak out
Because I was not a Jew
Then they came for me
And there was no one left
To speak out for me
*Martin Niemoller*

Joe now knew how the author had felt - unless someone made a stand then they, whoever they were, would always win. Use of fear, that was their weapon of choice. Hitler and other dictators had always used the same technique to take power. Having thought this out he pulled up outside the diesel pumps. After waiting his turn, he eventually looked down at Mike.

"Fill her up please Mike."

"Ok." He filled it up and then walked back to Joe. "Come into the office and sign the paper for it will you?" He seemed a little more pale than usual thought Joe.

"Everything alright?"

"No, I mean yes, look just sign the bloody piece of paper, will you?"

"Why can't you bring it here like you did yesterday?"

"Look just come in and sign the bloody thing." Joe, who knew that Mike hadn't sworn in his hearing so far, was indicating to him that there was probably something nasty waiting for him in the office.

"Ok, I'm coming." He picked up his jacket and put it on. Then walked into the office swinging the door firmly back against the wall of the shed. As the shed light wasn't on, Joe groped for the switch and at the same time a voice piped up.

"Ugh, my bloody nose. Give me something Fred."

"Shut it you fool." Joe stood taking in the scene that greeted him. Opposite him were two men and one of them had been speaking to him earlier. The third was climbing out from behind the door with what had been a clean suit on but there was blood on it everywhere. His nose was dripping blood ceaselessly.

"Well, well, what a group of slugs and other nastier things that creep out from under rocks."

"That was uncalled for Mr. O'Brian." Joe looked at the man with the suit.

Then Joe spotted a bottle marked 'ACID" on the table and quick as a flash picked it up and held it above his head.

"Now why was that uncalled for? I am waiting."

"Look we need to talk about this, but first put that bottle down."

"Why?"

"You don't understand what we are fighting for here."

"I know that you are giving Belfast a bad name. I only wish that you would leave. I would love to know what hold you had over Mike?"

"What hold do we have over Mike?"

"Do stop repeating the questions." He started to unscrew the bottle and they all moved back from him as one, with terror written all over their faces.

"Something the matter?" "Yes, don't open the bottle."

"But I was opening bottle, and besides the bottle only contains some acid, doesn't it?"

"No, not really. If you do open it then you would kill all of us and that would be silly, I mean do you want our deaths on your conscience."

"Well, I could throw it from the doorway, I may manage to get out safely. Whereas, your death, well I can live with that I guess since you are scum."

"Look, we beg you do not drop that bottle."

"Beg? Do the people you bomb have a chance to beg? Do they hell, it is far better that you are killed even if I have to die as well."

"Joe, look at this way, we are not just at war with Britain. Even if you kill us, others will come and take our place. Think about it."

"Then declare war on the Government and try and deal with the British Army and see if you can stand up to them, which I doubt. Anyhow this is academic, for you are going to die or my name isn't Joe O'Brian."

"We all have to die sometime, it isn't always up to us to choose, why not let us go and have a free conscience."

"What and then you kill me later, you must think I'm mad." "You don't have the nerve to kill us when it comes down to it.

Go on undo the bottle, but I should point out that it is not acid as marked on the outside. Once open and it encounters the air it quickly becomes a gas, a gas that kills. I doubt that you could get out quick enough. I may be wrong, so go ahead and throw the bottle and we'll all see."

"Let me get this right, this is a binary bomb?"

"My we have got technical all of a sudden, haven't we?" "Shut up. Now who is going to tell me about it?"

"Right, it's as you say, but don't open the top yet as we don't know the full effects of it. There are ten of them. Nine more like this."

"So where did you get these nice toys?"The three men looked at one another and the man in the suit spoke.

"A small break-in that we arranged; you would not read about it in the papers though."

"Thanks." Joe backed out and pulled the door closed and locked it. Then he turned to Mike. "Ok, what sort of hold did they have over you?"

"I like my wife, and the threat was enough."

"Ok, so what would have happened the next time?"

"The next time? They said there wouldn't be another time." "Oh, you are so naïve Mike, they would have returned with a worse threat. You would have given in and so it goes on."

"So, what do you suggest we do, give in and see our loved ones hurt?"

"But if we don't then an even larger number of innocent people will be killed or hurt. Does that make your decision easier?"

"You are not helping me at all, what about those three in there?" He jerked his hand towards the shed.

"Oh, those. Well one has a bloody nose, and the other two have become very nervous because I have this bottle." He tossed it lightly in the air and Mike dived for cover.

"Do you know what one of these things are?"

"Yes, but there are nine others and I need to find out the location of the other nine."

"How?"

"Well, this is where you help me. What I need is a bottle something like this shape and colour."

"I am beginning to get your drift; I am sure I can find something." He left Joe and returned a while later. "Will this do?"

"Perfect. What is in it?"

"Don't know." They undid the lid and an awful smell drifted out. Joe screwed the lid down tight.

"Let's hope that they don't call my bluff."

"If they did, it's unlikely that they would stay around to smell the contents."

"True." Joe walked out carrying the bottle before him in a careful manner as though it were the real thing. He could hear the shouting coming from within the shed. Mike quickly unlocked the outer door and Joe entered the shed leaving the door open. He bent down and placed the bottle under his foot. Then he nodded at Mike to undo the door.

Joe looked at the three of them as they flung open the door and then they all stopped dead in their tracks. How the rats change when they are in danger of being killed themselves, he thought to himself.

"Pay attention all three of you, the slightest lie or attempt to get to me and my foot breaks the bottle. I have been trying this on similar empty ones and it doesn't take much to break one believe me. That is not important, what is important is that you are going to write out the other nine locations for me."

"What if we don't agree?"

"Well, like you said, we all have to die sometime. I have made my arrangements; it may be a little painful though."

"But we don't have paper and pens."

"But I do."He produced them from behind his back and passed them across to them.

"What if we lie?"

"What if the earth was flat? It will not matter for your photos can be flashed around the world in minutes, as you well know, now write."

The three of them sat at the desk in the office and wrote quickly and Joe wondered if it was going just a fraction too easily. When they had finished, he nodded to Mike, who picked up the three pieces of paper and scanned his eyes down the list. Joe noticed that there were six names on each and in some cases the names were on more than one list. "So, I'll check these..." He didn't finish as the three pushed the table towards him and left the shed, banging the door after them. Joe stuffed the sheets into his back pocket and tore after them. Stumbling on some tools that lay on the ground outside he noticed that the area was now in darkness. Picking his way towards the exit in the darkness he was suddenly blinded by the lights coming on. "Dammit," he muttered to himself. He knew that the entrances to the fuel area would now be guarded by them. Looking around the site, a lorry would be passing him, so he crouched low and ran alongside it until he reached Mary's office. He bounded up the steps and into the office where Mary looked up in amazement.

"Where have you been Joe? Do you know how late it is? Are you in any sort of trouble?"

"Questions, questions. We need to go straight back to your mother's. Yes, I am in trouble."

"Ok but let me tell Sean first though."

"No, there is no time. Phone him from home." "Joe, something is wrong, tell me how I can help." "I'm being followed."

"Don't be melodramatic." "It's true I tell you."

"Ok, but you must fill me in as we drive home then." "Fine. Just tell me how I get to your car unseen?"

"Go out through that other door, bend down and get in the passenger's side, look here are the keys." She felt into her handbag and fished out a bunch of keys which she tossed over to him.

"I'll be out in two minutes."

"Two minutes." Joe did as she had instructed him.

A few minutes later, Mary appeared and got in beside Joe before she drove off towards her mother's. She turned to him as she drove.

"Once we get home the three of us are going to have a serious talk."

"Fine, but I need to have a bath first."

"Ok, but after dinner." She turned and concentrated on the driving.

+

Much later that evening after dinner Joe started to speak to them both.

"Right, now I'll begin at the beginning. It started when I saw an advertisement in a newspaper in Belfast…"

+

Colleen Kent drove on towards Oxford down the M40 but she was aware that she was being followed. However, she also knew the chances of her real identity being found out were slim to say the least. She had managed to swap the motorbike for the Jaguar again, in a layby she had previously parked it in.

While it was powerful, it was also very conspicuous, Colleen sadly knew that she would have to somehow get rid of it in Oxford. On the car radio she heard how a member of the ARI had been detained in Dover docks. She thought that it probably would be Michael or one of the cell. She could confirm her suspicions later.

As she continued to drive towards Oxford, Colleen tried to think of where the nearest phone-box was on that road. The sign for Forest Hill flashed by and she knew that she must be getting close to Oxford. She slipped down a small slip road and out onto a petrol station forecourt. She filled up with petrol and paid by cash. She glanced in her mirror and noticed with some amusement that the car behind her had pulled in and filled up with petrol, it had been following her from London. Colleen reached into her side bag and scribbled a note, before waiting for the driver to go and pay, then she tucked it under the windscreen wipers of the car following her. Deciding to drive through the back streets of Headington Quarry as it would make it that much easier to see if she could lose him somehow. She swung towards the south and drove until she saw the road sign for Quarry. Crossing the dual carriageway, she drove the car down through Quarry and out through Headington.

Colleen continued towards the city centre but the car behind still managed to keep up with her. At the last minute she turned sharp left to take her past Oxford Polytechnic. Then sharply turned right and down through the houses into St Clements. Smiling, she watched as she waited at the traffic lights as the car that had been following her shot past at speed.

Now she could drive straight to the railway station. Once there she parked the car at the far end of the car park. By running up the steps and to the station, she just caught a train to Reading. On the seat beside her was a copy of that day's paper.

Settling back in her seat, she picked it up and started to read it. The main story covered the bank robbery in Folkestone and she was amused to read that the police were looking for a blue Fiat. Since she had the compartment to herself and the next stop was Reading, it was unlikely that she would be disturbed. Colleen turned to the letters page and read on.

+

At the Oxford police station, a phone call between London was in progress.

"What the hell do you mean, she got away?"

"What I said, I followed her to Oxford and lost her in Headington."

"I would have thought that even you could have kept an eye on her. Good grief, Oxford isn't that big."

"So, what are we going to do about it?"

"We, we? What is this we? What are you going to do about it, now get moving as I want results and fast?"The Prime Minister slammed down the phone at her end. William turned to the officers in the conference room in Oxford.

"Thanks for the use of the phone."

"Think nothing of it, that was one angry Prime Minister." Said one of the Inspectors. Several of them nodded, they had all heard both sides of the phone call as it had been on loudspeaker phone. They all wondered how William would deal with the problem. He stood and looked at the note in his hand, the one that had made him drive like a lunatic to Oxford police station. To say that it was cheeky was putting it mildly. *It looks as though your date has stood you up, why not follow me to Oxford?*

"I think that we should start by looking in all the main car parks to see if we can find the car she was driving." said William out loud.

"That might sound fine in theory, but the number of cars parked in the city car parks both official and unofficial and on street parking add up to about twenty-five thousand each day." He stressed the figure of twenty-five thousand. Replied one of the senior officers in the room.

"Ok, point taken, but we won't find her sitting here." replied William with annoyance.

"No, you're right. Look, I'll call all the men on leave back and get them to start looking through the car parks, we'll start in north and east Oxford. You try the coach station and the rail station. Have you got a map?" he asked William.

"Yes."

"Good, then let's get on with it." They all poured out of the back of the police station and went their separate ways. William walked up to the coach park following his map. The car park was underneath a shopping and office development. He walked down and started checking methodically the cars one by one.

It was a very dejected William who walked down to the railway station two hours later. As he approached the car park, he was aware of the large numbers of police cars. One of the Inspectors ran up to him.

"We think we have found the car. It was parked at the far end of the station car park. It was the only car without a ticket on the windscreen."

"Where do you think she went from here then?" asked William.

"Could be anywhere sir. She could have changed cars or worse."

"What could be worse?"

"If she caught a train," he said softly. William stood silent for a minute thinking of the ramifications of what the man had said. There were unlimited destinations to go to. North and south and if she got to Reading, she could go either east or west. He turned to a nearby officer.

"Please can you find out how many trains have gone to Reading or Birmingham in the last two hours." The officer ran off and Bill turned to one of the other officers standing nearby. "At least let's get the forensics team to check the car."

"Ok, but I doubt if she will have left any clues sir."

"Let's find out first though, shall we?" William glared at the officer, who backed off and phoned forensics.

Bill walked over to the car and bent down and checked underneath. It all looked too clean. He began to wonder if they weren't chasing shadows. He turned to the Inspector on his left. "Get your senior men together, I think that we may be being had."

"In what way sir?"

"I'll explain it all in a minute." When they had all gathered, he outlined what had happened since he had walked out of New Scotland Yard with the tapes. How he had realised that she was following him to start with. At some point he set off to follow her wherever she led him. Bill pointed out that with the sort of cars and motorbike she had driven, it seemed that the ARI had supplied the money. That is, unless as he suspected, she was robbing banks to finance this trip. If this was the case, she still needed backup of some kind to arrange for the cars and motorbike to be in the right place at the right time.

All this time he was being drawn away from Folkestone and led all over the southern half of England. He thought that Folkestone still needed looking into, but still thought it was necessary to cover other parts of the investigation.

"Now what I suggest is this. We form three groups of specialist officers. One covers the railways. The second covers the buying of cars and bank deposits and any withdraws in the last ten days. The third group looks at the mass of material I have brought with me from London. It's in the boot of my car. Meantime I'll look at Folkestone angle. Any questions?"

"Why didn't you stop her sir?"

"Good question, I had managed to follow her for around ten miles but needed petrol. I pulled in and filled up, then found a note under the windscreen wiper when I got back from paying."

"Well, I'm dammed. What did it say?"

"It looks as though your date has stood you up, why not follow me to Oxford?"

"The cheek of it."

"It's possible that there may be another note in the car, where are those forensics people?"

"Well even if they turned up in the next few minutes it would be an hour or so before we could get anything out of them." A young constable ran up to the group of them.

"Sir, the ticket inspector at the barrier recalls seeing a lady who flashed a Gold National Rover ticket at him before getting on a Reading train."

"What is a Gold National Rover ticket?"

"It lets you go anywhere in the UK, saves having to queue and buy tickets at the station. The train left about two and quarter hours ago."

"Blast!" He banged his fist into the palm of his hand.

"She could be anywhere in the south or west or east by now." "While that's true, but consider this, there can't be that many of those tickets purchased, so let's try and see where she purchased it. We could try to get the stations to keep an eye open for anybody using those tickets, I mean they are very distinct from the main ones."

"Ok, let's check out these tickets and find out how much they cost."

"Six thousand and five hundred pounds."

"How much! That's more than a lot of people earn in a year. Ok, get to it." The officers moved off into their various designated groups.

+

Joe leaned back in his chair and looked at both ladies. He had just finished telling them how he had got the work at the tunnel and what was being asked of him.

"So that's the tale so far. Now I don't want to put either of you into any danger, so I had better leave."

"Leave, where would you go?"

"I'll find somewhere. At this moment, both of you are in too much danger. This is my fault. I can choose to make a stand, but it's not fair to involve you as well."

"Joe, I hear what you are saying, Why don't you phone your wife and see how she is. In the meantime, I have a couple of friends in Belfast who might be able to offer some sort of help.

"That's very thoughtful Mrs. Orchard."

"Fine, now go and phone her and then we will play cards for the rest of the evening and Mary will phone Mr. Bryan to put him in the picture."

+

"Reading, Reading, this is Reading. All change for..." The announcer's voice was lost in the usual noise of the station. Colleen Kent alighted from the train and looked up and down the platform, grateful that she could see no policemen. She walked over to the large timetable boards and ran her eyes over the trains to Exeter, noting there would be one in half an hour. She also needed to find out what had happened to Bill. Leaving the station, she walked across the road to a row of telephone boxes. Shortly she emerged visibly shaken. They had already worked out that the robberies were hers - she had expected that much. What she hadn't bargained for was the nationwide search. Realising that she now needed to move a lot quicker than she had originally planned, she ran back into the station and just managed to get on the train to Exeter.

All too soon the train was pulling into Exeter St David's. She jumped out and left through the main entrance, and on seeing a row of taxis, she jumped in the first one and asked the taxi to go to the head Post Office.

"Sure, no problem."

"I need a good hotel to stay in?" "Try the Red Mountain."

"Sounds Ok. The Post Office first though."

"We drive past the hotel on the way to the Post Office."

"In that case, I'll go and sign in first then." He dropped her off outside the hotel and Colleen told him to keep the engine running. She quickly ran across the road and up to the hotel. Shortly after she returned to the taxi. At the Post Office, Colleen paid off the taxi and queued for some stamps and the form for setting up a P.O.Box Number.

Leaving the Post Office, she walked down Princesshay taking in all the shops. Halfway down, she turned and walked through the pedestrian covered way to the High Street. She noticed that there were two banks near each other, National Westminster, and Lloyds Bank. Colleen went first to Lloyds and opened an account in a new name as well as cashing a cheque. Then she decided to take a walk around the city of Exeter and have a think about what to do. Obviously, she now needed to find some sort of work.

Exeter, like any city looks marvelous in the sunshine. The thing was that Colleen was not really taking in the history of the place. She wandered around the city lost in her thoughts. Eventually, she found herself near the main city library. She ran up the slope and entered to look up the history of Exeter. A glimmer of an idea was forming at the back of her mind as to what would be a good cover. She knew that it had been bombed in the Second World War, but that was about her limit. Here at least, it was most unlikely that the police would come looking for her. Colleen smiled at this thought and approached the main desk.

+

"Joe wake up, Sean wants to know if you are going in to work today?"

"What? Ok, I'll be right down in a minute."

`Well make it quick." She made her way downstairs and Joe followed shortly. He picked up the phone.

"Sorry to disturb you already. Are you wanting to come into work today? I know the new job doesn't start till this evening, but we are still short of skilled staff."

"If you think it is safe for me to do so, yes I'll come in and carry on working as before." He replaced the phone and looked across at Mary who was looking at him.

"Cheer up, nothing might happen, and if it does then cross that bridge when you come to it. Do you have the papers that those men gave you?"

"Upstairs in my room. I was thinking of getting them photocopied," Joe said. "Why?"

"I can do that at work, they would not think twice seeing me photocopying something. I do it all the time. Where is it? I'll run up and get it for you."

"On the bedside cabinet. Thanks."

When she returned, he looked across at her. "1 hope you know what you are getting into." "I think so."

"Good, because I can't see us getting out of this any time soon."

"Oh, I don't know, things could be worse." "How?"

"They could have your wife hostage."

"Right, but I hope they don't," said Joe as he followed her out to the car.

+

William, now driving back to Folkestone, was not a happy man.

If he had got a map, he would have gone the back ways. However, he didn't, so he carried on driving towards London. Five hours later he was at the police station in Folkestone. He ran up the steps and into the main reception area. An old sergeant looked up as he entered.

"Can I help you sir?"

`Yes, I wish to speak to Inspector Andrews." "I'll see if he is in, what name shall I say?"

"William Dawson." The sergeant left him to go and fetch Andrews. William was pleased to see the tightening up of security.

The officer returned with Andrews in tow. "William, good to see you. Come on through."

"Good to see you too. I see that the security has improved one hundred percent. I'm very pleased Andrews."

"Thanks, look, we have had a list of the binary bombs placed on the site or near it, so there is a bit of a flap on at the moment."

"What, I mean, where did you get that list?"

"It appeared on the counter and before you ask, I have already asked why nobody was on duty."

"You have been busy, look let's take a walk outside and I'll fill you in on what I have been up to in the meantime."

"Well, we have to drive to the works and see the bomb sites sometime, so why not tell me as we go?"

"Good idea." They left in Andrew's car and drove off in the direction of the tunnel workings.

## 9.28

In Exeter, Colleen Kent was very absorbed in reading up the history of Exeter. She had learnt that it had been around for about two thousand years, it was however the Romans who made the city. Unlike York however, which had retained its city walls, Exeter had seen fit to drive a large road through several sections. Other places had been hit by the bombing of Exeter over the fourteen different times that Exeter had been targeted Colleen had become so absorbed in the book that she was reading that she failed to see or hear the woman who had come up behind her.

"The history of Exeter is so fascinating, isn't it?"

"From what I have seen so far, yes, it is. Tell me do you know Exeter very well?"

"Know it? My dear, I was born here. Are you doing research for a degree, a book or just looking up your local history?" Colleen hesitated and thought about the question. If she said she was researching for a book, maybe she could write a book on Exeter as there appeared to be very few on the subject.

"Yes, I am researching for a sort of book which is based on Exeter, but it will have a fiction storyline. Though any sort of book with real background has to be well researched, you know how picky the readers can be if an author gets it wrong."

"Then may I make a suggestion?" "What?"

"Take a few days around all the important sites in Exeter. The Cathedral, Rougemont Castle, The Guildhall, The Underground Passages and what's left of the City Wall, get the feel of the place. Make notes and then go and use it in the book. History can be looked up, but it can become very dull if you aren't careful."

"But just now you said that the history of Exeter is fascinating, now you say that it can become boring, which is it to be?"

"When I said it was fascinating, I spoke the truth, it is. The difference is it could be boring if you aren't careful. I come here often, so I may see you again."

"I do hope so, you seem to know such a lot."

"Wherever you grew up, I am sure you know as much about that place as I do about Exeter."

Colleen went back to her books and started reading the history again. She would have to know it off by heart if she was to pass off as an author or local. Still one thing at a time. Colleen glanced at her watch - it was nearly five thirty.

"Blast" she muttered under her breath. She gathered the books together and walked over to the main desk. "I'd like to look at these tomorrow if possible, so can you keep them aside for me?" "Of course." He took them from her and she turned and left the library. It wasn't until she had gone that the librarian realised, she hadn't given her name. He bent down and filed them under"U" for unknown. He grinned somewhat wryly to himself - would she return tomorrow he wondered. As a lot of people said they would, but few did.

He walked over and flashed the lights on and off to indicate to the rest of the straggling readers that the library was about to close. Slowly the few walked out. Really, he thought to himself, you would think that people would be more considerate, he had to get home as well.

Colleen had walked out into Little Queen Street and thought of what the lady had said. It made a lot of sense when she reflected on it.

Walking briskly, she got back to her hotel in time for dinner. She had explained to the hotel management that she had come to Exeter at short notice, hence the lack of luggage at present. They had been extremely helpful especially when she had tendered cash. Colleen knew that hotels were in the main interested in only one thing, money. If you had enough of it, then it bought anything.

After dinner she retired to her room and read the booklets that she had picked up in the lobby of the hotel. She decided to draw up a list of things that she needed to purchase tomorrow. She knew that she would have to be careful where and how she spent her money to avoid leaving a trail for anybody to follow.

+

In Oxford, one of the three teams had been researching the documentation that Bill had brought down from London. Some interesting facts were beginning to emerge from the notes and files that the police had on this elusive woman, who it seemed could fly, drive, or use a motorbike or train. Already they had learnt that she had used her gold credit card only five times that year. Her bank account had a balance of around ten thousand pounds in it all the time. The list of people she seemed to have met, or it was suspected to have met, in the last five months read more like the wanted list.

What they were still looking for was an Irish or ARI connection, for none of the people listed were Irish or ARI members. They also had yet to find out who was supplying the cars and the money. It seemed she just had to want something, and she had it. "It looks as though she has a personal tap to the Bank of England."

"Say that again?" Said DI Rogers, his head looking up from the desk in front of him.

"I said, it looks as though she has a personal tap to the Bank of England. Why, is it important?"

"It might well be."The Inspector turned and called over to one of the sergeants in the room. "Anyone here checked to see if any of the banks or their senior staff are being blackmailed?"

"We checked the banks, but not for blackmail. Why, should we have?"

"I would have expected you to do so. Go and get on with it now, from the chairman to the cleaner, see if anybody is being threatened or blackmailed." snarled Rogers with annoyance.

"Well, yes, but don't we need..." "Just get on with it. Now go!" "But Sir..."

"Look, find all the banks in the ringed areas and check out the personal, their backgrounds, and so on. You have the power to do so, so now use it."The policemen rose almost as one and grabbed their coats from around the back of the chairs and left the Inspector in a very quiet room. Computer screens were left on and unattended and slowly the Inspector walked from desk to desk looking at the screens and the information on them. He sat down on one of the chairs and thought back to when he was young and ambitious, how he had climbed up to where he was today, but was it worth all the friends he had lost in the meantime? This case was becoming one of the more difficult ones to solve and he knew that the longer he took to help solve it the harder it would become. New cars, motorbikes, gold credit cards, good healthy balance at the bank on a no interest account. All pieces of a jigsaw, but as William had said it didn't fit. William had thought that they were being had, but what was wrong? He ran his eyes over the items that she had been supplied with in the last six months.

New car, new bank account, new clothes, second-hand motorbike, new rail card, new passport, new car license. Then it hit him. All the items were new except for the motorbike. The new items would have very little paperwork. But the motorbike, with some luck, that would have been registered at the DVLA in Swansea.

If it was stolen, then it may be on a list of stolen bikes that was constantly being updated. He leaned across the desk and picked up the phone. "Get me Swansea DVLA and a list of stolen motorbikes for the last six months. While you are at it, look at the list of insurance write offs, it may be there. Phone back in." He looked at his watch. "Say two hours." and then he replaced the phone slowly.

The Inspector smiled and then he picked up the phone again. "Get hold of the credit card companies and tell them you want to join their membership, not the run of the mill ones, but the exclusive type. What are the requirements? Got that? Good." He hung up again and the phone rang almost at once. He picked it up and groped around the untidy desk for paper and pen muttering about people keeping their desk tidy.

"Yes, who is it?"

"Listen, I don't have much time. Stop chasing the girl, you are looking for the wrong one. The men you need are..." there was a scream then silence. The Inspector looked at the phone.

"Hello, is there anyone there?" An ominous click fell on his ears and the line went dead. The Inspector phoned BT.

"Can you trace the last call to this number for me?" "No sir."

"What do you mean by that?" asked Rogers.

"What I mean is, that it is possible given enough time to set something up, but not just like that. What they say in the books is fantasy. When did you get the call?"

"A few minutes ago, why?"

"Well leave it with me and I'll see what we can do, but I don't hold out much hope quite frankly sir."

Rogers slammed down the phone and wondered who had been trying to tell him something. Obviously, he had to try and find out, but it was difficult given the tight security that went with the case. Suddenly over in the corner of the office the newly installed fax clattered into action. He had been opposed to it from the start, but the powers that be had ruled that it doubled as a photocopier, so that saved money. He walked over and tore off the piece of paper. Then read it and whistled softly to himself.

Running to the nearest phone Rogers asked for a direct line to the Prime Minister's office. While he waited for the phone to ring he re-read the fax. *If you are reading this fax, then I have been shot or killed by some other means but you are wasting your time looking for the woman. She is there for just one purpose, to lure you away from the tunnel workings. If you are looking all over the country your manpower is somewhat depleted. I think that you will succeed, given Mr. Dawson's help. He is no fool. Go to the locker on platform number one at Oxford station and you will find more evidence of where the bombs are and who is responsible. The number of the lock is......*

`Blast." muttered the Inspector. Just as we get somewhere the man gets killed. If I try to get the engineer to see if there is any means of tracing the fax, he'll say that"it's not possible." Then his eyes alighted to the top of the page noting there was a fax number on the top right. That might be a clue to where it had come from. He called up the engineer. "Is it possible to find out where a fax came from if there was no address on the paper, but I do have the number of the sending fax."

"Well, that will speed up things considerably I would assume. Re-send the number to this fax. 017865 999666 Then I can see if I can find the address for you."

In the meantime, the Inspector wondered if he ought to learn how to use the fax. He walked down the corridor opening doors and finding that nobody was in there, he made his way to the front desk sergeant and asked if he knew about fax machines.

"A little, why?"

"I don't know a thing and I want to send a fax. I need to know how to send one. Like to show me?"

"Well, to tell you the truth, I've only ever sent one and that was with a manual in my hand then. So, unless you have the manual?" He looked at the Inspector hopefully.

`No, I don't. Well do you know who can help me?"

"Try the offices over in St Ebbes. They are always closeted with their computers and what not, I wouldn't be a bit surprised if they had a fax machine already. Just a thought, the manual may be by the machine."

"Thanks sergeant." He turned and ran back up to the room that he had been in, but on opening the door he noticed that the lights were out. He reached out to switch them on and he received a hard knock on the back of his head...

... When he came round, the room was a buzz of people. He started to get up and then thought the better of it. He sat on the floor rubbing the back of his head.

What had happened he wondered? He could remember coming back to the office and finding the lights out. Then nothing, but why had he come back to the office?

"You alright sir? The doctor is on his way, just stay there and don't move. We have had some vandals turn the place over, nothing was taken though. Not even the fax machine. I mean you could sell one of those couldn't you?" Fax? Fax? Fax! That was it! The fax machine, he started to get up and found that he couldn't. Staying where he was, he looked at the sergeant and grinned.

"1 want you to see if there are any faxes on the machine." "Ok, sir." He walked off. The Inspector chuckled inwardly. "Bet he doesn't find anything." he said out loud.

"No nothing there. Not that it is surprising, I mean, no one wouldn't know our fax number would they? Well, they wouldn't, would they?"

"Well, that is where you are wrong, you see that is what was stolen from the offices."

"Pardon?"

"The fax, not the machine." Said Rogers with frustration. "You're having me on, nobody would go to these lengths to wreck the office if they were only after a fax."

"I'm afraid so, all this is a diversion." He waved his hand around the wrecked office. "Nobody would have thought of a fax missing. Just like you in fact. Now get me the officer in charge." The sergeant ran over to a middle-aged man who on being told who wanted him, visibly straightened his back, before coming over to the Inspector.

"Sorry we couldn't meet under different circumstances, what's this about a missing fax? I mean how do you know that one is missing?"

"I was in the office alone when the fax started to hum away, and when I looked at the fax the message was incomplete, I went to get somebody to fax back asking for more details and the sergeant on the main desk suggested I try the offices in St Ebbes, or that a manual may be by the machine. I came back to get the copy and that was the last thing I remember."

"Shall I fill you in on some details." "Do, I shall be most interested."

"You might think you will be but wait and see. First there has been a bomb scare in the police station, hence the reason why nobody was around."

"What about the sergeant?" "Not a real one."

"What!"

"Well, you see there is no office in St Ebbes." "What!"

"Don't keep saying 'What' Now where was I? Ah yes, also the bomb was a dummy one. The sort they use to fool the troops in Belfast. Very realistic I am informed. However, what is more important is can you remember what the fax said?"

"Well, I think so. First though I must speak to William Dawson." "Well, yes, that may be the case, but he is in Folkestone."

"So? I can fax him can't I?" "Well, you can't do that." "Why not?"

"Well, the fax has not been connected yet, That's why." He shrugged his shoulders as if to say,"there is nothing I can do about it."

"Listen to me, I heard, saw and read that fax, If, and I stress the word, if it is not connected, then how come I saw it working?"

"Sometimes a hit on the head does funny things to the memory, you may have tripped and fallen on the carpet."

"Now listen, I felt that thud across the back of my head. I would have a bruise on my face if I had tripped on the carpet, besides there is nothing to trip on here is there?" The other officer said nothing but asked for a mirror, and when he got one, passed it to the Inspector without a word. The Inspector held it up to his face and there for all to see was a large bruise over his left eye and forehead. "How did that get there?"

"We are hoping you can tell us that Inspector." "Well, I don't know how it got there."

"Well, don't let's worry until you have had a check-up at the local hospital."

"Can I ask you something?" said Rogers. "Of course."

"What time of day is it?" "Half past six at night. Why?"

"But that means that I have been knocked out for about five hours." "That's right."

"But don't you realise that there is so much to do about this enquiry. Have the reports come in, who was the voice on the phone and why was the fax used." He paused and the police officers looked around the room at one another with a worried look on their faces. The police doctor pushed his way through the group. He held a clipboard and pen and as he approached the Inspector, he looked down at him and smiled.

"Sorry about the delay, we'll have you up at the JR in next to no time."

"JR, JR? Why do people keep using abbreviations?"

"You must be joking, why everyone knows what JR stands for. Why it stands for..." The young policeman responsible for this outburst was silenced by a look from the doctor.

"Now look, this is serious, what does JR stand for?" asked the doctor.

"John Ross on Dallas. it's a TV soap."

"Yes, yes. But what else does it stand for?"

"It stands for..." He paused. "It stands for..." He couldn't remember for the life of him what it did stand for. "I don't know."

"Get him in the ambulance outside and keep it quiet, no sirens. Now get on with it." The doctor started to follow the Inspector out of the office. "I see you have installed fax machines here."

"But that is the whole point, I know a fax came into the office, yet I am told they haven't been installed." Insisted Rogers.

"Well let's wait until you are up at the John Radcliffe." "That's it. That's what JR stands for."

"Yes, but you wouldn't have known had it not been for my prompting, would you? Now let's go and get you checked out." "If it keeps you happy, Ok, but I really ought to be working on the case, but I have no doubt that you would say 'That is quite impossible.'"

"Quite right, but the sooner you do the tests, the sooner you can get back on to the case."

+

In Folkestone, Sean looked up as Joe walked into his office. "Good to see you, I know something is going on. Look I have a vacancy in the tunnel, not at the face but to the rear of the main TBM. The money is good, and you are good worker, so what do you say?"

Joe thought for a minute about what he was being offered. On the one hand he wanted to make a stand, but the other half of him wanted to turn it all down flat. He paused and asked Sean the question that would tip the balance.

"How much extra money?"

"That depends on your productivity, expect at least a thirty percent increase on what you are getting at present." Smiled Sean.

"Can I think about it?"

"What is there to think about? I mean the money is good, it's what you are good at, but if you want time to think, then I'll let you have until six tonight. I have problems of my own to think about." He waved him out of the office and Joe still in a daze, about what he had just been offered, walked out past Mary's desk and over to the machine enclosure but there he was jolted back into the present.

The compound was empty, but more than that, only the charred remains of the enclosure fence lay twisted and burnt like some horrible sculpture. He ran his eyes over the site and gasped out loud, for a large crater about twenty feet across and fifteen feet deep with blackened lines at the rim and a huge amount of foam lay in a decreasing pool at the bottom of the crater and on the ground nearby. Of the hut he had been in last night, there was not a trace. What surprised Joe was that Sean had not said one word about this. This sort of thing didn't happen every day, did it? He walked over to the crater and peered in, trying to visualize where the hut had been. Joe had just worked out that it was in the centre of the crater when one of the workmen walked up and joined him looking into the crater.

"'Tis a terrible thing that this should happen at the start of such a fine project." He turned to Joe. "What do you think caused it?"

"Are you talking to me?"

"Of course, I'd not be talking to myself."

"Must have been an accident of some sort. I mean nobody would want to do any damage to a hut?" Joe replied. "Do you know when it occurred?"

"Last night sometime between six thirty and seven o'clock, I think. I could find out exactly if you are really interested."

"No, don't do that." Joe stood looking at the crater. It must have happened only minutes after he had left the site. But nobody had been in the hut, so why blow it up? He began to shake visibly as he thought of how close he had come to being killed. "I wasn't even working in the tunnel," Joe muttered to himself.

"Pardon?"

"I'm sorry, I was talking to myself, it is terrible to think what might have happened if this had been the tunnel itself." He paused and wondered what reaction his neighbour would give. "Oh, I wouldn't worry about that. The security is watertight. The ARI must have been mad to think this would stop anything."

Said the man quietly.

"The ARI?" asked Joe, looking at him.

"Did I say that, no you must be mistaken. Nice to have met you, goodbye."

He turned and ran off. Joe looked in amazement and then walked over to the disc engraver's hut and knocked on the closed door. There was no reply, so he knocked again, this time harder. Still no reply. He turned his head as two police cars with sirens pulled into the site. Joe looked at the cars and then at the offices of Sean Smith. He made up his mind and walked over to the police cars. Two men got out and looked at him.

"Yes?"

"Look I know that this sounds silly, but this hut is locked and after last night's explosion..."

"Yes, we know about the explosion, now let's find either Mr. Bryan or Mr. Brooks, shall we?" All three turned and started to walk towards Sean's office. Just as they mounted the first step a terrific explosion from behind them threw all three of them against the office door and into the office landing in a heap on the floor.

"What the hell?" A second explosion went off, followed by a sheet of flame shooting up into the air. The heat and the explosion caused panic, everyone was running or shouting at the same time.

"I really don't think this would be the time to see Mr. Bryan. We should get out of here."

"You're right Andrews." The officer turned to Joe. "Where do you need to get to?"

"Anywhere but here!" He grinned and asked for a lift back to his digs. Then he thought of Mary. He turned and ran into the office's and looked at Mary where he could see she had been crying. "Mary, come on, this whole place could go up in minutes." She shook her head and waved him towards Sean's desk. He turned and looked for the first time at the shattered remains of Sean Bryan. He turned and pulled Mary out of her chair and pushed her towards the door...

"What did you want to do that for?" she asked, wiping the tears away.

"Come on we need to get out of here..."They both ran down and out across to the police cars. Across the whole site, offices and sheds were on fire and every so often there was a sheet of flame bursting into the sky. Men were driving lorries and trucks away from the flames. Joe pushed Mary into one of the cars and scrambled in after her. He told the police the address and the car left the compound with a screech of tyres and burning rubber as it swerved to avoid the incoming fire engines. Mary burrowed herself into Joe and tried to put the image out of her

mind. They pulled up outside her mother's house. Both Mary and Joe got out. Andrews wound the window down and leaned out.

"You two."They both looked at him.

"Yes, what do you want?" asked Joe, his voice sounding a lot steadier than he felt.

"I want to interview both of you tonight, is it alright if I come here?"

"Yes, that's Ok," said Mary. She looked at Joe and he nodded also.

"Eight?"

"Fine."They turned away and walked indoors. The car pulled away from the kerb. Andrews wound up the window and chuckled to himself. That should give themselves plenty of time to think up a good story. He started the engine and drove on back to the station.

Mary had insisted on telling her mother the whole story and her mother was visibly shocked. Joe wondered if he ought to pull out of the whole project. There were a lot of unanswered questions. He was curious as to who was going to replace Mr. Bryan. Was

Thomas Swift alive or dead and had anybody else been killed on the site and if so why?"

"Well Joe are you staying here or going back to Belfast?" "Staying."

"Thank the Lord for that. Right, I'll make a few phone calls. Mary will fill you in. I've no doubt that you have a host of questions to ask before the police come." Her mother left the room. Joe turned and looked at Mary.

"So do you know any of the answers or are you in the dark too?"

"All that I know is that I went into the office and there he was dead. 1 realised that something big was afoot and then you burst in and got me out of there." She smiled at the recollection. "What I need to know is what frightened you to death?"

"You know that I told you about the shed belonging to Mike O'Hara?"

"Yes."

"Well, it's gone and a great crater about twenty foot in diameter has taken its place, and that's not all. The engraving shed was locked and when I tried to make anyone hear there was silence. Then there were those two explosions. Now you know as much as I do. Now we must tell the police, as if my troubles were not enough."

"Get a grip on yourself, do you mean to tell me that both O'Hara's and Green's sheds have been blown away?"

"Well, O'Hara's has gone, but I didn't stop to see Green's after the first explosion. Mary who is going to run the personal office now that Sean is dead?"

"I expect I will, why?"

"Only this, the police will be treating this as an attempted murder enquiry in which you were in the same office, they are likely to make you the prime suspect."

"Oh, I hadn't thought of that. What do you think will happen?" "It's possible that they will take you down to the station and hold you for questioning. They can hold you for three days without charging you. I think that you ought to phone your solicitor."

"My solicitor? I don't have one. Never needed one. Perhaps my mother knows one."

"Maybe, but it needs to be a good one that could help you if you were arrested and charged."

"I'll go and check the yellow pages then." She left the kitchen to go to her room. A few minutes later she screamed loudly. Joe jumped up and ran up the stairs two at a time. He flung open the door to her room. Mary stood and pointed at her bed. On the bed was a note. He leaned forward and read it without touching it.

"Joe, look at the walls." He looked up from the note and took in the daubed wallpaper. Painted in large yellow capitals were the words: WE MAY HAVE MISSED YOU TODAY, BUT THERE IS TOMORROW AND THE NEXT DAY, WILL YOU RISK GOING TO

WORK? The question mark had dribbled into the dot under it and the message was nasty. Joe turned to Mary.

"We must tell the police about this. Even you can see that this sort of thing doesn't go on in Britain today."

"But if we tell the police, the whole thing will have to come out. Do you want that, Joe? Think before you answer." Mary walked over and touched the paint, but it was quite dry. "That's funny, the paint is dry."

"Let's tell the police all of the story." He turned and left the room and walked to his room. Mary ran after him and she watched as he opened the door and then shouted like she had done. She tore into the room. The walls were daubed in the same way as her room. She told Joe that they ought to have a little talk.

"I agree, but can you get a camera and take lots of pictures of all this." He waved his hands at the paint. "Both your room and my room." She left him while he packed all his things together,

Meanwhile she took the photos in her room. By the time she returned to his room he was ready. He had phoned the police. Mary finished taking the photos and removed the film cassette. The ring on the front doorbell indicated that the police had arrived. They and the police went into the front room and sat down.

Joe and Mary explained about the rooms and the fact that the paint was dry. Leaving Joe and Mary, Andrews and Bill went to examine Mary's room first and looked at the note then at the walls.

"Nasty, we'll get a forensics team up here fast." Then they returned downstairs to Mary and Joe.

"We are intrigued by you Joe, to say the least. You come from Belfast, find a room with the personnel's secretary's Mother's B & B. Then you happen to be seen leaving the site of the demolished shed last night, this morning you are looking over the remains of it, next you are in the office of a murdered man, Sean Smith and then you come here and lo and behold this is found in your two rooms. You don't panic you calmly phone us. And although you say you are married, we cannot trace your wife in Belfast."

"Oh."

"I'd suggest that you try and get hold of her first." Joe walked through to the kitchen to find Mrs. Orchard.

"Do you know where Sarah is? The police can't seem to get hold of her."

"Yes Joe, I do know where she is. She moved out of the house last night and some friends of mine are looking after her. Here is the telephone number, now give her a ring and tell her you'll phone again tonight." She passed him the phone and he did as she suggested. After that he went out to the police and Dawson and Andrews suggested that he should accompany them to try and shed some light on what was going on.

## 10.28

An hour later, both Mary and Joe had been put into a police safe house. A suitcase for each of them had been brought from her mother's.

He thought back to the messages, there was something sinister about the way that they had been daubed on the walls of the two bedrooms. Mrs. Orchard had sworn that nobody had entered the house or called all that morning. He knew that it could have been done while he was out. Then there was the fires and explosions at the site. He tuned towards Mary.

"What do you think happened this morning or last night?"
"Where, at the site or at home?"

"Both."

"Well, one or two bombs..."

"Stop, I know what you are going to say, and it will not hold water, there was no pieces of shrapnel or casing around the crater. Though the ARI are at the bottom of this. A workman let that slip when I was looking at the site. But when I mentioned it, he looked very worried. And you told me that the police took all the Irish files. They must know more than they are letting on. What I want you to do is to think back and try and remember if you can, if any Irishmen turned up for job interviews that were rushed through and subsequently got the job."

"Only one." "Who is it?" "You."

"Me?"

"Yes, look at the facts, you arrive at short notice and within a few days all of this happens. Well, you have to admit that it is rather a coincidence." Joe thought to himself for a few minutes and then chuckled quietly. What Mary said made sense in a weird sort of way, but his worry was that the police might think along those lines as well.

"What is so funny?"

"You, what you suggested about me being the man that fits the image. The police can come to the same conclusion."

"You should be worried then, not laughing."

"I would be if the attacks stop, but if they continue then they will realise that I can't orchestrate things from here, so I only have to sit tight."

"I hope you are right," Mary replied with a smile. "What do we do in the meantime?"

"Do? We do nothing but sit and wait. I want to get back on that site as soon as possible."

"But that is putting you at risk. You may even get killed." "Maybe but look at it from the ARI's point of view, it's the last place they would expect me to be." One of the guards looked over to Joe and smiled.

"You would be picked up the moment that you walked through the gates. You wouldn't stand an earthly of keeping in hiding there. I would strongly advise against doing it sir. You don't need to go back, not really, do you sir?"

"That's all very well, but I need the pay and bonus, and anyhow I am still on probation you know."The guard thought about what Joe had said and while it was true that there was a lot in what he said, he still thought that Joe's life was more important.

"I hear what you are saying, I still feel that you should stay here, but I'll put your point to the officer in charge."

"And just who is that?"

"A Chief Superintendent Rose. Why?" "Local man, is he?"

"Oh no, he is down from London. Why?"

"Well, if he was local, then he might know the local1ARI contacts down here."

"I'll mention that to him as well."The guard moved away, and Mary moved a bit closer to Joe to make sure the guard wasn't hearing what she was about to say.

"I want you to think of your wife and her future, it is very noble to think of going back onto the site, but what of your wife? I mean if anything happens to you, has she got enough to survive without you? Stop and think about that before you go heading off into that site. Think about my mother and us, we have lost our home for the moment and both of us are being kept locked up. Ok, I know that it is for our safety, but that is not the point. We don't know how long this will have to go on for. Now go and think over what I say."

Joe wandered away from her and went and sat down, his mind running back to when he had received the letter from the firm - now look at the mess he was in... He gave a lot of thought to what Mary said, because he could agree with most of it. He placed his head in his hands and leaned forward as if he was meditating. Mary watched him then walked over to the wall unit and helped herself to an orange.

"Does anyone else want a piece of orange?" A silence fell across the room. "Oh, well, all the more for me."

"I would like a piece please." said Joe. She offered him the plate, and he took a piece and started to eat it. She looked at him as if about to say something, then there was a knocking on the front door. Which brought any further conversation to an abrupt end. The guard motioned for them to be quiet, and he went and checked his monitors. He could see that outside there was Rose and a gentleman he hadn't met before. He opened the door and they both hurried inside, and the guard rebolted the door. Rose looked around the room and his eyes fell on Joe. He introduced the stranger to Joe and left them to get on with it. Rose swept the others into the kitchen. Leaving Joe and the other man to talk together.

"Mr. O'Brian, can I call you Joe?" "Yes."

"Right,first things first,I am down from London,MI5 and a new department that is being set up, LICD or London International Crime Department. It has a very wide remit. What I am about to ask you to do, you can refuse but I would like you to consider it first."

"Ok, but first can I say that I want to go back on to the site to work."

"But...but, that's what I wanted to ask you to do. My name is William Dawson. It seems to me that you are three jumps ahead of the rest of us. So perhaps we might stand a chance of winning."

"I am going back because I don't want to see them win, not because of you."

"Fair enough, now if we get you onto the site, how is best for you to pass out information to us on the ARI connection?"

"First things, first. What protection will be given to my wife in Belfast, for it is likely that they will get her to force me to work for them?"

"Good questions."William ticked off his fingers one by one. "One, your wife will be always under guard."

"Two nobody can guarantee complete safety."

"Three, the first time anyone starts to threaten you, we move in. Does that answer all your questions?"

"Nearly, how much do I get?"

"How much?" William looked at Rose, who had just re-entered the room.

"Yes, how much do I get for all this dangerous work?" "But is it dangerous?"

"I'll tell you after I know the amount." William turned back from Rose and looked Joe in the eye.

"Nothing."

`What! You must be out of your mind if you think that I am doing it for nothing, I'll go back to work and keep my eyes peeled and react like the three monkeys. See, hear and speak nothing." Joe left the room, leaving Rose and Dawson with an amazed look on their faces.

"Shall I go after him?" asked Rose. Mary entered the room.

"I have a suggestion to make." "Yes?" replied Dawson.

"Joe is stubborn, like you. Now why don't you offer to meet his expenses for his wife in Belfast, as he has been unemployed for a long time and I feel that he may need the money. It's unlikely he'll leave this job very fast. He is being accepted on site and is ideally placed for you. Given time he will provide the goods for you."

"Alright, how did you know that he needed money?" said Rose. "Don't be too long about it, for I had advised that he return back to Belfast just before you came." "What!"

"I wouldn't have, if I had known that you were coming up with a request for him to go back to the site."

"Quite so, now I'll go and put your suggestion to O'Brian." "Do that but don't say it was my suggestion. I mean it sounds real if it comes from you."

"Yes, I suppose you are right." He left her and walked in to where Joe had gone. After a short while he returned with Joe and told Rose that he had agreed to their plan.

+

Later that evening, Joe and Mary sat by the fire, both in their own thoughts. Joe looked across at Mary.

"Was this your idea Mary?" "Absolutely not."

"Something is bothering you. Is it that you don't want me to go back to the site?"

"Well, I just don't want you running any unnecessary risks, that's all."

"I don't intend to; on that you can depend."

"Ok, provided that you mean that, then I'll come back with you tomorrow."

"You will do no such thing."

"Who do you think you are to say that? I'll be going to work with or without you tomorrow. It will be quite safe, and I have nothing to fear."

"Nothing to fear. What do you think caused the damage in your mothers B & B? Who do you think caused the explosions at the site works? It's time to wake up and face reality Mary, look, you are one of the main suspects until the police are satisfied."

"Well, what about you? You must be one of the suspects too. I mean you came back with me instead of staying on site."

"Well, the police must be satisfied, or they wouldn't let me go free, would they?"

"I suppose not. Joe, did I ever tell you I didn't manage to get a solicitor on the phone."

"Why ever not?"

"Well, I had to go to the bathroom and then I popped into my bedroom, and you know the rest." Joe scratched the top of his head and looked around him. The fact remained that, as he had thought that morning while it looked nice. It was still a secure prison of sorts.

"Look, I suggest if you are taken for questioning, then ask for their list of solicitors, pick the youngest. See what he advises, that is what you are paying him for, after all. Stick to facts, I don't think that they would charge you, but if they did, then don't panic. Stay calm, Ok?"

"Yes, now that you have explained it all." Said Joe. It had been a long day and he needed to think. There was his wife to consider, was she as safe as they said? He also had to think about Mary and her mother. It wouldn't take much to work out the fact that he did feel something for Mary so he knew that he must keep his distance from her, if he was to avoid hurting her. Hurting her, that was a joke, ever since he had meet her, she had been hurt. First her boss killed, then her room damaged. As she had pointed out, this had all started happening only after he had arrived. He just hoped that things would happen overnight and then the police would realise that neither of them would be the one responsible for those acts.

Joe suddenly remembered that there had been something funny about the paint in the bedrooms and he knew what it was. He rose and walked over one of the two policemen.

"Look, I have an idea as to the sort of man who might have painted those threats on the walls."

"And who might that be sir?"

"I didn't say that I knew who it was, but the paint was a quick drying sort, and it was yellow. The sort of yellow paint that is used on the road. Double yellow lines, that sort of thing. Now there are very few outlets that would stock that."

"You may be onto something there. I'll make a note of it and pass on a message at once." He left them and went into the next room. Joe filled in Mary with his thoughts and asked Mary if there was anywhere on the site that painted road signs. She didn't think there was, but she could show him the paint store tomorrow. He told her that it was better that she didn't get seen with him. If she could draw him a map that would be a lot better. It would be useful for him when he resumed work as well, so he asked her to put in main offices. It may trigger some of the other locations for those bombs.

"But don't the police have the list of sites of the bombs." "Maybe, but is it a complete list?"

"Oh, I see what you mean. I'll get started."She went and cleared the table and then started to look for a piece of paper and pens. Joe knew he couldn't help her, so decided to go and have a rest, for tomorrow would be a long day.

A silence fell across the room and all that could be heard was a clock ticking and the scratching of Mary's pen on paper and muttering under her breath when she made a mistake. The day took on the appearance of a summer's afternoon when everything was quiet and peaceful. Suddenly the policeman's radio crackled into life, disturbing the tranquillity.

"SH3 receiving you loud and clear, go ahead."

"Home base, cover blown at SH3 go to SH2 at once, acknowledge."

"We are to go to SH2 at once."

"Over and out."The policeman turned and looked around the room.

"We must move out of here and fast, gather your stuff together and we'll move. I'll go and get Mr. O'Brian. Now let's move it." They all started to gather their bits and pieces together. Everyone except Mary who carried on as if nothing had happened. The policeman walked up and shook her by the shoulder. "Didn't you hear me? We must move out of here. Now go and pack."

"No."

"What do you mean no?"

"I mean it's time to turn and fight and not run, that's what." "I don't think that you realise whom you are taking on, fine sentiments though those are. We are talking about people that shoot people who kill or torture on suspicion of betrayal. If you feel you can stand that sort of pain then by all means stay and stand up to them. My orders are to protect the two of you and I have to consider the others, have you?" He left the room without waiting for an answer to his question. He thought to himself that there were times when he should have chosen a different career. People might knock the police, but they didn't carry firearms on the streets like in America and they were expected to cover anything from armed robbery to helping old ladies with enquiries.

He knew in his heart of hearts that was one of the reasons that he had chosen the police force anyway. He went and knocked on Joe's bedroom door and waited. Not a sound. He knocked again louder and tried the door handle. The door was locked, frowning he called out. "Mr. O'Brian are you alright?" Hearing no answer, he decided to break the door down. So he rushed up and threw his weight against it. It creaked under the impact, but all he had for his efforts was a bruised shoulder. He tried again and the door gave way to reveal an empty room. He looked in the wardrobe and then he noticed there was a note pinned to the bed and the windows were open blowing in the curtains. The outside bars were bent, and an opening had been made large enough for anyone to climb in or out, he thought ruefully to himself. He leant over and read the note.

"*You thought this was a safe house, by the way we know the other four safe houses in this area. Nothing will happen to O'Brian if he co-operates. I think that we will have no trouble in persuading him, do you? But don't try and find us, we have long gone. Let the others go as we have no quarrel with them, they will be safe as long as you don't try and find us.*"

"Oh, hell!" He turned and ran through to the phone. Picking it up he hit one of the buttons. It was answered almost at once. "We have a code one over here, now move!" He walked through to the living room where Mary still worked at the map. He approached her first. "Miss Orchard?"

"Yes? Oh, it's you officer, what do you want?" "A bit of bad news I am afraid."

"it's about Joe isn't it?"

"Yes, he has been kidnapped."

"Officer, you said this was a secure house. Some security this was, so it needs to be investigated and fast. What are the demands?"

"Just that we try not to follow them, and you are to be released with your mother as they aren't interested in you."

"Really? Why daub the walls of my room if that was the case officer? No, they are only saying that to think that we will go free. I think that you are naive enough to believe them. I think that we had better find a new secure house, don't you?"

"Hang on, a minute ago you were for staying and fighting. What's changed?"

"This has. Get onto your superior officer and see what we do next if we are to stay one jump ahead of them."

"Look are you going to make up your mind, for one minute you want one thing, then you change your mind. Now which is it to be? Think before you answer because if you go after O'Brian or the ARI you may get killed."

"True, but if we don't go after them, then the terrorists will always win."

"Hey, I'm not saying that nobody should go after him, just leave it to the experts."

"Huh, you can't even find him a safe house."

"Look, I have already made a phone call to my superiors, so that is taken care of, why don't you go and pack?"

"Ok, but you must tell my mother all of what you told me." Mary turned and left him to phone and break the news to Mrs. Orchard. She took it a lot better than her daughter he thought, on reflection later. The doorbell rang and after checking who it was, he let in Rose and Dawson.

"Who was snatched?" asked Rose.

"O'Brian sir. There is a note in his bedroom. I've not touched anything."

"Hell!" said Dawson.

"My thoughts exactly. Now I have told the Orchards that he has been kidnapped, Miss Orchard is all for going after them, but have them put into another safe house. I told her she can't have it both ways."

"Don't see why not. Look, we'll collect Mrs. Orchard and put her in the safe house and let Miss Orchard come with us. it's likely that they will want her anyway."

"The note doesn't say that." He led them through to Joe's room. They looked at the note in silence then Dawson turned and walked over to the window. He glanced out and walked out of the bedroom and around to the outside, to be under the window. He smiled quietly to himself, it was very well done, and would have had them fooled had it not been for a small piece of concrete off the path. Under the window was soft earth and he knew that it hadn't rained for some time. Somebody had made efforts to hide the way out of the house. The border was wider than a rake and it was the concrete chip which had given the game away, that they had used a ladder to lean on while clearing the border. He called out to the other two inside to come and join him. Once outside he pointed out his finds.

"If I had to say where Joe was, I'd stick my neck out and say the garden shed." said Dawson, smiling.

"Why do you say that?"

"Well Andrews, I think that this was to make us look fools and realise that they could easily take him under our noses, so to speak. They never intended to take him off the site. Now where is the shed out here?"The three of them started to look through the deep undergrowth. Rose was the one to give a shout first. The other two fought their way across the weeds and into the clearing where a shed stood. A dilapidated shed, but interestingly with a new shiny padlock. Dawson and Rose pushed against the door, but it held fast. The officer laughed at the pair of them.

"Look go for the hinges, they are unlikely to have been replaced." The three of them threw their joint weight against the hinges and the shed shook and the door gave way at the bottom almost at once. A second charge broke the top hinge and the door swung inwards to the shed, carrying the three of them inwards with it. Dawson looked around the shed and saw Joe on the ground, bound hand and foot. He walked over and untied him. Rose started to follow him in, but he was blocking out the light.

"Get out of here, I can't see with you in the way. Pull the door outside if you want to do something useful." Rose stepped out and turned to the officer.

"He seems touchy."

"Not surprising is it, he comes down from London and this all happens within forty-eight hours."

"How do you know that?"

"Oh, I listen to you two, I am a policeman after all." "I suppose so, still..."

From inside the shed, Joe spoke.

"Don't I count for anything; now could you get me out of here and we can talk about this."

"Sure, Mr. O'Brian. Let's go up to the safe house."

"That's a joke, it might have been safe once. But look how easy it was for them to snatch me. It will be much nicer though, I agree." They all walked up to the house and Mary threw her arms around Joe as soon as he walked through to the dining room.

"Let him alone Miss Orchard, we have a few questions we want to ask him." Joe walked on with Rose and the other officer and Dawson felt that he had cleverly been manipulated into doing the dirty work in telling the Orchards what they had planned for Joe and the two of them. They took the news with a degree of calm. Mary packed her few things and then turned to Dawson.

"Right Mr. Dawson, or whatever your real name is, I'm ready to go. Lead on." She picked up a small bag and followed Dawson out of the front door.

## 11.28

In Exeter, Colleen, having had breakfast and read the letter she had received from headquarters, saying she was to stay in Exeter for now. More details were to follow soon, most important was that she was to change hotels as soon as possible or better still, buy a flat or small house in Exeter and a small car. The car must be new. She should also keep the P.O. Box numbers going on a rolling basis. If needed she could write to the box number in London that she knew of, that would get a reply. She packed her few items and settled, paying with a credit card.

Once out of the hotel, she set off for South Street, apparently the place where lots of estate agents were based. Starting at the top of the street, she crossed over and went into the first one she saw.

"Can we help you?"

"I hope so, I want a flat in the centre of Exeter or a small house."

"How much are you prepared to go to?" "What do you have?" "Pardon?"

"The location is more important than the price."

"How about these new luxury flats that have just been completed in Southernhay West. If you are interested, then I'll get the brochure."

`Please do." He hurried away from his desk and Colleen took the opportunity to look around the office. After a short while the man reappeared with the brochure.

"I'm sorry that I kept you. Here are the prices of the flats that are still for sale." Colleen glanced at the price list and laughed inwardly to herself. "Are any of them the sort of thing you are looking for?"

"I'd like to see Flat 6, the two bedroom one, with the access to the garage in the basement."

"Of course, I'll get the keys and lock up here, it is only a short walk away, we can cut through the town." He went through to the back of the office and returned with the set of keys. She picked up her bag, and they both left the office, having first locked it. He led the way towards the apartments.

+

Two hours later, the initial paperwork having been done, he leaned across the desk towards her.

"Do you have the deposit?"

"Sure, here it is." She opened a bag and took out bundles of stamped and wrapped notes. He did a quick count and realised that she had the entire cost of the flat on the desk in front of him.

"Now please can you give me a receipt?" asked Colleen.

"Yes, of course." He reached down and produced a receipt book from one of his drawers. He made out the receipt and gave it to Colleen. "That should speed up things a bit."

"I'm sure it will, I'll be in the flat should you need me." "In the flat?"

"Yes, in the flat. Why is there something wrong in that? I mean I have paid you in full and you can't sell it to anyone else. So, I can move in, and the paperwork can follow later right?"

"It just seems irregular, that's all."

She reached across the desk and picked up the keys that he had put there.

"I'll be in touch. Goodbye." Colleen left the office, glanced at the brochure, and set off towards Southernhay West. She crossed the threshold and wondered if the expense was worth it.

+

Now, almost at the end of the day, having spent it organising the hundred and one things you need to do when you buy somewhere, she stepped into the hallway of the flat and locked the door behind her.

On the floor, was a long unaddressed white envelope She bent over and picked it up and opened it. Inside was a short message from the estate agents. "Should have given you the two sets of keys today, call around tomorrow and I'll give them to you or would you like dinner tonight, in which case I'll bring them with me."

She chuckled as she read the letter. Well she didn't want to cook a meal as well tonight, so she might as well take him up on the offer. She walked back to the offices and accepted his offer along with the keys. She asked him to collect her at eight o'clock after which Colleen went back and started unpacking her recent purchases.

+

In Oxford the pace of things was at last beginning to look up. The forensics department had finished their report on Colleen Kent's car and the report made interesting reading.

One of the many facts to emerge was that there had been a note left for Dawson along with a tape and a tape recorder. What they now needed were the other two tapes for a voice comparison.

"Folkestone police, can we help you?"

"Thames Valley police here, I want to speak to Mr. Dawson." "Just a moment I'll see if he is in the building, if not he will be out with Inspector Andrews." He hoped that William was still there, or he would have to start checking around the country. "Hello, look he isn't in the building at present, but I'll get him to phone you as soon as he comes in."

"Can I leave a message with you to pass on?" "Of course. Fire away."

"DI Rogers of Thames Vallety police requires the two tapes for voice comparison with a third tape. Do you have that?"

"Yes sir."

"Thanks." He hung up the phone and turned and looking thoughtful gazed around the room. "He isn't there and I wonder why?" he said out loud. One of his junior officers looked at him as he spoke.

"You talking to anyone in particular sir?"

"No, but if anyone has any ideas, now is the time to air them." "Well sir it may seem a little crazy." The officer stopped.

"No, don't stop, however crazy the idea I want to hear it." "Well alright. You recall that Simon said we were being fooled into thinking that this woman was important, and he said he would go back to Folkestone while we carried on looking for the car. We have done that and now found it. I wondered if her idea was to try and make us work our way back to Folkestone, when really, we should be pursuing her wherever she goes. That's all I have to say sir." Rogers looked around the room there were five officers and a few constables there. He knew that, like him, most were very tired, but what Dawson wanted he couldn't recall either.

"So does anyone here remember what Simon…"He stopped in mid-sentence as he recalled that Simon had, for security reasons, now become known as William Dawson. So how had the young officer known Williams real name? Had he, Rogers, been careless or was it a slip?"…as I was saying, if anyone can remember what William suggested about the three groups I would be glad to hear it."A silence greeted him then one of the officers called out from the back of the room.

"Check the credit card companies and the ease of getting top rated cards."

That opened the floodgates.

"Getting hold of the banks to try and trace the cards and the accounts."

"Seeing if we can trace where the cars were bought." "Where the motorbike came from."

"Where the National Rover ticket was purchased."

"What trains went from Oxford at the time she disappeared and their connections." The officer held up his hand and the noise stopped at once.

"Right, while I am as tired as all of you we need to get this woman caught. We have a lot of power at our disposal, so let's use it."

"You mean like now Sir?"

"Yes. I mean like now." Rogers left the room to the bauble of voices. A faint smile crossed his face as he entered his office and sat down and started on the huge pile of paperwork that lay spread out on his desk. He resigned himself to at least one hour of concentrated work. A knock on the door, followed by a young head appearing around it.

"Sir, William wants you on line two." The officer picked up the phone and waved the young officer out of the office.

"Well, this is a pleasant surprise, you got my message I take it?" "Yes, look things are getting hotter up here, I am coming up and will be bringing a couple of people with me. LICD and MI5 are both concerned that this could be the largest thing we have uncovered in twenty-five years. Are you free to meet tonight?" "Yes, why?"

"I'll fill you in then. Meantime, get your team to dig deep into the finances, it could have been buried anywhere from pension money to new money. Keep looking. I'll fill you in tonight."

"Just why do you need to come tonight?"

"Be patient." With that William hung up. The officer looked at the phone and wondered just was going on in this part of England?

The fact that William was bringing two people with him which was unusual in the least. He returned to the paperwork and had it finished unusually quickly for once.

Two hours later Rogers sat at his desk thinking to himself. What the police force were getting into if this could be one of the largest things in the last twenty-five years. He recalled that with the Great Train Robbery there had been a lot of promotion from that one.

He wondered if there was time to have a drink before they arrived, when there was a knock on his door and William and a man and woman entered.

"Let me introduce you to Miss Mary Orchard and Mr. Joe O'Brian they're here for two reasons. For their safety and to help us with the woman who gave us the slip. Mary here was secretary to Sean Smith and when he was killed..."

"Just a moment, who was Sean Smith? When was he killed? How does he fit into this?" asked Rogers with a puzzled look.

"Sean Smith was head of personnel on the channel tunnel site. I was his personal Secretary, Ok?" said Mary somewhat impatiently.

"I was talking to Mr. Dawson and if you could refrain from interrupting then we might all get on a little faster." He gave her a long hard look straight in the face, expecting her to apologize or at least look down at the floor. He found to his amazement that she did neither. She looked him back straight in the face.

"If that is your attitude, then we will both leave you to cool down and find your manners. Once you have done that, come and advise us. I had thought that by being brought halfway across southern England we might be helping you. It seems that we were both mistaken and misled by Bill. She turned to Joe and taking him by his hand led him out of the office leaving the two men standing there in amazement."

"Well don't just stand there, run and bring her back." Said Rogers to William.

"This is nothing to do with me. It was you, so go and sort it out. I'll keep well out of this." said William. Smiling went and sat down on DI Rogers chair and put his feet up on the desk, grinning. Rogers left the office slamming the door after him.

Dawson sat there in the peace and thought back over the last week. He wondered how they were getting on with researching all the leads that there are in a case like this.

He rose to find out, when the door swung open, and Rogers and Joe and Mary entered. He noticed that Rogers was rather red faced. Mary was looking triumphant to say the least. Joe just stood inside the door as if ready to fly out of there. "I trust you have sorted out your differences?" They all nodded. "Good. Now can we try and find that woman?"

"Yes." they all replied in unison.

"Let me bring you up to date with what is going on in Folkestone and London, then you can fill me in on what is going on in Oxford."

"Just a moment, Joe and I have both been brought here to help. While it is admirable to help and liaise with your colleagues, can't we be doing anything more constructive in the meantime?" asked Mary. Bill sighed and looked at them both.

"Alright, start by going through the mug shots of London, Folkestone and Oxford. See if there is anyone who you recognise at all. If there is, make a note of the number and carry on. I'll call on two officers who can show you where to go."

"Now that is more like it." said Joe"Though I doubt that we can help much."

"Well, you may see someone from Belfast and Mary might recognise the same face. Then we can make a connection and that just might, just might point us in the right direction. Start with the Oxford ones, I'll get the others couriered over to here."

An hour later the pair of them had been studying the photos constantly and both stood up and stretched for a few minutes before returning to the task in hand.

While along the corridor William was explaining to Rogers what had been going on to bring him up to speed.

"…that is what has happened so far in Folkestone in London. It seems that they have an endless supply of money for the first time and that worries me, it really does."William said as he finished.

"I don't doubt it, but what can we do until we have more evidence to convict or arrest?" asked Rogers.

"Enough of what we have been up to, what about here in Oxford?"

"'A' team are looking at the credit card companies and they are being obstructive to say the least. In the meantime,'B' team are engaged at looking at bank accounts and garages that sell motorbikes. We think the motorbike may be the way to get to her. All the other vehicles are new, that one wasn't. The DVLA are looking into its ownership. We are also trying to see where she bought the Gold National Rover ticket. That just about fills in what we are up to." said Bill with a shrug of his shoulders.

"I'll get the PM to apply some pressure on the credit card companies. They have to have a lot of personal details before they release a card, so that might lead us somewhere."

"Something else to consider. As a customer uses the card, the providers get a list of the businesses that are being used. They tend to sell that sort of information onwards to other firms. Armed with that sort of information, we might get an idea of what she is doing?" remarked Rogers.

"Very good, so what are we waiting for?" asked William. "You tell me, you are the one with the PM's ear."

"Right, I'll phone her on a secure line, you go and check to see if those two have found anything yet."

+

Joe had decided to take a decent break, they had been at it for hours and both were getting tired and cross.

"I am going to take a break. My eyes are tired, and I need a drink." Mary looked across to him.

"I think I've found someone." "Who is it?"

"Take a look at this man. He was one of the guards at the site." She said.

"Was? I mean are you sure? There must be hundreds of guards. Why remember this one?"

"Because when I came out of the office once, he was standing talking to a woman. Both were outside the main entrance to the tunnel site. She had a nice car, a red one if I recall it correctly."

"Ok, if that is the case then your security must be bad." smiled Joe.

"Why? Oh, I see what you mean."

"Hey, I have had an idea. Did you see who he was talking to?" "Why?" asked Mary.

"She may be the missing link in all this."

Mary thought to herself, had she seen much of the woman? Not really as she had her back to her, and the guard had walked straight out to her car, which meant that he had managed to do that when everyone was supposed to check in and out of the site.

"Yes, I saw her."

"Great." said William. He had entered the room quietly and had heard the pair of them talking amongst themselves and he now knew better than to interrupt them. They looked up at him. "I mean it. Can you remember what she was wearing?"

"Very little and that was unusual for the time of year," she laughed bitterly.

"What's the matter Mary?"

"I've thought I have worked out how they managed to get into the site."

"How?"

"Well human nature being what it is, if a male guard sees a pretty lady, he is more likely to go and speak to her. Then while she has him in conversation, in slips the other ARI member and wanders around the site finding out the place to put the bombs. Which he did to deadly effect as we now know. Then he confidently strolls out hoping that nobody challenges him, which they don't, as they are more concerned about people going in."

"We need to find out which guard was on duty and then we have to question him." said William with a frown.

"Ok, but what if he isn't there?"

"Let's worry about that when we get there, shall we?" "Ok but show him which one you have found." said Joe. "This one." Mary pointed at one of the photos.

"Oh him, now that is a surprise. I'll get on to Folkestone police right away." He left them alone in the office. It seemed to the pair of them that the long hours of looking at the hundreds of photos might just pay off.

"Shall we take the rest I suggested?" smiled Joe.

"Absolutely because I am really, really tired. Lead on." She followed Joe out of the room and down the corridor to the canteen, where they both sat down with drinks in front of them.

"Mary, what do we do now that we have finished here?" "Rest, then go back to work."

"You must be joking, if the ARI were after us before, now they will be really piling on the pressure. I know that we are supposed to be under police protection now. I do wonder though what the future is going to be like?"

"Well let's hope that the guard tells us what happened that day."

"He doesn't have to."

"But he is innocent until proven guilty."

"Right, but if he is silent, then he is presumed guilty." Replied Joe with a shrug of his shoulders.

"But that is awful."

"Right, but don't you recall that there was a lot of fuss about this in the paper last year?"

"I do recall something of that sort."

"Let's hope they find him, otherwise we are in difficulties." "It's not our problem though, is it?"

`No, but if the police don't get to him first, then ARI might beat them to it. If they remove him from the site before we get there that could cause real problems. It would also indicate that they know we are onto them. Makes it harder to find out about the ARI if he isn't there." said Joe.

"Why should it indicate that they are on to us? He might have left to get a better paid job than that one."

"Mary, the ARI don't go to the trouble of setting this up and getting someone in the site, past all the vetting procedures only to drop them at a moment's notice."

"And how do you know that?" "I read it in books."

"What sort of books are those?" "Thrillers mainly, why?"

"Well, I doubt that the detail is very exact, do you?"

"You have no idea of the amount of research that an author has to check before the book is printed. It might only be a novel, but the facts have to be correct, or people write in and complain."

They had been walking along to Rogers' office and they knocked on the door and waited.

"Come in." They both entered and stood in front of his desk. To the left of them stood William Dawson and to the right stood a police sergeant. Each looked grave and William was on the phone to the Prime Minister.

"We need the power to search the site now. Any delay and they will be gone by then. You have the authority to get things moving, get them moving. You say you want to combat terrorists, now do something about it. We have been up all night trying to find this man, now move." said William, on phone.

"What is going on?" Mary whispered to the sergeant, behind her hand.

"Quiet, Rogers is trying to get permission for the Folkestone police to move onto the site. He has his hands tied by the fact it's in another area to his. If it goes through the correct channels, it will take about a fortnight. The terrorists will most likely get away and we will be back to square one. Why don't people realise that this is the most important thing to deal with this decade. Thousands of jobs and many millions of pounds from this country and around the globe depend on this project. All that could be at risk if this gets out. Doesn't the Prime Minister realise that?"

"I expect she does." said Joe with a smile.

"What do you mean if anything got out?" asked Mary.

"Why it would close the project down as fast as that." He clicked his fingers together. "Lack of confidence in the project."

"By whom?"

"The underwriters would pull out of the project and the money would dry up. The result would be no jobs for anybody. Then the French would probably sue for loss of earnings, cost of tunnel works and other associated costs."

"Like what?"

"Oh, I don't know. Like the buying of the land for the Paris to Lille railway."

"But isn't there already railway there?"

"Yes, but not a high speed one, which would need new track. For that you need new land and the farmers have done very nicely out of that. You see by the year 2000 there is supposed to be a network of trains and roads linking Europe. It is supposed to mean that you could in theory go by train from Liverpool to Naples uninterrupted."

"Well then, we must stop the terrorists from winning." said Mary defiantly. They both looked to where William was still on the phone, he waved a hand at them impatiently. Both Mary and Joe went and sat down without another word.

William knew that the Prime Minister could be either helpful or obstructive, depending on the mood she was in. He put down the phone and looked at them before turning to Joe.

"The PM has said that we are to send you back on to the site as you wanted. She thinks you might just learn something. If we rush in, we might get some of the members, but not all of them. The one's that we capture will be replaced with ones that we don't have a file on. Making it twice as difficult to find out who they are. Her idea is if you go back to work, you can listen to the talk on new members and report back."William paused for a minute and looked straight at both Joe and Mary.

"I've been asked to point out that you do not need to do this if you choose not to. Don't make your mind up now but go and sleep on it. You both look all in as it is."A silence fell across the room as they all knew that for Joe to go back to the site was like signing his own death warrant. He rose and turned towards the door. Mary caught his eye and rose as well.

"You said something about sleeping?"

"Yes, sergeant get them to the secure house in Oxford."

"Yes sir. If you both could follow me and keep your eyes closed when we get in the car, it's not far, but it would be best for reasons of security."

"We quite understand." said Mary. They both followed him out to the waiting car.

Half an hour later they were settled into a very nice secure flat in the centre of Headington and sleeping the night away.

+

The following morning Mary had said to Joe to contact the disc engraver on his return to the site, as she knew him as a friend.

Joe was to stay out of dark areas and try to avoid from being caught alone. If he was changing his working clothes, then change in the company of others, for although there were Irish there, he wasn't to assume they are all ARI members. She told him that if he used his common sense then they might win. Then William and the car that would take him to the tunnel workings came and collected him.

William Dawson turned to Joe as the car speed along the M40.

"You know, you can still pull out if you want to. Nobody would think any the less of you."

"I could,but if I do,then hundreds,maybe thousands of people, innocent people would be hurt or killed. The terrorist must not be allowed to win. If we don't make a stand then there is no hope in the world. We all say how bad things are, but nobody really does anything!"

"Ok, but why should it be you?"

"The answer most people give would be, why me? I say why shouldn't it be me?"

"Well, you are married and just starting a new job and trying to clear a load of debts..."

"While all of that is true, I still feel that I ought to make a stand."

"Then look at this file of information on the ARI members in the Folkestone area. I want you to try and memorise it by the time we get to Folkestone."

He passed Joe a file and Joe settled down to read it from cover to cover. Eventually the car pulled up outside the works and Joe got out. He picked up his case and walked on into the site and showed his pass and identity disc.

Bill had watched Joe enter the site then he said to the driver. "Drive me to the Folkestone police station. The real search is about to begin, and I don't want to be late."The engine roared into life and pulled away into the direction of Folkestone police station.

## 12.28

William Dawson arrived at Folkestone Police Station and ran on up the steps and inside, where he was stopped by two officers. Showing his pass, he walked on in and through to Andrew's office. He noticed as he walked there was a sense of freshness and a new paint smell hung in the air.

"Come in."

"I thought the place had been bombed but it all looks the same as before."

"It was, but we need to move faster than the ARI. Hence the fast redecoration. How can I help?"William bent over and wrote on the desk blotter, 'Is this place clean?' Andrews looked in amazement until the penny dropped.

"Yes, it's as clean as a whistle, one of your lot came and checked it out today."

"One of our lot?" said Bill looking surprised. "Yes, why the strange look?"

"Let's take a walk outside."They both rose and left the office and walked around to the car park. Once outside William turned to Andrews.

"We don't have anybody as far as I know that checks offices for bugs. Hence why I brought us out here. Did the bomb disposal branch manage to move the second device at the house? The one that had the bomb exploded when we were there."

"They did manage to stabilize it, and then took it away to be checked over. When the disposal team got it back to their headquarters, it was late at night, so they put it in one of the research huts but during the night it went off. The research hut was obliterated completely. In the morning the team measured the pit that it left. It was five hundred feet across and fifty deep. The worrying thing was the small amount of explosive that was needed for that size. I mean it would fit into the palm of your hand. If you clenched your fist, it would be completely hidden." William looked at Andrews as he took in what he was saying, it meant that a device that small could be placed anywhere in Britain and nobody would know about it. All that would be needed was a detonator and a timer. He knew that Joe would have a hopeless task trying to find something that small.

Security at the site would become worthless. Something that small could be thrown over the fence to a waiting person.

"Security at the tunnel is being stepped up on our side of the fence, but we don't have enough officers to do the job properly." added Andrews with a shrug.

"So, we have a probable insider, giving the ARI information about this case. Also, we have, as far as you know, only limited information on the number of houses that might have been bombed down here, correct?"

"Yes, but there may be more information stored down in the files."Andrews led Bill indoors and down to the file room. Racks of shelves ran from floor to ceiling.

"Where do we start?"

"B" for bombing I assume."The two men started, one at each end of the room. It became quickly apparent that files were stored in number sequence.

They looked at each other and sighed. It had been confirmed that there was an ARI informer in the police station. Andrews had a good idea who it was and had started to feed them false information on a regular basis.

"Look, this is going to take ages, I suggest that we call in the person who deals with this."

"If you can vouch for him."

"Sure, just wait here." Andrews left William in the store he looked along the shelves, just in case, but it was to no avail. A few minutes later Andrew returned with a constable who looked across the room and walked unerringly to one of the shelves. Then he turned to the pair of them.

"You two been messing things around in here?" "No and add a sir when you address us."

"Well SIR, they have been removed. However, they were there two days ago."

"How do you know that?"

"Well, someone asked for the file like you are; I found it and he said it would be replaced when he had finished with it. I can't understand why he didn't?"

"I can, the fact is that he was no constable, but someone impersonating a constable."

"Oh. Just a thought, it may have been transferred to the computer transfer office in Folkestone. You know, we are trying to get these all onto the computer, but it is taking a long time." The officer turned and left the two of them still looking at the files racked high all around them.

"Is it worth trying the computer, in case they have been transferred already."Asked William, scratching his head.

"Well, let's go and find out."They left the room and made for the nearest computer terminal. Andrews sat and typed his code number into the computer and asked it for any information on bombings. A silence, then a line of text appeared rolling across the screen. "THIS HAS BEEN HACKED INTO AND EVIDENCE DESTROYED ON INSTRUCTIONS RECEIVED... THIS HAS BEEN

HACKED INTO AND EVIDENCE DESTROYED ON ..." Andrew snapped the computer off and turned to William. "You do realise that all the evidence has gone on that case?"

"Yes, but the house remains are still there." said William. "Look, you can't simply bag up a house and take it into court and parade in front of a load of witnesses." He paused. "Come on, they will be too far ahead of us if we aren't careful."

"Why the rush?" asked William.

"Without any evidence we will have no case, but we do still have a lot of valuable witnesses. Witnesses that the ARI may go after."

"Oh, come that is a little far-fetched, isn't it?" laughed William. Then he looked at Andrews. "You really think they may get our witnesses?"

"Well, I hope not, but I am going to check first. Do you want to come with me?"

"Just try and stop me. Anything connected with this case I want to know about." Replied William.

They both left and went out to Andrew's car, just as he was about to turn the ignition, William placed his hand on Andrew's. "Wait a minute. We'll both get out of this car slowly and look at the underside of it."

"Ok, but this had better be worth the delay." Both men got out and peered under the car. Where, taped to the exhaust, was a long black tube. They looked at one another. `So how did you know it would be there?"

"Guess. Now they have most of the details about this case, they know who was in charge of the case."

"So, what do we do next?"

"Call in the bomb squad, then we drive on and announce to the world in general that there was an explosion on one of the roads leading to the house." replied William with a smile. Andrews looked puzzled for a minute before smiling at him.

"You want us to be one jump ahead of them for once." "So, let's get a new car and get moving."

Thirty minutes later they pulled up at the ruined house and Andrews looked at William.

"Something bothering you?"

"Yes, where are the signs and police tape warning people to stay away from the site?" He climbed out of the car and made of in the direction of the shed. Andrews climbed out and followed him over to the shed.

"What do you think you will find?" he asked William.

"I don't know, but it might be something that shouldn't be here." Approaching the shed William turned to Andrews and pointed out that a new device might have been planted in the meantime. When they got to the shed, they found that the door had been replaced with a much stronger one as well as a new padlock securing it. "Strange, that wasn't there last time."

"Well, there is a window, but where is it?"

"Under that." Bill pointed at the huge pile of compost, that was piled high against the side of the shed.

"How do we uncover the window with that there then?" "Move it with spades, but I'll throw this in for good measure.

It would be very easy to back up a lorry and dump the compost here now that the house is no longer in its way. Anyhow, all this is unimportant, more to the point, why the new door and padlock?"

"I don't know, but if we are to come back, then I suggest we bring a warrant." They walked back to the car and got in and slammed the car doors.

Almost at once there was an explosion from the direction of the shed. The car physically shook. They both got out and looked at the spot where the shed had been. It was just a crater.

"Blast!" said Andrews in frustration.

"I know, but let's get back to the station, I think this was a diversion."

"Some diversion." Andrews gripped the wheel and speed along the roads to the police station. William said nothing, this was the first time that he had come that close to being killed on the mainland. He had the feeling that they were being suckered. He turned to Andrews.

"Andrews, I think we should try and create a diversion of our own out of this. Call up the bomb squad and announce that a large device has gone off in Folkestone. People are to stay indoors. Also, move sixty percent of your constables from normal work to the area around the bombed house, doing a door to door. Has anybody seen anything suspicious, that sort of thing? If anybody from the ARI is watching, they might make a mistake or two.

Also, I need a phone to London. A secure line mind you." William leaned back and thought as the car sped along the small back roads that it was time to call BOTOG. The police car swept into the station and Bill was the first out and bounding up the steps two at a time. Waving his ID card at the two officers, he walked in. He quickly entered Andrew's office and checked it for any bugs that may have been planted since they went out. Picking up the phone, he dialled a long number and waited to speak to the chairman of BOTOG.

"Hello, Dawson here, this line may not be secure." "Ok, scrambler now on. So, fill me in."

"it's looking far more like a very well-orchestrated affair, than we first thought. We have had a second explosion and I am expecting a third shortly. What do you want me to do?" asked William.

"Stay put, I am coordinating the three centres of London, Folkestone and Oxford and it is possible that we could have a three-way phone link between the three centres."

"Ok, do we know any more about the woman who escaped in Folkestone?"

"She may have gone to Europe; I'll take a look into it from here in London."

"Thanks, now what else? Yes, look I am on the move mostly, here are the two number's you can get me on." He gave him the car phone number and a Folkestone number, then rang off. It worried him that Andrews had yet to turn up, so went off in search of him. As he walked past the gents, he heard a groan. He entered and saw Andrews on the floor moaning. He splashed some water in his face and pulled him into an upright position.

"What happened to you?"

"I think I have found out who our mystery man is." "Who?"

"Get me back to the office and I'll tell you." They walked down the corridor and back into the office.

"I think that there might be another explosion, they will start to feel confident and may think that we were killed up there today. Now who is our mystery man?" asked William.

Andrews opened his mouth, and the phone rang on his desk. He picked it up and listened without saying anything. Then he replaced it and looked at William in amazement.

"Well, I think that you are too psychic for your own good." "Why?"

"That was to inform me that the goods wagon where we found Beehive has been blown up and a crater of twenty five feet across and ten feet deep has replaced it. However, worse than that is the main line tracks were damaged so there will be long delays. You know what that means? The national news. What do we do now?"

"Phone BOTOG." "Who?"

"BOTOG it stands for Boot out the Terrorists of Great Britain. It has enormous powers. I'll phone to arrange a news blackout."

"Can you do that?"

"Oh, yes. Now who is this inside man?"

"Oh, it has to be..." He stopped short as a bullet was fired through the window. "What gives?"

"Get down and get out of here, before a bomb follows the bullet." The two men crawled across the floor and then shut the door after them.

Once in the corridor, William was quickly on his feet and running towards the car park but as he passed the main desk, he was conscious that nobody was there. Running down the ramp outside, he raced around to the area outside of Andrews' office. He arrived just in time to see a figure dressed in blue jeans, dark green sweatshirt, blue balaclava. The man was in the process of swinging his arm back to throw something but whatever it was William didn't have a chance of finding out, he was too mesmerized that this was happening on mainland Britain.

"Stop, police." Yelled William as he stood taking in the scene. The man turned and threw the bomb at Bill. Then he ran off towards Folkestone.

Bill dived for cover, and a second later there was an explosion. Raising his head from the ground he saw that a few police cars were on fire, and he knew that the petrol tanks would explode soon, if they hadn't already. He made his way to the reception area. Andrews was already by the counter.

"So, who is the man on the inside?" he asked.

"Who is missing?" replied Andrews, waving his hand at the empty front desk.

"Point taken." "Now what?"

"We contact the bomb disposal people as I suspect any messages I gave were not passed on." said Andrews gloomily.

"Quite likely. I'll phone BOTOG and see where the nearest bomb disposal unit is based, be that the police or the army." William picked up the phone and got through to BOTOG. He explained that he wanted to know if there was bomb disposal squad nearby.

"No, not that I know of, but I'll check for you. You might want to know that the banks have released the fact woman on the run has a gold card so we are trying to find out if she is still using it. British Rail tell us a National Rover ticket was purchased in Folkestone using it. The man who served her has confirmed it, as he hadn't seen a gold credit card before."

"How much do one of those tickets cost?" asked William. "Six thousand five hundred pounds."

"What!"

"So, someone has money to spend don't they."

"It seems so. It is imperative that we know who the card belongs to and where she is using it. It will guide us to where she is holding up." William replaced the phone and looked at Andrews, who looked at him.

"Well, he thinks that there is no bomb squad down here, and now tell me who did you place in the tunnel operations. We didn't need to risk Joe O'Brian if there was anyone already on the site."

He stood there looking at Andrews. "Well, I am waiting for an answer."

"You recall that we sent some men to go around the houses that we suspected the ARI might have used in the past. Using the excuse of the Crime Prevention Officers; I think that you were in on the briefing."

"Yes, get on with it." Snapped William in annoyance.

"One of the houses turns up to have been in a place called Wood Cottage Street. When we visited it, we couldn't get access because the place was boarded up and looked as though it hadn't been used for months. But on forcing an entry around the back we discovered that the door to the kitchen was locked with a padlock, a new padlock at that. Once inside we discovered the door had three new bolts at top, bottom and middle. So, the house could be lived in, but shows no sign of being lived in yet. It was almost as if it was set up ready for someone to come and live in but remain hidden. If you get my drift?" said Andrews.

"Get on with it, we've not got all day."

"Taking a good look around we find a used British passport with a photo inside of one of the ARI wanted men. We used one of our officers and made him up to look like the ARI man and put him in the house in the hope that the real one will turn up and we can substitute them. Anyhow, nobody turns up. So, it was suggested by somebody higher up, a senior officer, he infiltrate the camp. That's all really."

"Do you have a picture of this officer when he went off to the camp?"

"Most likely, it will be in our record department." He left the room at a run and returned shortly with the photo. "Here it is." He passed it to William.

"Thanks, now I'll fax it to BOTOG. I'll send copies to Oxford and London as well."

"What good do you think that will do?"

"It might just bring either the real one to the surface or their accomplice."

"Their accomplice?"

"Yes, the ARI would not risk just sending one person on a thing like this."

"Right, now what?" asked Andrews.

"Well, I'm off to London, then Oxford. My car phone number is on this card." He passed a small square black and gold card to Andrews. "This is to be used only in an emergency." He left the police station and as he would be passing Folkestone railway station decided to stop there first.

William asked to speak to the person who had sold the gold ticket and asked if the man would go and look at the police files at the station tomorrow. He replied that he would be happy to help in any way he could.

William then got back into the car and drove off towards London.

+

In Exeter, Colleen Kent had finished unpacking and placing the pieces of furniture that had been arriving all afternoon. She had been and placed an ad in the paper so that more money would come in due course. She was now having a nice bath and wondering about her next move.

So far, she had been very lucky, but she wasn't stupid enough to realise that it might not last forever. The lady she had met in the library had given her a gem of an idea - perhaps she would give the idea of writing a book based on Exeter with facts twisted to fiction a try. This then would enable her to go anywhere around Devon or Exeter. The more she thought of it, the more she liked it.

She rose and wrapped a towel around herself and went and dressed. Then the entry phone rang. She looked at the clock and swore to herself. It was only five in the afternoon, the phone buzzed again, longer this time. She picked up the phone.

"Yes?"

"Green here, now let us in." "Us?"

"Me. "

"Alright, come on up." She heard the door click three times and she walked to the front door and opened it. Outside stood Green and two men that she hadn't meet before. "Who are you?"

"Friends, now can we come in?"

"Of course. Come in." She led the way across the hall into the living room and closed the bedroom door as she went past, a fact not unnoticed by the three men.

"You have company?" asked one of the two men. "What makes you think that?"

"Only that you closed the door to the bedroom. I just wondered."

"Well, I haven't, so you can stop wondering, can't you?"

"Alright."

`Now Mr. Green, why are you here and not at the estate agents signing all the paperwork for this flat, and who are these two apes?"

"Well, I got a phone call telling me to come and sort out your paperwork on the purchase of the flat. I assume that you want things speeded up as you always do. These two are here to protect you."

"Look, I am supposed to merge into the background and live down here, I can hardly do that if those two are following me around everywhere?"

"Oh, I don't know, they could be useful. Look there are only two ways out of here west and east go west and you soon run out of land. Go East and you have only two railway lines to go out on. You need help."

"Not that sort of help. If I did need some help, I would have told you. I've been here a few days and I have already a gem of an idea how to go into deep hiding."

"How? Patrick will want to know your plans."

"Never you mind, the few that know the better. Now please can all three of you go? Unless you have something else to say?" "Only the papers need signing tomorrow at the estate agents at eleven, OK?"

"Fine, I'll see you there. Don't be late."

"We won't." She showed them to the door, and they left. She picked up the packing that lay around the room and then squashed it into the bin bags that she had bought earlier. She walked down to the rubbish areas and noticed that outside the two men still stood guard.

Colleen decided to lead them a nice walk all over Exeter. Starting by walking down Princesshay and into a coffee shop, she bought some coffee and positioned herself so she could see anyone in the reflection of the glass of the shop. So, they were still following her, she thought as she counted four of them.

Drinking up the coffee, Colleen set off for the top end of Princesshay and into the British Telecom shop. Colleen sorted out the paperwork for going on the phone. Then she went towards the cathedral and it was obvious to a trained eye that they were still following her at a distance.

For the next three quarters of an hour, she led them all over Exeter and ended up in the underground passages. It was there that she finally lost them, for if you dodged down the stairwell quickly, nobody could see where you had gone.

It was about an hour later that Colleen emerged and made her way back to the flat. It dawned on her that they only had to make their way back to the flat and wait for her. At least she had thrown them off her trail in Exeter, which would indicate to them that she could do it at any time.

Meantime Anthony Brown, the estate agent, had arranged for a meal at the "Triple A Restaurant", it was a little more than he had planned, but the restaurants that were within his price range were already fully booked. He had booked the table in his name and now knew how to get there. It had opened on the quay, near the new Shilhay estate and he had read good reviews of it in the"Express & Echo" where, over time, he had found that they were very good and accurate. He bent over his desk and re-applied himself to his work.

+

At the tunnel workings in Folkestone, Joe sauntered through the main gates and over to the main temporary shed to hang his jacket with the hundreds of others in there. He wandered out, wondering where he was to work that day. Joe ran his eyes over the site and noticed that the two craters had been filled in and Sean Smith's office had been dragged to one side, where it was unceremoniously lying on its side. New metal sheds had replaced the ones that had been blown up and a much larger office had been put there in its place.

He walked into the personnel office and found nobody inside, however there was a list of new jobs and a piece of paper telling all the new workers to go to the engraving office.

Joe left and walked across the dry and dusty site, recalling what one of the policemen had said about footprints. There wasn't much of a chance of seeing a footprint in this dust bowl. He entered the engraver's but ducking under the door as he did so, for it appeared with the explosions so nearby the foundations had been shaken and the but had sunk a little. Inside there were two men, one of whom Joe didn't recognise, the other was Thomas Swift, the Engraver.

"Hello Thomas Swift, I'm back."

"Great, look meet Mr. Meadows, he is the head of personal. Things are going to be toughened up around here, though I believe the higher up are bolting the stable door after the horse..." His voice trailed off and he bent back to his work. Meadows looked at Joe.

"So, I understand you haven't been well. Now are you fit? I want you working in the tunnel, the sooner we catch up the better."

"Thanks, look can I think about that for an hour and let you know?"

"Sure, I'll be in my new office over the way there." He left the engraver's but and Thomas Swift turned around with a surprised look on his face.

"I thought you were dead."

"When did you hear that?" asked Joe.

"About two days ago I think it was. It was when they were filling the bomb craters in, I walked over and one of the lorry drivers said, wasn't it terrible that Mr O'Brian had died? I said I wasn't aware that you had died, and he said you had been too close to the place where the bombs had gone off. He had emphasized the too. I wondered why."

"Who else knew about the bombs?"

"Nobody, it seems that the general word is that the fuel dump exploded because someone threw down a lighted match. You have any ideas?" Joe remained silent, he had plenty, but not for the telling yet.

"No, I just was off sick for a couple of days. It now appears that I am working on the tunnel face or something. Is the large work board still around?"

"Behind you." Joe turned round and looked at the list of names. His was there, but Mary's wasn't.

"What happened to Mary Orchard?" Joe asked, to see what the answer would be.

"She died and was buried two days ago." Joe stood there stunned. Either there was a huge cover up, or else they were trying to see just how much he knew.

`Well, I must be getting on." He made towards the door and Thomas Swift called out to him.

"Hey, you haven't had your other disc done yet, and sign on the board over there." He jerked his thumb at the board and Joe hurried over and signed on. There were hundreds of coloured pins dotted all over the map of the site, green for topsoil removal, blue for Folkestone cliff, black for the tunnel itself. red for the sidings. Joe picked up a black pin and stuck it into the board. He walked back to Thomas Swift who was engraving a tag for him. Anyone working underground had to have two tags. He passed it to Joe and said.

"Joe they probably already know you are back on site. So, get down the tunnel tonight as they will not expect you to do that on your first day. If you need me, you know where I am." Then he bent over and carried on engraving and Joe walked on out of the hut.

## 13.28

Joe entered the mouth of the first tunnel where could see a string of light bulbs stretching far into the distance and running along one side of the tunnel was a huge silver pipe, pumping air down into the tunnel to the front-line workers. Set into the ground of the tunnel were some railway tracks, not the ones that would be used when the tunnel was finished, but a narrow-gauge railway. This took the men each day deeper under the channel.

He could see the seven sections loaded behind the TBM that made up the tunnel and where the concrete grout had overflowed and run down the sides of the tunnel.

Taking all this in, Joe made his way back to the engraver's hut, where he borrowed paper and pen and wrote to both his wife and to Folkestone police giving details of the lack of security and how the terrorists could hit bits of the tunnel and still cause delays in the building of it. He would need at least another week to find out more details for them. This was all written in code previously agreed with Dawson. Thomas Swift looked up from his desk.

"You ought to post those now, I'll come too, if you like." "Thanks, I'd like that."

"Wait for me to get my jacket and we'll go." He reached out and switched off the engraving machine, then rose and took his jacket from behind the door. After they had gone through the main gate, Thomas told Joe that the only mailbox was two miles away.

"Well, can't we walk?"

"Ok, but we'll have to walk both ways." "Why?"

"Too few buses and too few passengers on them, you would be remembered."

`Well, let's get going then." They set off at a brisk pace and after three quarters of an hour, arrived at the Post Office. Having posted Joe's letters, they saw a rather full bus load of passengers, so Thomas stopped it and as it was crowded, they had to stand all the way to their stop.

On the way to post the letters, Joe asked Thomas Swift if he knew of any place to stay. He knew that he had to find somewhere else, now that he wasn't staying at Mary's mother's B & B.

Thomas wondered to himself about letting Joe live with him, for he slept in an old fairground caravan, and it was large enough. He had an old fairground lorry to pull it with, on which were mounted two generators. They walked back to the engraving hut. Joe collapsed on the small bed, While Thomas sat down and switched on the engraving machine and bent over to start work again.

+

"Well, well. We have already heard from O'Brian. He asks for more time to find out what we want to know. About a week is what he wants. Do we let him have that much time?" asked Andrews.

"Well, he has given us some information already, and he has only been there half a day. I would say let's meet him halfway, give him half a week and say we will review it from what he sends us. We could send one of those Government safety inspectors to look over the site, that way it is unlikely that anything would happen."

"Do you think so Bill? It could be exactly what the ARI are waiting for, something to embarrass the Government. This is the first undertaking of its kind in the UK. Also happens to be one of the largest projects, therefore the risks are increased. Security is weaker because of the size of the site and the fact that everyone is working faster to try and get it open on time, and to get some of the shareholders' money paid out as soon as it begins to show a profit. Coupled with the fact is there hasn't been a project like this before and that brings its own risks. Then there is the fact that the tunnel sections are made at a separate location and sent here does mean that the security at that factory might not be up to the required standard. The Insurance premiums keep on rising, year on year. Is there anything I have missed?" Andrews folded his arms and looked at William, who smiled and ticked off his fingers as he spoke.

"Plenty. First, they may be infiltrating from the French end. Second, we are looking for a respectable person who has been here a long time and built up a respectable lifestyle that wouldn't be challenged. Third, it may be a corrupt policeman. Forth, oh why go on. The list is endless. Let's get back to what we are discussing here. What to do with O'Brian."

"Well, let's suppose an Inspector could come, where would that get you?" asked Andrews.

"Well, while they are at one end we can look at the other end of the site. The problem is the sheer size of it." He waved his hand over a map of the site that was pinned on Andrew's office wall.

"How do I get in and not be noticed, any ideas?" asked William. Andrews doodled on a bit more paper and tossed it into the bin, to join the already overflowing contents. They had been in his office ever since the letter had arrived. It had been Bill's suggestion that the local post boxes were emptied and sorted separately from the rest of the mail. Once sorted any unusual mail addressed to the police or any of the families of workforce on the tunnel would be kept to one side for the police to see first.

"Get yourself one of the identity discs that they all wear" "Fine, now any other ideas to back it up?" The silence was deafening, he took off his tie and rolled it up and stuffed it into his jacket pocket which he had taken off long ago. William slammed his fist into the palm of his other hand.

"Blast it, they are making fools of us. I must have something to tell Thatcher when I go back to London, anything is better than nothing, well?" Andrews stayed quiet, partly, because he didn't have an answer, and he knew it was a rhetorical question anyway. The phone rang making both men jump. Andrews reached out and snatched it off its cradle.

"Andrews."

"Now listen carefully and do not interrupt." Andrews threw a switch and a tape started recording.

"We know that you have a man on the site and unless he is removed, you and you alone will be responsible for him and his lovely wife. Don't think we are bluffing; he would tell us everything before he died. You have just three hours." The phone went dead, and Andrews snapped the switch off and rewound the tape back to the beginning, then he grinned and smiled at William.

"I think we have them rattled, don't you?" "Pardon?"

"I think we have them rattled."

"How do you make that out? Why don't you get the tape analysed to see if we have the voice on file?" said William.

"They will have used someone who isn't yet on our files. Still, we'll do as you say." He picked up his phone and asked for one of his officers to come in and take the tape away to be broken down and remove the background noise. Only then the team would try to identify the voice.

Andrews leaned back into his chair. "So now you have something to tell Thatcher."

"Not quite what I had in mind. I was looking for something more positive."

"This is positive news. Already they know we have someone on the site, yet how do they know that? Answer me that and I'll be pleased." The phone rang on his desk again and he snatched it up at the same time slamming another tape in the recorder. "Inspector Andrews, Folkestone Police."

"Oxford CID here, I have a Detective Inspector Rogers for you."

"Fine, put him on."

"Andrews? Rogers here, look we have heard from the credit card company head office. The lady seems to be spending in Folkestone and Exeter. Do we call in the Devon and Cornwall police?"

"Hang on, let me think about this." Andrews paused, thinking what the implications would be if yet one more force had to be drawn into the web that already had London, Folkestone & Oxford entangled in it. But of all the places to go, why choose Exeter? He decided that two forces were more than enough to deal with at present.

"No, don't inform them, just arrange to get someone down there and follow her around. If we ask Exeter to follow her, they may have to arrest her and then we lose control of the back-ups and any information about them in that part of the world."

"Ok, if that's how you want it. By the way what do you want us to do with the woman?"

"What woman?" "Mary Orchard."

"Keep her down there. Why is there a problem?"

"Only that she has slept with Joe during the night that they were in the safe house down here."

"Slept with in the real sense, or in the same flat?"

"In the same two-bedroom flat, but the ARI probably know that he was in the flat with a nice-looking girl. And looking at the picture of his wife, I know who I would have rather been with!"

"How did you get a picture of his wife?"

"Sent over by fax last night. Did I ever tell you about the robbery of the faxes out of our fax machine? No? Well, I'll tell you next time I see you."

"Hang on, what fax robbery?"

"Look, I'll send you a fax all about it, today. Goodbye." He hung up and Andrews turned to William.

"What do you make of all that?"

"I think that I had better pay a visit to Oxford before making my report to the Prime Minister. If I get any more information, I'll let you know. By the way, I'd still keep watching that ARI safe house you discovered." Said William.

"Which one?" asked Andrews.

"The one that's ready for anyone to move into, I want to be informed when the ARI turn up."

"What's with the 'when'? surely you mean if?" said Andrews, looking puzzled.

"No, I do mean when. It's obvious that they are coming over to England sometime, the question is when. Our biggest problem we have right now is that they are so well funded. First a house down here, not cheap, then they obviously have had to buy somewhere in Exeter, again not cheap, throw in a New Jaguar car at a cost of thirty three thousand, excluding delivery or number plates."

"That much!"

"I am afraid so. So, you see, it seems that they are spending money for some long term campaign, and we haven't yet found any arms."

"That would be expecting too much."

"True, but it is the cost of the operation that bothers me, the money must be coming from somewhere."

"I wonder if they have a safe house in Oxford?"

"I doubt it, if they had, she would have gone there instead of to the station. They may have a contact in Oxford. Stands to reason, why go there otherwise? I mean you could drive up to London, pop over to Paddington and catch a train straight through to Exeter. The car wouldn't have been found as quickly that way. Come to that, why didn't they do that?"

"Perhaps they wanted the Jaguar found?" said Andrews.

"You could be right. Look get on the phone to both Oxford and London, tell them that I am coming to London, then on to Oxford, before travelling down to Exeter to see what I can dig up there."

"Not literally I trust?"

"That depends, look I'll keep in touch. See you."

With that William left Andrews alone in his office looking at his overflowing desk.

Swiftly he gathered all the unwanted paperwork together, too much to shred he decided. Having got a large bin bag, he filled it and took it out to his car to drive to a corporation dump outside Folkestone. Knowing it would be fair drive he settled back and listened to one of his cassette tapes as he drove.

+

Bill had borrowed another car from the fleet of the Folkestone police force. He drove to the Eurotunnel exhibition at the main tunnel works. After he had reached the top of the viewing tower, he could grasp the real size of the site.

Reading about it was one thing but a visit made it seem real. In the distance two lights flashed on and off, indicating the entrance to the tunnel. Plain daft that was - why it pointed out the entrance to anybody or any member of ARI for that matter.

Shaking his head sadly, he returned to his car and drove off towards London.

+

Anthony Brown had cleared his desk in Exeter and was now walking towards his flat. He lived in the same block as Colleen Kent but hadn't told anybody of the fact that he lived there, or they would be always running to him with their problems.

He also owned properties scattered around Exeter, which were let to students, in the main they were near the university. He crossed Cathedral Yard and the mound of grass that was in front of the west end of the Cathedral.

There had been a church on that site, and when it was pulled down there had been uproar. The archaeological dig on the remains had revealed all sorts of wonderful things and there had been talk for some time of it being on permanent display. However, it had come to nothing, and after the archaeologists had finished with the site, it had been refilled carefully and grassed over.

He walked on around the Northern side of the Cathedral and past Richard Hooker's statue and towards the eastern end of Cathedral Close, through to Southernhay and on to the new block of flats.

He entered, completely unaware that he had been spotted by the two men that were watching the flats.

"Who was that?"

"Haven't a clue, but we are here to watch only Colleen." "Right, but have you seen how many empty flats there are?"

Both looked at the windows of the block. Colleen was at one of the windows and she waved to them. Without thinking one of them waved back at her.

"Idiot."

"Who me?"

"Yes, now she knows that we are here watching her." "But she knew that anyway, so what's the problem?"

"We didn't tell her that we were opposite her flat, did we?" "No."

"Well, now she may have to leave by a different way. We don't know how many exits or entrances there are in the block?"

"That's true, so what are we going to do about it?" "You ever seen the programme 'Blackadder'?" "Yes why?"

"Because you remind me of Baldrick, now shut up and let me think."

Colleen had seen the two of them and had waved to see if they were the two that had been to the flat that day. She hoped the estate agent would be on time. She kept wandering around the flat, arranging the few items that she had purchased that day. Already the flat had the lived-in look. The entry phone buzzed, and she jumped up and answered it.

"Hello?"

"Anthony Brown, estate agent."

"I'll be right down." She walked through to her bedroom and picked up her handbag and after checking to see if she had her keys, left the flat and ran down the stairs. Anthony stood at the bottom waiting for her. He escorted her out to his car, and they drove off towards the "Triple A" restaurant.

After they had finished eating, Colleen was wondering what this man was like when he wasn't selling houses, flats and the like. She knew that although he had been very generous and kind, he had said very little about himself tonight.

It had been a mostly one-sided conversation with her doing most of the talking. She had been constantly on her guard in case anything let slip. Now he had sent the waiter to get the bill. The meal had been perfect and she wondered if he was planning to spend the night with her or did he have something else in mind?

Anthony placed his credit card on the tray and the waiter took it away without a word. Shortly he returned and he signed the slip. The top copy was signed and handed back to Anthony. Then the pair of them left the restaurant feeling replete.

Colleen recalled that she had once traded all of this for helping with the ARI. Had she any regrets she wondered to herself? Anthony burst in on her thoughts.

"I'll get the car and then I'll drive you home." "Fine, and Anthony …"

"Yes?"

"Thanks for such a smashing meal. It was lovely. How did you find it?"

"Yellow pages."

"Let your fingers do the walking kind of thing?"

"You could say that."He smiled and they both walked to where the car was parked.

They drove back to Southernhay in silence, and she wondered what would happen next?

"Look, you can drop me at the end of the street. I can walk the rest."

"Wouldn't hear of it. Besides I live nearby."Anthony pulled the car into the flats' car park and got out and walked around to Colleen's side, but she had already opened the car door.

"Thanks again for such an evening, I didn't realise that estate agents went to such lengths when they made a sale." Anthony locked the doors of the car and followed her into the flat entrance hall and staircase. She turned.

"Where do you think you are going?" "I thought I'd come in for the night."

"Being a bit presumptuous, aren't you?" "I don't think so."

"But I do. Just because I get taken out for a meal, doesn't mean that it gives you the right to come in for the night."

"No?"

"No."

"What if I told you, I lived here?" "Don't believe you."

"But it's true, look here is the key." "You can get the keys for all the flats."

"True, but would I go to the trouble and expense of furnishing the flat to my style. Here, come and look if you want." He led the way upstairs and on towards his flat. He unlocked the door and threw it open but as he did so he got thrown to the floor as a masked man swept out and knocked them both for six. After Anthony had picked Colleen and himself up from the floor, he made his way into the flat and over towards to the phone.

"I'll phone the police." Picking up his phone he found out it was dead.

His eyes followed the lead and saw it was cut and the plug was still in the wall socket. About as useful as a cooker in the Sahara. "Damn."

"What's the matter?"

"The phone has been cut, look can you lend me your phone?" "I would if I could, but I haven't got on the phone yet."

"Well, I guess that I'll have to go and try and find an unbroken phone box."

"What about me?"

"I suggest that you get back to your flat and lock the door." "What if anyone is there?"

"Unlikely, but I'll come and check for you if you want." "Thanks, and Anthony…"

"Yes?"

"I have had to think up reasons for men getting into my flat, but this takes the biscuit."

"Hey, this wasn't planned you know." "Really?"

"Honestly."

"Well, if that is the case the security here is lousy."

"That's true, here is your flat. You going to give me the keys or are you going to go in yourself?"

"You go in first, that's why you are here." Anthony led the way into the flat and wandered around the flat switching on the lights and checking out the rooms.

"Look, it is completely empty, I'll go and search out a phone. When I return I'll knock on the door three times like this. That will signal that is me. Just let me in, understand?"

He left her in the flat and walked down to his flat, as he stood in the doorway, he really saw the mess that it was in. It had been really turned over as the police would say later. He didn't touch anything but closed the door after him and then he went in search of a phone box.

+

Later, having written and read his statement, he was being asked if he had anywhere else to stay that night?

`Look, if you can wait a few minutes, I'll go and find out."

"Be my guest." Anthony ran down the stairs to Colleen's flat and knocked on the door three times as arranged.

"Anthony, is everything alright? I was wondering what had happened to you, since you hadn't come back."

"Look, can you do me a favour?" "What?"

"Can I spend the night here?" "What a question to ask. Why?"

"It seems that the police don't want me to sleep in the flat." "Well in that case I don't have any choice, do I?"

"Not really." He ran back up to his flat and asked if he could pick up a few items of his?

"What did you have in mind sir?" "Shaving stuff and the like?"

"No, I am afraid that is quite impossible, there may be fingerprints on it. We've asked for forensics team to come as soon as possible."

"How soon is that?"

"About eight in the morning, if that is convenient?"

"Being broken into is never convenient, so here are the keys and you can call me on this number at work tomorrow." He handed the policeman a business card before he left the flat and walked out without a backward glance.

"Right, now he has gone let's get on with it. Phone forensics, CID, British Telecom and Scotland Yard."

"Why London?"

"Don't any of you read the faxes that come through the system? There was a request from London that any break-ins at flats and new houses were to be reported direct to London. Something to do with tightening up the crime prevention."

"With respect sir, if you believe that, you will believe anything." "Yes, I know that son, but I just get on with my job and don't cause waves, understand?"

"Ok, I'll go and get the phone humming." He walked over to the phone in the flat.

"You would have a job phoning from that one, the line has been cut."

"Ah. Well, I'll phone from the car then, shall I?"

"That might be a good idea!" The young sergeant left the room and made his way towards the stairs. The officer sighed contentedly, that was more like it, no point in doing things yourself, if you could delegate them. Looking from the open doorway he knew that with a deep shag pile carpet like this one no footprints would show.

Each of the five rooms would probably be in the same state. Thoughts began to float through his mind as to the unusualness of this break in. You could hardly call it forced entry, and although the rooms were in a mess, it didn't somehow look as professional as a real thief would have left it. The one thing that niggled at the back of his mind was the fact that the outer door had been locked and yet someone had gained entry before making their way up to this flat and then without forcing the door got inside and ransacked the place.

In the distance he could hear the sirens wail as the police cars drove up Southernhay. This would give the *Express and Echo* something to write about tomorrow, he glanced at his watch, today he corrected to himself. It was well after midnight when the forensics team arrived on the doorstep of the flat. They were followed by the police photographer. Knowing they would be there all night he left them to it. He had a report to write, and they didn't write themselves.

+

In the Colleen's flat, she called through the door to his bedroom.

"Antony, what time do you want waking up?"

"Not before Six."He turned and went fast asleep, a few minutes later Colleen was also fast asleep.

+

The forensics team had finished looking over Antony's flat. Now the long tedious business of studying what they had collected could start. The problem was compounded by the fact that the inspector wanted a report unusually quickly for him, namely that morning. They packed up their equipment and made their way quietly down the staircase. Any other time the overtime would have had to have been considered. Not this time though. They knew that the cost was being shared by the Met, and they wanted to know what was going on. They really didn't know themselves, which irritated them.

An atmosphere was growing in the station and once that happened anything could fly around. Rumours abounded. The DI in charge of the case was looking at his notes and wondering what to say to London when he phoned them. He sat at his desk and looked at the report he had just finished writing. It was the rough draft that was compiled before checking for mistakes. Now he corrected his mistakes and placed it into his out tray and turned to see what was next.

He was agreeably surprised to see that he had completed everything. He stood and stretched his arms. He was stiff from writing so long, and was it any wonder, it was now four thirty in the morning.

Gathering the reports and other paperwork to be typed up, he put it in the pigeonhole for the typist to see later that morning. He couldn't fathom quite how the person had got in. The locks on the doors were supposed to be "one hour thief proof". He wondered how many keys there were to all the flats, empty and in use.

He had noticed that about three quarters of them appeared to have "For Sale" signs up in the windows. He would go and ask the estate agent tomorrow if he could have a set of master keys to the flats.

When he arrived the block of flats the place was very quiet and it seemed that everyone was asleep, and the police had also left. The two men who had arrived with Green were still sitting in the car opposite and had been amused by the comings and goings of the police all night. Now it was quiet, one nudged the other.

"Time to go."

"What if the police are in there still?" "No chance, they left hours ago."

"Right, lead on then."

The pair of them approached the block of flats in the shadows, some of the streetlights had been 'conveniently' broken before they had come on. This way they could get to the flats and keep from being seen.

The previous day they had gone to the estate agents and spun them a tale about measuring the flat with a view to purchase. He had asked them for a small deposit and passed the original keys over to them. A quick visit to the flats and they had gone around all the empty flats trying out the keys to see if they opened any other flats. This led them to finding that the same key opened Anthony's flat as well as one of the other flats. Copies had been cut and after trying them out, they had returned the originals to the agents. They had also purchased a few items for using in the flat.

The two now entered the block and walked up the carpeted stairway. They made their way to their flat which was on the floor directly above Anthony's and opened the door. Apart from the two new camp beds and sleeping bags, the flat was completely empty.

The camping equipment had been bought that morning and brought there to see if anyone would show any interest in them, but they hadn't, for which they were very grateful. They bedded down for the night, having first set their wristwatch alarms.

Beep,beep,beep.... Both men awoke and switched off their alarms. Having dressed, they quietly ran down to Anthony's flat. "Look at the way that the police have left it, dust everywhere,

I mean, it's enough to make you write and complain."

"Ok, enough of the wise creaks, let's look for a connection with Colleen and this man."

"That'll be the day, she is far too clever by half to leave anything around. Besides, I don't think she came into the flat for long enough to leave anything here, do you?" His companion looked around the flat and could see what he meant.

"No,but we have been asked to check it out and that's what we will do."They set to with a will and after ten minutes confirmed what they had first thought, that she hadn't been in there. They left and went to report what they had found out.

+

That morning would see several things happening all at the same time in different locations.

+

Anthony awoke to the sound of the alarm ringing beside his bed, and he started to get out only to bump into the wall. He must have been in one hell of a state last night, last night? Where was he? He looked at the bed and he could see the sleeping form beside him. It came back slowly, the break in and the need to sleep here. He climbed over her recumbent form and quickly dressed and let himself out of the flat, but not before leaving the latch up. He ran up to his flat to be there in time for the police to arrive to question him.

+

Detective inspector Armstrong having placed his report in the typist's office, little knowing that by the end of the day it would be out of date, made his way over to the forensics department where he could see the lights were all on in the office block.

The number of cars outside gave him an idea as to the size of the team who had just finished their night's work.

They had finished bagging the last of the samples of soil that they had found in the flat. Plastic bags littered one of the benches and the men looked and felt exhausted. Suddenly they were aware of Armstrong's presence in the office.

"Carry on, don't mind me."

"We have just finished; I was going to write up the report."

"Suppose you give it to me verbally first, then write it up."

Armstrong sat down at a desk and took out his pipe and lit it up. Despite the protests of his colleagues, he always did and always would, besides his wife said he smoked more matches than tobacco.

"Ok, well having gone over the flat with a fine-tooth comb, we have only found clay."

"Clay?"

"Clay, which comes from the centre beds of Southernhay, That's the flower beds sir."

"How the hell did you find that out?"

"Hunch, but we sent someone to obtain a sample and compare it with this one." He rummaged on the table and produced a bag with a flourish, rather like a conjurer producing a rabbit out of a hat. "It's about two hours old."

"Then I am looking for a man or woman who has walked across a flower bed and then into a flat two hours before we found it had been broken into?"

"Yes, that just about sums it up sir."

"Well, I'll see the owner and question him today. Anything else?"

"Only if he has been in any clay lately let us know so we can cross him off our list."

"Fine, now go and get some food." He left the room and the team in the office smiled and followed him out.

+

William was driving on to Exeter. He had learnt that night the purchases on the credit card were the sort of thing if you were setting up a home somewhere.

It was her first mistake, he thought with a smile on his face - she should have bought them in shops across Britain. But she hadn't and now he was heading down there to stop anyone from rushing in and sending any of the ARI off in another direction.

Bill carried on towards Exeter on the A34 before turning onto the A303. He knew that this could sometimes be a slower road, but it gave him time to think and that was a good thing. He continued driving.

## 14.28

Anthony stood and looked through the front door of his flat at the mess that still lay inside. He suspected that whoever had been in the flat before the police were called, had now returned while the police were not there. Frustrated at the police not securing the flat, he drove his fist into the framework of the front door.

He wandered back up to Colleen's flat and re-entered it. He walked over to the dining room, where a smell of fresh cooking was drifting across to him.

"Hi, I was wondering where you had gone."

"Up to my flat. It looks like as though there was another raid last night."

"What are you going to do?"

"Go and contact the police again I suppose." He left the flat and made his way towards the lift and then out to his car. He then drove out to the police station in Heavitree Road where he parked it and went inside.

"Can I help you sir?"

"I hope so. Look I called you out last night when I discovered that my flat had been broken into. Now it appears that the flat has been broken into again. Why weren't the police there all night?"

"If you will wait a few minutes, I'll go and find..." He stopped in mid-sentence as Armstrong walked in. He looked at Anthony in amazement.

"What are you doing here?"

"The flat has been broken into again, unless your men leave it in a such a mess."

"What!"

"Come and see, if you want."

"But we have been and checked it out already."

"Well in that case I suggest you come back and look over the rest of the flat."

"All right. But look someone must have a key, who did you purchase the flat from?"

"Myself."

"Pardon?"

"I work for one of the two estate agents that are selling the flats. I chose to purchase one of them."

"I see, could you tell me who the two estate agents are?" "Certainly, Buxley's and Smythe and Smythe."

"Who do you work for?"

"Smythe and Smythe, look here is one of my cards."

"I see, look, I'll get one or two men together and come with you."

"Ok." Anthony turned and left the police station. As he drove back, he let his mind drift over what was the most likely way to obtain the keys and he suddenly saw how they might have got in. He put his foot down and drove back to the flats. He would call in at Buxley's to see if there had been any interest in the flats in the last few days.

Armstrong was having much the same thoughts at the same time and left a message on the blackboard of the forensics team. "*RETURN TO THE SAME FLAT AS BEFORE AS SOON*

*AS POSSIBLE, WE HAVE A PROBLEM*" Then he left and drove towards the flats.

Anthony had arrived at the flat and was standing outside like a dog guarding it. He wondered if he had been dreaming. He hadn't. Now he was thinking about the woman downstairs, he couldn't recall such a thing happening in his career before. But his thoughts were soon disturbed by the arrival of Armstrong and his forensics team complaining bitterly to him.

"We have done this one."

"There wasn't much here the first time." "We are unlikely to find anything new."

"Shut up all of you." Said DI Armstrong. "There has been a new development and now if you will step this way." He led them through into the flat.

"We didn't leave it like this sir."

"I didn't think you did, but I want you to go through it again." He turned to Anthony. "You wanted some things last night; I suggest you buy some replacements."

"If you say so. Do you want me to sleep in the same place again?"

"If you could, then we'll stay until we finish checking it." "Isn't that bolting the stable door after the horse has bolted.

Oh, what's the use."Anthony turned and left.

+

Downstairs Colleen was worried. She had tried to blend in and now all this was going on around her, at the back of her mind she suspected that Green might be behind all this, but this was quickly put from her mind as she realised, he wouldn't know where Anthony lived. He was another man who kept his cards close to his chest.

Clearing away the breakfast things, she decided not to change for she was only going to sign some papers for Green. Then she could return to more of the history of Exeter in the Library again.

In Folkestone at the tunnel workings, Joe awoke and looked around him and could hear the rain beating down on the metal roof. He wondered where he was, then the whirling to his right brought things back to him.

He sat up and looked to where the noise was coming from and saw Thomas hunched at his machine.

Swinging himself off the bed he stood up and stretched himself, goodness he was stiff. He would have to find somewhere else to sleep tonight or he would be fit for nothing. He coughed quietly and Thomas looked around.

"Awake then?"

"Only just, my back is aching, I must find somewhere else tonight, that was awful."

"Well, I have been thinking about that. You see, the way I see it, your problem is that after a long day's work it's going to be hard to start looking for somewhere to stay."

"So, what do you think I should do?"

"Well, you could move into my van, it's one of those old caravans that the fairground people use to use. I have an old generating lorry to pull it from site to site. What do you think? If you like the idea, I'll show you around as soon as I have finished this disc."

"Like the idea? I love it." "Hey you haven't seen it yet." "What rent do you want?"

"See the caravan first before we talk rent." "Do I still report to Martin Andrew?" "Who?"

"Martin Andrew the man in charge of the earth movers." "There is no Martin Andrew on this site, I should know for I cut the discs. In fact, I would suggest that you inform the site manager of that fact, in your absence the security has been tightened a hundred percent."

Once dressed, Joe left Thomas and turned his collar up against the rain. Two new portakabins were being lowered close to where the site managers office had been before. Two large portable cranes suspended them a couple of feet off the ground as men tried to bolt the two huts together. Mr. Brooks was looking worried, but Joe pressed on and made his way up to him.

"Do you have a few minutes where we can talk?"

"Look around you, does it look like it? Come back in half an hour and I may have an office." He paused. "At least I hope I'll have an office. If one of the cranes lowers too fast all this will have been a waste of time."

"Fine, look I'll come back in half an hour." "Ok."

+

In Exeter Library Colleen had approached the main desk. "Do you have any books on the history of Exeter?"

"You left a pile the last time you were here." He reached under the counter and looked in the"U" section before finding them and passing them over to Colleen.

"Thank you, I didn't expect that kind of service from down here."

"Oh, you are not from around these parts then?" the librarian asked. Colleen could have kicked herself, that piece of news would soon go around the library, she was sure.

"No, I am from London." She replied with confidence that if anyone did try to check her out, probably there would be hundreds of Colleen's up there.

"Never been there, bit too large for my liking. Me I like somewhere about the size of Exeter."

"But Exeter isn't that small, is it?"

"Look if you want to see Exeter and its history, I could show you around if you want me too." He looked down at his shoes a trifle self-consciously.

"I'd like that, perhaps we can fix a date?"

"Sure. Now do you want to take over a table here or do you want to go through to the research section?"

"Here is fine."

"Ok, well if there is anything else you need, just ask." He was rewarded with another of Colleen's smiles.

"Thank you." She made her way over to the empty table and sat down, with the books on the table, she looked the part of a student she thought to herself.

Bending down, she removed her notebook and pen. Then pulled the first book towards her and finding out that there had been a city on or near to Exeter for the last two thousand years.

After half an hour she was so engrossed in her reading, that she didn't hear the lady come up behind her.

"Still here then?"

"What? Oh yes, I have been reading and making notes." "That's wonderful, I might suggest you go and get the feel of

Exeter. Take in the FLESH of Exeter as it were. You know what I mean?"

"Look at the buildings, that sort of thing?" "Exactly."

"That gentleman has offered to show me around." said Colleen. "Ah, in that case, you are in very good hands then. He is one of the best." She moved away and Colleen thought about what she had said. Lost in her thoughts the librarian sat opposite her looked across and spoke. "Penny for them?"

"I was wondering when to see what remains of the original Exeter. It appears that the people of Exeter are very keen to show off their city."

"Why who else has offered?"

"That lady over there." Colleen pointed out the lady to the librarian.

"Old busybody, she runs the Keep the Historical Exeter Society."

"Well, she thinks you are good as a guide." "That's a first."

"Why, what's the matter with her?"

"Look there is a lot of Exeter that needs keeping and we all agree on that. However, if a building is in the way of progress, it must be considered on its own merits. If it warrants keeping, then move it."

"Move it?"

"Yes, you see it has been done down here before and we could do it again."

"When was that?"

"Oh, about..." He paused in thought. "Nineteen sixty-one it was. It's an old house near the bottom of Stepcote Hill."

"Stepcote Hill?"

"Oh lord, I'll have to take you all over Exeter, when are you free?"

"More's the point, when are you free?" "Tomorrow afternoon."

"Then that's when we will meet." He moved away and she muttered"Stepcote Hill" under her breath and pulled a book towards her and turned to the index.

+

Anthony opened the office and after he had sat down at his desk the first person through the door was DI Armstrong.

"What are you doing here?"

"I want to know if anyone has bought or shown an interest in those flats in the last five days. Or if you know of a way that anyone could get into your flat without your knowledge." He waited for an answer.

"Personally, I have sold only one flat in that time, but as you can see there are two estate agents."

"I am seeing them next."

"Good, then please can I get on with some work. Oh inspector." "Yes?"

"There is one way that the flat might have been opened." "How?"

"If the key to another flat matched mine." "But that's not likely, is it?"

"Probably more likely than you would believe, once the flats are built and occupied, who is going to go around trying doors with keys?"

"I take your point. So, we need to try the other doors with your key?"

"That's it, and before you ask, here's a copy of my own key." He tossed it across to Armstrong.

"Thank you,sir."He left the estate office and walked to Buxley's. Before he had left the office that morning, he had passed the fax machine and had seen that there was a message addressed to him. A trouble shooter was on his way to Exeter.

Armstrong was soon at the flats,and started trying all the doors, but after about half an hour he gave up and left having tried just half of the flats. Keeping going for just two more flats, would have resulted in finding the two men's camping equipment.

He made his way back to Buxley's, on arriving there earlier, he had found they were still closed. Now they were open and a gentleman of about fifty rose from an oak desk as he entered. He had noticed that most of the properties had"SOLD SUBJECT TO CONTRACT" stamped across them.

`Good morning, can I be of any assistance Sir?"

"I understand you are selling the flats in Southernhay?"

"Yes, in conjunction with Smythe and Smythe, we have had a lot of interest in them. Considering the low price that they are priced at..." But Armstrong cut him off in mid-sentence and produced his badge.

"DI Armstrong. All I just need to know if anyone has bought or shown an interest in the flats in the last week."

"Quite so, I'll get one of the ladies to find the register." He came back with a book under his arm and Armstrong grabbed it and opened it. He looked across at the old man.

"Had a lot of enquiries, have we? There are only four names here."He tapped the page. "Why no dates for the last two names?"

"Well..."

"When did they call?"

"The day before yesterday. They left a sizeable deposit for the flat and then they took the keys and came back after half an hour saying it wasn't what they wanted."

"What!"

"What's wrong with that?"

"Let me tell you that probably, due to your slackness, someone managed to get into one of the sold flats and wrecked it last night. Now can I have a complete set of keys please?"

"Well, I don't know about that." Armstrong leaned across and grabbed the man by the lapels of his jacket and lifted him off the floor and looked him in the face.

"Pay attention. If you can let two total strangers off the street have keys, then a simple matter of helping the police force should be an easy decision for you." He whispered firmly.

"Ok but put me down first." He let him go and the estate agent dropped back into the chair. Then he got up and went and opened the cupboard of keys. Armstrong took a plastic bag from his pocket and pushed his hand into it and grabbed the keys indicated and pulled them into the bag without touching them. He sealed the bag and gave a chit to the estate agent.

"You will get them back. I'm taking this for fingerprints. So don't panic." He turned and left the office very well satisfied with the day so far. He made his way back to the flats and around to where he had parked his car. He got in and dropped the keys on the seat beside him and drove off towards the forensics department.

+

In Folkestone, half an hour later, Joe knocked on Brooks office door.

"Come in." He entered the almost bare office, save for two new desks and a swivel chair. He saw that Mr. Brooks was busy painting the drab grey interior of the hut. Joe coughed discreetly and Mr. Brooks turned around. "Be with you in a minute, take a pew. I'll just finish this bit." He turned back and put the finishing touches to the bit around the window. "There, now I can give you my full attention."

"It's like this, I was talking to Thomas Swift, and I mentioned to him that I had last reported to Martin Andrew, and did I still report to him but he said there was no such person working on the site and he must engrave the discs for everyone. He suggested I saw you, so who is he?"

"That's a good question. I'll go and call the Folkestone police, you had better come with me since you are so observant." They both left the half-painted office and climbed into the nearby Land Rover Defender before driving over to the main three huts in the centre of the main site.

+

William Dawson had arrived in Exeter and like so many before him, was desperately trying to understand Exeter's one way system. Eventually he saw some traffic signs indicating the way to the police headquarters. He cursed himself as he found he was caught up in all the evening commuter's traffic. He knew he should have driven the more direct route, but it was too late for reproaches now.

Having retuned the radio, he turned the cassette over to play the other side. He was surprised to find a voice interrupting what should have been playing.

"Hello Simon or William, pity about your flat in London. Are you still chasing all over the place or should I say places? Since you are in or near Exeter you really ought to drop this case before it gets nasty. Oh, I'd get out of the car if I were you." He grabbed at the cassette recorder and flicked the tape out. Braking hard, he pulled into the side of the road and leapt out of the car.

A few seconds later it burst into flames. Now what he wondered to himself. The car behind tooted his horn at him. He walked over to the driver.

"I have already called the fire brigade and the police." Great, thought William, just what he didn't want on his first visit to Exeter.

"Thank you. Must have been the engine overheating."

"More likely the petrol feed broke loose and ran over the engine, then all you need is a spark and there you are."

"Well thanks again for phoning." Bill made his way along the verge to await the fire engines and the police. What a way to start a visit to Exeter, yet how did they know he was down here? No mention had been made other than at Folkestone. Folkestone - everything kept leading back there. William slammed his fist into the palm of his hand, it couldn't be that obvious, could it?

+

Colleen stood up and stretched her arms above her head. She had been writing all day and now was very tired indeed.

"We are closing up the library now. Do you want us to keep the books aside for you?"

"What? Oh no you can put them back; I have finished here for the moment."

"Already?"

`Yes, but I'll be back sometime though, then you can help me again."

"`You haven't forgotten that we are going over Exeter tomorrow?"

"No, but will we be able to see all of it in an afternoon?" "That wouldn't be possible, but we could see but most of the best bits. The bits the city planners didn't break up." "Break up?"

"Well in the 60's deciding to 'improve' things, they drove a road through a part of the old city wall. This at a time when other cities were preserving theirs. However, that's not what I wanted to talk about. Where shall we meet?"

"How about here?"

"Fine by me, now would twelve noon be alright for you?" "Yes, that would be great. I really must be going. I'll look forward to it. Goodbye." Colleen rose and left the table. At the exit she looked back but he was already gone as were the pile of books she had left on the table. Leaving the library, she went in search of a shop that sold computers. It had dawned on her that if she looked in the Yellow Pages, she might find a computer shop much quicker than walking all over Exeter. She made her way to the BT shop in Princesshay.

"I wonder if you have a Yellow Pages, I might take a look at?" "Look at? You can have one for free. Here you are." He reached down and picked one off the top of a pile of them under the counter. Colleen thanked him and left the shop and walked back to the flat. As she approached, she saw three police cars parked outside the flats. Now why were they there? Did they know she was in Exeter she wondered to herself? She went inside and made her way to her flat. On each floor a policeman stood waiting. Walking past them, she entered her flat and closed the door and slid to the floor shaking with fright. There was nothing that she could think of, that would link her with Folkestone since the money from the robberies had been long laundered.

+

The fire brigade had arrived and put William's car fire out. So now the police had started to question him. He was adamant that he wasn't going to give any statements yet. The car, or what remained of it, had been winced up onto a police lorry and taken away.

William knew that this would make the local, if not national press and that was not the best way to keep quiet. He was interrupted by the senior officer coming up to him.

"That was your car sir?"

"Yes, and I have already told someone that I will only talk back at the station, when I..."The detective cut him off.

"You'll get your chance to speak later, in the meantime I suggest you come down to the... what did you say?"

"I'll only speak at the station." "Then let's go."

"Fine, oh what will happen to the car?" "Why?"

"I imagine that Folkestone police force will want to know." The policeman gulped and looked at William.

"You are a policeman then?"

"Not exactly, but I do work for the Government."

"I see, at least then let's go on ahead of the rest of the team." As they drove around the car park in the police station Bill was still wondering what to say. They walked through and entered the detective's office.

"Look, can you slap a 'D' notice on that accident?" asked Bill. "Do you know what you are asking?"

"Of course, but I do have the clout, right up to the Prime Minister."

"Then that is what we'll do sir." The detective scuttled off and William chuckled for the first time that day to himself. Why did the average man in the street or anyone else come to that, always jump at her name? He sat down at the desk and phoned the PM to put her in the picture. Meanwhile, the car would be checked over by the forensics team.

+

In Folkestone things had quietened down and Andrews was using the time to catch up on the dreaded paperwork. He had worked out that Folkestone was only one part of a much larger picture. While it was an important part, there were some pieces missing.

That morning he had heard from Bill that they had planned a spectacular entrance for him in Exeter. Whatever that was supposed to mean. Ah well, only time will tell, he thought to himself, and bent back over his desk to deal with the dreaded paperwork.

+

Brady had arrived in Paris, and he was fed up. He didn't speak the language and until he had grown a beard and a moustache to match, he couldn't venture out. That there was nobody to talk to about the cause was frustrating.

He was missing Colleen because he couldn't drive. He hadn't realised how much he had depended on her until now. But he had his hope up as he had been told that he would get some new clothes delivered to him before he returned to England. Through the tunnel apparently. He would have to wait and see. Later that evening he returned to the flat with a feeling of elation, for his contact had told him he was returning to England that night. There was a way through the service tunnel now that it was complete.

He had a new passport and special passes for both sides of the workings. But the best news was he was to go to the site tonight. He went through to the bedroom and stretched out, falling asleep in minutes. His internal alarm would wake him in good time.

+

Chief Superintendent Rose looked at a map that covered most of southern Britain. He had flagged the bombed sites in Folkestone, and he felt in his heart of hearts that if they were to catch them, it would be through a mistake and that was very unlikely.

Picking up a ruler off his desk he drew a line between Folkestone and London. Then he drew another line between Oxford and London and Oxford and Folkestone. He was about to draw straight lines intersecting from the points into the middle of the opposite lines when the phone rang. He grabbed it.

"Rose."

"William Dawson here, I am in Exeter, I think we have a lead down here, can I fill in the local force?"

"Why are you asking me? You carry more weight than I do." "Didn't want to tread on your toes."

"Go right ahead. You remember the forced entry at Scotland Yard?"

"Do I!"

"The man we have in custody will say nothing, it's due to this damn law about being nice to them and their rights. Any suggestions?"

"One or two, Look I am returning to London once I finished down here, by train."

"Why, what's the matter with your car?"

"I'll tell you in London. Will you arrange for someone to meet me off the train?"

"Funny if I didn't know you better, I would say you were frightened."

"Damn right I am. Look get someone to check out my flat as well, and to be prepared for a bomb."

"What's all this about?"

"I got a warning on the car cassette tape recorder." "Like the other two."

"That's right..." William stopped as he recalled he hadn't told anyone else other than the man who had been killed in the computer room.

"Look, I really must go now, I'll fill you in when I next see you." "Ok, you might want to know that some of the money from the robbery has turned up." "In Folkestone?" said William. "How did you know?" "Guess. Bye-bye."

Rose replaced the phone and got out of his chair and looked again at the map. So, Exeter now had to be drawn into the web of connecting lines. He quietly did so and wondered if they were looking in the right place.

+

One month later…

Joe had been working in the tunnel for over a month. Nobody had approached him yet. He had moved his equipment in with Thomas Swift and they got along very well. He hadn't seen any sign of the ARI and for that he was grateful.

+

Colleen having been taken all over Exeter and shown almost everything, now realised she might be in love with two men at the same time.

Both the librarian and Anthony Brown had been so helpful in what they could do for her.

She had also started to write a book that was half fiction and half fact partly based in Exeter which gave her the need to stay there.

Mr. Green was just happy that she had merged into the background so well. He hoped the same would happen when Brady got back from France.

A new flat had been purchased and equipped and a phone installed. It had been a lot easier with Colleen doing the shopping for them. Now, for the moment she sat typing at her new Apple computer that she had purchased over a month ago.

+

In her safe house Mary Orchard had grown tired with the Thames Valley Police force. They were keen to let her go, and she could see why. It appeared that their hands were tied under instructions from the higher ups. She knew that their budgets were being cut and they wanted to shift her to save money. Mary had repeatedly asked if she could go, but they said no each time.

The phone rang and she answered it only Thames Valley knew the number since it wasn't printed on the dial and Mary wondered who it was.

"Folkestone police here, we are releasing you tonight Mary and you will be reunited with your mother. You can check this call by dialing…" It then gave her a long number to dial.

Mary phoned the Thames Valley as she had been taught if a call came to the house. They verified that the number was genuine, and they too had been informed of the fact she could go. Mary was over the moon with delight.

Joe had decided to make one of his rare phone calls to his wife. Using a phonecard, he phoned Belfast.

"Hello Sarah, just taking a few minutes of quiet to phone you. You ok?"

"More than ok Joe, you are going to be a father." "When, I mean, really?"

"It's true Joe. In about seven months."

"Then I must work that much harder, wait till the lads hear this."

"I wouldn't tell anyone Joe, at least not yet anyhow. Just think of where you are working."

"True, I hadn't thought of that. Still, it's great news. Look I am going to have to work some overtime to build up the money, how much do we owe now?"

"We don't, and we have started to save some money, so isn't that great?"

"It is love. It truly is."

"I must go, the milk is boiling over on the hob, I'll be seeing you. Love you. Goodbye Joe."

"Goodbye Sarah." Joe walked out into the cold night air, but he didn't feel it, he jumped into the air and punched it yelling "whoopee" and he then ran all the way back to the site caravan of Thomas Swift's and made it in the quickest time ever.

# 15.28
## ONE YEAR LATER.

Colleen left the flat and made her way to the library as she had done regularly over the past year. Since Michael Brady had joined her in Exeter, she knew that the risks had now greatly increased. So, Michael had changed his face, undergone plastic surgery, and had new papers.

He now was ensconced in his flat. Although he had grown a beard and looked different, the police had put out a rough lookalike to him on the programme 'Crimeview'. She had been courted by both the librarian and the estate agent for the whole of the twelve months. The more she got engrossed with them, the better the cover.

Colleen had changed her route to the library several times. Consequently, she now knew the quickest route and the longest route and the most unusual route. Her book had been mostly written and she had to admit that she enjoyed doing so.

She knew that Green would come for her one day and that was the one nagging question at the back of her mind. Should she give up the cause? But a voice at the back of his head would answer "*but you couldn't have done all this without the cause behind you, you know.*" Sighing she entered the library.

Collecting the usual pile of books that she had set aside the night before, she made her way to her table and bent down to start work.

Half an hour later she felt a shadow fall across the desk, she frowned it was most unusual to disturb any of the researchers. She turned and looked up, and a gasp fell from her lips.

"Brady, are you mad?"

"Don't think so, I wanted to see where you went each day. So this is where you come is it?"

"Yes."

"What kind of answer is that? I want a full explanation of why you are here."

"Brady be quiet, people are looking at you, and that's not a good idea, is it?"

"Alright, so tell me what you are doing?"

"Writing a book on the history of Exeter, fact and fiction." "What!"

"Look, be quiet, everyone is listening."

"So I'll be quiet, but where can I meet you to talk this over?" "Rougemont Castle. Before you ask there is a map downstairs,

I'll meet you by the war memorial." "Fine. When?"

"Half an hour." She turned back to her books, but her heart was not in it, why did he have to find out? She knew that he would question her and then the threats would start. She had sometimes wondered what the victims' families felt like, well now she would find out.

Colleen collected her books together and took them to the desk. "Keep them for me, I'll be away for two days at the most. If I am not back by then put them back."

"That's ok Miss Kent, that man, he wasn't troubling you was he?"

"No, not at all." So even he had noticed. She knew it was far too risky for Brady to be there.

"You sure you are ok. Only you have come over all pale." "No, I am alright." Deciding to go a different way to Brady, she soon was able to see that Brady was already there waiting for her, but he couldn't see her.

Occasionally, he glanced at his watch, as if that would make time go any quicker, she thought to herself. Then she walked out to meet him.

"Well, what do you think of all this?" she asked him.

"What I have seen I like, and I can understand what you see in the place, but I can't understand you working in the library each day. I mean you are asking for trouble, aren't you?"

"No, I don't think so. You see I have been accepted down here and regularly going in and out for the past year to the library, nobody has questioned my motives. So why are you worrying?"

"I still think that it's too risky, you must give it up." "Give me a good reason as to why I should?"

"Why? Well for starters you may have to return to Folkestone." Colleen turned her back on him.

"Never! I have burnt my boats there. You saw to that. No Brady I am not going back. I have a nice new flat and a new name and a new city, what more do I need?"

"Me?"

"No, not even you Brady. In fact, most certainly not you." "What!"

"You heard. Now I think that you had better go back to your flat and have a meal."

"Couldn't we go out? I am tired of having meals in the flat." "No, already someone has questioned if you were bothering me, it's too risky."

"Well in that case you leave me no alternative."

"What do you mean?" Her heart pounded away, and she wondered what he was going to threaten to do.

"Oh, I'll have to have you moved." "Brady I am not a piece of furniture." "No, but 'The Cause' needs you still."

"I moved down here to get away from all that."

"Exactly, but you owe us for all the flat and the belongings." "Wrong,I have paid, paid in ways that you wouldn't understand. Look, I had to leave everything I loved in Folkestone and that wasn't easy."

"But once in the cause, you are in it for life." said Brady, with a worried look.

"Not me, I am now out of it." "The world is a small place."

"You think so? So where did Lord Lucan go then?"

"That was a one off, now don't try and change the subject."

"Look, I don't want to fall out about it. I am staying here and that's the end of it."

They set off back to the flats and as they walked across the Cathedral Close the sunlight was catching the Beer stonework on the west front.

Colleen looked across at it. The thought that she may have to move on from here soon and since she always seemed to be doing that, she wondered whereabouts she could settle for good and not be disturbed at all.

She would phone Green when she got in. They got back to the flats, and she unlocked the door and walked in. Once inside she made for the phone and rang Mr. Green. He picked up the phone.

"Hello?"

"It's your friend in the south west. I need to meet you." "Well, it is a bit far for me to come."

"I'll come to you. Usual place in Green Park." "When?" he asked.

"Three days' time. Two in the afternoon." Colleen replaced the receiver and took a deep breath to relax.

+

Upstairs in his own flat, Brady had heard all the conversation. He had bugged her phone the first time he had been in her flat. Now with a frown, he looked at a map of London and then dialled a number in Belfast before going down to speak to Colleen about the call she had just made.

He knocked on her door and turned the handle, the door opened, so he walked in and shut it after him. Colleen looked up as he entered her flat.

"What do you want now?" she asked nervously. "Who were you talking to?" Brady asked quietly.

"What did you say? Have you been listening to my calls?" "I said who were you talking to on the phone then?" "Never you mind."

"Oh, but I do. Who was it?" He lunged at Colleen, but she dodged him and grabbed his arm and twisted it behind his back. "Agh!"

"Now tell me where the bug is, and fast if you know what is good for you."

"Obviously it is in the phone, I planted it on my first visit." "Right, well, you can go and remove it."

"Right." croaked Brady. "And Brady."

"Yes?"

"I want you to cook me a wonderful meal today in your flat. But don't get any ideas."

"No of course not."

"Right, I'll leave you to it then." "Good."

+

In Folkestone Andrews was reviewing the last twelve months files of their cases in readiness for filing. He looked up at the Sergeant.

"We never managed to find that woman who went from here down to Exeter. I wonder what she is doing now?"

"More to the point sir is why has there been no threats against Mr. O'Brian for the last twelve months."

"You do have a point." He tapped the files. "Maybe we ought to keep this one file out for a few more months. He knew the names of the ARI members that were still working on the site. He hadn't removed them for the same reason that he had given months ago, namely, if they were picked up then they would be replaced by people they didn't know.

"You have to put your reason on the docket on the front sir."

"Yes." He thought for a moment and scribbled the reason on the top of the file.

"Do you want the other files stored sir?"

"Might as well."He got up and opened the door for the sergeant as he had both hands full of files.

"Sergeant, get the names of everyone who was working with us on that case and the names of the known ARI contacts."

"Right sir." He left the office. An hour later he had returned and was holding a list of the people that had helped them in the case. He handed it to Andrews who was looking out of the window onto the car park.

"You'd think that with all our resources it wouldn't be that difficult to catch just a couple of people whose one aim is to bring maximum disruption to the tunnel. We should have used HOLMES." said Andrews thoughtfully.

"But sir, you didn't want to at the time."

"I know that, but I was wrong. I see that now." "Fine, but what can we do twelve months on sir?"

"Well, I was wondering what you said about Mr. O'Brian. Look what if he has been approached, but one of the conditions was not to contact the police, what would you do with a wife and child?"

"Do as they said I suppose."

"Exactly, so let's try and get hold of his wife. See how she is. See if she is getting all of his money that he sends her."

"And if she isn't?"

"Go to Belfast, and urgently. And draw some expenses from the office, here's a chit for them." The sergeant's eyes bulged when he saw the size of it.

"Anything you don't need you have to return. But I don't want you not being able to follow something up, because you didn't have the right sort of money." The sergeant left the office and Andrews took the file off the chair and put it on his desk. He sat down and put on his glasses, then he pulled the file towards him and started to read.

An hour later he had finished, and he now knew why he had wanted the file kept back. There had been too many loose ends for his liking and no arrests. Threats to the tunnel, the writing in Mrs. Orchard's House, but apart from that, nothing sensational.

He decided to write to Joe at a place they had already agreed on. He pulled out one of his drawers and took out two sheets of paper and a sheet of carbon paper, then he went and called down the corridor to the typist's office.

"Bring me a portable typewriter will you someone?" A few minutes later his secretary walked in and put it on his desk.

"Why don't you indent for your own?"

"Then I wouldn't have the pleasure of seeing you."

"What you need is one of those word processors. Then you could juggle the text until you had it to your liking."

"Do you own one?"

"Yes, but not here, only at my house." She flashed him a smile and he nodded at her.

"I might come and see it one night if that's ok?"

"Certainly sir." She turned and left the office." Andrews went and closed the door, then sat down and started to type Joe's letter.

†

Joe had been working steadily underground and had not been approached since he had started there. He was earning a lot more money and most of it was being sent back to Sarah. Now that he had a son, he had increased the amount that he sent back.

He received regular letters from Sarah and had a small photo of their son which he always carried with him. He was thinking of him and wondering how he would have to adapt if he brought Sarah and his son over to England.

He had been somewhat apprehensive about working underground to start with, but now he was working up near the front of the TBM or Tunnel Boring Machine. The machine had a long rear section on which a series of conveyers kept plying the front of the machine with the seven segments of tunnel. A small narrow gauge railway track had to be regularly added to as they pushed further towards France.

He was now putting in the last of section of a segment of the tunnel. This one had a square hole which grout was pumped into to line the rough tunnel and the smooth sections. He held the hose as it pumped in the grout, the surplus, running down the side of the sections.

Water ran everywhere as the hoses used to pump water out of the tunnel were in constant use. Even the best hoses and pumps in the world can give way, and these leaked with the enormous pressure it was under.

At the end of the shift that night, Joe had been on the small train going home along the tunnel and happened to glance to his right and his heart dropped like a stone. One of the two men he had run into on the site a year ago, was sat on his right. He turned back, but it was too late - he had been spotted.

"Hi there, we have been looking for you for ages. I want to talk. Now tell me where we should meet."

"I have nothing to say to you."

"Maybe not, but you might want to listen and learn. It may concern your new family." Joe turned back and listened; if you didn't listen to them, then that was at your peril.

"So, what do you want?" asked Joe in a sullen voice. "To talk, simply to talk Joe."

"Where do we meet then?"

"Outside the site opposite the supermarket." "Which one?" asked Joe.

"You choose."

"Then the main one opposite the main entrance to the sidings. What time do you plan on this meeting?"

"Eight O'clock tonight."

"Fine, how will I know that you are there?" asked Joe.

"I expect we can find you like today." He turned his back as the train broke out into the fresh air of Folkestone. Joe decided to go and change and get to a phone as soon as possible.

Joe having freshened up, was now busy eating a meal at Thomas Swift's caravan when Swift walked in.

"Is that dinner I can smell?"

"It is, yours is in the oven keeping warm." "Thanks, I'll change first though."

"I need to talk to you."

"Isn't that what you are doing?"

"You know what I mean." He left Joe to finish his meal and start washing up. When Thomas had changed and was eating his meal Joe sat opposite him.

"What do you know about the ARI Thomas?" "Only what I have seen on TV, why?"

"I'm having pressure put on me underground by them and I have to meet someone tonight, I think that they are about to threaten to hurt my wife and son, if I don't do as they say. What do I do?"

"We go together to this meeting?" "I hoped you would say that."

"Good, if anyone starts to force you to go anywhere, I'll go to the police."

"Fine, but I expect that by tonight they will have my wife and son, and I bet one of the conditions will be 'Don't tell the Police'."

"But Joe, you aren't doing that. I am."

"Ok, and if the Police come, who do the police look for? An Irishman? How many are there on this site? A hundred? A thousand? You know how big the changeover points are under the tunnel, why someone could hide out for days down there especially if you have the friends they have."

"Ok, but what else can you do?"

"I was going to phone Sarah, but I thought they might be keeping an eye on me, so could you phone her? Tell her to get out of Belfast and bring only her passport and the money I have been sending and our son. She isn't to tell anyone, not even her mother."

"When do I do this?"

"When I am meeting this man." "What!"

"Look I intend to say no to whatever they want." "Why?"

"Because I want to make a stand, and if I don't, then they will win. Someone has to make a stand at some point."

"Why you? Look let me go and talk to them."

"They wouldn't want you. They need someone who is working underground."

"How do you know that?"

"Because just after I started, I was approached by two thugs and offered the chance of going and working underground."

"Why didn't you say anything to me?"

"I didn't know then who to trust. It was at the time that those bombs were used to blow up different parts of the site if you remember?"

"As if I could forget that. What did you do?"

"I felt that if one didn't make a stand at some point, then what happened in Germany in the last war could then easily happen over here. People being frightened, it's a great weapon, fear. Now twelve months on, I have a son, and I am not hesitating this time. That's why I am asking you to phone her. I don't want her at home when I turn them down."

"What if they have her already?" asked Thomas, frowning. "Then I may still sacrifice the three of us, better that, than the thousands who will or could be killed." "What thousands of others?"

"The thousands who will be caught when the tunnel is blown up."

"Blown up, but the security…" Thomas stopped in mid- sentence. "…so that is why you are going to say no. Look, why don't I phone your wife before you meet this man? Then you would know exactly where you stood."

"Ok but be quick."

"I'll run in both directions." He grinned and left the caravan after looking around him. He made his way to the new cardphone phone box and post box outside the site and phoned from there. He could hear the ringing tones in his ear and muttered to himself "pick it up".

`Yes?" said a man's voice. Thomas's throat tightened as he realised that they must already have Sarah.

"Can I speak to Mrs. O'Brian please?" "Wrong number, I am sorry."

"What number are you?"

"Belfast 12445768 Does that satisfy you?"

"That's the number I have, now put Sarah O'Brian on the phone."

"Look, there is no Sarah O'Brian here." A scream ripped through the air, followed by a baby crying, then the phone went dead. Thomas guessed they were professional terrorists then. Ruthless people who killed or maimed if they got paid to do so.

He waved down a waiting taxi and told the driver to drive to the police station.

+

The phone rang on Andrews desk, and he snatched it up. "Andrews."

"We have someone in reception who thinks that he can help with the tunnel enquiry."

"Hold them there, I'll be right up, in the meantime find an empty interview room." He ran out of his office and up to the interview rooms.

"In room three sir." Said one of the sergeants. He opened one of the doors and Andrews entered the room. Thomas jumped right up.

"Thank goodness you are here, we must move fast, if you want to catch the ARI. that is."

"Look, start at the beginning and work through what you have to say." Sitting back down, Thomas did as he was asked.

"So, you see, we must act quickly." he added at the end of his explanation.

"Thanks for coming in, look you go back we will take over now, I thought we could let it run, but I think the time has come to move."

"Ok. Thanks for believing in me." "That's ok, now go." He watched as

Swift left and then Andrews returned to his office and pulled out the maps for Folkestone, Exeter, and Oxford. He had learnt more about Joe in the last half an hour than a whole year of keeping him on the site. Leaving the office, he drove to a public phone box and phoned Dawson in London.

After Dawson's flat had been bombed, he had moved, but was still ex-directory. Andrews knew of two numbers to call if this was an emergency. He tried both and got one of Dawson's bosses.

"Yes?"

"DCI Andrews of Folkestone CID." "How can we help you?"

"A year ago, William Dawson helped us with an investigation, I have some new evidence, he should be told."

"Is this that important?" "Very."

"Ok, I'll get back to you." He hung up and Andrews, who wasn't one to sit around doing nothing, then rang Oxford and Exeter and asked for their case notes to be transmitted to Folkestone. In each case they agreed to do as he asked.

Each of them asked what the rush was, and he told them that he had new evidence. Both wanted a share in the glory, but if the other stuff hit the fan, then he was solely responsible. Still beggars can't be choosers. He put down the phone and it rang almost at once.

"DCI Andrews Folkestone CID."

"Rose here, I need to come down, Bill is abroad, and he is coming back to see you, it had better be good."

"It is, but how did you hear about it?" "Phone tapping."

"Blasted cheek." said Andrews.

"That way I know what is going on. See you shortly."

+

Thomas got back into the caravan and found Joe looking at a bunch of Sarah's letters. He looked up as he came in.

"What took you so long? Have you spoken to Sarah? What is going on? Tell me!"

267

"Give me a minute, will you? Sarah and the boy are alive - she screamed, and he cried. But they claimed it was a wrong number."

"Well, they would say that wouldn't they?" said Joe. "Are you armed?"

"No."

"Ok, there is a gun here somewhere." He rummaged around and produced a small gun. "Do you know how it works?"

"No."

"Then you had better learn." They bent over the table together before going outside to practice.

+

DCI Andrews was putting the finishing touches to his moral boosting speech to his men. He had told them they were going to try and capture an ARI cell tonight and had a good tip off as to where they would be. He had shown them where to hide and there would be getting on for over a hundred officers and soldiers out there, slowly getting into position. They were to shoot to injure rather than kill if they could help it. Then he left them and went to look at the new files that he now had.

# 16.28

Brady was cooking in his Exeter flat and wondering what to do about Colleen. He felt that he ought to get in touch with Green, he might know what to do. The problem was he didn't have Green's telephone number, and he couldn't very well ask Colleen for it. Perhaps if they could go for a long drive in the country, it would be away from the city, and nobody would recognise him. He would put it to Colleen later over the meal. He finished preparing the meal.

After they had eaten, Colleen looked at the maps around the south west and started to add the figures of the distance they would be travelling if they went for a drive around the west country.

"Alright where do you have in mind Brady?" "Ilfracombe and Lynton and Lynmouth." "Fine, how far is that?"

"About seventy-five miles give or take a few."

"How far?" said Colleen with a concerned look on her face. "Seventy-five miles, but that isn't far, we could make it stretch to two days if you like."

"What's made you change your mind?"

"Brady, the difference is that we would be in the country and not in the city were you would risk being recognised."

"What about your book?"

"A couple of days off will not matter for once." "Ok, but where will we stay?" asked Brady

"Guest houses and hotels. If you have cash, they are happy." "Right, let's eat, then." He led Colleen through to the dining room where they discussed the details of the trip.

+

William Dawson had arrived at Dover and hired a car and was now exceeding the speed limit as he drove towards Folkestone. He knew that he had to meet the schedule that had been set up for him.

Driving into Folkestone eventually he pulled up in the police station car park. Getting out, he ran over to the entrance and cleared the three steps in one bound and entered the building breathless.

"Can you tell me where DCI Andrews is please? I'm William Dawson, he is expecting me."

"Yes, we know, if you'll follow me, please." He was led down to the large double office that was being used. "If you can wait here, I'll go and fetch him, I'll not be long." He left and Bill wandered around the room looking at the maps and information on the walls. A few minutes later Andrews appeared at the doorway.

"William, how great to see you again. Look, come down to my office where we can talk a little more quietly."

"`Great to see you too Andrews. What has made all this fuss?" "Wait a few minutes and I'll tell you." They walked down to Andrews office and went inside. William closed Andrews office door after them and looked at him. "Well?"

"We have had a tip off that the ARI are moving on to Joe. We think that the reason is that they now have his wife and child."

`Hang on, what child?" asked Dawson with a frown. "Joe has a son."

"Since when?"

"About three months ago I think." "Right, carry on."

"Well, I think they will ask him to place a bomb in the tunnel sometime, and given the fact that they have his family, what would you do?" asked Andrews.

"Me! Look what I would do is not important. Do we really know what is happening at the works?" asked William frowning. "He says that if he is trying to stop them, then it's better to stop them by dying and saving thousands of innocents."

So, if that means that three people die, then so be it." Replied William, shrugging his shoulders.

"It sounds fine but is it likely that he has thought this through? Let's assume they carry out the threat and kill his family, and he still doesn't do as they want, all he will have achieved is his and his family deaths. The ARI will just go and find some other person to do this." replied Andrews with a frown.

"Reading between the lines on what you have said about him, I think that he feels that if anything happens to him, then we can pick up the cell of the local ARI. Which could stop any attempt on the tunnel." said William.

"And you think we have enough men on the ground to stop this attempt?" replied Andrews, frowning.

"Remember this is the biggest civil engineering project going on in the world now. I bet the ARI have had their eyes on this ever since it was first announced."

I expect we will catch them. replied Andrews.

"Just don't count your chickens yet, that's all I am saying." Said William.

"There are over two hundred men out on the streets around the area where they are going to meet. They won't get away." said Andrews confidently.

"Ok, but just don't get too confident." "Why, what do you think will happen?"

"They will switch the location at the last minute." "If they did, where would they go?"

"Ah, but that is the sixty-four-thousand-dollar question, isn't it?" said William with a frown of his own.

+

Thomas was starting to wake Joe up, when the door of the caravan burst open and two hooded men stood in the doorway. One had a gun in his hand, and he motioned towards the door with it.

"Get outside and wait." He said waving the gun at Thomas Swift. He left and walked over to the lorry, but as he did so, he saw two of its tyres were now flat. Obvious that they were professionals he thought. Inside Joe was standing looking at the two men.

"I thought we were meeting later."

"My aren't we quick, I hope that you are as quick later tonight. The reason we came earlier is that we tend to live longer that way. I expected the place to be crawling with the police and Army by now."

"I don't intend to help you."

"Well, they all tend to say that to start with. You see we have your family."

"I still don't intend to help you."

"Well, maybe a visit to Belfast would help convince you."
"Unlikely, besides I would need to get the tickets first." "Here are your tickets, you will be on that flight tomorrow."

"What!"

"You heard, have a good flight."They backed out of the caravan and into the night. As they passed Thomas they smiled in a cruel manner. "Don't go interfering in things that don't concern you, understand? Next time the lorry might not be the only target." Thomas nodded his head slowly, but they had already disappeared into the dark.

Joe was standing inside the caravan wondering what he should do. He went to the door as Thomas Swift came in.

"So, what did they want?" "Me to plant a bomb."

"But that is what you expected." "Yes, and I said no."

"What did they say then?"

"Then they gave me this return flight to Belfast. I have to go and see Sarah."

"Are you going?"

"I don't have a choice."

"I suppose not. What about work?"

"I am due some leave, but they probably know that too."

"I had better inform the police that they have already had their meeting. They won't like it, but what else can you do?" said Thomas.

"Look, if you are speaking to them, make sure that none of them tries to follow me to Belfast, policemen have a way of looking like policemen even when they are in plain clothes.

"Ok." Thomas left the van and Joe went off to bed to have a rest. He soon had drifted off to sleep.

+

At the police station, Andrews was inwardly furious. He had listened to Thomas and then had returned to his office.

"Apparently they called on Joe earlier than arranged. I have hundreds of Policemen and Army at my disposal, can't we do anything right."

"I did warn you not to be too confident, didn't I?" smiled William.

"Yes, you did warn me, but how did you know they would do that?"

"From past experience."

"So, draw on your experience, where do we go next?" "I go to Belfast."

"Not going to happen, Apparently Joe emphasised that he didn't want any plain clothes policemen around him." Said Andrews.

"I agree, but you see I am not a policeman." replied William. "Oh."

"So, we can obey him, but keep a watch on him as well. I'll fly over there tonight and can be in Belfast before he arrives tomorrow morning. Then I can follow him. I do photography as a hobby and therefore I can take my kit with me." said William forcefully.

"Well, I have no say over what you do. It sounds fine if Joe doesn't find out that you are out there. I'll keep the higher ups informed." Replied Andrews with a shrug of his shoulders.

"Keep in touch." With that William left the station and made for his car. He swung the car out of the car park and drove off towards London. He had copies of all the material that was sent from the different sources and he could read the material going over on the flight to Belfast. He phoned ahead to his office and got them to arrange the tickets and to bring his file and an overnight bag to Heathrow.

"Do you want assistance?" Assistance meant both in person and with a gun. He was asked.

"That would be useful but do go a different route to me." "Anything else?"

"Money, lots of it. And some help reading papers." "Nothing else?"

"Yes, check the answer phone and see to the messages." "Ok, then I'll see you in Belfast."

"Thanks." He switched off and looked at his on-board computer which was telling him that the M20 was blocked with traffic but quickly worked out a cross country route.

"So, Andrews, how the hell did the ARI get on and off the site without being seen? Answer me that." Asked CS Rose angrily.

"They don't walk around with ARI badges on their jackets. It is near one of the many crossing points for tourists from France and Europe. A lot of the workers are both from France and the

UK. The Irish contingent had been the first to be offered work, an attempt to try and bring stability to the province."

"Ok, but it makes me furious that we are being played for suckers. They seem to know what we are planning at every stage of the proceedings." Said rose with a frown.

"Get the men off the streets and back here, I'll bring them up to speed." Said Andrews to his sargent who was standing in the doorway.

"Right, you are sir."

Half an hour later Andrews was standing in front of all of his men.

"Look, we blew it, no, I blew it. Now I do not intend to let all the talent assembled here go to waste." Much laughter. "So please look through all the material that is on the tables down here, if anything strikes you, however small and insignificant it might seem, please bring it to my office. I'll be in there until you all have finished." He turned and left the group clutching his copy of all the material in the room.

An hour later there was a knock on the door to his office and he got up and opened it to one of his constables.

"Come in."

"You said to come if anything sprang to mind or if we saw anything that might have been missed."

"Yes,, well what did you see?"

"Well, I was wondering why neither you nor Exeter hadn't collared the bank robber, you know the female one. She robbed two banks in this district, and it never went further."

"Remind me of which two banks."

"Well, when the bombs went off in that house, about the same time there were two robberies in Folkestone. You were on the ARI case so you may have missed the details. Anyhow the poster sketch is supposed to be a close likeness to the driver that drove that ARI man off out of here. Assuming it was the same person, she would now have the means to go and live in any part of the world. What if she went to, say Exeter, it would be easy with the money for her to stay hidden? The real problem is the money."

"Why?"

"Well, the robbery of each bank took place just before closing time, therefore a lot of the notes were unknown. At the first bank, though, most were a consignment of new notes. Unusual for a bank, but it was its first day of opening."

"Alright, I get the picture. That's the sort of insight I was looking for. Constable, get hold of Exeter and ask them to find out if any estate agents had sold any properties to anyone for just cash. You know the sort of questions to ask, get the men out of bed if need be. If she is living down there, have her tailed and thank you for spotting it. Now go and get on with it."

The constable left the room and Andrews noticed that he was walking out a little straighter. He chuckled to himself, but it seemed that just had opened the floodgates.

Every suggestion was acknowledged, and it would be followed up, although he knew some of it was a waste of time. He felt that at the end that it was time to call on Joe and fill him in on what was going on. He picked up the internal phone.

"Andrews here, I need an unmarked car out the front in five minutes."

+

At the same time, Joe was being driven to London by Thomas. Thomas had said to Joe that he could catch that night's last plane to Belfast and perhaps be one jump ahead of the ARI. They would have assumed he was going to fly in tomorrow.

+

Andrews ran out of the doors of the station with a sergeant following. They both jumped into the car and drove off in the direction of the tunnel works.

"Where do you want to go when we get there sir?"

"Let's just get to the main entrance first, and I'll take it from there." The car soon swept into the main entrance, where they were stopped by the guards. After showing them their badges, they drove on to the site office. Andrews ran up to the door and opened it rudely. Inside Sam Brooks looked up at the sudden intrusion.

"Who are you and what is the meaning of this interruption?" "We'll ask the questions; we are Folkestone CID." He showed his badge at him, but not long enough to see what it said. "How can I help you?"

"Where are Mr. Swift and Mr. O'Brian right now? "At this moment, I haven't a clue."

"I really need to know if they are working or resting or off the site altogether, and are you telling me you can't get that information?"

"That's right, if you want to you can wander the site at will and you may look in the tag room to see if they are on the site." "WHAT! Why didn't you say that at first?" asked Andrews with his voice dripping with sarcasm. "When I said at this moment, I did mean as of this minute, every second is important."

"Oh come, that is a little too much to believe, don't you think?" "Is it? What would you say if I told you that they were trying to..." Brooks interrupted"...Blow up the tunnel? Plant a bomb? Infiltrate the site? Really Inspector, do you not think that we haven't thought of that already? Here look at those." He got up and pulled open the top drawer of a filing cabinet. He removed a file and passed it to Andrews.

"It's all in there, take it and look at it at your leisure. Go on, take it." Andrews took the file and sat down. "No, don't read it here, take it back with you. Believe me that every one of those threats have been followed up and taken very seriously indeed. Nothing has happened yet."

"When did you first start to get these sir?"

"About a year ago, look at the first one, they have all been date stamped with the date they were received. There was some threat of bombing one of the site workers homes, but nothing came of it."

Andrews said nothing, but recalled it was about a year ago that the bombed house of Patrick O'Shane had been found. He recalled the body had been dead for some time, later he would look out the file.

"So, if you can just point out the tag room, I'd appreciate it." "Sure, see this map? Well, that's the tag room."

`Thanks, and where do Mr. O'Brian and Mr. Swift live?" "Swift has a caravan in this area somewhere."

"Right, I'll go there first. Thank you." He left the site office and walked over to the car. "Let's go to the caravan, I feel that I am wasting time, but let's do it anyhow."

"Ok, but don't you need a warrant?"

"Most likely, but if there isn't anyone there, then they won't be around to query it."

Both men carefully searched the caravan in record time. They were about to leave when they heard voices outside. They went still.

"This is it?"

"Yea, look we know that both of them have gone to London so let's give it the once over shall we?"

"No, we wouldn't find anything, that Joe is too clever by half. He needs to be taught a lesson. What if his home isn't here when he returns?"

"If he returns you mean."

"He'll return, we have his family. When he sees what we intend to do he'll give in."

"Maybe, but the site talk is that he is going to stand against us." "Then he'll find that he has bitten off more than he can chew." "Alright, so do we fire it or wreck it?"

"Fire it. I'll go and find some petrol." Andrews looked at the sergeant.

"I'm going to make a dash for one of those two as soon as I leave the caravan you dash for the car and turn it around. If I don't make it, head straight back to the station and don't stop for anything."

"Let's go sir." both men exploded out of the caravan and onto the second of the two men.

"What the hell?"

"Police, you are under arrest. Anything you say may be taken down and used in evidence against you."

"I'm saying nothing." By now Andrews had him in an arm lock and had marched him to the car.

"Cuff him sergeant. Then let's get the hell out of here."

"Right."They drove off with their arrested man seated beside Andrews in the back. They saw the other man walk up to the caravan,by the site road. They had to pass it again in a few minutes only this time there was a wire fence between them. "Phew, I am glad we are well away from that sir."

Both men could now see that the caravan was well ablaze. Already in the distance there was the sound of fire engines as they raced towards the scene. "Yes, but we do have one of them. So much for the site's security. Drive on."


Ten minutes later the Irishman was still in handcuffs and cuffed at his ankles.

Andrews intended to keep him for the full thirty-six hours. While he could keep him for longer, if he did so then his senior colleagues would have become a little more interested in him. That was something Andrews wanted to avoid. For the first time, he felt that they had the upper hand.

A knock on his office door made him look up, as his light indicated that he wasn't to be disturbed.

`Come in."The constable who he had spoken to about Exeter stood there.

"I've phoned Exeter and gave them your request; they are looking into things down there. They want to phone you direct, I offered to take a message, but they wouldn't hear of it. When would be the best time sir?"

"Now, if possible, I'll phone them."

"Right, and Sir, I can't find the file on the Folkestone bombings."

"Why do you need it?"

"Chief Superintendent Rose asked me to find it."

"I thought he had a copy of one in his file in London?"

"I do." said Rose entering the office,"but something made me stick around here. I thought that you might pull something out of the hat so to speak."

"Well in the morning I may be able to help you. I thought that you were heading back up to London."

"I was, but a large fire on the site made me turn around." replied Rose.

"I expect they were burning scrap wood."

"With three fire engines racing to the scene. Come off it, I wasn't born yesterday you know."

"I never said you were." "So where is Joe O'Brian?"

"I only wish I knew. I think he has headed towards London." "Right, I'll leave you to it. Phone me in the morning, will you?"

He left the room and the young constable looked at Andrews.

"About the man you brought in, do we feed him, only if he is handcuffed?"

"No, we do not feed him, and the reason is that when he has gone without food for a period of two or three days, he will probably sing like a bird."

"Right, goodnight Sir."

"Goodnight." Andrews picked up the secure line and dialled Exeter's police phone number.

+

Early the following day, Brady and Colleen drove off towards North Devon, without anybody else knowing…

+

When DI Armstrong had spoken to Andrews the day before, he had pointed out that all the woman did was to go to the library and look up books on the history of Exeter. They had left her alone as she didn't seem to be contacting anyone. Andrews had asked them to hold her. Also, once arrested, she wasn't to be given any food for at least a day. Hungry might make her more talkative, at least that was what Andrews had thought last night.

+

Armstrong was at his desk and took out his pipe, matches and tobacco and when he had lit it and it was going nicely, he leaned back in his chair and thought to himself. Why was everything going to Folkestone? All the usual enquiries went to London. Why didn't these? He buzzed the internal phone and got the desk sergeant.

"Get me the best twenty men and tell them I want to have a meeting at two, this afternoon, to discuss things. All of them must be able to handle a gun."

"Right sir."

"Then get on with it."Armstrong replaced the handset and sat back in his chair; his pipe had gone out again. Sighing he set about trying to relight it.

+

William had parked his car at Heathrow Airport and after a small wait his colleague, Gail, showed up.

"What kept you?" he asked her.

"Nothing, I was here first, but you were followed."

"I know that, look let's split the money and you can give me the ticket." He ran his eyes over the airport lounge as he got the feeling that he was being followed. Before he could do anything about it,Gail spun round and grabbed the man following William. "Why are you following us? Who do you work for? What are you following me for?"

"Questions, questions, agh…." he shouted as she twisted his arm right up behind his back, it cracked, and he cried out again. William walked up and rested his hand on Gail.

"Enough. The man will talk, I think. Right, it's your lucky day as we work as a team. Any more resistance and we will all regret it."

"Why will you regret it?"

"Because I dislike physical violence."

"Ok, I'll fill you in." said the man, rubbing his arm in pain. "Good. Come with us to this small room over here."They led and half dragged him into the room. A short while later they left him but the information they had learned was useful though. Smiling, they walked out onto the concourse towards the flight for Belfast.

# 17.28

The plane landed at Belfast Airport and Gail and William looked at each other. During the flight they had quietly discussed at length what the details of the case were and had come to the same conclusions that there was a"cell" of three to five on the mainland as well as somebody within either LICD or the police who was keeping the terrorists informed of the progress of the LICD.

William had heard a whisper of a rumour that Folkestone had managed to capture a member of the cell. So, if this was the case, why hadn't he been consulted?

"Penny for them?" "What?"

"You were miles away and we are last to disembark the plane." "Sorry, let's go then." He unclipped his seatbelt and rose from the seat and took down the two cases in the locker above them.

"Why did you have to bring all of this?" He asked her.

"Because the item I don't bring, will be the very thing I need, besides these cases are important and I never let them leave my side." They left the plane and with a speed that took Gail's breath away cleared customs.

"Friends in high places?"

"Yes, you could say that." Said William. "Where now?"

"Find the third taxi and take that one."

"Right." They left the airport and made for the third taxi and got inside. He tapped on the driver's shoulder.

"Hotel Londonderry and make sure no other taxi follows us."

"What, as in the films?"

"Right."

"Why did you choose the third one?" asked Gail.

"Because this way we live a little longer. Probably the first would have taken us anywhere but the right Hotel. The Second one would probably have followed it, then the occupants would have killed us. Remember we are on their territory now and they will always have the upper hand. Therefore, always go for the third or fourth taxi in the row. It's very unlikely that they will have four cars marked."

"Alright, but how did they know we would be here so quickly?"

"The phone is very quick and the fracas on the concourse at Heathrow didn't help. I know we got some useful information out of him, but it was always unlikely that he was working on his own."

"Sorry to interrupt, only it appears that we are being followed," said the Taxi driver, glancing in his mirror.

"Will you be able to shake them off?"

"Doubtful, how about I drop you about two hundred yards from the hotel and then drop the bags at the hotel?" the driver helpfully suggested.

"Ok, but add the lady to the plan, by that I mean drop her and the bags." said William

"How will that help?" asked Gail.

"They may think we are just sharing a taxi."

"Look go via the M2 and go around the roundabout twice, when they are on the other side, pull down the slip road and go like a bat out of hell." suggested Gail.

"Fine by me." She was banking on the large mound of the roundabout concealing them for those vital few seconds. That is exactly what happened. The taxi's radio crackled into life and since the driver had managed to re-tune to their frequency, they could now hear the some of the other taxis conversation.

"Hell! They seem to have given us the slip; the boss, I mean Patrick, isn't going to like this at all."

"It's not our fault, I told him that we needed more backups, but would he listen? No, not him."

"Heard enough sir?"

"No, keep it on, we might learn something." "…if we can get the girl that is."

"He'll come running as soon as we have her. Those sorts always do, they fancy themselves as some sort of James Bond."

"Look, let's go and have a drink first at 'The Border Inn'." "But that is off limits."

"Only at nights and if the security forces catch us." The radio went quiet, William turned to Gail.

"Do you want to go back?" "No."

"Right, then let's get moving."

"What do you plan on doing?" asked Gail with a grin. "Find their car and cause a small diversion."

"What with? Alright, I know, don't ask."

Bill turned to the driver. "Do you know where that is?"

"Yes, but it is not a place that ladies would frequent. Why, do you want me to take you there?"

"Please. Can you pull up alongside their parked car and keep our car engine running please?"

"No problem. Just leave it to me." He drove on towards 'The Border Inn.' and soon spotted their car and pulled up alongside it.

"This alright sir?"

"Perfect." William opened one of the two cases and removed a small magnetic mine complete with time delay and a can of pressurised paint. Leaving the taxi, he ran over to the other car. William slide under the back of the car and carefully placed the mine between the petrol tank and the exhaust pipe. Spray paint blended the whole thing into the underside of the car.

Then got out from under the car and wedged the remaining bits and pieces into his pockets and ran back to the taxi. Once inside he removed a small remote detonator from his pocket and told the driver.

"Now get out of here and fast."

"Right sir." The back wheels skidded as they pulled away from the car park. William smiled grimly and pressed the remote detonator as the car drove away.

"Wasn't that illegal?"

"Probably." They had driven about a mile when there was a large explosion and Gail turned around and a mushroom cloud arose from where they had just been. She turned pale and looked at William.

"Was that nuclear?" Her voice trembled as she spoke.

"No, just a device that looks like it. Most people will think that it is. Would you go near something like that?"

"Not likely!"

"Neither would most other people. Besides, the ones who want to look closer wouldn't have the right equipment at a moment's notice."

"So?"

"Well,by the time they have,the car will have been transformed into thousands of small pieces." Said William with a satisfied look on his face. Taking out a small radio transmitter, he tapped the small button twice and then put it away.

"What happens next?"

"The TV and radio will now give out messages to advise people to stay indoors. The army takes over and it looks for all the world like a real nuclear attack."

"What does this achieve?" asked Gail.

"It gives us a lot of time, puts us on the first foot for a change and throws them into confusion, as they won't be able to leave the area. Neither will they be able to find out if we are killed or not."

"Ok, I think that I am beginning to understand."

"Good, look, here is the hotel." He paid off the driver and took the cases off the floor in front of him as Gail climbed out and stretched herself.

"Come on. I'm tired."

"Coming." He followed her into the hotel, and they looked around in amazement. The place was empty and deserted. William leaned over the counter and noted the room number.

"Room 345 is ours."

"I thought I booked a suite?"

"You did, that is the suite number, now come on, I want to be up there and settled in as soon as they come back."

"Where is everybody anyway?"

"Probably ran off as soon as the radio or TV were interrupted, I shouldn't wonder."They got to their room and Gail went to turn the handle of the door.

"STOP!"

"Why?"

"Just keep quiet until I have finished." Opening both cases, he removed a small silver piece of metal, which he placed against the door.

Next, he took from his second case a pair of wires with a clamp at one end, and a probe at the other. He attached one end to the metal, the other ends were attached to a machine in the second case. A meter gave a reading as soon as the second wire was connected. He bent and adjusted the knob to bring the needle back to the lower end of the scale. Slowly he worked the metal probe over the whole of the door. Satisfied at last, he put his equipment away and turned to Gail. "Was there anyone else in the office when you arranged this room?"

"No, nobody at ..." She stopped. "What is it?"

"... I thought that someone had passed the door of the office, but door was nearly closed. I only thought I saw a shadow of someone."

"That explains it. This door is primed to explode as soon as it opened. I could eventually get in there, but it would take time, it's better to go to a different hotel. You go and see to that, while I'll leave a small device to make it look as though we tried to get in."

"Fine, I'll go and do that." Said Gail.

"Ok, I'll be down shortly."They both went their separate ways. A short while later both were in a new taxi heading towards another hotel. A small explosion went gone off as they had pulled away. William thought it was small enough not to have caused too much damage. The taxi driver looked in his mirror at the pair of them.

"Are you two something special?" "Why do you say that?"

"Take a look at the traffic."They both looked out of the window and saw for the first time the large traffic jams of cars driving the opposite way. William said nothing but looked at Gail and smiled.

Half an hour later they were settled into a new hotel. Like the first one, it was almost empty, and the manager had rubbed his hands together like Uriah Heap. He had explained that most of the staff had left as soon as the news of the bomb had been given, he had stayed as had one other member of staff, but alas he didn't have a chef. At this he had looked at them both and William had said nothing but smiled and acknowledged the fact that he would take his part in cooking.

Now both he and Gail were talking at length, having first swept the room and found it wasn't bugged and had set up a device on top of the HiFi.

"What now?"Asked Gail.

"It appears that more people believed the fake news broadcast than I thought. The upside is this will give us a bit more time to do what we came for."

"It may make them panic, have you thought of that?" asked Jane.

"If that had been the case, this hotel would be totally empty. Though it will be a lot easier to find out where they are hiding." said William, rubbing his chin thoughtfully.

"How do you plan on getting in touch with Joe? He is unlikely to act rationally when he arrives here is he?"Asked Gail,frowning. "No. So, he'll make straight for his home. Giving us the opportunity to grab him before he enters it." "Fine, but how do we get there?"

"Walk, it will be quicker than waiting about for a taxi." "No way, what about bicycles?"

"Alright, but only if you organize them, while I'll go and prepare the dinner."They went their separate ways and agreed to meet in about two hours.

+

Not twenty minutes' walk from the hotel, a masked man stood pointing the gun at both Sarah and her baby boy.

"Pay attention, your husband and father will be arriving tomorrow, at least that is what he has been strongly advised to do. If he turns up on time all is well, if not..." He left the sentence unfinished.

"But why us? There must be hundreds on the site." asked Sarah, tearfully.

"There are, but not all are married with a nice young child." "Are we really the only ones?"

"No, but you fit the bill in as much that..." He was interrupted by one of the other two men.

"Shut it, you talk too much." He jerked his head towards Sarah. "Go and get us some coffee."

"Alright." She left the room, glad to be out of their presence. "Why aren't the rest here yet? They said they would be here ages ago. It's so unlike him to be late. What shall we do?"

"Wait, be patient, don't get rattled. If we do then we lose everything that has been put in place for this. The British Government will have to deal with us on this one. Then they will be swept out of office for breaking their promise of 'We never do deals with terrorists'." he said in a bad imitation of Thatcher. Sarah brought in the coffee and picked up her son. He needed changing. She looked at the three men.

"I have to change him."

"Ok, go ahead, Pat can keep you company." She walked up the stairs to their bedroom and Pat followed them both. Up until now not one of the terrorists had spoken when she was alone with them. He did now though.

"You do realise that your husband must come and agree to our terms, or we are all stuck here."

"But what if he doesn't?" she whispered.

"Then let's hope for your sake that he does. He should, the air tickets were supplied, and he was given money. Given those things wouldn't you come here?"

"Yes, damn you. Yes." Sarah turned and busied herself with the boy. Pat walked over to the window and thought back to what he had joined all those years ago, it hadn't been like this then. He knew it was very unlikely he would live to an old age. Once in the ARI you were there for life. He turned to speak to Sarah, but she was gone. He ran down the stairs and found her with the boy asleep.

"Some guard you are, what were you doing?" asked the other gunman looking at him.

"Thinking."

"You don't think, you do as you are told. Right?" "Right sir."

"Good. Now go and get some food and steal a van and park it within two hundred yards of here. Then walk the rest of the route."

"I'll be as quick as I can."

"And just be sure you aren't followed." "Ok."

+

William had finished preparing the dinner in the hotel kitchens. It was almost ready for eating, the thing was, where was Gail? He looked up as she suddenly cycled in, with one hand on a new bike alongside her. He stepped into her way and grabbed the bikes.

"Thanks, I couldn't think which brake controlled which wheel. I didn't think until I started, it's years since I last cycled, but they are quite right, you never forget."

"Come and have some dinner." He led the way across the kitchen to the table.

"My, we have been busy. Look, I got a small radio. It appears that you started more than you thought. Some of the shopkeepers are staying. However, they are charging a huge amount for basic items."

"Thanks, look, I have to bend someone's ear, you carry on eating." He left the kitchen and ran up to the lobby and phoned the Prime Minister's office.

"I'd like to speak to the Prime Minister, it's William. Yes, I'll hold and before you ask, no, the line is not secure." He waited till the dulcet tones of the Prime Minister came on the line.

"Have you any idea what you have started?"

"I have a good idea, but I need the Armies help." "How?"

"I want them dressed in nuclear survival suits and carry out a house-to-house search."

"How long for?"

"As long as it takes. We can pretend to look for stored food, but at the same time who knows what we might find." He knew that she would get the drift of what he was saying. That an unauthorised search could lead to lots of juicy pickings of hidden weapons.

"Have you thought about the size of the operation?"

"Yes, I need Rose over here and I mean like yesterday." Said William.

"I don't think that is a good idea." "Why not?"

"If someone that important is seen flying into Belfast then people may start to put two and two together. I assume you don't want that to happen?"

"No, not really."

"Look, I'll try to get him in through Southern Ireland, but no promises."

"When?" asked William angrily. "Ten hours?"

"Too long, make it two."

"Have you any idea as to what you are asking?"

"With BOTOG working as well, no problem." He hung up and dialled the other number to Ian McKenzie a retired Army bomb disposal expert. One of the few in Belfast that knew of his cover name.

"Ian, it's William Dawson."

"You have started something haven't you William? It's got your handiwork all over it. Where shall we meet?"

"The Belfast Hotel kitchens." said William. "Twenty minutes?"

"Fifteen?" "Fine."

"See you, and bring your gear, we are hunting big ones tonight." added William.

"Right, I'll be there in fifteen minutes." Ian hung up. William went up to his room and took two guns out of the case along with ammunition, some of which he loaded in readiness. He just hoped that Ian had some of the new 5QUAB, for he was fast running out of it. After that, he went down to wait for Ian.

Ian turned up five minutes early. He peered around the kitchen door and took in Gail sat eating.

"You're not alone?" asked Ian. "No, this is my assistant Gail." "What do you want me here for?" "Eurotunnel."

"Ha." Laughed Ian bitterly. "Exactly, now can you help?" "You have found a bomb?"

"It hasn't been planted yet, but what I need to know is what sort of bomb the ARI are likely to use."

"I see. If you can get hold of the current list of the last ten devices they planted, then I might be able to tell you."

"Fine." William rose and left the room to phone his department head. By the time he returned, both Ian and Gail had finished eating. Ian looked up at William, who nodded that he had the list.

They both fell to talking to each other over past times and catching up with past times. They had met first on a ARI campaign in London and just as they were getting close to the main suspects, they had been taken off the case. Both had suspected there was an inside member of ARI and Ian, as a bomb disposal person, was disgusted with HMG, so decided to retire. He had gone to live in a village on the border, just outside Northern Ireland, but still managed to keep his hand in if he was asked to work a 'Black Op' on the quiet.

+

Once back from their trip to North Devon, Colleen had driven to London through the country roads. She assumed, correctly, that her flat would have been watched. With the access to the garage directly from the flat, it had been an easy matter to get to her car and drive out under the cover of darkness. Mr. Green would be waiting at their usual meeting place, but she aimed to try and get there first, if only to scoop the place out.

"Colleen?" She turned around and saw Mr. Green.

"Hello. You turned up then." Then she saw there were two other men with him.

"Your problem is you now know far too much Colleen." Green said, shaking his head sadly.

"You can't shoot me here, far too risky. I have left a list of contact names with…"

"I don't want to know. Now shut up and come with us." "No!"

"Bring her along with us."

"But the boss said we were to arrange her…" "Shut up, she stays alive."

"And the car?"

"Leave the car, go and hire a van. The place across from here does hire vans. Sort it out and meet us later."

"Right. Where shall we see you?"

"Charing Cross railway station. Now get going." He waved them away and turned to Colleen. "I think you are bluffing, but you might be telling the truth, so you live for now. But if you try to run, then you are dead."

"If you say so. Off to Folkestone are we?" "Are we?"

"Yes, Brady said so." Said Colleen with a brave face.

"He is another one that talks too much."said Green thoughtfully.

They had started walking to Charring Cross and flagged down a taxi to take them there.

A few minutes after they had arrived at the railway station,they were soon all in a blue hired van driving towards Folkestone. She drifted off to sleep and the two men and Green talked in low tones.

"We have to talk about the getting the stuff onto the site." said Green.

"Are you sure he will do it?"

"We have to assume he will." replied Green.

"If you haven't seen today's papers yet, maybe you should. Nuclear Explosion in Northern Ireland ARI? reads the heading and then they go on about the fact that the ARI have always said they are armed with nuclear weapons."

"But we don't have such weapons. Unless something has changed." Said one of the two thugs.

"This might change things, but who authorised its use?" said Green with a frown.

"You mean we have such a thing?" "Have done for some time."

"So where did we get it from?"

"The first one, indirectly from the Russians. Call it a gift. After that we decided to buy our own."

"And now it's been used?"

"It would seem so. The high council didn't want to use them though. They feared a public backlash from using one." Green stroked his chin thoughtfully.

"Let's think about this." They were silent and then Colleen woke up. She saw the paper and the headline. She shook the paper in front of Green.

"Is this your doing?"

"No way!" said Green in a shout.

"Well, I would suggest that the ARI go on the record as saying it isn't anything to do with them."

"Good idea, now listen. You have two choices in Folkestone. One, look after Sarah and her son or two, we'll hand you over to the Folkestone Police."

"Not really a choice, is it?"

"No but you will love the place we have for you." "You are sure about that?" Colleen asked doubtfully.

"Yes." Colleen settled back and waited to see what would unfold in time.

## 18.28

In Exeter, Brady woke and dressed and had breakfast. Then he made his way to Colleen's flat. Banging on the door failed to make any impression. He made his way down to the car park under the flats, but her car was not in it's usual spot. Next Brady went to the library but then found that she wasn't there either. Now he was starting to get worried, it looked as though Colleen had left him in Exeter and gone he didn't know where. Best thing to do was to clear out of Exeter as soon as possible he thought to himself. Once back at his flat he gathered the few items of his together and placed them in a small rucksack which he placed outside the door of the flat. Then he slipped out to a nearby shop and bought strong bottles of cleaning fluid before returning and wiping down all the surfaces in the flat that he may have touched. He pulled the front door closed pushed the keys through the letterbox and wiped down the door, picked up his rucksack and made his way down to the car and set off driving towards Folkestone aiming to get away as far as was possible from Exeter.

At the same time, Detective Inspector Armstrong and his team had planned an early morning raid on the flats. They pulled up outside the flats as Brady was already joining the M5. Armstrong's team of men were too late. It was apparent that nobody was in the flat. Armstrong turned to his men.

"There is nobody in the flat, so I need that door opened in a quiet and safe manner."

"It will take a few minutes; I'll get my tools sir." One of the young officers ran off and came back with a large tool kit. A kit that any crook would envy.

"Quiet, please." He said and bent to his task.

A few minutes later the doors were both open. Just as they were about to step into the flat Armstrong spoke.

"Stop!"

"What?"

"Don't go inside." "Why not?"

"Forensics are always on our back moaning that we mess things up for them. So now is our chance of seeing how good they are. Get onto the phone and get them up here as soon as possible." said Armstrong with a sound of irony in his voice.

One of the brighter men made off towards the car phone and called up the forensics department.

While deep groans about the extra work greeted the news at the forensic team, but they also knew that they were being offered a very unusual and rare chance. On the way to the flats the team talked among themselves.

"The locals will be wondering what there is about these flats, this is the third trip and questions will be asked soon."

"We will soon know more about the flats than the owners I should think."

"Though, if we find anything nasty, this time we can't blame CID."

"Neat trick, mind, getting us to go first. If there are any bombs or such like..."

"Oh, shut up, we have moaned about being called in late for years and now we are being given a chance to go in first we are complaining."

"Ok, let's go for it." The team had pulled up and they poured out and with their equipment ran in and up to the flats.

Four hours later they had picked the flat clean of any clues. It looked as though the people who had been in both flats had been there for some time. There were piles of food and loads of female clothes in one flat. The other flat was completely empty of everything except an old money belt found on a shelf at eye level. It had been pushed to the back, which probably explained why it had been missed. They would examine this later.

What they found in Colleen's flat excited them more. There had been a pile of notebooks written up in a spidery hand. These would have to be deciphered, but it was something to go on, and only one type of fingerprints. Armstrong was pleased with this and told them so. He asked that the notebooks be deciphered as soon as possible. Adding it would help if he had a selection of pages to show London.

"I now need some volunteers to work on those notebooks." "No sir! We have worked for seventy-two hours straight. The team are now more likely to make mistakes. Bring in another team from Somerset or Cornwall, then we can be of more help or else we rest for twenty-four hours. After which we would be a lot fresher."

"I take your point. Although you shouldn't have spoken like that sergeant. Let's get hold of a team from Somerset and I'll take one of the notebooks to London. Pass me the last one will you someone?"

"Sure, here you are sir."

"Thank you. Now, you stick around and the rest of you go home." There was a sigh of relief as they left the flats.

Armstrong had asked two of his men to guard the entrances, in case either of the two occupants should return, although he knew it was very unlikely. "Right, now come with me." He led the way into the flat's kitchen. "Notice anything unusual?"

"No sir."

"Why the locks on the kitchen door?" "Ah."

"Right, now tell me why the freezer is so full?" "If they both worked..."

"...but they didn't, well, one didn't anyway. He or she was too busy sealing cans."

"Sealing cans?"

"Sealing cans as they do in a factory, look here is the gadget. What do you think they were canning?"

"Not fruit sir."

"Would it help if I mentioned ARI?" "Oh, so it could be explosives?"

"Could be, which is why you and I are going to call on the Marines at Lympstone. They will have the right equipment for making these safe."

"Right, so we take them two at a time?"

"Yes." He picked up two and looked at Armstrong. "Ready sir?" "As ready as I'll ever be. "Lay on Macduff, and damn'd be him that first cries.'Hold, enough'!"

"You know Shakespeare well then sir?"

"Enough to quote correctly, rather than in error."


Half an hour later they had loaded all the cans into the boot of the car. Armstrong looked at the young officer, who was looking at the ground in front of him.

"Sir, can I come with you?"

"Of course, now let's get going."

They drove down to Lympstone and drew up at the barrier and produced his badge.

"DI Armstrong of Devon and Cornwall Police. You should have heard from my office by now."

"I have sir. You can go straight down to the hut. Number ninety six. Look for the number on the top of the posts, each one is numbered on from here as one follows two and so on." They thanked him and pulled away at a slow pace, eventually coming upon hut number 96. They pulled up by the door and parked the car.

"It seems to be in total darkness sir." "That doesn't mean anything." "They or he might not be there."

"Of course, there will be someone there, take one of the tins and follow me."

They entered the office and a man in a white coat came up to them.

"I understand you want to know the contents of these tins." "That's right."

"Well, bring them through into the lab."Armstrong turned and the young man sighed.

"I'll bring them, shall I sir?"

"Thanks. Look I don't even know your name yet." "Michael Digby sir. Devon forensics department." Armstrong turned to the man in hut ninety-six.

"Just to be clear, whatever you or we discover it does not go on any files or computer records. Only we three will know what is in the cans, understand?"

"Yes." "Good.

"So first off, where did you find the tin, if you don't mind me asking."

"In the kitchen along with the rest of them. Michael is bringing in the rest now. Why, how does that help?"

"Well, if they had been stored outdoors, I would think it more likely they would be bombs, but let's see shall we. It also makes more sense to have all of the tins."

"Why?"

"The contents of all of them might make something much larger. It, whatever it is, might have been broken down into small parts to smuggle in somewhere."

"I see, well that would make sense, for we found a machine for canning them."

"Good, for there must be the rest of these cans somewhere. I mean that you don't just buy fifty, so where are the rest?"

"Good point, I'll put someone onto it as soon as I get back." "Let's get on with this first. Bring one of the tins over to this machine, it shows what's inside and not just the outline but the actual item. It's better than the X-Ray machines at airports. We take the photos and wait like so." He waited for a few minutes, then the photographs popped out the side of the machine already developed. "They are working on a field version of this, but I can't see it being around for some years yet."

"So, what is in there?" "Not bombs."

"What then?"

"Let's open it and find out, it's some form of paper. At least this one is, that much I do know." He went to get a knife off the bench and Armstrong was studying the photographs.

"Wait. There is a bit of dark red in the bottom or top of the tin. Here you have a look."

"Then it's probably money, and that is a dye that would render it useless on opening the tin. Used by security people carrying a lot of money around, the dye can't be got out of the money, and it therefore renders the money useless."

"Then how do you get the money out?"

"I am not saying you can't, it is just that I need more time." "How much more?" asked Armstrong with a frown.

"Four hours."

"That much! Hell, I need to know how much is in there long before then."

"Well, it would speed things up if I had some help."

"Alright, I'll go and see if I can find anybody." He walked out to the car and phoned Andrews in Folkestone.

"Andrews, it's Armstrong from Devon and Cornwall, do you know where William Dawson is right now?"

"Sorry, he is out of the country. The nuclear explosion in Belfast..."

"What explosion?"

"It's all over the media, a nuclear device went off and we thought the ARI would never use it."

"Well, well. So how do I get hold of him?"

"Why do you need to?"

"I need him to waggle the ear of the Prime Minister." "Look, if he phones here, I'll pass on the message, ok?"

"It'll have to be. Tell him I need to speak as soon as possible, if not sooner." He put the phone back and went back into the lab. "There appears to have been a nuclear explosion in Northern Ireland."

"What!" They both exclaimed.

"You heard, but I don't think it fits, it would be counterproductive, nobody would be able to live there for years and years." said Armstrong with a sigh.

"So, are you thinking that it isn't real?"

"Could be, except for the fact that it takes a lot to fool all of those people."

"Fake bomb, looks like the real thing, but isn't, if you get my drift." Said the man from hut 96.

"Do we have such a thing?" asked Armstrong with interest. "Yes. It could be that this man in Northern Ireland has gained some sort of access to it." said the Marine from across the bench. "Never!" said Armstrong.

"Why are you so sure?"

"Well..."The phone rang in the lab and Armstrong waited for the Marine to answer it.

"It's for you." He passed the phone over to Armstrong. "Armstrong."

"William said to send his apologies but has arranged for extra help to be sent to you. He also said something else."

"A fake explosion?"

"How the hell did you know that? Only a few people know the existence of it."

"Can't tell you, classified." He hung up and looked at the Marine behind his bench. "Right, how did you know it was fake and I want an answer right now."

"London asked for us to develop a bomb along those lines some time ago. They reasoned with the Army already here, it would be the last place anybody would look for a research project of any kind. For five years we got nowhere. Then three months ago, we made the breakthrough. London requested three of them and although I had misgivings we did as we were asked. I knew if they were ever used, panic would ensue. What appears to have happened is that somebody has let one off, to force the ARI into an awkward situation."

"What sort of awkward situation?" asked Armstrong, looking worried.

"We think the ARI have a nuclear device, one from Eastern Europe, but are afraid to use it."

"So, I repeat. What awkward situation do you think they are in?"

"First, the public will assume that it is the work of the ARI or some other group. If on the one hand the ARI deny it, no one will believe them. Then on the other hand, if they step forward and claim responsibility, every country in the world will condemn them. And if they say they haven't got it, then even if they have it, they would be unable to use it in the future. So, I wonder what they are planning to do tonight?"

"Well explained, now can you start to make that machine that will open it?"

"Yes, and if either of you are handy with your hands?" "I'm not, but Michael might be able to help."

"I do a little bit of DIY sir."

"Right, I'll drive back to Exeter and you two start work."

He had a pile of paperwork on his desk. Most of it he knew needed just his signature. He drove onwards, while thinking about what he had learned as he drove.

+

In Belfast Pat Doyle was caught in a long queue for traffic heading out of the city. He hadn't had the radio on, so hadn't heard about the explosion, so was quite prepared to sit there and wait.

Meanwhile, the terrorists and Sarah, had heard the news on the radio about the explosion. They knew that it was unlikely that the ARI would have bombed a pub they frequented regularly. They had also heard the news that nobody had claimed responsibility. That was not surprising, it was the usual ARI response to start with and much later they would admit responsibility, but not until there had been a lot of speculation.

This however was different, there had been a note of panic in the presenter when mentioning the bomb was of the nuclear type. The others in the room had at once all started to talk at once.

"Quiet, I want to listen to the weather forecast." "What! A nuclear bomb goes off and he talks about..."

"Shut up! If we know which way the wind is blowing the radioactivity, then we go in the opposite direction."

" ... And now Northern Ireland. Forecasts of rain spreading to the north east from the south west with heavy winds. Our listeners in and around Belfast are urged to stay indoors."

"They are on to us, I don't know how, but they are. We have to get out of here."

"Just a moment where is Pat?"

"Still not here? We will just have to go on without him." The phone rang and he snatched it up. "Yes?"

"Pat here, look I'm stuck in traffic. What do you want me to do?"

"Come straight here, bring as much of the food as you can carry. Ditch the van and walk."

"Ok, it seems that everyone is on the move."

"We are moving too; it appears that some sort of nuclear device has gone off."

"What! So, what is the next move? Has Joe arrived yet?"

"He was supposed to be here hours ago, but this has put a whole different complexion on things."

"How about leaving the woman and kid and getting out of here fast?"

"Are you mad? This has taken years to set up, while it's true that I hadn't forecast this, we can sort something out."

"Ok, I'm on my way."

"Fine, look there is someone at the door. See you later." They all looked towards the door and watched it as it opened, and Joe walked in.

"Well, I am here as you said I would be." He walked over to Sarah and his son and wrapped his arm around them both. "Now what?"

"I suggest that you make the most of being together for unless you do as we say, she is going to die slowly and in agony."

"You don't need to draw a picture. Now do you mind if I talk to my wife in private?"

"Not at all. You don't mind being searched first though?" "No."

"By saying that, I know you are clean. Right, go on upstairs and talk away."

Joe led Sarah up to their bedroom and closed the door. "I have missed you Sarah, what do I do?"

"Talk it through like we always have done."

+

William and Gail were cycling on the road towards Joe's house. Empty cars littered the roads. It was evident that this was going to take a lot of sorting out. He was grateful that it wasn't his job. He had talked to Gail at length about this and they knew that looking for Joe was like looking for a needle in a haystack, in fact that would have been easier. Bill was quite happy as he had managed to get the Prime Minister to evoke the Emergency

Powers Act.

To be used in times of war and other dire emergencies, it gave both him and the Army very sweeping powers.

+

Joe and Sarah had left a message scribbled on a bit of paper before putting it in a bedside drawer. Now they were back downstairs waiting to see what would happen next.

"Mr. O'Brian, or can I call you Joe? This is what you are going to do. Go back to work on the site and in due course you will be given the bomb and told where to put it. We will still hold your family as hostage and if we find the bomb has been found or tampered with in any way, we will kill them. When you have placed the bomb in the tunnel exactly as we tell you, then we will deposit half a million pounds into a Swiss bank account in your name."

"But I don't want the money, it will look as though I did it for that reason alone."

"Exactly." "Oh."

"Now you can leave ahead of us, your plane ticket was booked a long time ago, think yourself very lucky that you have a ticket, I hear they are like gold dust."

"Goodbye Sarah. Take care." "I will think of you always."

"Goodbye." He turned and left the house.

"Let's go, pack a few things for about a month, we are going away from here."

"Which way?" "Due south." "Then where?"

"By boat to England, the usual means. Now come on." The other terrorist walked in as they started to get their gear together.

"What gives?"

"Apparently, we are off to England. How close is the van?" "Half a block away."

"Good, we walk, and then ride."

"No chance, it has no petrol and it's over-heated." "Blast. We walk until we see another car that has been left."

"Oh, you'll see plenty of those, but they all have the same problem."

"So, what do you suggest?" "A bus?"

"Silly suggestion, look go and see if you can find any petrol." said the leader with a sneer.

"Right. Pack my gear while I am gone."

"Sure." He went off to look for petrol. Half an hour later he returned.

"Well, did you get anything?"

"A Landrover 120 it's full to the brim of petrol, it's got two spare tanks full as well."

"Ideal. It can go off road as well. Come on, let's go." They left and walked down to the Landrover and climbed inside. "Right drive straight across country and stop for nothing. Any roadblocks we go around."

"Sure."

"Then what are you waiting for?" They drove on towards the south of southern Ireland and down to the southeast coast. In a small village they knew very well, they pulled up outside a thatched cottage. They went inside while their leader stayed to negotiate the means of getting to England with the owner.

"I thought you would have turned up sooner." "What's that supposed to mean?"

"Well with your nuclear bomb going off, I guessed you and your lot would want to make your way south. The going rate is five thousand, per head."

"What! Last time it was five hundred in total."

"Last time there wasn't a nuclear explosion or a reward on your head was there?"

"No, but it wasn't us."

"Is that so? Treat it as inflation, if Thatcher hadn't brought it to our attention, we would never have realised how easy it is to make money. Supply and demand. We supply, you demand. The only difference is the price. Get it?"

"Yes, but I'll not pay. I'll go someplace else." "You will be back, I know it."

"Sure." He walked off towards the other houses and the owner of the boat walked back into his house.

"He turned me down" he said to his wife. "Oh dear."

"But he'll be back, and I told him as much."

"Do you think so? I think you asked too much, three thousand would have been enough."

"We will never be able to return here. Go and get the money and be ready to go."

"Right." She rose and walked through to the kitchen. The leader opened the door and came inside.

"Like you said, no boats. Is this your doing?"

"Of course not. Now have you got the money or not?"

"Yes, half now, half once we get to England, Bude to be exact." "About time too." He watched at the man counted the money onto the table, before he gathered it together and put a rubber band around it. "Right, let's go." He called to them all to follow him and his wife came down the stairs with their suitcase. He handed her the bundle of money, and she put it away in the case. But not before the terrorists had glimpsed the stack of notes that filled it inside.

They all walked down to the boat and untied it. Minutes later they were heading for south west England.

# 19.28

William had found the note in the bedside table. Now Gail and he were standing while the Army forensics team searched the house for any clues. While they knew each second delayed meant the terrorists were getting further away, they also realised that any clue left would help them, so this would be time well spent.

"Why can't they work faster?" asked Gail. "Mm?"

"Nothing, I just wish they would hurry up."

"We haven't found anything else sir." said one of the forensic team coming to where they both stood.

"I want to phone London and Folkestone first."

"Ok, we'll meet outside." Gail turned and left. William picked up the phone and told Folkestone to inform London that it was most likely Joe was now heading back to Folkestone and going to plant a bomb. He was to be watched around the clock and if anyone went near him, follow them. William looked up as he was aware that Gail stood beside him and watched him speaking. Once the phone was replaced, she asked him.

"Why do you know more than anybody else?"

"I've have been on the case longer; do you want to travel back with me or…?"

"You, I might learn something then." "Oh."

"You will tell me all about it on the plane?"

"No, but I'll write it all down for you to read sometime." "Clever."They left the house and drove to Belfast airport,where they were soon on the aircraft and heading towards London.

+

Andrews walked into the police station and made his way down to the cells, to the one containing the ARI prisoner.

"Well, how is he?"

"Very quiet for him. It was noisy to start with, but he has been quiet since last night. Do you want to go in?"

"Yes. But be ready to slam the door closed after me if I come running out. Understand?"

"Yes?"

"Good, open the door." He braced himself and walked into the cell. What greeted his eyes was not a pretty sight. The man was spinning around on a rope that was attached from the light cord.

Although the body was suspended upside down, he could see a mark around the neck. He guessed that the prisoner had been hung and then taken down and put the other way up. Andrews left the cell.

"I need a list of everybody who visited this cell in the last three days. I want it on my desk in half an hour, got that?" he snapped at the policeman by the door. Walking fast to his office, he decided that he could get on with his paperwork.

Half an hour later the list was brought in and placed on his desk. He ran his eyes over the list and the one name sprang out. Mr. Green. He had been admitted late last night. Booked in as the solicitor of the prisoner, not his killer. He had been in there half an hour, ample time to kill somebody and hang them upside down. It was time to look for this elusive Mr. Green. Andrews pulled the phone towards him and called in the forensics department, after which he left the office and phoned London and left a message for William on his answer phone.

## 20.28

Ten hours later William walked in with Gail on his arm. He knocked on Andrew's office door and pushed it open.

"Hi, any problems need sorting out?" asked William. "Don't be funny, it doesn't suit you." snapped Andrews. "My we are upset."

"You haven't been home yet and got my message, have you?" "No, why?"

"We now have a dead ARI man in the cells." "How?"

"Apparently, first he hung himself, then once dead, he took himself down, turned himself upside down retied the rope and stayed that way for another twenty hours."

"But that's..."

"...of course, it's impossible. We need to seek out and find a Mr. Green."

"The ARI solicitor?" "Right first time."

"Well things really are moving and fast."

"Wait a minute, we have a dead man here and you say things are moving?"

"To bring you up to speed. In Belfast, the ARI are probably heading south, and Joe is heading back to Folkestone. He was on the same flight as us, but we made sure he didn't see us."

"Oh."

"And at Exeter they found tins of money." "Tins of money?"

"Yes, the stuff you spend to get things with. Weapons, bombs, cars and houses for example?"

"Where are they getting it from?" asked Andrews with a perplexed frown.

"By this time tomorrow, we might be on the way to finding out. A small team are in the West Country looking at the tins now."

"Anything else?"

"Only once Joe has planted the bomb, no doubt he will be killed and then the problems will really mount up."

"Cheerful aren't we."

"I like to think so. Now I intend to phone Exeter and see what they have been up to while I have been away." Said William.

"Fine." Andrews watched him hit the number on his cell net phone.

"Armstrong? William Dawson here." "Now what do you want?"

"Update, is what I want, phone me back on this number in ten minutes."

"Right, ten minutes."

William replaced the phone and strode over to a large map of the whole of southern England and traced his finger along a line between Exeter and Folkestone and London and Folkestone and Oxford and Folkestone. Then he drew lines between Exeter and London and Exeter and Oxford. Finally, he drew lines from the centre of each town towards the intercept point of the other lines. A triangle developed within three places. Salisbury, Andover, and Winchester. Within the triangle there were about forty villages of different sizes. He decided that the time had come to start looking for a place which would be a good centre for driving to all four places that had been seen in the wider picture so far. He tapped a pencil on the map.

"I think that we should look in this area for the main hideaway, don't you?"William said, glancing at his watch.

"No, they would stand out too much. In a town they could disappear into the background." Replied Andrews wearily.

"Such as?"

"Southampton or Bournemouth."

"You could be right. Though I still feel that we should look in the villages. Let's do both, you go and arrange for your counterparts to search Southampton and Bournemouth and I'll throw a cordon around that area."The phone rang on Williams mobile and he snatched it up. "Yes?"

"Armstrong here, look we have a mass of stuff for you. I suggest you switch on the recorder."

"Done that. Fire away."

"Fifty cans of money have been opened and the dye has not been sprayed onto the money, we have looked at the serial numbers and they mostly come from a bank robbery in Folkestone. The flats have both been checked over. We know whoever used one flat was clearly a professional. The place was clean of fingerprints and the key pushed through the letterbox." "Now the owner of the other flat was called Colleen Kent apparently. But she has not been seen for five days. Known to be researching for a book she was writing about Exeter. Has written a fair bit too by all accounts. Any developments in Northern Ireland?"

"Nothing, we think that the ARI cell from Exeter may be heading for a place somewhere within the triangle of Salisbury, Andover and Winchester."

"Why there?"

"Get a map of the South of England and look at it. At the same time bear in mind there are four places that we have had sightings of one or more of them."

"Right. And the Irish cell, if they fled Belfast where do you think they will go next?"

"Bude."

"Where?"

"Bude in Cornwall." Replied William. "I know the place, it's just so quiet." "Just what they want then isn't it?"

"Any particular reason? Before we go chasing off to Bude?" "We had captured a ARI member here, but he is now dead.

Killed."

"Oh, you think they might be tidying up the loose ends?"

"It is starting to look that way. We were hoping for a flood of information when he was captured. We have several questions that need answering. Any member of the ARI would help give these answers."

"How are you so sure that Bude is the place they will head for?"

"Look at a map with Ireland and Devon on it. Draw some lines. Look, I have to go, thanks for the update and keep us posted." Willaim switched off the phone and looked at Andrews.

"I want to re-run the events with you, you might spot something we are all missing. So, let's go outside to walk and talk."The two men got up and walked out into the sunshine.

"Fire away." Said Andrews.

"To start with, we both agree that there is a plot to blow up the tunnel at some point."

"Agreed"

"We need to look at the reasons, something that nobody has done yet. Joe O'Brian, for reasons we didn't know at that time, is selected as their candidate, maybe as early as the interview, I don't know. He gets the job and joins the firm. A few days later he is approached and offered work in the tunnel. He has previously done some work in a mine some years ago. This offer is unusual in coming so soon after he has started working as a JCB driver."

"He ignores the offer and carries on working on the top site, by the sidings. Suddenly he gets promotion, this he correctly guesses will bring him to the attention of quite a few people. Well he isn't wrong about that."

"He is now approached again and told that if he wants to avoid his wife and child from being hurt, he must work in the tunnel. Joe weighs up the consequences and for reasons we don't yet know about, he turns them down and then he tries to get in touch with his wife, but he can't, he talks this over with Mary Orchard and her mother."

"I think that he realised they were all at risk from that moment onwards. The people who approached him could kidnap them and this might be a breaking point. Everyone has a breaking point, some better than others. Anyhow, Joe is offered a large pay rise to work in the tunnel and he is tempted as he has debts at home. He at the same time manages to get a list of bomb locations on the site, don't ask me how."

"We learn about that time of Sean Smith's death. Painted messages appear on the walls of Mary Orchard's bedroom. You place all three of them in a safe house. We want him to go back to work and by a stroke of luck so does he. Before that can happen, he is 'kidnapped', I know he was found again, but I think it was to show us how easy it was for them to kidnap him." "Joe agrees to go back to work; Mary Orchard goes off to Oxford while her mother goes to another safe house."

"What next? Ah, we look at the blown-up house that seems to have been blown up to do two things. One to show the ease of how the ARI can carry out bombing on the mainland and the second was to cover the body of one of the ARI members. We learn that there has been an insider here in the police station all along, it made life a lot easier for them. Joe moves in to share Thomas Swift's caravan and he is feeling nervous as he hadn't been approached for a long time."

"A year goes by, during which there are threats to the tunnel, ignored as it happens. We think that they were building up a supply of men working in the tunnel. Joe is re-approached and told they now have his wife and child. He is told to fly to Belfast and see them. Swift tells us that the meeting between Joe and the ARI is going to be set up that night, but they give us the slip. We track them to Belfast and after we have set off the look-alike bomb, we just miss them."

"Joe returns here, All that I know, now from here onward I am guessing. I think that his wife and kid are heading for Bude in Cornwall. Personally, I think that they will then head for the triangle set between Winchester, Salisbury, and Andover. there are loads of villages where they could hide out. There that's about all I know for now, have I missed anything?"

"Only that we went through the site files and found a hundred and fifty or so, ARI suspects. Couldn't prove anything though, so we had to release them. Why Bude and that triangle?" asked Andrews.

"Look at the map and I'll explain. Bude is in straight line from the Southeast of Ireland and is one of the few places you could land a boat. I know that there are harbours, but they tend to be manned. Whereas a beach like Bude is far better bet. The triangle is at the centre where the lines cross when you take in the four centres where ARI have been. Folkestone, Oxford, Exeter, and London. Both you and Armstrong in Exeter think that Southampton and Bournemouth is a better location for them to make for, on the mainland."

"So, tell me, how do we stop Joe from planting the bomb?" "We don't."

"What!"

"No, we let him plant it and then we go in and defuse it. Then leave it safely in its place. If we take it out, then either they get Joe to plant another one or use another person who we don't know. This way, we do at least have an idea as to who we are dealing with. We also know the person they have got to plant the bomb."

"You have it all worked out, don't you?" "it's my job. That's what I get paid for."

"Is that all we must discuss? I take it you are going off to search that area of yours?"

"Yes. By the way all of this was off the record." "I quite understand."

They turned and walked back to the office. Once inside Andrews looked at Gail, who had remained there while they had talked.

"You both had better get going."

+

Brady had arrived at Folkestone town centre and parked. He knew that there was house in the town that he could use. He had a gut feeling that Mr. Green was based here too but that worried him.

He could distinctly remember an ARI safe house down here. He walked along the sea front until he came to an unoccupied seat and sat down and began to think. Where was he to go?

He could try to get work on the tunnel but realistically Brady knew that was very unlikely, security would now have been increased tenfold. The only thing was that he already knew of three members of ARI working on the tunnel, who could probably get him in. Brady realised that the police may have infiltrated the site, but that would be a whole lot better than Mr. Green chasing him to kill him.

First things first, he would start to look for that ARI safe house. An hour later he had made his way up to Cheriton Road and was turning into Firs Road where after a few minutes he turned into Wood Cottage Lane. He looked for about half an hour before it dawned on him that it was over a year ago. The house was most likely sold. He turned around as he reached the last house and was taken by surprise as two men rushed out and pulled a hood over his head. They dragged him indoors and upstairs.

"Don't try to remove the hood."

"Ok, whatever you say. Who are you?" said Brady in a muffled voice.

"Do you think we would tell you?"

"Suppose not."A voice sniggered from the doorway.

"Well, well, Brady, what a pleasant surprise. Kind of you to join us. Now I don't have to go looking for you."

"It's Green, isn't it?" "Mr. Green to you."

Brady tore off the hood and looked him in the face. "So, what are you doing down here Mr. Green?" He spat out the name with contempt.

"More to the point, what are you doing up here? You got away from Exeter then. Such a pity, as you don't fit into my plans at all."

"Why pull me off the street then? I could have walked right past here and been none the wiser. Now by bringing me here, you risk a lot, I'm sure that they will be proud of you. Now where is Colleen?"

"Why do you ask that?"

"She wasn't at the flat. Do you know where she is?" asked Brady.

"Tell me, what happened to her possessions?" replied Green, ignoring Brady's question.

"I don't know, I left Exeter in hurry and cleared out of my flat PDQ I can tell you. I wonder how you feel, knowing that you probably have two of the most wanted people. The police will be pleased with you, but you don't plan on going to the police, do you?" said Brady sadly.

"Ok, you have guessed most of it. We are waiting for the last piece to fall neatly into place. We have a man to plant the bomb and are holding his wife and kid. He'll do as we want."

"But why would you bring them here?" "Did I said they were going to?"

"If they were going elsewhere, Colleen wouldn't be here." "Did I say she was?" replied Green, frowning.

"You didn't say she wasn't either." He grinned and sat down on the bed.

"Comfy."

"That's as may be, but you are not going to be using it very long."

"Shame."

"Ok, so we may or may not have Colleen here, but that doesn't mean you get to know all the facts."

"A delay in getting mother and son to arrive?"

"All right you know everything or have guessed most of it. I do have a plan but as I said I haven't thought of where you will fit in yet."

"Look, this morning I was in Exeter, now I am in Folkestone and am tired."

"Go and rest then for a few hours. I think of what to do with you in the meantime."They left Brady in the room, and he heard them lock and bolt his door.

+

The boat landed at Bude, and they were met by an ARI sympathiser. He walked down to the group.

"Move quickly, I have a van waiting. I didn't know that there would be so many of you. Should have guessed though when the bomb went off that the boat owner and his wife would want to come as well."The leader looked at the van and whistled.

"Where did you get this, it's brand new isn't it?"

"Of course, that way we don't bring attention to ourselves, don't just stand there, get on board and we'll talk as we drive."

"What about the boat?" asked its owner. "Leave it where it is. It will be safe."

"So where are we off to?"

"Folkestone. So, settle down for a long trip."

"By the way, we'll need this to be altered. It must seat eleven and with the extra space, you can fit two extra petrol tanks." said Patrick O'Conner with a frown.

"Fine. I doubt that Ford would have liked that, but it can be altered."They drove on.

+

The police had arrived at Bude beach twenty minutes after the van had driven off. The abandoned boat was poured over by the forensic team. Ten hours later, all far too late, they had most of the names of ARI members who had come over to the mainland. There were little things they had found on the boat as to who they were. Details were sent by fax to Exeter, Folkestone, London, and Oxford.

Five hours later, records from Belfast and London had confirmed the names of most of them and photos of three of them. A raid was carried out on a small village in Ireland. The house was empty with the door left open. Neighbours said the boat belonging to the owner was not in the harbour.

One person didn't appear to have a record or a photo but was known locally as 'The Boss' so it was assumed he was the leader of the cell.

+

In Folkestone Joe was back at work and was busy placing the last one of the seven pieces of the tunnel into place and then swung the pump hose for the grout into place and indicated to his colleague to switch it on. The grout poured out into the space between the outer ring of concrete and the wall of the original cutting. He wondered to himself where would they fit a bomb; the security had been greatly increased of late. The pump automatically stopped as the hole filled to overflowing. One of his colleagues leaned over to him.

"Someone wants to talk to you Joe. I'll cover for you. He is back there." He jerked with his thumb. He walked further back to the place that he had indicated, and his heart sank. He saw it was one of the two men he had met before.

"About time. This is how you are going to plant the two bombs." The terrorist took a piece of chalk from his pocket and drew a diagram on the wall of the tunnel"here and here. The pressure will be so much greater down here, so we need to be sure."

"You said a bomb, not two." "One, two, what does it matter?" "A lot."

"Just remember that we have your family." "Not likely to forget am I?"

"We are very unhappy that the security service found your home so quickly."

"Well, they could have found my records." "Unlikely, we made sure they were destroyed." "How do I plant the two of them?"

"Drop them into the filler hole of the key piece, one each side of it. Just before you do that, hit the red button. Once they are in there, you can pour the grout on top of them."

"How do you expect me to manage that? The team are working with me all the time."

"You will be on an emergency relief team for the next fortnight. There will be an incident that requires you to attend. That will give you time to do the work."

"Ok, but what about the TBM?"

"It will break down. For a ten minutes only." "Really? They are checked two times a day."

"It will break down, and you will manage to do what we ask and fix it. The whole thing shouldn't take you more than five minutes maximum. Then the TBM will be fixed and working again, with

306

a bit of luck the management would not even notice. "But we are behind schedule already,every minute is docketed.

Reports have to be made."

"Then give your team some of this." He passed Joe a small foil packet. "Just one of these per person at the start of the day shift. You will be amazed by the results." Joe looked at the packet and then at the man offering it. "It's poison, isn't it?"

"No, not at all. It helps to get you through the day. Look, I'll take one myself." He swallowed the small pill and smiled at Joe. "If it were poison, then I'd hardly be likely to try it myself, would I?"

"Suppose not."Said Joe, looking down at the floor of the tunnel and scuffing it with his boot.

"Just one more thing, make sure you do it right. There can be no mistakes or a second chance."

"Alright, when do I get the bombs?"

"We'll get in touch when we need to hand them over, watch you pour in the grout on top of them and the job is finished. You get a large sum of money for doing five minutes' work. Remember to give yourself and the team that pill in the morning."

"Right." He walked back and carried on working.

## 21.28
## TEN DAYS LATER

Joe awoke and looked around the hut. Ever since his return to the site and finding the caravan burnt out, he and Thomas Swift had been forced to live in the basic accommodation provided by the companies building the tunnel.

While Brooks had been sympathetic, he had explained that as their accommodation could have been provided for by the firm, he would be unable to provide any compensation for the loss of the caravan. He did agree to investigate how the two men had managed to both get onto the site and set fire to it and would contact the police. With that they had to be satisfied.

Joe swung himself up out of his bunk and dressed, he was working a back-to-back shift today. That is where a worker works all day, then goes on to work all night. By doing this you then work night shifts. Though the disadvantage is that you get extremely tired. The reverse happened when you came off the night shift, a nice long break.

Joe caught the workers bus going over to the 'hangman's room' so called as with all the clothes winched up high, it looked like a lot of hung bodies.

Then he took the small working train and travelled underground to the back of the TBM now working on the second main tunnel. It was now actually possible to walk from France to England, using the service tunnel. The main two tunnels were yet to be finished. He joked with the rest of the team as he travelled the miles underground. Then they all disembarked, after which the train took the slurry in the wagons back the way they had come.

Joe worked on through the day, though down here the only means of telling how long was to wear a watch.

It was late in the morning that a tap on his shoulder indicated that he should turn around. The two men stood there wearing hard hats and muddy overalls, as if they had been working all morning.

Without a word, the first one passed him a sketch of the tunnel and two marks where the two bombs were to be placed. The other put his finger across his throat to indicate that he had better not fail or else. Joe nodded and went back to his workstation.

He had yet to figure out a way of getting anywhere near to the front of this massive, nearly two hundred metre long, machine. By mid-afternoon, he had worked out a way and at seven that night the conveyor broke down and all hell broke loose.

Wasting no time, Joe moved swiftly across and scrambled up the machine to the last segment which had just been placed in readiness for the grout that had yet to go into the hole. He dropped the first package in the hole and scratched the surface of the key stone with his initials. He had been doing this on every keystone he put in since he knew that he would plant the bombs, but this one he ringed around. Then dropped the second down through the hole, the only difference was that he hit the button on this one.

He hoped that if just one explosive ever went off, it would be insufficient to do any serious harm. He could now relax knowing that he had done as they wanted.

He finished the shift and after he had returned to the surface and showered, he made his way to his bunk as he was dead tired.

Joe stopped in his tracks when he saw who was on the bunk. One of the two who had originally approached him.

"What now?"

"You are coming with us." "Me?"

"Yes, we are going somewhere for you to see Sarah and the kid."

"Fine."

"Did you plant the bombs?"

"You know I did, you said you would watch me do it. Didn't you see me drop them in the hole?"

"Somebody did. Now stop worrying and get some of your clothes together." He watched as Joe quickly gathered his few items and put them in a rucksack.

"Good, now keep quiet, we are going out in a Landrover." "I won't disturb anyone."

"Sensible man." They left the hut and walked over to the Landrover and climbed in. They drove off towards Cheriton Road. Joe knew that he was too tired to really take in where he was being taken.

They pulled up at the house and bundled Joe inside and the driver drove off to abandon the car.

"So now I have done what you want, you can release us all can't you?"said Joe in a tired voice, once he was inside the house. "No. Your family yes, but you know far too much I'm afraid." said Green with a frown. He motioned Joe upstairs and Sarah was left looking helpless as Green followed Joe up the stairs. "You can't do this to him." she called out.

"No?"

"No of course you can't. Look he did what you wanted." "Agreed, but he is too big a risk." Green motioned Joe into a bedroom. "Like I said you are just too big a risk." He levelled a gun at Joe's knee and shot it, then while Joe rolled on the floor, he shot him in the chest. Then leaving the body in the room, Green locked the bedroom door and pocketed the key. He went downstairs again and noticed there was a silence. He waved the gun at Sarah and the rest of the group. "Now let's get out of here, the van is round the back."They all left through the back of the house and climbed into the van and drove off towards Oxford.

+

Andrews stood looking at the map of Folkestone. A phone call had been received saying a neighbour had heard shots being fired. From which house it was impossible to say. It was close to the tunnel works though. Andrews groaned aloud. That of course covered hundreds of houses, He just didn't have the manpower to do a house-to-house check. He opened his office door and called for one of his Sergeants.

"Where do you think the shots were fired and where might they be hiding?"

"Around this area sir?" He indicated the area that took in the house they had been in.

"How many houses are in that area?" "I don't know, but I can find out sir."

"Well do that and if there is under a couple of hundred, get as many officers on the 'knocker' as possible."

"Right sir."

"And don't come back and until you have something positive to report."

"Yes sir!" He left and Andrews sat down and applied himself to his paperwork where for the first time in weeks the out tray was higher than the in tray. He bent over his desk and carried on…

+

Three hours later, in Oxford, the van pulled up at the centre of Headington at the traffic lights and then drove to St Leonard's car park. A rented a house in Windmill Road lay just across the road from the car park. Mr. Green had told them where to go. Sarah looked at Patrick.

"What have you done with my husband?" "He'll follow on later."

"Don't believe you, I heard shots in Folkestone."

"Suit yourself." Patrick shrugged his shoulders and locked up the van. He took her by the hand and with a gun in the small of her back made their way over to the house and unlocked the door. Once inside he turned to the group.

"We have had to come here as Folkestone was getting far too risky to stay there. I want one of you to take her and the kid upstairs to the room at the back, it has its own toilet." Sarah and the child were bundled up the stairs into the room and the door locked. Back downstairs a conversation was in full flow.

"…but as a larger group here in Oxford, don't we run a larger risk of being found out?"

"Possibly, now does anyone have any ideas on what we should do with the wife and kid?" asked Patrick O'Conner.

"Not yet, but have you seen the kitchen, it's wonderful."

"Well, we are here for as long as it takes me to find a suitable very large old property. I want us to be undisturbed for at least the next year. If anyone sees anything at all suitable, let me know." He left the group and went out to the car park and picked up one of the two cars he had bought and drove to Summertown.

Pulling into a lay-by, Patrick made his way over to the phone box and stepped inside, he reached into his back pocket and discovered that although the phonecard was there, his wallet wasn't. He tried to recall when he had last used it. Oh well, the phone call came first…

+

Andrews was tired and wanted to go home and rest. As for the first time ever, he had managed to clear his desk completely of paperwork. He leaned back in his chair and sighed. He knew that he had a hundred men out there on a door-to-door fact finding basis. The problem was that although it was only two hundred houses or so, it would be ages before they had been all checked and cleared.

Andrews knew that he had a long night ahead of him. The phone ringing beside him bringing him back to reality.

"Andrews."

"William here, I have been through this area with a tooth comb, but nothing here, I must have got this bit wrong."

"That's a first." "What is?"

"You admitting you got something wrong. So, you had better come back, all hell is breaking out."

"In what way?"

"Just come back and I'll tell you all about it."

"I would, but after I'll have been to Oxford and then to Exeter." "Oxford and Exeter! What do you think that you can see there that they haven't already faxed to us here?"

"Oh, I don't know, maybe there is something. Besides I want to see the tins."

"Oh, the tins." "Yes, the tins."

"Well, don't be too long." He replaced the phone and slammed one of his drawers closed. Why should he have to be stuck in the office, when Bill was out in the field enjoying himself? The phone rang on his desk, and he snatched it up.

"Andrews." "That you sir?"

"Yes, what's happened?"

"We think we may have found the house. The forensic team are on their way, I thought you ought to know."

"Thanks." Picking up the phone, he dialled the forensic desk. When he didn't get an answer, he got up and ran down to it. The officer who was supposed to be behind the desk, wasn't there. Andrews walked around behind the desk and looked down. The man lay on the floor on his back with a plunger of a syringe stuck into his heart. The plunger was hardly pressed in, and the rest of the tube was empty. Just air into the heart then, thought Andrews grimly to himself.

Bad though this was, his more pressing question was, who was supposed to be driving out to the house? Certainly, it wasn't the forensic team, a glance at the desk made him realise that the desk signing in book was missing too.

Standing up, he raced out to his car. A quick glance underneath the car and then got in. Then using the car phone,he phoned one of the on-call police doctors and told him to sort the problem that he would find in forensic depart. Then he drove on towards the house.

He knew it was the right house by the blue flashing lights and as soon as he was inside, he told them to go and turn them off. Running upstairs, Andrews peered into the bedroom through the now open door at the body of Joe and turned to the policeman.

"Stand everyone down except the man who discovered this house."

"Right sir. Sir, do you know this man?" "I did."

"Oh, we have phoned the police doctor. He says he will be a little late."

"Yes, that is not surprising." "Oh."

"I'll tell you all about it someday. Make sure you look after that body."

"We will. Is there a reason sir?"

"We have a real problem now and life, if it wasn't going too well now, then it is not going to get any easier."

Right sir."

"Now leave me alone, I need to think. Is there a car that is available right now?"

"Yes, use mine." He led the way out to his police car. Andrews got in and wondered what he was going to tell William Dawson when he turned up.

He had been complaining that he wasn't out in the field, ha! That was a joke. He sat in the car and put his head into his lap to think over what was happening all around him.

+

The next day, William arrived back in Folkestone and swung the car into the police station's car park. He got out and slammed the door after him, then he marched up to the station on inside. Anybody could see that he was upset, and that was putting it mildly.

The desk sergeant got a curt acknowledgement. He strode down the corridor towards Andrews office, flung the door open and marched up to the desk and placed both hands on it and looked at Andrews. Andrews looked up; he wasn't surprised that William had come in so abruptly. Andrews had told the police force to stop his car and get him back to Folkestone.

What did surprise him was William's temper. Still, it was better to let him vent his temper and then he might see reason. So, Andrews waited.

"Of all the stupid, crass, idiotic, bungling, inept, farcical, downright dangerous things to do. Anyone could have been listening and intercepted me. Then where would you have been? Also, we had been managing to keep this to four forces, now the whole country knows. Let's broadcast it on the news. What is so important that I get dragged back here? I know that you didn't want me to go to Exeter or Oxford, but there was no need to go to these lengths. Ok, let's hear your version and it had better be good."

He flung himself into the other chair. Andrews rose and walked to the office door and closed it, then looked at Bill.

"Don't you ever do that again. I don't care if you come from the MET or Mars, nobody but, nobody tells me off with the door to this office open. Got it?"

"Yes."

"Good, now you listen for a change. Some of those questions of yours will be answered in due course."

Andrews walked over to the window and looked out across to the houses. He thought to himself, we don't really know what goes on in people's houses. What made them kill Joe like that, he wondered? He continued looking out of the window.

"They have shot Joe, so obviously he has planted their bomb." It had started to rain again, he watched as two rain drops raced down the windowpane, that's how he felt, propelled by other forces. He heard the intake of breath from William.

"Oh!"

"Quite. So where do you think they fled to?"

"Well somewhere within that triangle." He looked up. "You are holding out on me, what else has happened?"

"A duty officer has been killed here." "What!"

"Oh, don't let it worry you. You were off to Exeter and Oxford, so you are in the clear."

"I didn't think that I would be a suspect. What I meant is how did he get killed and by whom?"

"Well, my sergeant is so keen to get everyone involved, and there were over a hundred men out on the knocker so the station… "Andrews left the sentence unfinished. It was obvious what had happened. What was not so obvious was who had done the deed.

"What do you intend doing about it?" asked William softly. "That is what you are going to tell me I hope." He looked at

William who saw that here was a man who was exhausted and needed rest.

"When did you last have some sleep?" "Two days ago, why?" replied Andrews.

`Then go and rest, you are no use to me until you are awake and fit, understand?"

"Yes, if you say so." He rose and picked up his coat. He walked to the door and turned. "Where will you be if I need you?"

"Folkestone, Oxford, Exeter, London and Europe. Oh, I forgot to mention Belfast."

"Well superman, I'll see you in four days' time." He watched from the office window as Andrews left the car park. William took out his mobile and phoned the Met.

"Get me CS Rose, it's Dawson from Folkestone." "Chief Superintendent Rose is in conference."

"I don't care if he is talking to the bloody Prime Minister, get him on the phone and tell him it's important."

"Alright, just hold."

"This had better be good Bill, or its your neck," said Rose once he had picked up his phone.

"It is not good, in fact it's as bad as can be. Joe is dead. The bomb has been planted and we have no way of finding it."

"No way whatsoever?"

"None. They have gone into the country somewhere, where to nobody knows. I know you wanted a closed lid on the whole affair, but it looks as though we may have to go countrywide on this one. We have four forces already knowing sketchy details, what they don't know, they are probably guessing and close to the mark too."

"Well, I don't know, I'll have to talk to the PM on this."

"Why? The Government aren't in any way concerned with the project. Talk to the backers and the makers. Tell me when you have the permission for me to use the whole of the force."

"I'll try my best, where can I get you?"

"I'm on this number." He gave Rose the number and told him not to phone during the next five minutes.

"I'm not likely to, she is at Brighton, opening some conference. Then she is returning to her hotel."

"Well, isn't this more important?"

"Of course, but would it win her any votes?"

"No, but when she has finished opening the event, get her to move and tell her to get up here and make some real decisions for once in her life. It wouldn't hurt her, but I know she doesn't have much practice."

"That's enough, I'll pass on the gist of your message, and get back to you."

"You had better, or I'll phone her direct."

"That would be the end of your career." "There are always other options."

"No there wouldn't be."

"Whatever, use your pals, and the old boy network. Get on the phone and speak to her majesty." He switched the phone off and looked at it.

Here was a crisis of national security and he was being fobbed off. He didn't like it one bit.

He phoned Exeter and got through to Armstrong. They had found that most of the money in the tins tallied with a lot of the money stolen from Folkestone bank robberies. At last they could make a firm connection of the robberies to the ARI woman. This revealed how they got the money for such a large operation. William thanked Armstrong before he drove out into the countryside and phoned a contact that should be always at home. This time the phone just rang in his ear. He sat at the wheel of his car and tapped the steering wheel. What next, he wondered.

He started the car and turned it back towards Folkestone. As he drove along the phone rang. He answered it and drove one handed.

"William Dawson."

"OK I passed your message to the PM. You are to be in Brighton at ten thirty tomorrow morning."

"Afraid that I can't make that time." "What did you say?"

"I can't make that time. Try about three in the afternoon." "What! Now you look here, you are darn lucky that she has fitted you into her schedule. What are you doing in the meantime?"

"I have to see a man about a clutch of bombs." "And that of course, is much more important?"

"Don't be sarcastic, it doesn't suit you. What I mean is by then I will have more information to give her."

"I'll put it to her, but don't hold your breath." The phone was slammed down, and Bill replaced his phone on the hook in front of him.

He swung on to the main road and accelerated off towards Folkestone, where he eventually arrived back at the police station, walked into Andrews' office and shut the door and sat down with his feet on the desk. He placed his hands behind his head and leaned back and let his mind run over the past year....

+

In Oxford the group were getting angry with each other. Sarah had already realised that with only two women in the group they might expect her to do the sort of "women's things" in a totally sexist manner. She also thought that they had already killed Joe but didn't want to believe it. So, she carried on the pretence of believing all they said. When they locked her in her room, she got down on the floor and would try and hear what they were saying, but she could only catch snatches of conversations.

Sarah thought that they may be in Oxfordshire somewhere, and decided to leave a note if possible, it would serve as a guide for anybody else when they had gone. She knew that they were planning to move on. They had been discussing houses in the country and Oxfordshire had been mentioned. The other woman had questioned all the money that was being spent.

Apparently, they had already written off two flats in Exeter, a house in Folkestone, a flat in Folkestone (hers). It wasn't as though they had unlimited resources, they should go back to Belfast. At this there had been much shouting and chairs had been pushed back noisily. Then the leader must have entered because it went very quiet.

"Right, we move tomorrow." "Tomorrow! Why so soon?"

"Because they feel that there is too much heat around here." "Are we going back to Folkestone then?"

"No, we are heading to an area that they wouldn't look for us." "Where?"

"You will find out in the morning." He walked out to the kitchen and started to put the food in the cupboards. Colleen followed him.

"Pay attention, I want out." "What!"

"I'm sick to death of running and I want to settle." "After this there will be no more running."

"That's what you say each time, but it's not true is it?"

"No." He paused. She looked wonderful with the light shining through her hair. "I am afraid that it's out of my hands now, I'm sorry."

He turned and walked back to the rest of the group. Colleen reluctantly followed, now knowing that all her good work at Exeter was wasted. If only Brady hadn't turned up, still it was no use thinking of ifs. She closed the door and joined the others in the main room, but she found that she couldn't settle, so she picked up a book and went upstairs to lie down.

Downstairs, on the phone, Mr. Green and Patrick O'Conner was going over what they would do in the morning. They were to head

North towards Scotland and use the two new cars that were in the car park. In a convoy so to speak. Once on the road, they would be told where they were to go by the car phone. It meant an extremely early morning start. Patrick told them he was turning in for the night and advised that they did the same. He retired to bed, though he didn't like the fact that they had to split into three groups and hide up for two years, but that was what he had been told, so that's what he planned on doing for now.

He sat in his room and looked at the piece of paper he held in his hand. During the last couple of years, he had heard on the grapevine that there was a new synthetic drug that the USA army had developed to stop fatigue setting in. At first, he hadn't taken much notice of such talk.

Then a cell in Ireland had said they had tried it out and it made them not very sleepy, but more alert and able to stay focused for long periods of time.

His interest now reawakened, he set about trying to get a list and instructions on how to make this new drug. He could see long term financial gains if it did all that it was supposed to do. After a lot of work and some research, Patrick had managed to obtain the list of all the items needed to produce it. The only item that he had not been able to source was something called sheepsbane, only found in the north of Scotland apparently. It also was very toxic in the raw state and handling of it had to be done with extreme care. A chemist he knew of had been approached and had been 'persuaded' to make some up.

While it was true the first two or three attempts had not been that great, the most recent had been a real success. Ok, there was the small matter of it being a bit addictive, but that probably would be a good thing in the longer term. Repeat business was a way of making money, at least that was what he had been told once. Patrick smiled as he recalled arranging for it to be given to Joe and his small team of tunnel workers.

Results had been so much better than he had hoped for. They all had been at the point of giving up their jobs due to fatigue. The difference was measurable. From his sources working inside the tunnel, those that had taken the drug had increased their work rate by sixty seven per cent. Something that the tunnel management had failed to notice.

Once the results were confirmed after a second dose, the chemist had met with an unfortunate accident and died.

Then a Russian, who Patrick had known, could also see the commercial benefits of manufacturing such a new drug. They both had been looking for premises to manufacture the drug in. So far it had been a bit difficult to find anywhere suitable that was close enough to the main routes to and from London and not be noticed by any local person.

A possible site was in Eynsham, he would check that out later that night. The associate though, thought that somewhere near the river Thames would be a better option. Patrick would have to wait and see, first a few hours' sleep and then he would slip over to Eynsham and look at the empty storage unit.

+

Andrews was in the morgue, and he looked down at the body of Joe, it was obvious that the ARI had killed him. Despite a few days' rest, he had managed to arrange for the house to be searched from top to bottom. The only thing they had found was a wallet lying just under Joe and that was being examined closely. He felt that what the most likely outcome would be, that it was a stolen one. He wondered what William was up to.

+

William was at that moment was striding angrily into the site manager's office and demanded to speak to Mr. Brooks. His secretary offered to page him. He duly accepted this and sat and waited for Mr. Brooks to appear. It was an hour before he did.

`Sorry I am late, only I was in the tunnel, and it takes longer each day to get out."

"We now definitely know that a bomb has been planted in or near to the tunnel."

"Any idea where? I need a much closer proximity than that vague description."

"Well, if you could let me talk to the other men on the shift who worked with Mr. O'Brian"

"Which one?" "Joseph O'Brian."

"Ah, funny that, he hasn't been for a few days now and he was most proper in phoning in if he couldn't make work."

"If you know more than you are letting on, heaven help you." "No, I don't. Why has something happened to him?"

"You could say that, now those men he worked with?"

"Ok, but first you had better come and get kited out for going underground." He led William towards one of the sheds and got him kited out, then he drove him over to the entrance to the tunnel. They climbed on to the narrow-gauge railway and after a short while they were at the TBM with the rest of Joe's team. The men in the team told them that since Joe had disappeared the sections that they had last laid with Joe were a hundred and twenty-five metres back from the front of the machine.

Since they had been taking the new drug that was being given out, they had increased the amount of tunnel dug and finished. Unfortunately, due to the length of the TBM, that it wouldn't be clear until the end of the TBM had passed it by and that wouldn't be for a few days yet. It depended on two things -one, the type of rock that was going to be in front of them and two the amount of material that could be loaded onto the conveyor belts. They had the paperwork from the engineers, but that wasn't the same thing as working down here, was it?

William asked if he could see how the segments fitted together. "Of course, it's a bit of a climb along here though. Come on."

He led them down the side of the whole length of the machine until they arrived at the front where the segments were arriving by conveyer belt. A machine scanned the rock face behind the cutters and then selected the right piece to put into place. Six pieces were butted one into another, before the smallest and last stone was fitted to hold the other six in place. It was the key stone. This had a square hole in the centre for it was here the grout was pumped in between the outer wall and the outside of the segments.

"Could anything be dropped between those two surfaces?" asked William.

"Not without us knowing it." "But it could be dropped?" "I suppose so."

"Thank you, Now where was Joe when he was last down here?"

"Like we said, halfway back the length of the Machine. But none of us were watching him. We all had our own work to do. Piece rate, you work hard to earn the bonus. We have already overtaken the French for rock we have moved down here."

"Does the speed vary then, how many pieces you fit and seal?" asked William thoughtfully.

"I should say so, in the early stages we were behind the French side, now in the last couple of months we have overtaken them. It's a bit of rival working that gets the tunnel dug and finished. If you get my drift?"

"Thank you,you have been helpful."William turned and walked back the length of the TBM and looked down the tunnel and the lights shone on the segments. He looked across at Brooks. "How many segments on this side of the tunnel?"

"What?"

"How many segments on the British side and find out how good the security is on the French side too."

"Our security is very good on this side."

"You joking or something? A bomb has been planted and we have no way of knowing where it is. Come on, I have seen enough." He walked on back and got on the train to take him out and back to fresh air.

+

An hour later, Brooks had spoken on the phone to the Isle of Grain where the segments were being made and stored. He replaced the phone and looked across at William.

"Four hundred and seventy thousand segments are being made for this side of the project. I really had no idea of the sheer number of segments."

"So, we can use metal detectors to find the package."

"I am afraid not, you see the tunnel segments are all reinforced, every one of them would react to the metal detectors."

"Bugger!"

"It is a bit of a blow, I am sorry, now if there is nothing else, I can do?"

"Not that I can think of. You have been more than helpful. I'll find my own way out." William left the office and walked back to the car. That number of segments, he whistled to himself as he tried to visualise what that would look like. Meanwhile he had an important meeting to attend with the Prime Minister. He got into the car and drove off towards Brighton.

+

The policeman on the door outside her suite, opened the door and passed in the card that Bill had offered. He waited a few minutes and then was ushered in to meet Mrs. Thatcher.

"Do come in and sit down here." She led the way into the front room. Tastefully decorated in pale blue. He waited until she had sat down, then he sat and started to tell her the whole story, not the edited one that would have been passed on by Rose…

"…and that's about it Prime Minister." He looked at her and wondered if she would decide to release the resources to him to find them. He thought not. He wasn't disappointed.

"I have listened to what you have said, but the fact remains that the British taxpayer shouldn't have to pick up the bill for this one. I have every reason to think that the security is good enough for this project. You are welcome to talk to the construction firms, it may be that they will be able to help you. I have said publicly that the taxpayer's money would not be used on this project."

"I know it hasn't had to be used yet, but it will be."

"Didn't you hear me? No money from the taxpayer will be used in the way you describe. I think that this interview is over." He rose and stood and looked at her.

"There may be a time when you will call for me to urgently come here, I hope you remember this interview then." William left the room and walked out to where he had parked the car.

He kicked the nearside front wheel and looked back to where he had just come from. It was so short sighted of her.

He drove out and turned right to drive to Oxford but something still niggled him. Typical politicians, think they know the answers till something goes wrong, then all hell breaks loose. Smiling to himself, he took a small tape recorder from his jacket pocket and placed it on the passenger seat beside him and played it back.

*"I have listened to what you have said, but the fact remains that the British taxpayer shouldn't have to pick up the bill for this one. I have every reason to think that the security is good enough for this project. By all means you can talk to the construction firms, it may be that they will be able to help you. "I have said publicly that the taxpayer's money would not be used on this project."*

*"I know it hasn't had to be yet, but it will be."*

*"Didn't you hear me? No money from the taxpayer will be used in the way you describe. I think that this interview is over."*

*"There may be a time when you will call for me to urgently come here, I hope you remember this interview then."*

+

Andrews jumped as the phone rang on his desk. He picked it up slowly. He had been working through the night,only being supported by tea or coffee and he didn't expect any calls at this time of night.

"Yes?"

"That you Andrews? Said the head of forensics of Northern Ireland police.

"Yes."

"We are sending over details of what we have found in O'Brian's house. Can you get him to talk to us?"

"That's a bit difficult, as he is dead. Shot twice. It is not general knowledge yet though."

"Oh."

"In the meantime, we will try and find out as much as possible from the files. But I can't promise much." Said Andrews.

"Anything at all is better than nothing."Andrews replaced the phone and left his office.

He needed some fresh air and a thought that if someone else read the file, they might spot something he had missed. He walked down to the desk sergeant and asked for a list of who was on duty that night. He picked out one of the officers and arranged for him to look at the file then Andrews went home to have some well-earned rest.

+

The house was quiet in Oxford as Patrick O'Conner crept down the stairs and towards the front door. The sitting room door was ajar, and the TV was on quietly. Then a voice pierced the night.

"How much longer do you plan on keeping both of us locked up here?" asked Sarah.

"In due course you will be released, till then we need you. I am sorry it's a bit uncomfortable, but it will be more spacious when we have arrived. I will say this though, you are going to be with us for the next two years, so you might as well get used to it." Said Patrick with a shrug of his shoulders.

"Two years!"

"That's what I said." Now I must go out, goodnight." He closed the door after him and got into his car and set off for Eynsham.

+

William realised that there was no way he could check all the segments. He wondered if he could work out the answer from the money angle now that the tins were open. It might help if he knew the sort of total amount they were talking about.

People had to be paid after all. He phoned Lympstone direct and waited until he had the right person.

"Can you send one of the money tins up to London please." "Sure, what do you want us to do with the money? Each tin has contained about a thousand pounds." "Then keep them in the safe."

"Will do."William gently replaced the phone and looked at the desk. He was behind again on the paperwork, but first he made a call to a bank friend.

"Hello Mike, it's Bill, sorry to bother you this late, can you spare a few minutes? You can? Right, what I need to know is how easy is it to trace money?"

"What sort?" "British."

"It depends if they have consecutive numbers or not. If they do, then it is somewhat easier, but if not,it is virtually impossible."

322

"Thanks."

"Any time." He hung up and phoned Lympstone again.

"Put me through to the department dealing with the London Met."

"Can you hold?" "Sure." He sat waiting. "How can we help?"

"Are those notes varied or consecutive?" "Varied, well the ones we have opened are."

"Don't rush over sending them here. I think it's the end of the line for us. Thanks for your help." He replaced the phone. He sat and phoned Folkestone, Oxford, Belfast, and Exeter and told them it was all over. He thanked them for their co-operation. He knew that a few details were still unanswered, but what could he do? Already over a year old, the trail was too cold. William sat and pulled the paperwork towards him and started to catch up on the past few weeks work.

## 22.28

Patrick got out of the car and stood and looked in the moonlight at the large warehouse in front of him.

The industrial estate was one of the new ones that the government had promised would be opening all over the UK to encourage growth and employment. He grinned as the many 'For Sale' or 'To Let' boards on the site revealed the truth. Taking a torch from the boot of the car, he was now walking up to the small staff door set to the left of the roller door. Noticing that the padlock lay cut on the ground, he approached cautiously at first.

Pushing the door open, Patrick stepped into the dark interior. He flashed the torch around the warehouse. To the left were the kitchen and toilets and a small staff room. In front of him were five long and tall rows of metal racking, standing ready to receive whatever products were to be stored on them.

He walked further in, picking up the pace as he did so. At the back of the unit was a winding staircase that led downwards. Curious he started to go down it when he heard the roller door being winched up. He returned through the warehouse and moved into the shadows, keeping as near to the front as he could, but the warehouse lights had been switched on.

Peering round one of the racks, he saw a lorry reversing in a trailer unit which had three canvas sides and a top. Patrick moved closer to see what it was and learn just what was going on. For he had been told the unit was empty and unused.

"Be quick, we don't want the police to find us."

"Jack, turn the engine off and get that trailer uncoupled, will you? Now all of you move out of here. We'll come back tomorrow evening and split the stuff five ways as agreed." A low murmur was heard and then minutes later, the lorry roared back out of the warehouse and the rattle of the roller door coming down was heard in the silence. The lights went out and a door was slammed. Patrick moved quickly to the front of the warehouse and across to the side door. He tried the handle and found it was now locked. He returned to the shadows as the handle was turned downwards and the door re-opened. A shadow moved across to the trailer end and then re-appeared carrying a number plate before it left and relocked the door to the warehouse.

Patrick waited for ten minutes to see if anybody was going to return, but nobody did. Sighing, he made his way to the door and risked flashing his torch at the wall. A bank of switches, all nicely marked, could be seen. Deciding not to switch any on, instead he moved to the rear of the trailer. The tie down straps were not locked, so he loosened three and then made his way in.

Once inside, he put his torch back on. In front of him were 12 identical pallets and each one had a large plywood frame screwed to it. The ply looked old and dusty. Slowly, checking all the pallets, he made his way towards the front of the trailer and tried all of them to see if any of them had been opened, but none had. He did spot a faded piece of paper lying trapped under a pallet near the middle. Patrick bent down and tore the paper away.

Это часть ... общей партии. Чтобы быть в безопасности, пока война не закончилась. Затем он будет возвращен в свой первоначальный дом и отображается, как и было обещано народу ... [6]

[TRANS: It's part of ... the general pieces. To be kept safe until the war is over. It will then be returned to its original home and displayed as promised to the people.....]

He would need to find somebody who could translate this. Stuffing the paper into his pocket he retraced his steps and carefully replaced the straps as he had found them.

While the place was ideal, he felt it was too large for what he had in mind. Patrick walked over to the small door and the bank of switches and found the one that operated the roller door. Patrick pressed it until it had opened enough for him to crawl under and return to his car parked in the shadows of the industrial estate. An old newspaper page had blown against the car door handle. About to throw it away, he read the headline. Man murdered in

Marlow Industrial Estate. Police confused as to motive. Marlow, there's a place that is near the river and not too far from London or Oxford. Once in his car, he reached down to the glove compartment and took out an A-Z map. He traced the roads to Marlow and then smiled and turned the engine on and drove off, leaving the warehouse in darkness once more.

A man stepped out from the bushes and watched as the car speed away. Then he made his way across to the warehouse and bent down and went inside. A few minutes later he locked up the warehouse and phoned his contact.

"He must have been inside all the time. With the small door padlocked the only way out would have been using the roller door, which he did. He had left it open, as he couldn't have lowered it again once outside."

"Did he get into the trailer?"

"Doesn't seem like it, the straps are all intact and tight as we left them."

"Who was it? Did you get his number plate?"

"Yes, I'll pass that on to Roger tonight. He will track it for us."

"Well, make sure you do so. I wouldn't want us to lose all this after all the trouble we have had to recover it."

"But it is not all of it, is it?"

"No, but we can make a start with this part. Now lock up and get over to Roger."

"Will do." The call went dead and after a few minutes a car was heard driving away leaving the warehouse in darkness once again.

+

Patrick swung the car into the Marlow Industrial Estate and parked at the rear of the row of units.

Police tape was across the door of two of the units, but other than that, the place was in darkness. He picked up his torch and made his way over to the rear doors of the units. Helpfully, each one had a number and the business name printed on a metal plate by the rear door. He tried one or two, but they were locked. By walking the whole length of all the units, he reached the end one and paced out the side of it. By Patrick's rough calculation, he thought it would be around 4800 sq ft. Perfect in size for a small factory producing his new product.

An old display 'For Sale or Let' board was lying against the rear wall of Unit 12, the last one in the row. Currently it didn't have a business name on a board, so he moved around to the front. It was next to a firm that produced industrial diamond drill pieces. Better and better,

Patrick thought to himself, they may supply the tunnel machines, if not, then surely, they soon could. Noting the agents number off the board, he smiled.

He would make enquiries as to who had leased or bought it in the morning. Then it would be a case of simply applying the right pressure against the firm's weak spot. He also needed to find a translator for the piece of paper in case it said anything important. Humming to himself, he turned the car and pointed it in the direction of Scotland.

## 23.28

## Two weeks later. Marlow.

Patrick drove the minibus up to the rear of unit 12 and turned off the engine. He looked behind to the people sat in the seats. Most were not even aware he had stopped.

He got out and walked over to the rear door of unit 12 and unlocked the padlock, then he disappeared inside for a few minutes, only to reappear holding a clear bag of white and red tablets.

Walking back to the van, he smiled as the ten people in the minibus started to stare and drool as he approached them. Once inside the minibus he looked at the ten faces, now riveted on the bag he held.

"Right, pay attention all of you. I need you to do some serious digging for me, it is hard rock and to start with it will be by hand tools. In a short while I'll organise a small machine to help, but for now it is all by hand. The waste is to be bagged in black bags and tied off with a cable tie. Is there anybody who does not understand what I mean?" Silence greeted his question; they were still transfixed by his swinging bag of tablets.

"Then follow me over to the unit. Tools and so on are inside." Obediently, they followed him over and once inside the unit, he shut the door and gave them one tablet each.

Then he stood back and watched them work. His research had already proven the tablets worked, bit addictive though, Patrick thought as the work progressed. He glanced at his watch and smiled, no knocking off tonight, they would stay awake working, as long as he supplied the precious tablets. His only worry was where to get hold of the sheepsbane that he, or more accurately, his associate, needed to make more of them.

Patrick moved outside and walked over to the adjoining unit. His contact in Russia had supplied the money that would buy out this company, if they accepted his offer that is…

…Two hours of serious talking later, resulted in Patrick now owning unit 11 as well. The previous owner had handed him the keys and a list of outstanding orders to be delivered to the channel tunnel workings. He couldn't believe his luck. Once the factory was making his precious tablets, he could also get them onto the tunnel site as well. Rubbing his hands together in glee, he pulled out his phone and tapped in the code for Russia and a long set of numbers after it.

"Ivan, it's Patrick here, yes I know what the time is, we now own both units twelve and eleven. They also had a contract to supply their product to the Eurotunnel works. How lucky is that? I just need to find a supply of sheepsbane, a regular supply mind you, if we are to up production."

"Just be careful. Good work getting the second unit. Now get up to Scotland and get a contact to regularly supply you with this Sheepswool."

"Not sheepswool, sheepsbane. It is a very toxic weed that only grows in Scotland, the North of Scotland that is."

"A weed that is funny, no? I'll send some more cash to you, same way as before. And Patrick?"

"Yes?"

"I have some students in Oxford who will be great distributors of this new drug."

"We need a name for it, one that is easy to recall." said Patrick.

"That can come later. Get the factory started and get the supply of sheepsbane arranged." The phone went dead, and Patrick looked at the rear of the two units, smiled and got into his car and drove off.

Inside the unit, the ten were working like there was no tomorrow. Already about a metre of rock had been roughly cut and bagged up and still they worked on, not wanting to stop for food, water, or rest.

+

The following morning, around three o'clock, Patrick drove up to unit 12 and opened the door. Ten eager faces peered out at him. He looked past them and saw that over five metres of rock had been hand cut and bagged. The bags were lying outside the unit, all tied as he had wanted.

Smiling, he passed the tablets around and the work started again. Patrick beckoned to one of the men to pick up the bags and take them into unit 11. Bending down, the man gathered four in each hand and walked quickly across to the rear of unit

11. Curious, Patrick tried to lift one of the bags, he couldn't get it off the ground. He gazed as the man returned and repeated the task.

A new effect of the drug, one that the chemist and the earlier trials had overlooked. He took out a small notebook and recorded what he had seen and dated it for future reference. For now, he had to get back up to Scotland. Patrick had arranged for one of the team to come and keep things ticking over here in Marlow while he drove north, perhaps via Oxford? Patrick wondered to himself.

## 24.28

November 1992.

The service tunnel is now completed. Despite all the scares and furore, nothing had happened that made the police force seem worried. The only person still concerned is Simon Reed, (aka William Dawson when undercover) and he isn't saying anything at present. The ARI cell hasn't been found and are still holed up in different parts of the country.

Inspector Andrews is just happy that nothing happened. The security around the newly built railway stations are not as good as it was when the project first started. The shareholders and banks are feeling more confident each day and are looking forward to getting a good return on their investment.

+

In a flat in London, Simon heard the newspaper being forced through his letterbox, and getting out of bed, he walked down the hall and picked it up off the mat. Going into the kitchen, Simon made himself some coffee.

He flicked his eyes over the headlines - nothing much of interest there, the pound was on the way down again, unemployment was on the way up. He grunted to himself and turned to the inside pages. He had done this daily ever since he had been told to leave the investigation.

Simon still felt that something bad would happen to the tunnel one day. Probably when they were least expecting it. He stopped at page seventeen. An advert at the bottom gave a box number and told anyone who was interested in the tunnel to write to it. Going to his desk, he took out a file. This was just one of five that he had on the tunnel project; he had been keeping cuttings on any mention of it ever since he was pulled off the case.

Sitting at his desk, he wrote to the box number. He had a gut reaction that something might be about to start. He would need a lot more than that though to re-open the case.

+

In their various hideouts and houses, the ARI members had received their new instructions. Now, for the first time in years, they could start to finish what had been planned a long time ago.

In Oxford, Mr. Green arranged to post some letters to each of the directors of the tunnel company and to the bank underwriters. Having done so, he drove back to the others. They all looked up as entered the room.

"The letters are posted. We just have to wait and see." "What if they ignore them?"

"If they ignore our letters, we move to the next phase. The large adverts advising the public of the bomb in the tunnel will be placed in strategic places around the underground and such like."

"But I thought we couldn't advertise."

"True, but we have a group of workers on the underground who change the posters each week One or two of them have been 'persuaded' to put our poster campaign into motion, if they hear from us in the next seven days."

The group fell silent as they began to realise the full implications of what they were now doing.

+

Next morning the letters arrived at their destinations. Secretaries opened them with the rest of the mail and then took them fast through to the directors, who were each visibly shaken.

They phoned one another, only to learn that they already knew. Then it was decided after some talk to ignore the letters and throw them away as the work of some crank. Only one of the older directors decided to file his letter in a desk drawer.

+

One week later large adverts appeared in the Underground and informed the population that the security at the tunnel workings had been infiltrated and a bomb was already planted. That was all it said.

Andrews, Simon, the directors and shareholders all learnt about the adverts when they saw they had been photographed and printed in the daily newspapers.

Simon re-read the article and felt sick. He had known that it hadn't gone away and that at some point it, the tunnel, would be a target. Two years ago, he had warned them. He dug out the files and stacked them on his desk. The phone rang and he picked it up.

"Simon Reed."

"Rose here. You are to get yourself over to the Prime Minister's office fast. You may well be the only person in Britain who knows more about the tunnel than anyone else. And bring anything you have on the tunnel with you."

He replaced the phone and went a selected two box files. These two would be sufficient for what he wanted. He drove towards Downing Street and through the Iron gates and up to the front door. It was already open. The policeman outside ushered him in.

"They are expecting you inside in the cabinet room sir."
"Fine." He walked in with a file in each hand. The current Prime Minister looked up as he entered. Thatcher had long since gone. "Now Mr. Reed, we appear to have a problem. I presume you have read the papers?" "Yes."

"From what I have been told, you came here when my predecessor was here and asked for help. I am now saying you can have whatever you need to stop these people."

"Now is far too late. Have you any idea as to what is happening out there Prime Minister?"

"Yes, the share price is now one pound and fifteen pence." "So?"
`So before the adverts appeared, it was eight pounds and fifty pence."

"It fell that much overnight?"

"I am afraid so. The adverts have made our investors nervous."
"How does that affect me?"

"You are to find the organisation behind this, and the bomb and make arrangements to defuse it, remove it and/or make it safe. You have unlimited resources from HMG but only on a need to basis. Any questions?"

"A few." Bill ticked off his fingers as he spoke.

"One. I need a helicopter at my disposal twenty-four hours a day."

"Two. I need the ability to slice through red tape, if I need to fly from one country to another, I do not have to wait for passports or visas."

"Three. I need a small and very select team and they will consist of the following: Inspector Andrews of Folkestone CID, My office assistant; Gail Rose of the Met, Chief Superintendent Rose of the Met and Detective Inspector Armstrong of Devon and Cornwall Police force."

"You have them, now go and find them and the bomb." "How much time do I have?"

"As long as it takes."

"Then I had better get started. Goodbye Prime Minister." "Good luck." The Prime Minister watched from the window as he drove off. "You are going to need it," he murmured to himself. Simon drove out, knowing this was a potential gamechanger in his career. Returning to his flat, he packed a case and put the remaining three files in the car. Then he phoned Andrews in Folkestone.

"Andrews, it's William Dawson from London. I am coming down there. I assume that you have read the papers?"

"Of course. I was expecting you. We got a phone call from the PM saying you were on the way. What can I do to help you?"

"I need you as part of my small team. I'll collect you as soon as I arrive. Suggest you go and pack a few things for a couple of weeks."

"Who do I answer to?" "Me!"

"Right. I'll see you when you arrive, and thanks a lot."

"No problem." He replaced the phone and phoned the others.

+

Andrews sat thinking at his desk. Then he picked up the phone and spoke to one of his sergeants.

"How soon could you put a large room for ten people together, with full facilities, phones, fax machines, photocopiers and a direct phone line to the Met's computer?"

"With our budget?"

"No, assuming there is no limit on the funds." "Then quite quickly."

"Get to it, you have very little time." "How long exactly do I have sir?" "Three hours."

"What!"

"You heard. Now move."

+

William had over the years equipped himself with a small arsenal of weapons. Now he had collected both his assistant Gail and his new NoMax credit card. He had a small amount of the new SQUAB hidden in the car, but he didn't plan to tell anyone of this just yet.

Pulling the car up at London's Helicopter Airport, he and Gail got out and they both looked in amazement. There stood in front of them was a brand-new police helicopter. He snorted in disbelief.

"I'm not going in that." He turned to the manager as he came forward. "Do you have anything else that is available either for selling or hire?"

"We do have this small Bell helicopter that an American gentleman has instructed us to sell for him."

"Fine, I'll buy it. Here is my NoMax card it will cover its price."

"Is this for real?"

"Try it and see." He watched as the man walked off. After a short while he returned and smiled.

"I'll send the paperwork on shall I?" "Do that."

"I also assume you can't fly this?" "Correct."

"I've found you a pilot to fly it. He is good I can assure you of that."

"You a magician or something? We need a helicopter, you have one. We need a pilot and surprise, surprise, you have one."

"Just lucky."

"I'll believe you." He turned to Gail. "You go to Folkestone in this. Book a couple of rooms at a nearby guest house, it's unlikely we'll use it, but it's better to be safe than sorry. I'll drive down, give me some time to think things over on the way.

"Right, you are"She watched as he drove off, then Gail climbed into the helicopter.

Halfway there,William pulled in and phoned a secure number. "Duty Officer."

"Simon Reed here. Can you please find out if any of the directors has been contacted about this bomb first, or if they are being threatened at all. If ARI want to bring the tunnel into financial ruin, then they have already almost done that. We know that it is bigger, a bomb or some sort of similar device. Whatever it is, I want to know what it is. Understand?"

"Sure. How long do I have?"

"You have just about three hours, phone me at Folkestone CID or on this number."

"What!"

"Now move yourself."

+

Armstrong was at home when the call came through from William. Once he had replaced the phone, he looked across at his wife."

"Have to go to Folkestone." "How long are you going for?"

"About ten days to a fortnight." She got up and went and packed a case.

+

Gail had arrived and booked into a guest house. She had then phoned Ian MacKenzie from the nearest cardphone, why William had insisted on that she didn't know. Still, this was the number she had been given.

"Ian MacKenzie here."

"Hello Ian, Gail Rose, you met me once. William Dawson told me to phone you and say that both yourself and your wife are needed in Folkestone asap."

"Is he in trouble?"

"No, but the country is."

"Right then I'll be over as soon as I can arrange things." "Would it help if I said that both tickets were ready for you at the airport?"

"Confident, wasn't he?"

"No, I was." He laughed and put the phone down… Then she phoned Folkestone police to tell them where William would be staying while down there before returning to the guest house and lying on the bed dreaming of helicopters being chased by fast cars.

+

William swung his car into the police car park and narrowly missed hitting the new two large office cabins. Picking up the two files, he ran up the steps and into Andrews office.

"It looks great."

"I am glad you like it. It's good to see you again my friend." "Good to see you too. What remains to be done?"asked William with a smile.

"I can't get beds for the rest of your team unfortunately; the guest houses are fully booked."

"All of them?"

"Those that are within my budget."

"What if I said go for the top of the range?"

"They would have rooms free, but who is paying for all this?" "HMG."

"No!"

"Yes, so let's make the most of it." "I will, don't you worry."

"And when you find a hotel that has rooms, book the whole place."

Andrews picked up his phone and did that very quickly. Then he turned back to William.

"So, tell me what is the meaning of all this?"

"That's what we have to find out. My brief is to find the people responsible and find and defuse the device."

"Not too much to do then." said Andrews with a sarcastic voice. I thought that you told the Prime Minister about this two years ago…"

"I did, but there has been a change of Prime Minister since then." Said William with a grin.

"So where do we start?"

"We do know is that a device of some sort has been put into the tunnel by Joe, at least we assume so, as he was killed."

"Ok, do we know which one though, as there are three tunnels."

"I am aware of that. Let's find out which one he was working on when he was killed. That is the most likely one that the bomb is planted in. I think we should look for that before we start trying to find the ARI cell. Don't you think so?" asked William.

"On reflection, you are probably right."

"You have worked wonders in such a short time." said William with a smile.

"Thank my sergeant."

"Then all I can say is he is very good." "I'll pass on the message."

"Talking of messages, anything for me?"

"Not that I know of. There may be at the front desk."

"Right, you read these two files I brought down with me. Something might spring to mind."

"Such as?"

"How should I know?" William walked off and Andrews took the first file in his hands and placed it on his desk, before removing the top page and starting to read…

+

William phoned Gail, who answered after a short while. "Yes?"

"Gail, get yourself down here to the police station asap. Did you get hold of the other team members?"

"I talked to Ian, and they are on the way here, via London, I mean."

"Good, I'll speak later. Bye." He hung up and decided to have a meal and when he returned, he noticed that the rest of the team had all arrived.

He outlined to them what he had been asked to do. Andrews raised his hand.

"Yes?"

"An update for you. Apparently the directors and banks were given notice a week before the adverts. Asking for a ransom. Most of them threw the letters in the bin. One of the older directors filed his. We are looking for fingerprints on it."

"Good. Now all go and have a good night rest. Meet at the tunnel in the morning. Seven sharp."

"What are we looking for?" asked CS Rose.

"If I knew that I would go straight to it sir. Till tomorrow." "Goodbye." They all left the office leaving Andrews and William. "What do you think will happen next?" asked Andrews. "They will ask for more money and they will set a time limit.

This time they have the upper hand." "Real trouble then."

"I fear so, I really do."

+

First thing the following day another series of adverts appeared carefully placed in the more popular papers:

334

The ARI demand the release of 26 of its members in the next 24 Hours. If they are not released, the ARI will demonstrate by detonating a device somewhere in the UK at a time and place of their choosing.

We suggest you lobby your MP to do the right thing or the British Government will be responsible for any deaths that will occur.

William walked into Andrews office and flung a copy of the paper down on to his desk.

"Read that and weep."

"Thanks, but I have already done so. You are to ring the PM and tell him what you have done so far. I said you were out of the office." William snorted his disgust and went to his office and picked up the direct safe line to the PM.

"How can I help you Prime Minister?" "Find the ARI and defuse the bomb."

"Don't you think I would, if I had any idea as to where the device has been placed? I have a bomb disposal squad sitting here doing nothing, but if anything is found they will sweep into action. Can you arrange to stop all the Eurotunnel trains for now. It would mean that if a device exploded in the tunnel, at least there wouldn't be any deaths on my watch."

"The freight ones too?" "All of them."

"But the cost."

"Less than if you had to compensate the people who might die if they are in the tunnel when the device explodes though." "Ok, leave it with me." Said the Prime Minister with a heavy sigh. Bill replaced the phone and sat looking at it before getting up and going to discuss things with Armstrong and Andrews.

+

"Isn't this playing into their hands? I mean nobody knows for sure that there is a bloody bomb down there." said Armstrong with a shrug as he lit his pipe.

"That is true, but we can examine the tunnels more easily this way."

"But you tried that two years ago, so what's changed?"

"Well, there is a new machine for detecting bombs? We now have the means to detect Semtex after all."

"Is there such a machine?" asked Andrews curiously.

"Find out. Speed is of the essence here. Look, I only was given this job yesterday, I am still trying to get to grips with everything. What I want is for the tunnels to be searched from one side to the other."

"Fine." said Andrews

"Well?" said Gail looking at William. "Well, what?"

"You haven't read inside the papers have you? No, I thought not. Everyone is now using Heathrow to fly abroad, but the air traffic controllers can't cope now any more than they could in the eighties. The number of ferries that have closed since the tunnel opened is alarming. Nobody expected the tunnel to get opened by the revised deadlines set by the banks. When it was everyone was surprised. The banks are now wanting their money back right now not the next twenty years."

"I know that. What do you expect me more to do?" "Phone the PM?"

"Ok, I'll do that and say I'm sorry, I have been on this for less than a day and I really can't cope. He would love that." He turned to her and looked her in the eye. "I'm sorry, it's not your fault. Just too much pressure of the job." He leaned across the desk and picked up the direct phone to the Prime Minister. There was a pause, then he came on the line.

"Any news?"

"Not much, I just want to know if the Government would concede if it came to it?"

"Why do you ask?"

"We may have to fall back on the final analysis for the first time ever."

"Why?"

"The sheer volume of segments and it could be behind any one of them. In the meantime, please can you supply me with a list of the most up to date explosives. World-wide that is, I have an expert here who may be able to disarm the bomb if we can locate it."

"We can't use metal detectors since there are too many reinforcing rods down there, the instruments jump all over the place, unless you know of a new top-secret machine?" He paused hopefully.

"No. Look, if we give in now, they can do this again and again," said the PM.

"Or it could end up being like a row of toppling dominos Prime Minister. Since the tunnel opened the number of passengers using the air or ferries is well down. The consortium is made up of a lot of well-known companies. If the tunnel is blown up, then they will go bust as well.

"We could choose to buy it off them, the tunnel I mean?"

"At a price. But right now, would be a good time to do that, the share price is so low." Replied William. Smiling as he thought of what Thatcher had said about no public money being used.

"What sort of price would you think that would be?"

"No idea Prime Minister. Use some of your backroom office staff to check prices and run the figures."

"I've already had the consortium on my back wanting help. I've told them no Government is going to bail out a private company. We didn't with Lloyds and that would have been far better for Britain. How would it look if taxpayer's money were used now? Who do you think is really behind this campaign?"

"Could be who they say they are. The ARI."

"But from what I gather from London and MI6 nobody of any significance has come to their attention in the last six months." "This has been planned for years. We are talking at least four or five years here. The coastline of Britain is large, over eleven thousand miles. Anybody could land almost anywhere they chose, Prime Minister."

"Look can I get back to you on that?"

"Of course." He replaced the phone and turned to Gail. "They are playing CY."

"CY?"

"Cover yourself. Politicians are notorious for it. Particularly when something nasty comes up."

"Like this?" she replied with a smile. "Right."

"So, now we have to sort out the mess that they have made." He nodded and kicked an empty wastepaper basket across the room with a look of pure hate on his face.

"If only we could catch the bast.." He stopped and looked at Gail. "Sorry I was forgetting you were here."

"Don't worry, I have heard worse, get it out of the system." "No, it's passed."The phone rang, making them jump. Gail took the phone and answered it, then she reached over and switched on a tape recorder and handed it to him.

"It's them." Gail said quietly. "What!" He took the phone. "Simon Reed?"

"Yes." He was stung by how much they knew. "What do you want?"

"We do know that you have been seconded to this job and have been keeping files on this ever since you got kicked off it all those years ago." Now he really was shaken-that information was supposed to be classified, as it was only available to a few people.

"So, what do you want me for?"

"As a person who can talk to both sides." "I am really no good at that sort of thing." "You or nobody."

"Who are you?" asked Simon trying to gain time. "No questions, are you going to do it or not?"

"Call me on this number in half an hour and I'll tell you." "And you set up a bug on the line! No thanks."

"No, you keep the call short and sweet." "Well at least that sounds honest." "Who are the hostages?"

"Nice try. No deals till you are on the team."The phone went dead. He rewound the tape and took it out of the recorder and handed it to Gail.

"Get that analysed. I want a small recorder as well as a supply of tapes. Think you can do all that?"

"Of course."

"Good, then off you go." He shooed her out the door and phoned the Prime Minister again.

"Prime Minister's office."

"Tell the Prime Minister that William Dawson has some very bad news, and it will not wait."

He cradled the phone on his shoulder and fished a pen and pad towards him. He started to doodle designs at the top of the pad. "Hello Prime Minister. I have some really bad news I am afraid."

"What could be worse than their demands?" "First question, do you know my real name?" "No, why?"

"The terrorists did,they phoned me at Folkestone on a number that has only just been set up and knew which name to use."

"I am beginning to see light at the end of the tunnel."

"Then let's hope it's not an oncoming train! Look, somewhere near the top there is a big breech in security. I want it found and found fast. The terrorists also want me as a negotiator."

"So, what is your problem?"

"I like to stay out of the spotlight, and if I am a negotiator, I can hardly do that can I?"

"While I can see what you mean by that remark, I think you should agree to talk. Say, if you are to be the go-between, then there must be no publicity. It's either that or another negotiator."

"Good thinking Prime Minister, I'll do that."

"A small thing you might want to know, the banks have been loaned a large sum of money to keep their pressure off the consortium. However, do keep that to yourself."

"Will do." He replaced the phone and found that he had doodled all over the page, he tore off the page and walked over to the wastepaper bin and dropped the screwed-up page into it. Gail burst into the office.

"Got you the small tape recorder." "Thanks. Much appreciated."

"Good." She turned and left the office. After a couple of minutes, he followed her down the corridor and outside.

+

In Oxford and Scotland, the two groups of terrorists had been waiting to hear if Reed would agree to be the negotiator. If he said he wouldn't deal, they would use the bombs. However, that meant they would have to get within five miles of the bombs. They walked around in a restless manner. Colleen Kent was making dinner in the Oxford groups kitchen.

+

Some members of the ARI wondered what would happen if HMG gave in to their demands. They, the Government, had always said "The Government would never talk to terrorists."

This was the largest threat that had ever been made. Then the front door opened, and Patrick walked in. It was pouring down with rain, and he left a puddle where he stood.

"I have to phone back in half an hour. I think he'll agree though. Using his real name shook him. Us having somebody inside the Government has really helped this time."

"Did Simon understand the demands?"

"Didn't really fill him in on those yet but given the number of adverts we have placed I don't think he would not be aware of the cost.

"I agree, with the cost of the tunnel being shut is huge. Why every minute it is shut they are losing money. He will be aware of the cost, both in time and money." Said Mr Green from an armchair by the fire.

"I can't see the Government giving in, they might supply the money to buy off the banks and then we have no lever." Said Seumas with a yawn.

"But we can blow it up." Said Lorcan.

"True, but it wouldn't get the prisoners out of there. Isn't it time you left and made that second phone call?"

"Alright, I am going, I just thought that you would like to be put in the picture as it were." Patrick went out and got into the car and drove off. The others watched from the window until the red rear lights had disappeared. Then they went and had some dinner and preparing to wait for a long time.

# 25.28

Simon stood waiting by the phone to hear from the ARI. With the equipment in place to record and analyse the call, he just needed them to call back. The phone rang making him jump. He snatched it up.

"Yes?"

"Simon, I presume that you have spoken to your bosses?" "I have, there is one request."

"There always is. What is it?"

"Well, I am prepared to do as you say." He paused. "But?"

"Can we use the official spokesman?" He waited with bated breath a lot hung on this answer. If he said no his cover was blown, if he said yes, his cover remained intact.

"I'll check for you, but there is one condition." "Like you just said..."

"You trick us, and we blow your cover and kill the two hostages."

"You said one thing,That's two."

"Maybe your hearing isn't so good, the message is to be treated as one."The phone was replaced, and Simon felt that this was a professional he was dealing with. If the roles had been reversed, he would change phones and call back.

+

Somewhere in England Patrick was busy looking for another phone box. Finding one, he stepped inside and picked up the phone and dialled the number...

...In Folkestone the phone rang again, and Simon snatched it for the second time. He waited for the message.

"The answer is yes." said Patrick.

"Now phone me back on this number." said Simon as he gave a new number to Patrick before replacing the phone. Then Simon quickly put the phone down, unclipped the microphone and ran out to his car. The number he had given was his direct car phone number. It already had recording equipment built into the car phone. Simon knew that it was a dangerous game he was playing. Although with a cell phone number, the ARI could not be a hundred percent sure where he was based.

Simon was hoping that the terrorist might start to make mistakes if he was the one under pressure for a change.

The phone rang and he picked it up slowly. He waited before answering.

"Simon Reed here, how can I help you?" "Ok, wise guy, don't you do that to me again."

"Oh, but I thought that you didn't want the call traced. BT can't trace one that was that short you know."

"Yes, we know. Meet me at the House of Commons by the entrance to the underground car park. "said Patrick slowly.

"Fine and the time?"

"Tomorrow morning at ten thirty." Simon hung up. He phoned the tunnel complex and asked for an update.

"They have been checking the tunnel area that Mr. O'Brian was last working on. We sourced a spare sample of one of the segments of the tunnel to see how much of the reinforcing there is in each segment. The results will be sent to you once the contents have been analysed."

"Thanks, and let's hope that something is found."

"I hope so as well, or all of this is a waste of time." Simon hung up and left the car to return to his office. He looked at the noticeboard that ran down one wall of the office. He got up and walked over to it and wrote on it in large print: Check all the workers on the tunnel, their background and when they were signed up.

He then underlined the all to make sure it was taken up. Then he added: Also, try to get hold of a Mr. Sam Brooks who was the Site Manager or Miss Mary Orchard, his secretary.

The phone ringing on his desk brought him back to reality with a jolt.

"Simon."

"London here, you have sent us into a flap with that tape that Gail gave us. We have been storing and analysing voices for only a short time, by that I mean keeping records."

"Have you found out anything yet?"

"Yes, it belongs to a little-known ARI man. He is called Patrick O'Conner. Apparently, he moved house three times in the last four years."

"Do you know where he is now?"

"No."

"So, we know who it is, but don't know where he is?"

"That's right. He could be anywhere. And Bill, just because it is him, doesn't mean the rest of the cell are nearby."

"Not great news then?" "That's right."

"Well thanks for what you have done." Bill replaced the phone and looked thoughtful.

+

In Scotland the terrorists had been waiting for Patrick's return. He came in through the front door and took off his jacket and flung it over the back of a chair.

"Well?"

"We meet tomorrow outside the House of Commons." "How do you get down there in time?"

"I drive through the night as do the rest of us. It is time to move on from here, so we may as well leave right now."

"Fine." They left to pack their few belongings and give the property a deep clean. No need to give the police any clues as to who had been living here. After an hour they had left the house and were driving south.

+

Very early the next morning they were driving into the centre of London to the West End. They parked the cars in the NCP just off Shaftesbury Avenue. Then walked over to a nearby restaurant that was open.

The owner was sympathetic to the cause. He ushered them to the rooms upstairs.

" I know why you are all down here. You should read the papers, for it is all over the front pages." He pointed at a small pile of newspapers onto a table and walked out. They picked them up and started to read. Colleen noticed that most of the papers were at least two days old, so she decided to go out and see if she could get a more up to date one. Leaving the rest of the group, she walked down to the front door and let herself out and went in search of a newsagents. Finding one, as she entered the bell over the door jangled. An old man stepped down from a pair of steps and stood behind the counter.

"Yes, how can I help you?"

"Do you have yesterday and today's papers, I need to catch up with what has been going on." She watched as he bent down and brought a bundle of papers onto the counter neatly tied with string. He untied the knot and removed the top paper. Then retied it before placing it down behind the counter. He pointed to a pile of that days papers that stood ready for putting out on display.

"Take one off the top of those, then it will be two pounds please." He held out his hand expectantly. She took out her purse and counted out the coin into his hand.

"Thank you." He turned and put the money into the till, but by the time he looked back around, she had left the shop already taking in the headlines.

Colleen re-entered the room and flung down the papers.

"I think we ought to know how much is really being covered on this project in the media. By the look of things, an awful lot."

"Is that a problem?"

"Only for Brady, because he is too well known - nobody else will be known. Well, will they?" She gazed at the group in front of her.

"No."

"Good." She sat down and started to read the headlines on that morning's paper. Patrick looked at her and then went and made a quick phone call. After which he went and tapped Colleen on the shoulder.

"A word please?" Putting down the paper, she got up and went outside with Patrick.

"I think we should give them a surprise, by them I mean HMG." he said.

"What sort of surprise do you have in mind Patrick?"

"I think you should go instead of me. I doubt they have you on file and it might just make them a bit more nervous."

"Ok, but don't bet on it. I don't think they have anything on me right now, but who knows?"

+

The next morning found Simon at the House of Commons. Having parked his car in the underground carpark. He walked up the ramp into the daylight and stood outside waiting for Patrick O'Conner to appear. He knew that he had very few advantages - knowing the ARI man's name and having a photo, all be it a bad one, from his file were a couple of them. In due course he was tapped on the shoulder and a woman stood there in a check shirt, blue jeans and a pair of trainers completed the picture.

"You Simon Reed or would you prefer to be called William Dawson?"

"Yes, but how do you know?"

"Good, we'll take your car as it is nearest, being parked here." She jerked her thumb in the direction of the House of Commons. "Besides, I wouldn't want you to have to whistle up the helicopter that you have on twenty-four-hour basis."

"Don't miss much, do you?"

"No, that's how we stay one jump ahead of you." "Where do you want me to drive you to?"

"I'll direct you. You will know the way." They walked back to his car and Bill drove up and out of the car park. He looked and wondered what sort of person his passenger really was. Oh, well he would soon find out, he assumed.

"Right, lets first drive to the flat."

"Which flat?"

"Don't stall or play games, your flat."

"Fine." He gunned the engine and drove to the flat and after parking the car, he opened the door and ushered her into the flat.

"Right, the reason we choose here was that you probably would not have the flat bugged. So, sit down and we'll talk terms."

"What terms?"

"The ones outlined in the newspapers."

"Look, I can act as a go-between, but I don't have carte blanche you know." Said Simon.

"Different to what I hear. I understood that you had all the resources at your disposal."

"You seem very well informed."

"We are. A lot of people have been involved in this project. Now are you going to give in or not?"

"So lay out the terms on the line in full."

"All twenty-six prisoners released and full pardons for all of our group involved."

"What!" shouted Simon in amazement. "I can't give out pardons."

"Alright, so calm down, let's start with the prisoners."

"I have a figure in mind." Said Simon.

"Let's hear it then." said Colleen

"Five."

"I'll see myself out." Colleen started to get up.

"No, alright ten then."

"Twenty."

"Twelve."

"Fifteen." Said Colleen.

"Fourteen." countered Simon.

"Done."

"Now as to the pardons, I'll need someone's authority for that." "Well, I expected that, I would point out that we do have a couple of hostages."

`Yes, I was wondering about that." "Who has been missing for two years?" "Tell me."

"Work it out, they are connected with the tunnel." "You mean that you still have Joe's family?"

"Yes. Meet me again tomorrow. By the lions in Trafalgar Square. Now drop me off in Cambridge Circus." They both left the flat and he drove her to where she asked. Once he had done so, he drove back to his flat and sat down to take in what they knew, make some notes and decide what and who he had to ask.

Half an hour later, he picked up the phone and rang Downing Street.

"Get me the Prime Minister and fast, we have a problem." "Who is speaking?"

"Simon Reed. And I need to speak to him in the next ten minutes."

"Then you had better get here in the next five or you don't get another chance today."

"I'm on my way."

"Good."

+

In a newspaper editor's office, a young reporter was talking to his editor.

"Look sir, at a college ball that I attended last weekend, the word going round was that the Government were about to bail out the consortium over the tunnel. Well, that's a story, isn't it?"

"No son, it's a rumour. It's facts that are needed first."

"How do you set about getting the facts?"

"Not me, you can though. I'll give you three days to dig something up on this that is based on facts and then I may print it. I mean hard facts, I don't want a"D" notice slapped on it, just as the presses are ready to roll."

"Where do you suggest I start?"

"The banks, the underwriters, Lloyds the insurers; if they will not comment, read them that is what you will print. If they grant you an interview, take notes and read it back to them before you leave. If it's off the record, then memorize in your head. If it's on the record, write it down. Now get out of here."

The young man walked over to his desk and picked up his jacket from around the back of his chair.

He went down to the cutting room. The young woman in charge smiled and he was instantly entranced by her.

"Something I can do for you?"

"I can think of lots of things, but right now I need to know about the channel tunnel, all you have on it."

"Right, well it is in five large folders, which bit did you want?"
"The financial side."

"Look how about I'll look out the relevant bit for you and meet you for lunch about two."

"Fine."

"Meet me outside the main door then about ten to two."

"Thanks." He turned and left the newspaper library. He would go to the British Library. He was looking for was a suitable quote, even if it was from another newspaper. Once he had got there, he spent a lot of time pouring over back newspapers printed when it first opened.

After an hour and a half, he found what he wanted. A quote from the Prime Minister in parliament when the service tunnel had been connected. *"This has not had, nor will have, any public money put into it. For the first time this century we have a civil engineering project that we can be proud of. Mr. Speaker, we have agreed The Anglo-French Treaty and the concession set the framework within which Eurotunnel operates. Article 1 of the Treaty states that 'The Channel tunnel Link shall be financed without recourse to government funds or to government guarantees of a financial or commercial nature›, something that this Government should be and will be proud of."*

He knew that this opening line was the key. If the Government did put any money into it at any stage to prop it up, then this story would strongly damage the Government's credibility.

He noted which paper and the date before checking that they wouldn't mind an acknowledgement in his paper. Then he glanced at his watch, he had to fly. An important lunch date would be waiting.

+

In Downing Street, the Prime Minister sat looking at Simon.

"What do they want from us, really I mean?"

"Well Prime Minister, they are asking for fourteen men to be released and a full pardon for the gang responsible for this."

"Completely out of the question. We might give the terrorists a bit of money and some of the fourteen, but not a pardon."

"May I remind you that you said I was to have unlimited resources and point out to you that I got the number to be released down from twenty six to fourteen."

"I know I said that. But a pardon, that is too much. No, I'll have to think about it."

"Well don't think too long, two lives are at risk. They do have hostages."

"Who exactly?"

"O'Brian's family."

"I'll be in touch with you shortly."

"You can get me on the special mobile number."

"I'll have a cabinet meeting before then, so I'll make sure that this will be placed at the top of the agenda."The Prime Minister indicated the meeting was over. Simon stood up and left the room. He shook his head in despair.

Then he drove back to the flat and phoned Folkestone to see what if anything was going on down there.

"Folkestone Police."

"Get me Andrews and tell him it's Simon Reed or William Dawson."

"Right away sir."

"William, good to hear you. The good news is that we now know what sort of plastic they used. The bad news is that it is manufactured in France."

"Could you be a little more specific please?"

"Sure, it's located just outside Paris."

"Just perfect, given the current relationship we have with the French over this tunnel closure."

"There is more to come."

"Break it to me."

"The tip off came from a Thomas Swift."

"Didn't he share a van with Joe?"

"Yes."

"Ah."

"But, before you go any further, he has a perfect alibi."

"I distrust perfect alibi's."

"You will in this case, It's us."

"Oh."

"And there is worse, after he had told us he was killed."

"Oh."

"Is that all you can say? Oh."

"No, but what else can I do?"

"Not too much I suppose." He hung up and the phone rang in the flat almost at once. It was the Prime Minister.

"We are going to agree to the conditions."

"But..."

"Don't interrupt, we will continue the search after they have been released."

"That will make the Government implicated, won't it?"

"Not really. You see we have arranged that the consortium admits that all the money has been given to you and paid for by them."

"And who dreamt up that half-baked idea?"

"Chief Superintendent Rose, I think. Why?"

"I'll tell you later, thank you." Simon hung up and left the flat to walk towards Trafalgar Square. Arriving, he went up to one of the lions and stood and waited.

He had his mobile phone on him. He stood there for half an hour getting angry, why hadn't he been phoned? He walked around the four lions in a clockwise direction. Unknown to him at the same time Colleen set off from the opposite lion and went at the same time in a clockwise direction around the lions. This of course led to both missing each other. In the end each went back to their flats and sat very angry with one another.

In Simon's flat the phone rang, and he snatched it up. "Where were you?" asked Colleen in a voice of steel.

"Where were you more like it?" replied Simon, equally angry.

"I was at the lions." Colleen replied

"So was I."

"But I walked around all four." said Colleen angrily down the phone.

"And I did likewise." Simon paused for minute. "Hang on a minute, what if we both had walked in the same direction at the same time.." He left the sentence unfinished.

"I suppose that it's possible. Stay in your flat, I'll be there as soon as possible."

"Fine. Coffee will be ready when you arrive." He hung up and busied himself in the kitchen. A short while later Colleen arrived and entered the flat. She stood and looked at Bill.

"Well, do we have a deal?"

"HMG have agreed to give you the fourteen prisoners. On condition that you agree to admitting that a money deal has been done with the consortium instead."

"Ok, and what about the Pardons for us?"

"You must appreciate that only the Queen can give those out."

"True, but she only does what the Prime Minister says, so is it yes or no?"

"If you agree to the rest of the deal, then the answer is yes, but you must show us where the bombs are first, and you can't contact your friends."

"Oh."

"And Colleen, you only have a short time to think about it." He watched with delight as he saw a look of shock fall across the women's face.

"How do you know my name?"

"From Exeter, you were very careless in how fast you left your flat. You have until nine tomorrow morning."

Colleen rose and left the flat. Bill was left wondering if he had done the right thing.

## 26.28

The ARI group sat playing cards, in the corner a television was on while they half listened to see what, if any, mention might be made about them on the news. So far they had heard nothing. Seumas rose and turned it off.

"Where is she?"

"She'll come back."

"What if she doesn't?"

"Then we have a problem, don't we?"

"We ought to plan in case she doesn't." The front doorbell rang twice, and they all stopped talking.

"Well, it is the signal, aren't we going to answer it?" asked Barry. "Yes, of course." Lorcan made his way to front door and let Colleen in. He double locked the door once he was inside. "We were getting worried."

"We have a small problem."

"Oh. Haven't they agreed or given in to the demands?"

"No, it's not that, it's security of this project. You see we have a mole." Colleen said as she looked at the group in front of her.

"Never!"

"Well, you know we were all recruited by different people."

"Yes."

"This was so nobody knew who we were. It was supposed to be the most secure project for years. What happens? We agreed the deal and then finally just as I was about to leave, he puts the knife in and calls me by my name. He said they have a high-level source."

"He's bluffing."

"Really? Then how did he find out my name, tell me that? He said it was me being careless in my flat in Exeter. The flat was supposed to be empty and deep cleaned after I had left it. So now they have my details on file. I think somebody else needs to go tomorrow. Patrick, maybe it should be you."

"Ok, I'll go tomorrow, but we need to find out who is leaking information to HMG."

"We could look into the Belfast angle, I always felt that we were hustled out of there far too fast."

"So were a lot of people. We didn't know that the British would let off a nuclear device."

"I still don't think they did. Look how many people are back living in that area already, and you know what has been rammed down our throats for years, how dangerous the bomb is with radioactivity lasting hundreds of years."

"We take your point."The group fell into silence.

+

Simon had requested the Prime Minister summon an early morning meeting of the members of BOTOG knowing he had to act fast.

"Well Simon we trust there is a good reason for this meeting?" "Oh, I think you will agree with me that it was worth it. I have a list of the clients who were supplied with the explosive identical to that which has been found to be used in tunnel." "So just round them up and start from that angle."

"I did. The problem is there is only one customer. Which is Her Majesty's Government."

"Good grief!"The Prime Minister looked around the room and then at Simon. "Will you leave the room please?"

"No way!"

"Pardon?"

"I said no way! I am staying here."

"May I remind you that you are employed under the official secrets act. You do as we say."

"No, you listen to me for a change." He ticked off the points on his fingers as he spoke.

"One, I kept lots of files and cuttings, when all of you didn't want anything to do with the tunnel at all."

"Two, I have gathered the very small, trusted team together." "Three I now know how they kept one jump ahead of us." "So, tell us."

"Not yet. But I stay in the room, it's my neck out there." "Then we agree?"asked the Prime Minister,looking first angrily at Bill then at the rest of the group. They all slowly all nodded their agreement. Simon wanted to see who would be the last one. He thought he knew who it would be. As he thought, he now knew who the insider was. Simon was sad but it confirmed his suspicions. He salted away this information for use at a later stage.

"Well now, I shall want a list of all the places that this has been stored at on my desk…" said the Prime Minister, but he stopped as Simon laid the list on the desk. "This it?"

"Yes, Prime Minister."

"What do you suggest?"

"Well Prime Minister, we could give them enough rope to hang themselves so to speak."

"And how do you propose that we do that?" asked the one who Simon knew was the insider.

"Let all the prisoners that we have agreed to free, go free then promptly re-arrest the lot."

"What of the pardons?" asked the insider. Ah, thought Simon, that is your first mistake, I haven't mentioned pardons to anyone except the PM.

"Didn't I mention that the pardons only apply to the main four members?" Simon said out loud to the group sat in front of him.

"I didn't know we knew that there was a team of four."

"Neither did I until today. It may be five. I need to check a few things."

"Well, this isn't getting us anywhere, Mr. Reed has put an idea is on the table, let's vote on it." said the Prime Minister in a business like way.

"May I ask who is underwriting the tunnel, Lloyds?" said one of the BOTGB members from the back of the room.

"No, we are." Said the Prime Minister. "We have no choice."

"Since when Prime Minister?"

"Since yesterday. If anything happens to the tunnel, we pick up the tab. Right, if that's all?"

"One thing Prime Minister. If you agree to my idea, I want a complete free hand." said Simon.

"Oh no we can't have that, we must have reports at least to the PM's office." said the insider quickly.

"I'll write up a full report when everything is done Prime Minister. Just four copies though."

"Sounds reasonable, so let's vote on it." said one of the team. They all raised their hands slowly and as before, Simon noticed the same person was last. Simon gave a satisfied smile at the Prime Minister.

"Right. First things first, I want to speak alone to the Minister in charge of Transport."

"Why?" asked the insider.

"You will know the reason soon enough. Now I have only two days left. Goodbye gentleman." He left the room, and the rest just looked at one another.

+

Patrick O'Conner had decided to phone Simon's flat. The phone rang and only got the answer machine. He left a message saying that the he would phone again to re-arrange a new location for the meeting. He replaced the phone and turned to Colleen.

"Where is he?"

"Could be an early morning jogger?"

"Might be, but I somehow don't think he is."

"So where is he?"

"I don't know." The phone rang and they looked at one another.

"Who knows we are here?"

"Find out. Pick up the phone."

"Hello?"

"Is that Patrick?"

"Yes, who is this?"

"Never you mind. Simon has been at an early morning meeting of BOTOG in Downing Street."

"What about? We met and agreed terms yesterday."

"They all have been told where the explosives came from."

"What! And anything else?"

"He is talking to the Transport Minister."

"About what?"

"Goodness knows, he wouldn't say anything at the meeting. It could be that he may be planning to close the airports and ports."

"He hasn't got that much authority?"

"He has now. They voted it to him this morning."

"Damn!"

"There is one place that wasn't mentioned. The hovercraft in Dover."

"Thanks." Patrick hung up and looked at Colleen. "They are getting a lot closer than I would like. They seem to be learning an awful lot about this operation very quickly."

"What do you mean?"

"Well, they have found the factory that supplied the explosive, and they already know that it only supplied it to the Government."

"You know, in years to come, someone will write a book about this." Said Colleen with a smile.

"They'd better not, if they want to stay alive that is, anyhow only a few people know all of it." replied Patrick. "That isn't really important. What is important is to get hold of Simon. Shall I try phoning the flat again?"

"Yes. If you manage to get to speak to him, try and arrange a new meeting place." said Mr Green from his usual chair by the fireplace.

"Where though?" asked Patrick with a frown.

"What about a station on the underground?" Said seumas with a smile.

"Brilliant! They couldn't trace him if he is wearing a mike down there and we can change trains frequently. I'll buy a couple of those Rover cards." Said Patrick.

Colleen picked up the phone and rang Simon and this time got through to him at once.

"You have been naughty, haven't you?" said Colleen. "What do you mean?"

"We know that you know where the explosive came from and who owned it."

"Look, I have my job to do. All I want from you is where are the bombs and how to defuse it. Where do we meet?"

"The underground station at Paddington station. Three hours' from now."

"Fine." He hung up and went to change clothes.

Colleen replaced the phone and looked at Patrick and said nothing. He nodded and looked around at the group.

"I think that something is going to happen to you."said Seumas, standing up.

"Rubbish, I am the only one who knows where the bombs are planted." replied Patrick. "That's why it has to be me that he meets."

"I understand that, we all do. However, what if Simon captures you or decides to kill you?" said Colleen.

"What are you suggesting?"

"Leave a set of the details in Exeter. Write out everything you know and post it to a P.O. Box. When I was based down there, I opened a PO Box, it is still in operation. I'll get the number for you.

"0k, I'll do it. Give me pen and paper."

"Here you are, now I'll leave you in peace." Colleen left the room.

+

Simon turned to Gail, his secretary, who had been sat listening to his side of the call. "Well?"

"I think you are being set up. Take someone with you."

"Don't be silly, I know the woman, and I am certain I know who is leaking information."

"I know you do. But if you are the only one that knows, then you could be killed."

"Self-defeating. The ARI could then be hunted openly. They wouldn't do that though."

"You could dictate to me all you know, I'll type it and lodge it in a bank deposit box."

"Alright, if it makes you happy." He nodded to the two chairs and they both sat down, Gail took out her notepad and nodded to Simon and he started to talk.

Two hours later they had finished and looked at his watch. On his desk was a pile of typed paper and a large envelope beside it. He put the paper into the envelope and sealed it. Then he tossed a small card to Gail. "That number can get me if it is really important." He turned and left. She watched him go, unconsciously crumpling the card in her hand.

+

Almost at the same time, a similar thing was occurring at the flat of the ARI. Patrick had stated that he should go and had sealed up the envelope. Colleen had long since written the address and stamped it.

Now, having picked it up, he left the flat and started to walk towards Paddington.

Both men just made it on time, and they said nothing until they were on the circle line train. When Simon started to speak, Patrick interrupted him.

"You do know that you are being set up by your own Government?"

"I know." replied Simon with a shake of his head.

"As long as you do. I was shocked as to how far you have infiltrated us. What else do you know?"

"A lot, but nothing that you will learn about until I know the place of the bombs."

"Well, I am the only person who knows the true location. I hope that the Government will trust me?"

"Don't you mean the consortium of banks?"

"No. I understand that now it is the Government who are now underwriting it. Since it was now their property." Said Patrick.

"You have just given away your inside source. It will make my job easier to collect and arrest the members of the group and those inside that helped you." replied Simon with a laugh.

"You are bluffing. You might not live to do that." said Patrick. But he felt a bit concerned, nevertheless.

"Think so? I wrote it all down and deposited it in a safe before coming to meet you." said Simon.

"Stop trying to look for more evidence, it might mean you or somebody close to you gets hurt."

"What more evidence is there?" asked Simon.

"You know what I mean. Now as to writing it down I did the same, so in a way it's stalemate. I suggest that we each make our own way down to Folkestone, and I will contact you there." said Patrick.

"Fine." Said Simon. He got out at the next station and left Patrick on the underground, looking pensive as the train pulled out of the station. Simon slowly made his way over to the other platform and back to his own flat.

He pounded up the stairs, opened the door, then put the chain on.

"Did you have any visitors while I was gone?" he asked Gail.

"No, why?"

"Only that I have to keep off looking for evidence, or they will hurt you."

"Did they mention me by name?"

"Not by name, but indirectly."

"What will you do? You can't stop looking it's against your nature."

"I'll try and think of something to keep you and the hostages safe." replied Simon.

"Why don't you let me look for evidence?"

"Do you know what you are letting yourself in for?"

"Probably, I did read what you wrote. Also, remember that I work in the same department as you. So, think I can handle things in my own way safely."

"Ok. So please try and get me the details of who exactly bought the explosive, by that I mean the individual. I think I know who it will be, but I want the facts."

"What about you?"

"I shall go to Folkestone as soon as possible."

"What do you want me to do if I find out?"

"Fly across to France and get the documentation for purchasing the explosive from them, how did they do it, who delivered it and so on."

"How do I do that?"

"Use the helicopter. Here, I'll phone and arrange it." He pulled the phone towards him and did that. Then he said to Gail. "Be there in three hours. I don't care how you do it, just be there."

+

Patrick had made it back to the flat and Colleen opened the door with the chain on it. Once she saw who it was, she let him in. He removed his jacket as he came through the door. He walked through to the kitchen and took a beer from the fridge. He opened it and looked at her and the rest of the group.

"Well, how did it go?" she asked him.

"Not too bad."

"So, what next?"

"We go to Folkestone. By the way, it appears that the factory that we got the explosive from has blown up."

"How convenient."

"Yes, I thought so too."

"Now Patrick, unless we get our demands starting to be carried out by this time tomorrow, the rest of the gang are going to announce where you are hiding and who you are."

"But they already know who some of us are." He glared at Pat Duffy.

"Alright, go to Folkestone. But heaven help you if they don't release the men."

"They will. You'll see."

"Why should they? Look, once the bombs have been defused, the threat is gone."

"But we have the hostages."

"In the end they are expendable."

"Right, then how about if I'll find one bomb and then tell them to release half of them. The other half to be released when the other bomb is found. Does that suit you?"

"It will have to." Colleen said and looked at the others, who nodded their agreement.

"Phone Simon and tell him, I bet he doesn't agree. He is on their side for all his nice manner."

"I'll phone and see." He called Bill but getting no answer, he frowned. Then recalled that they were supposed to be meeting in Folkestone. So, it was most likely he was already on his way there. He replaced the phone and turned to the rest. "He'll be on his way to Folkestone, as we agreed."

"Then you go to Folkestone,I'll keep trying to contact anybody else, who may be at the flat."

"Fine." Colleen dialled again and was happy when the phone got picked up at the other end.

"Hello, who is this please?"

"I need to speak to Simon, its urgent."

"He is out right now. I can take a message and try and forward it to him. Alternatively, I have a number you could try."

Colleen beckoned Pat Duffy over to her. Then wrote on some paper by the phone. *He has gone to Folkestone, but he has left the Gail girl in the flat, she can contact him, or you can on a special number.* Nodding at Colleen, Pat wrote underneath. *"Let me have the number."*

"Ok. Can I have the number please?"

"Certainly. 007006009004 if you are phoning from outside the UK drop the first two zeros off the number and replace it with a 69."

"Thank you." Colleen hung up and turned to Pat. "Here it is, I wrote it down." Pat dialled the number on the paper and when Simon answered, Pat spoke slowly.

"We want half of the prisoners released when the first of the bombs are found."

"Fine, and?"

"And nothing. We will release one of the hostages at the same time."

"Right you are." said Simon.

"Goodbye." said Pat as he replaced the phone and smiled at the rest of the group. "That was easy."

"Maybe a bit too easy?" thought Colleen to herself.


# 27.28

Once in Folkestone in his office at the police station. Simon picked up the phone and dialled the Downing Street direct number he had been given. The phone rang for only a few seconds and then it was answered.

"Hello Simon. What can I do for you?"

"We seem on the point of a breakthrough, I was wondering, can you arrange for the security of the tunnel to be tripled…"

"What for?"

"…and when we have found the first bomb, seven of the fourteen are to be released."

"I think that I had better come and see you."

"I'm on the way to the tunnel, if you want to see me, you have an hour."

"I'll be there, I'll fly down. I'll meet you at the tunnel entrance."

"Sure."Bill hung up and looked at the phone. "Damn politicians," he said to the empty office.

+

The Prime Minister sat and looked at his fingertips. He pressed a bell on his desk and his secretary entered the room.

"Find out what Simon likes, and what it will cost us to buy him off, when the time comes, that is."

"But Prime Minister, you were elected on a cost cutting platform!"

"Just do it!"

"Alright." The secretary left the room and the Prime Minister rose and walked down to his car.

"Get me to the heliport as fast as possible."

"Yes sir."Twenty minutes later he was on his way to Folkestone.

Forty minutes later the Prime Minister's helicopter touched down near the entrance to the tunnel and he bent low as he left the helicopter and ran out to meet Simon who was standing there waiting.

"Prime Minister."

"Simon. Do you know what you have agreed to do? We have always said we wouldn't deal with terrorists and here you are letting seven go free in…" he looked at his watch.

"…in thirty minutes to be exact Prime Minister. I know that but there are some circumstances that you will think it makes it worthwhile."

"This whole project could have been bought off using the contingency fund."

"But the cost of buying it off would have been billions." said Simon frowning.

"We would have managed."

"Prime Minister, now you have had your say, let me at least have mine. The following are facts:"

"One, a person on the very small select team in your Government is feeding information to the ARI and has done for at least the last five years. Two, the explosive came from France and was sold to one client. The British Government, apparently. Three, we have a link with Europe for the first time in history. Four, I have put together a good small, but deadly team, including people who have come back from retirement.

Five, I have done nothing but worry about this for five years and almost got killed in those five years. Now I intend to finish it, even if it kills me in the process. Now don't repeat to anybody what you have just heard."

"You have gone too far!"

"On the contrary, I haven't gone far enough. However, when I get there, you will be the first to know.." Simon stormed off leaving the Prime Minister standing by the helicopter opened mouthed. He wondered if he had chosen the right man for the job.

+

In London, the young reporter had made his lunch date with minutes to spare. She suggested that they eat in her flat. He nervously

358

agreed and followed her across the road and up to one of the upgraded old warehouses. Inside it was like something out of a Sunday colour supplement. He wondered what he was getting himself into as she didn't appear to have a file of cuttings with her.

"You don't seem to have brought the file of cuttings with you."

"No, I have a direct link to the office, I can call up the files from there by computer."

"Oh." She led the way into her office part of the flat and switched on one of two computers.

"Now let's see what I found out for you this morning."

+

In Folkestone police station all hell was breaking loose as Andrews told the other three what message Simon had sent to him.

The only two missing were Simon and CS Rose. He outlined that there was now a need for increased security and money and arranging for MacKenzie go into the tunnel with Simon. He turned to MacKenzie.

"Do you agree to that?"

"Well, I'll have to talk it over with the wife."

"What is there to talk about?"

"Well, I am retired, and I came out of retirement in Belfast to help Bill. However, this is a whole different ball game. What if I should die defusing the bomb?"

"I think that we can give your wife a good lump sum to live on."

"You could charm a snake."

"I know." He laughed. "So you'll agree?"

"Don't have any real choice, do I?" said MacKenzie, with a smile.

"Not really, you already know too much."

+

In the flat in London the young reportetr was being shown the computer screen.

"There are all the details of the cuttings you wanted. You open each folder and extract what you want, then send it to the printer."

"Fine, leave me to it."

"I'll get some lunch." She walked out to the kitchen and left the reporter reading the files. The structure of the financing interested him. He soon was reading the last paragraph. *The Shares in the tunnel have hit a new low today with adverts appearing in newspapers all around the country, one wonders how the managed to get the money for such a high profile campaign? One of the most pressing questions is how far in advance were the adverts booked and paid?* The article continued:

*At a time when the Government was thinking of repealing the ARI law banking publicity, many backbenchers have already voiced their opinion that it was a bad law in the first place. Now the major banks who put up the money are demanding the loans be repaid and fast. Since the time they were taken to allow repayment was large and long.*

*Now this is clearly unattainable. That is unless the unthinkable happens and the Government steps in to bail out a private company, all be it a consortium. It will be remembered that at the beginning of the project we were assured that no public money would be spent. What are we to believe now that this has happened?* It concluded.

"Come and have some lunch, or do you want to eat there?" She looked over his shoulder. "I thought you would pick that up."

"Who wrote this?" "Man called Williams." "Can I meet him?" "I'm afraid not." "Why not?"

"He's dead. He was parking his car on the top of a multi-story car park and as he backed it into the car space, his brakes failed."

"And?"

"He reversed through the low barrier and straight down to his death."

"How terrible."

"The car was examined and there were no faulty brakes at all." "So?"

"The car had been tampered with and put back to normal. All I am saying is, do be careful whom you talk to. There is one other thing."

"What?"

"This fax, never mind who sent it to me, look, go to the factory and ask questions. Don't quote me on this one." They both sat down and started to eat, his head buzzing with questions.

An hour later they both pushed the chairs back. He stood up.

"Look I had better start to get back, do you want a hand or anything?"

"No, I only have to load the dishwasher."

"Mind if I use your phone?"

"To phone who?"

"The editor."

"There is an internal line." She nodded her head in the direction of a green phone on the desk. "Just dial his number."

"Thanks."

"I have to go now, do let yourself out when you are finished and make sure the catch is down." She walked down the stairs and out of the apartment. Smiling, she removed her mobile phone and dialled a number. "He has taken the bait. Just sit back and let him do the work for us." She switched off her phone and smiled in a nasty manner.

+

Inside the flat the young reporter sat and phoned the editor. "Hello?"

"You sent me off looking into the Folkestone tunnel item this morning."

"What about it?"

"Well, I have a couple of leads. A new kind of explosive was delivered to the tunnel back in the day. Apparently the HMG paid for it. Now the banks are wanting their money back..."

"It seems that you may be onto something. Now go and get some francs, your passport and get yourself to Folkestone. There will be hovercraft tickets waiting for you at the booking office. Now go!"

"Right sir."

"Goodbye." The reporter left the flat and went to the offices and did as he had been told. He didn't bother to check and see if anybody was following him. He collected his paperwork and money and made his way down to the hovercraft booking office in Dover.

+

Simon stood at the entrance to the tunnel waiting for the rest of his team to arrive. The first was Andrews.

"You were right, there is something bad going down."

"How do you mean?" asked Simon.

"Well, every time that Rose is in the office chaos breaks out, when he isn't there, it runs like clockwork."

"So?"

"I think we are being set up as a target, and we have found the link of who is supplying the money." said Andrews angrily.

"Who?"

"Get in the car and I'll tell you." The two of them got into Andrew's car and shut the doors.

"I've got some news for you too. But you carry on."

"Well, the money is coming from Switzerland."

"They have never shown any interest before in the ARI."

"Ours is not to reason why...."

"Quite, we had better cover that angle. Now how many down here have noticed that Rose may be the problem?" asked Simon, concerned.

"Most of us."

"Oh dear."

"Is that a problem?"

"Could be. Look we have found out that the bombing of that house in Folkestone is linked with this new substance. " added Simon.

"It seems that five years ago the ARI got hold of a large quantity of a new substance but unlike Semtex, this didn't give off any smell. It was supposed to be much more powerful, so the user didn't need as much. However, they needed somewhere to try it out. If they chose Belfast, they would have been found out in no time with all the experts over there. They decide to try it out over here instead. What we have found out since is that it gets very unstable in a damp environment. We doubt if they know that about it though."

"Ah." said Andrews.

"There is one other thing, I have been tipped off that we have a young reporter looking into this." added Simon.

"What sort of things is he asking?"

"He is seeking some confirmation to the questions.'Were the explosives bought by the Government?'That sort of thing."

"Can we stop him?" asked Andrews, looking worried.

"Not unless we want the whole of the press pack down here. If we stop him, the story of the stoppage would spread."

"It's better to let him feel his way then?"

"Yes, he is a new young reporter. Maybe he will not find out too much." replied Simon.

"Maybe, but he will probably be very keen and may chase any lead."

"In that case let's put a tail on him and if he tries to leave the country, stop him." replied Simon.

"Alright, I can agree to that."

"So where did he get the news from, we have only just got it ourselves?"

"We could approach him and ask him."

"Do we know his address?"

"No, but we have his phone number."

"Get on to BT and get the address. They will give it to you if you say who you are. If need be, we can drive across to Dover and catch him in time." Simon replied.

"Right." Simon left the car and wandered over to the quiet sidings by the entrance and walked down the length of one of the trains. Wondering where they were hiding the hostages.

"Where are you?" He said out loud. "Pardon sir?"

"Oh,Armstrong I didn't see you. I was wondering where they were keeping the hostages."

"Could be anywhere."

"I don't think so, look it has to be within a half day of driving from London."

"Why do you say that?"

"Well, they wanted the meeting the next day early in the morning." said Simon.

"Could be that was to fool you."

"No, I don't think so. I feel I know this man."

"We'll know soon anyhow."

"True." Simon wandered over to the service tunnel entrance and met McKenzie there.

"Are you all ready?"

"Yes. I have all my equipment."

"Good. Then let's get in here." said Simon, tapping the steel doorway.

+

In Dover, the young reporter swung his car into the car park for hovercraft and parked in one of the last few spaces. One of the last few hovercrafts to be still in service and queues stretched out onto the road and back for over a mile.

He wondered how his editor had got the ticket so quickly. All around him were hundreds of police and army personnel. He made his way to the booking desk to wait for those with advanced bookings and queued with the rest.

After ten minutes, he collected his ticket and walked out into the sunlight. Gail had already spotted the young reporter and had followed him and saw him collect the ticket. She now followed at a discreet distance.

+

The ARI gang had been on edge since Patrick had gone off to Folkestone. They knew things were nearing the end and always that was the worse bit of an operation. Pat Doyle rose and turned the television off.

"We must move from here, he hasn't phoned to say what he is doing. I don't know about the rest of you, but I am feeling like a rat in a cage."

"Hey, we are all the same you know." said Seumas.

"And some of us the police don't know anything about." added Barry.

"What's that got to do with anything?"

"Oh, wouldn't the police love to see you lot now." said Lorcan. "If we move then how does he get in touch with us?"

"There is a way as it happens, Seumas. Tell them Colleen."

"Well, we have a portable phone, but it can only be used once. Each call is logged and then the police could trace it."

"So, we could make the call, then leave here?"

"You've got it Lorcan."

"Let's do that then. We can then leave here." Each of them nodded their agreement.

Pat went off to get the van and Colleen went and told Sarah and her son that they were moving. She also told them it would soon be over.

The rest set about picking up all the items and litter that they had brought into the flat and bagging it in rubbish bags. These would be thrown into various skips that seemed to be dotted all over London now.

+

Patrick arrived in Folkestone and was looking for the usual contact that he had used in the past when he was in Folkestone. It was a pity, but it was looking as though they would have to tell HMG where the bombs were. Still the prisoners would be released. He eventually found his contact and arranged for a bed for the night.

Then he entered his room and knowing that he had two hours before his meeting with Simon, he had time to rest.

+

He awoke an hour later and found himself handcuffed to the bed both by his feet and his hands. His contact was looking at him down the barrel of a gun.

"What are you doing? Untie me, I must be at the tunnel in less than an hour."

"You aren't going anywhere; you see those bombs are going to explode along with Bill and his team. It will greatly help us."

"But the prisoners that are being released?"

"There aren't going to be any released prisoners."

"You can't say that. This has been years in the planning. If you let the bomb off, then all this has been a waste of time and money."

"No, we can cause massive waves of disruption and kill off these top men as well."

"But why let us think this is the plan for the last three years?" "We didn't intend for this to happen. It's only recently that we have been advised to change the plan."

"Oh."

"Well, I must be off." He turned and left Patrick laying there. "Oh, I have arranged for someone to untie you tonight some time, no longer than five hours from now."

364

"Five hours!"

"Yes. Goodbye."

"But look..." But he had gone. For a minute Patrick tried to get free, but it was impossible. So, he finally put his head back and drifted off back to sleep.

+

The group had left the flat and the door ajar. They would have got away completely undetected, had it not been for a couple of schoolboys who needed some shelter from a rainstorm and had suddenly seen the door swing open.

They had dashed across the road and ran up to the flat. They were surprised to find it was furnished but not locked. They checked out each room and then went and phoned the police. It wasn't until much later that the police would make the connection.

+

A man entered a phone box and placed some money in the box before dialling the Folkestone CID number.

"Folkestone Police how can we help you?"

"A man you want is at 169 Tower Avenue, off Tower St. Folkestone. He will be there for some five hours." The phone was replaced, and the man moved out of the box and walked purposefully towards the tunnel sidings. Dressed as he was, nobody challenged him.

+

"Where is he?" Muttered Simon under his breath. "We can't wait any longer."

"Let's call back to see if they have contacted us again."

Having done so, they then learnt that there had been a tip off about a man in Tower Avenue. Once Simon knew this, he grabbed his coat and fled out of the office towards the address.

+

The reporter stood in line for the last departure of the hovercraft.

Gail looked at her watch - where was Simon? Should she follow the reporter or wait for him? The loudspeakers announced the departure of the hovercraft.

She ran over to the telephone boxes and phoned Simon's portable phone number.

"Hello?"

"it's me Gail, that reporter is getting on to the Hovercraft, do I go with him or stay for you?"

"Follow him. I have a problem here. I'll stay in touch."

28.28

Patrick was getting worried. He knew if he didn't turn up, then the bombs would be exploded, and the last ten years would be totally wasted.

He struggled at the handcuffs, but it just made his wrists go red. The phone had rung twice in the last hour and he wanted to know who would phone here. He heard the front door open downstairs and the sound of feet running up the staircase. There was a furious knocking on the door.

"Ok, we know that you are in there, just open the door slowly." He laughed.

"I can't do that; you will have to break the door down." "Stand back." There were two crashes, and the door gave way

and Simon and two other men stood at the bedroom door gazing at Patrick lying handcuffed on the bed. "What gives?"

"Some other branch of the ARI wants to blow the tunnel. They tied me up and left me here, how come you knew where to come?"

"He tipped us off."

"Then it may not yet be too late. Unlock me."

"Do you know about the unstableness of the explosive?" "What! You mean it?"

"It's true. We don't know what sort of effect being down there for so long will have had on the explosive. It can become unstable if it gets damp or wet." Said Simon sadly shaking his head.

"Did you know that there was a reporter who is looking into this Simon?" asked Patrick.

"Yes, but he is being followed, why?"

"I think he is leading you a merry dance."

"If you say so. Now where are the rest of the team?"

"I don't know."

"Well, we'll leave you here and maybe you will remember."

"But the bombs? I mean you need me, don't you?"

"I don't think so. You see we have the place sewn up tight. If the other ARI man comes near, then he'll be spotted. Goodbye." He turned to leave, and the portable phone rang on desk. Simon picked it up and listened, then without a word he held it close to Patrick's face.

"Patrick where are you? The rest of us are moving on. Tell me where we are going to meet?" Simon indicated that he should tell them to come to the house. Patrick felt sick, for he knew that if he did that then they would walk right into the trap, but there was little else he could do.

"Come to the following address. We have used it before a long time ago." He gave the address and then Bill pushed down the aerial and switched it off.

"Very good. I must go to the tunnel, you, Patrick, stay put." He laughed and left two policemen on guard,with strict instructions not to release him at all.

Simon left and drove like a bat out of hell towards Dover. He got there just as the last calls were being made for the passengers. Gail saw him and waved at him.

"Come on, this is the last call."

"I'll mange to stop the ferry, you get that reporter off it." "Right you are."She disappeared into the crowded deck. Simon ran to the harbour master's office and knocked on the door. "Come in." Simon walked in and quickly told him why the hovercraft had to be stopped. He showed him his card and was impressed by the speed with which the harbour master acted.

On the deck below Gail had managed to get hold of the young reporter. Once the paperwork had been sorted out, both Simon, Gail and the reporter drove back to Folkestone, all the while asking how the reporter had got hold of the files on the tunnel. Once back at Folkestone, Simon told Gail to fly back to London with the reporter and return to the girl's flat. Then he turned and looked at the reporter as the car pulled up by the helicopter. "You would never have got it printed; a 'D' notice would have been slapped on it. But it was worth trying." "Thanks for nothing."

"Don't worry, you'll realise that this could never come out in the full version. The big stories never do. Anything that might harm any government minister will soon be stopped from ever being printed." He got out and opened the door for Gail. "I'll see you in London sometime."

"Sometime."

"I promise, when this is over, we'll have a nice dinner."

"Alright, I'll hold you to that." She ran with the reporter over into the helicopter while Simon watched them go.

+

At the tunnel entrance there were police everywhere. Simon grinned and looked at Armstrong and McKenzie.

"Bit like bolting the proverbial stable door, isn't it?"

"Not really, while we don't know exactly where they planted the explosives, we now do know where Joe was sent and worked. So, we can concentrate on where he worked for the last three weeks of his life. I have a map showing where he worked, so let's move it." said Armstrong.

"What if they blow the explosives while we are down there?" asked Simon with a frown.

"Then we will be in the most expensive tomb in history." smiled Ian as he lit his pipe.

+

The members of the ARI cell arrived at Tower Avenue and entered the house. Once inside they called out to Patrick and moved forward to the different rooms. Once that they were all in the house, did the police slam the front door and arrested the whole of the group. The two hostages were safe.

Patrick looked back to where he had seen the rest of the ARI enter the house along with the two hostages.

The phone call telling the police to release him had been very opportune. Not one to hang about, he had left and waited behind a car parked near the house.

He knew his luck couldn't last that long but wanted to make sure the rest were alive. He remained crouched down, peering through the car door windows to see what would happen. Twenty minutes later he saw five police vans pull up and most of the ARI members were marched out of the house into the waiting vans.

+

Simon and Ian had got half-way towards the middle of the tunnel when he had the message brought to him that the group had been captured. He passed back the message that he wanted Patrick brought to the tunnel forthwith.

Twenty minutes later a sullen Pat stood alongside the group of men in the tunnel.

"Right Patrick, where are the bombs?" Said Bill, his back to the man.

"I don't know. I am not Patrick; I am Pat. Patrick is not here." Bill turned around and gazed at Pat.

"You are right, you are not Patrick, now who knows where the bombs were placed then?"

"Not any of the group, Patrick did learn where they were placed from two of his men. Both have now died, sad isn't it?" Pat smiled wickedly at Bill.

"So, who knows then?"

"You might already have your suspicions, let's just say somebody well connected."

"CS Rose?"

"You said it."

"So how did you recruit him?"

"His daughter. That's his younger daughter, she is called Jane Rose. She is the apple of his eye, and you already know older daughter Gail. We just had to threaten to harm the younger one."

"I didn't realise that Gail and Rose were related. So he helped you? But didn't that go against all his principles?"

"Of course, but what could he do?"

"How long has he been helping you?"

"Since before the Brighton bombing." "You can't mean that?"

"You aren't married, are you?"

"No."

"Children?"

"No."

"Then it makes it difficult for you to understand what men will do when their young daughter is put under pressure. Look, you like Gail, right?"

"Yes."

"Well, if we said unless you do as we say, we'll harm her."

"You fiend!"

"You get the picture." Pat shrugged his shoulders, as if to say, I couldn't care less.

"So, I have to find first Rose and arrest him, not easy."

"No, but then that is not my worry."

"No, that is my job. Right, I'll go in search of him."

"Goodbye William or do you prefer Simon? Do any of you have any painkillers on you by any chance? The wrists are sore where the handcuffs were put on.

"Goodbye Pat. One thing, I doubt I'll see you again, so do have a couple of these aspirins." He passed him a pair of small capsules. "Thanks Simon, I wish we could have met in some other way."

"Me too." He turned and left.

+

It was more than ten hours later that the police were to find Pat Doyle was dead in his cell.

Simon phoned CS Rose and waited in the Folkestone office for him to arrive. He wondered how to tackle this and decided that head on was the best approach.

"Good afternoon Chief Superintendent Rose, we seem to have some problem finding the bombs."

"So?"

"I wondered if you might assist?" "Me? How should I be able to help?"

"Well, let's put it this way, if I don't get your co-operation over this matter....."

"You are going to the PM?"

"No. I'd let slip to the ARI that you had told me everything and your young daughter might die."

"You bastard!"

"I don't think that this is the time for name calling. Where are the bombs placed?"

"They'll kill her." "Do they have her?"

"No, but they could snatch her anytime. She works in a newspaper library. You have no idea, no idea at all." He bowed his head in shame.

"That may be so, but you already know that I have enormous powers I can use.

"Try to solve the problem in Northern Ireland and that would be something. They wanted money to start with, then information on new weapons, then on explosives. As Minister of Defence, I had the right sort of access to that information."

"So now let's go to the tunnel and you point out the bomb sites."

"But if I do that then I sign my daughter's death warrant." "You will be signing your own if you don't, I'll force it out of you." Said Simon grimly.

"Ok, they are behind the segments that are signed with his name but have a circle around it. I watched him do it." said Rose with a resigned look.

"And yet you did nothing."

"I had my hands tied so to speak."

"Listen there is a way your daughter wouldn't get harmed." "How." he asked eagerly.

"I'll leave my gun here unless you have one of your own?" "You really would do that, wouldn't you?"

"Yes."

"Then you are leaving me no option are you?" "No. None whatsoever."

"Then leave me alone. You are quite right; I should have done this a long time ago. I will miss all of this." He waved his hand around the office. "There is one thing you should know about though first."

"Which is?"

"The leader, Patrick O'Conner, has other plans. Ones that do not run with the approval of the leaders of ARI back in Ireland. Follow the money and look at his record, such as it is. We don't have much on him, but what little amount we do have, do use. Now can you leave me alone please?"

"I'm sure that they will write you a good obituary."

"Thanks. You were too good you know." said Rose as Simon turned and left him. A few minutes later a shot rang out.

+

Simon returned to the tunnel and told the team where to look and what to look for. It took the team about half an hour to find and two days to remove safely.

## A Fortnight later.

The day after the tunnel reopened Simon Reed walked to his office and reviewed all the evidence of the past five years. Now he knew the key players, and most were either dead or would soon be in prison.

He had to give a report to the Prime Minister, so spent two days re-reading all the documents before typing up the shortened report of what he wanted to say.

Simon then phoned Downing Street and asked if he could see the Prime Minister? He could? Well in that case that afternoon would best suit him.

Then he made five copies and addressed one to each of the following: DI Rogers, DI Armstrong, DI Andrews and a copy addressed to himself at his bank. The final copy he slid into a folder to give to the PM.

On his way to the Prime Minister, he called in at a newspaper office and spoke to a lady working in the newspaper historical records department to check something.

Now he was ready to meet the Prime Minister.

+

"Good afternoon Mr. Reed." "Good afternoon Prime Minister. Why did you want to see me?"

"To hand you my report on the channel tunnel threat." said Simon as he passed the folder to the John Major.

"It was a shame that Chief Superintendent Rose died in trying to find the bombs. His obituary was a good one though, wasn't it?" said the Prime Minister, as he looked at the report in his hand.

"I tend not to read them sir. Otherwise, are you happy with how things worked out?"

"To be frank with you, no."

"Why not?" asked Simon.

"I think you already know the answer."

"You are right, I do."

"Then tell me."The Prime Minister sat back in his chair behind the desk and put his hands together and listened to Simon speak.

"Some years ago,when the tunnel project had been announced by your predecessor, the ARI decided that they could plant a bomb to explode in the tunnel at some time to be decided in the future."

"They found a person and blackmailed him into doing what they wanted. At this point only a select few knew the full details. The service tunnel was connected, and things started to look good for the backers and underwriters of the project."

"Then letters were posted to the directors of the banks and the tunnel company. Most ignored them, so adverts appeared, this time on the underground. Panic set in and share prices and future ticket bookings dropped like a stone. The Government had already stepped in and picked up the bill of the tunnel costs that the banks were demanding be paid. Eurotunnel had come cap in hand to the Government and had not been turned away despite the rhetoric of the earlier Prime Minister when the first sod was cut." Simon paused and looked at the PM.

"So now you have a tunnel on your hands and the Government thinks the consortium will buy back the tunnel once everything is resolved. Then you learn that the banks don't want it back. After all, who really knows how many bombs are down there?" "It's become a very hot potato. Then a person,a well connected person, comes to you and whispers that if you decide to let it be destroyed, everything about the purchase of it will be swept away in the deep recesses of Government departments. This sounds a great idea, until I upset the apple cart by telling you that I have managed to negotiate with them to release of fourteen of the twenty-seven prisoners. You, PM, hadn't planned on releasing any, right from the start. Now you would have to release fourteen prisoners. Well, that really spoilt your neat little plans."

"You knew I was on the right trail of the explosive when I had informed you that HMG were the only customers as far as I could ascertain. Chief Superintendent Rose knew lots more but said nothing. He looked at you at the meeting and you very slightly nodded your head at him. His unknown job was as a government adviser in security, meaning that he could go almost anywhere unhindered. Just as we start planning to visit the factory that makes the explosive to look at their records, it is blown up. Coincidence? Could be, but I doubt it somehow. I then learn that the explosive used for the two devices can become unstable if left in a damp atmosphere and the race is on to find them."

My meeting with the ARI member is somehow delayed and a new, and I emphasis the word new - reporter is thrown enough bits of the story to make them start to find out things. A quick phone call to his editor and you thought that with a reporter at my heels I would get tangled up in them.

You choose the wrong reporter, someone older would have been better. He is introduced to Jane Rose, the younger daughter of CS Rose. I think she already knew or had guessed the pressure her father was under. She shows the reporter a series of files on a computer that covered everything in full documentation and he heads off towards France. On the only hovercraft. With tickets at a premium? I wasn't born yesterday. Then I get told that Patrick has been captured. By pure chance a phone call is made to him just as I am about to leave. The rest of the cell are all to come to him. I return to the tunnel and ask for Patrick to be brought to me. He isn't, another member of the ARI is, somebody called Pat Doyle. Apparently Patrick was authorised to be released just after the rest turned up. Pat indicates that I should ask CS Rose. Which I had suspected for some time, as well as most of the DIs in the team. How long have you known about Rose, Prime Minister?"

"Two years."

"I point out how helpful it would be if he points out the site of the bombs. He tells me where they are and how they are marked, claiming he watched Joe do the deed, something I doubt very much. The bombs are defused. Somehow, he dies during this time." Simon took a sip of water from a glass on the PM's desk and carried on.

"The tunnel is now declared safe. But now the Government must explain to the British public how it used taxpayer's money to buy off the banks. What do you plan on doing with the tunnel Prime Minister? It won't be used now."

"Why ever not?"

"People's worse fears have been justified."

"Only if the whole story comes out that is. A much more pressing question is what are we going to do with you?" He looked at Simon across the desk.

"Do? You can do nothing as I have decided to resign." "Resign? O no, I really can't allow that. You know too much."

"But I wouldn't talk."

"They all say that, until the pension runs out. You only have to look at Peter Wright to prove it."

"So, what can you offer me?"

"Well, I know that you are unlikely to accept a bribe, so treat this as a package."

"Go on."

"There is a new organisation the Government has just started up. LICD or London International Crime Department to give it the full title. A new unit that has connections with both the USA and our European counterparts. With your skills you would be assigned a good position in there. And a good package to go with it."

"Who is on the team?"

"A very small select few, let's say. I would like you to consider joining them?"

"A bribe then in any other language."

"Not at all. Let's just say I would rather keep you where I can still see you working for the good of the UK."

"And if I say no?"

"I wouldn't ask, but there are dangerous jobs on nuclear power plants. Accidents occur now and then to the best of them. I understand that one is about to be decommissioned in a few years' time in the far north of Scotland. I understand they will need a full-time security officer up there."

"I don't have much of a choice, do I?" said Simon sadly.

"Not really. The Prime Minister smiled and took a folder off a small pile on his desk. He looked up at the map of Great Britain on the wall.

"There is one man we would like to know a lot more about. He has no real record to speak of. He also managed to avoid being caught when almost the rest of his cell were. All that is known is that he is called Patrick O'Conner or aka 'The Boss'. We are very concerned about his whereabouts. See if you can find him for us."The Prime Minister pushed the file towards Simon.

Simon looked at the file on the desk and paused, then reached out and picked it up and looked at the Prime Minister in the eye.

"You don't want much do you? Just so you know, there are four more copies of the full report out there, one of which is in my name, in a bank vault. However, I ask only one thing."

"Which is?" asked the PM with a frown.

"Jane Rose really wants to work for the Police. She is bright but doesn't have the right connections or the right parents now." He let his sentence hang in the air. The Prime Minister nodded slightly before making a note on a piece of paper in front of him. "I recognise the name. Just don't push your luck too far. One final thing, there appears to be a new drug on the street, seems to give people the ability to work longer and more efficiently. But there may be side effects we are not aware of yet. Let me know if you know of any information that might come to light Simon."He watched Simon turn and leave him alone in his office.

# Chapter 20

Moscow 1994

The IT officer sat at her desk looking at the screen in front of her. Surrounded by old monitors, computers and keyboards, her desk was almost hidden from anybody who looked in the door. She had sorted the computer as Ivan's secretary had so nicely asked her to. However, she was now very concerned with what she had found on it. She had kept a copy for her own use, a firm believer in some knowledge may save her life one day.

Now she was looking at the screen as it filled with pages of information about a new drug. It seemed from reading the file, that Ivan had his hands in a nice little earner in south England.

An atlas was spread out in front of her, open at the page showing Marlow and part of London. She could see the location was perfect, river and road connections were so near. A noise in the corridor made her look towards her closed door. As the door opened, she reached for the button on the computer and pressed it to delete what she had been looking at. The floppy disc lay on her desk. Swiftly she put the atlas on top of it and pushed her chair back and stood up as Ivan walked into the office, unannounced as usual.

"I have a small problem that I need you to solve for me."

"If I can, I will. What is the problem?"

"While I was away recently a file on my personal computer was downloaded and deleted. At least that was the message I received."

"And you want me to retrieve it for you?" asked the IT Officer.

"No. When I got back here, I opened my computer and downloaded a copy of file from my office laptop. Now here is the strange part. My computer seems to still have the original file on it. Despite it being downloaded and deleted. I wonder if you could find out who would do such a thing? When you have found them, please arrange for them to be downstairs in the lower interviewing room. I know you wouldn't fail me in this matter." Ivan turned and walked to the door and then looked back. "Are you planning a journey to England?" He pointed at the atlas and left the room, closing the door after him.

The IT officer sat at her desk for ten minutes not moving at all. How could she have made a mistake that Ivan could find so easily? She ran her hand through her hair and wondered how to get out of this mess. If she told Ivan the truth, he would smile and then he would arrange for her to be killed, and not too quickly either if the talk about the lower interviewing room was to be believed.

She reached for her phone to ring Ivan's secretary, but then replaced it without doing so. She turned on the computer and brought up the live image of what the secret camera that she had installed in Ivan's office showed. The desk was empty as was the room. Nodding her head, she reached out and took a computer, identical to Ivan's, off the shelf to her right. Then walked out and up to Ivan's office.

It was the work of ten minutes to install the replacement and take the original one away with her. Once back in her own office she stored the computer among the others on the shelves beside her. The replacement computer on Ivan's desk was just a slave to the one that she had installed in his office. Now everything that Ivan thought he was doing on the computer was being stored and backed up on two other computers. At least she knew what Ivan was up to or planning.

Ivan sat in a small office and smiled as he watched his IT Officer change the computer. His suspicions were correct. He had arranged for another company to install secret CCTV cameras both in the IT room and his own office. In time, he would arrange for her to be a "guest" in the lower interviewing room.

Now though there was the more pressing matter of sourcing a new centre for the distribution of the new drug. Also, he needed to find the person or persons who had set fire to the Dacha. Ivan picked up his phone and dialled a number in London. He needed an update on what was going on.

+

In London Ruth Sanders was in early that morning. Busy at her desk doing the usual paperwork, she kept an eye open through the open door to see if Bill and Jane would come in to work today. She didn't expect them to, as the last she had heard was that they were heading north to Scotland, via Oxford it seemed. The phone rang on her desk, making her jump.

"Hello?" Only a few people knew her outside line.

"Ruth, nice to speak to you again. An update would be useful, no rush, sometime today. And I need you to do me a small favour, concerning two of your officers. I will fax you details later, an accident or something similar will do." The phone was replaced, and she sat shaking at what he had asked.

Information was one thing; this was quite another. She rose from her desk and left her office; she needed some air.

+

Ivan picked up his phone again and spoke to his top henchman.

"Two things. One, I need to know who started the fire at the Dacha - if you don't know by midday, then you had better look for another employer. Two, collect both my secretary and my IT officer at some point today and invite them for an interview in the lower interview room. I need to know what information they have and who put them up to stealing it. Also, make sure they tell you which one is my real computer in the IT officer's office. Understand?"

"Yes, find the person who destroyed the Dacha and why. Also find out why your secretary and IT officer did what they did and for who."

"Exactly. You have until midday for the first and five o clock this afternoon for the other."

"I'll be in touch later." The line went dead, and Ivan sat back in his chair and smiled, before opening a drawer and taking out a bottle of vodka. Not bothering with a glass, he took a swig, put the top back on and went back to his office.

+

In Cowley near Oxford, Justin had finished looking at a new, half built, industrial unit. While much larger than the group needed now, it could be sub-divided and let, leaving the remaining part for their own operations. If in time their business grew, then they could expand if needed without the need for moving again. Being half built, if they bought it now, the additional alterations would be easy to have made. He made a note of the company selling the unit and walked back to his car. He needed to find a phone box and call her.

+

The New East Sutherland was now properly open. Patrick had agreed with planning that the work at the rear of the hotel could be finished later in the year.

Patrick smiled as he watched the first of his guests drove up the tarmac drive and stop at the bottom of the steps. A woman got out and his porter went and took her keys and arranged to park the car and unload her luggage. The front of house team was well trained. They knew what was required of them. Patrick had spent a fortune doing the hotel up and wanted it to be the first place anybody would want to stay if in east Sutherland. Of course, a reason to come here would be good.

378

He stepped out on to the steps and shook hands with the lady as she approached him. A member of staff offered her a drink and she took it and followed the staff member towards her room. Patrick glanced south towards Dunrobin Castle, bits showing in amongst the treetops. That was what most tourists came to see, but he knew that he needed some other hook to keep them here longer than just a night or two. Another car swung into the car park, and like the first, stopped at the bottom of the steps. This time a man got out and smiled at Patrick.

"May your troubles be less, your blessings more, and nothing but happiness walk through your door. Patrick, it's good to see you. I heard that Pat had come up here to speak to you. I have tried to get hold of him, but not been able to do so. Have you seen him at all?"

"Barry? Barry Ryan? Is it really you?" asked Patrick, looking slightly shocked. He hadn't expected to see any others of the original group up here any time soon. "No, I have not seen any sign of Pat for over a week. He came and stayed a night, then went south, at least that is what I think I heard him say. Now come in and I'll get you a drink and you can fill me in with all the news from over the water."

+

The phone rang on the woman's desk. She leant forward and pushed the door shut, then picked up the phone.

"Hello?"

"Justin here, I think I have found our ideal base. It's an industrial unit still being built, half complete and if we buy it, we could sub-let the half we don't need to use."

"Where exactly is it?"

"Oxford, well a suburb of Oxford. Use to be part of a large car manufacturing plant. It's being reduced in size and the land is being built on as a business park. I tell you it's ideal for what we want."

"Price?" she asked.

"Twenty-two thousand, give or take a bit. Probably can get it for less if I haggle. Have you heard anything from Kenneth about the other property he was looking at?"

"Funny you mention that I only learnt a short while ago that he has been killed in a road traffic accident. I'll try and find out the address he was looking at and perhaps you could go and look? Before we decide, that is."

"Where was it exactly?"

"Eynsham Industrial Estate, near Oxford

"Not too far for me to go. I'll drive out and look. The other place sounds better though."

"I agree that it sounds ideal. First look at Eynsham, see what you think, then go and find out what each one is wanting for outright purchase. And Justin?"

"Yes?"

"Phone me next time at home, not here." Smiling, she replaced the phone.

+

Justin replaced the handset and went back to his car. He got in and drove northwards toward Eynsham industrial Estate.

An hour later he had arrived and was walking and shaking his head in annoyance. Three units were for sale and four were for letting. He walked back to his car and took out a small tool kit he kept in the boot. Then looking up and down the quiet estate, he made his way towards the unit located the furthest from the entrance to the industrial estate.

Justin banged on the small door set into the metal roller door and waited. A bell was fixed to the wall. He pressed his ear to the door and pressed the bell. He could not hear anything. He waited for a couple of minutes then broke the lock and pushed the door open slowly.

Inside the warehouse was empty except for the blue and orange racking reaching up five levels. Just inside the entrance, he saw a piece of paper lying on the ground. Picking it up, he held it to the light and saw that it was in some foreign language. Justin stuffed it into his back pocket for checking later and moved further into the warehouse. His footsteps echoed back at him as he walked the length of the building. At the back he saw five doors all open. It seemed that four of them were small offices, the fifth led to some stairs going downwards. He flicked the light switch on the side at the top of the steps, but nothing happened. Annoyed, he returned to his car and collected a large heavy torch.

Once back inside, he took a closer look at a bank of switches just inside the door to the warehouse. All were in the off position. Justin pulled one marked warehouse down, and all the lights slowly came on. Smiling, he looked for one marked basement, but didn't find one. Shrugging his shoulders, he walked the length of the warehouse and down the steps, his torch flashing on the walls of the stairs as he did so.

At the base of the first set of stairs were two doors. One blue and one red. Slowly he pushed the handle down on the red one but it didn't move. Then he tried the blue one and it squeaked open slowly. He shone his torch into the space and saw several wooden containers of different shapes and sizes. Shinning his torch on the floor, he saw footprints in the dust. Justin stepped back and closed the door. Then retraced his steps back up to the warehouse. He had just got into the warehouse when all the lights all went out.

+

In Moscow the IT officer and Ivan's secretary were out for a walk. Both had agreed that outside would be far safer and away from prying ears and eyes.

"So, what is it you want to say?" asked his secretary with a frown.

"Ivan knows that someone tampered with the computer and the memory."

"How does he know?"

"No idea, but he has asked me to find out who did this and get them to the lower interview room. You and I know what that means."

"You have a problem then, don't you?" replied the secretary with a shrug.

"Wrong! We have a problem. I don't intend being silent if he does find out it was me. I'll mention your part in it. Now let's try and think what this is about and how we are going to sort this out." Both fell silent and carried on walking. Then his secretary looked across at her companion.

"I found a small piece of paper saying, 'amber file.' But that was all."

"As in colour or something else?"

"No idea, I would look on the computer, but don't really think that it a good idea at the moment."

"Probably not." The two women walked on and before they knew it, they were back outside his offices. They looked terrified as his leading henchman, Boris, walked towards them followed by two of his staff.

"Ladies. Care to join me and my friends for a small interview?" He smiled and stepped aside as the two ladies were led down to the lower interview room. He then followed them down the stairs and then once inside, closed the heavy lined metal door. "Now ladies, I need to learn what you both have been up to. We can do it the easy way or…" He paused and indicated the rooms bits of 'furniture' that had been adapted for a totally different use. "…the hard way. Now which is it to be?"

+

In the warehouse, Justin was slowly feeling his way along the back wall away from the offices and basement. At the front he could hear the murmur of voices. Anxious to hear what was being said, he carried on moving through the racking towards the front of the warehouse.

At the front two men were peering into the darkness of the warehouse. One looked at the bank of switches that his companion had just turned off.

"I didn't leave the lights on."

"Never said you did. The lock is broken, so somebody has been inside. Now if they have been downstairs, well then, we had better make ourselves scarce. The fewer people that know we have stored the items there the better. Yes?"

"Ok, I agree that we need to take a look, but can't we put the lights on to make it easier to see?"

"The person may still be inside. If we put the lights on, then they will know we are here. Better to wait and see what happens. This is the only way in and out after all. If we start to go into the warehouse, then they could leave without us knowing." Justin had heard the last bit of the conversation. He had wondered if there was another way out from the basement, the red or blue rooms perhaps. Now though, he realised that unless the two at the front went away, something that was very unlikely to happen soon, he was trapped. He sat down on a pile of disused packing cases and waited to see what would happen.

+

In the hotel, Patrick led the way to the bar, with Barry following behind. His case had been taken to the room that Patrick had given him. The bar manager looked up as Patrick entered.

"Your usual sir?" He reached for the large bottle of Golspie whisky from behind the counter.

"No, get me two Irish ones. A special large one for my friend here," Patrick said, as he slapped Barry on the back.

"As you say sir." The manager turned and filled the two glasses before slipping a non-tasting pill into the glass, which dissolved almost at once. He turned and put the two glasses on the counter in front of them.

"Sla'inte." said Barry.

"Sla'inte." replied Patrick smiling at the bar manager. He watched as Barry downed it in one.

"Give me another, just like that one." said Barry.

"Just like that one." The bar manager looked at Patrick, who nodded. The same procedure was followed twice more, then Barry looked at Patrick.

"I don't feel great, can you help me get to my room."

"Come on, it is this way." Patrick led the helpless Barry away from the bar and down the hall before slowly climbing the spiral stairway to the first floor. He looked up and down the hall to check that nobody was about and leaned Barry against the railings. Then he moved and unlocked the room that he had allocated to Barry. He turned to watch as Barry was now climbing the railings and with his hand outstretched on either side, tried to balance as he took a step forward…

…An hour later, the remaining tablets had been removed from the bar and stored safely where nobody would find them.

The bar manager had been given the rest of the day off. Barry still lay on the floor of the hallway, a sheet covering the body.

Patrick scratched the back of his head. At present the only guest was the lady in the top floor apartment. She hadn't appeared when Barry had screamed on the way to hitting the floor, so he assumed she was asleep. He stepped forward and removed the sheet, then went to his office and phoned the local police.

"Is that Golspie police station?" "Yes."

"It's The New East Sutherland, I want to report an accident. One of the guests has fallen and appears to have killed himself."

"Don't move anything, we will be right there."

Patrick replaced the phone and smiled. This time he would not get anything wrong. He had already spoken to the two men from Ireland. Now with three of the original cell dead he felt he was starting to regain the upper hand. He sat at his desk and wrote a short note to a certain Russian that he knew.

†

An hour had passed and the two men at the warehouse door had grown tired of standing, so one had remained, and the other had gone for a smoke outside. Justin sat and waited. He knew the longer they waited without anything happening, the better the chance they might leave, and then he could get out. A noise at the front, made him reach for his torch.

"Watch where you are going, you nearly crashed into that pillar." said one of the men.

"Are you surprised? We have been here over an hour, and nobody has appeared. I think we should look at the items and then if they have not been touched, lock up and go."

"It's true that nobody has shown up. They would have by now. Right, we'll do as you suggest." One of them moved to the bank of switches and pulled a couple into the 'on' position. Justin sat and listened as the footsteps grew quieter. Then he made his way quickly along the front and outside. Once outside, he sprinted across to his car and got in. No sooner had he done so, than the door opened, and a hand reached in and took the keys out of the ignition.

"Come with me, we need to have a little chat. We guessed you might be inside. My colleague walked down the warehouse and I walked outside and stood watching. I saw you come out and dash to your car. Well now, we need…" Justin rose out of his seat and jabbed the man in the kidney with his torch. The man reeled back grabbing at his kidney as he did so. Justin reached down and took the car keys off him and then got in and drove off. He needed to find a phone and soon.

Inside the warehouse basement the other man was unlocking the red door. He pushed it open and breathed a sigh of relief, nothing had been touched. Closing and locking the door, he peered into the blue room and as far as he could make out, there were no new footsteps in the dust. He pulled the door closed and returned to the front of the warehouse to find his companion lying on the ground outside.

"I thought you were supposed to catch him. We knew he was in there somewhere."

"I did, then he hit me in the kidneys, grabbed the keys and took off. Did he get into the basement rooms?"

"Doesn't appear so. No new footprints on the floor in either of them."

"That's a relief then. Now let's lock up and go."The two men did that and then got into the van and drove off leaving the warehouse alone with its mystery stack of boxes.

+

Spotting a phonebox, Justin pulled in and dialled the same number as before. Since it went to answerphone, he left a message.

"Cowley would be better. Eynsham is being watched. Although there are some boxes in the basement. I didn't explore as there were others on site at the time. I'll drive back to Marlow."

In London, the lady listened to the message then deleted it. Rising from her desk, she made her way out of the office and down to her car. She was soon driving towards the industrial estate in Marlow.

+

An hour and half later in Moscow, Ivan looked at his phone with annoyance. He had asked that he didn't get disturbed, yet here it was ringing. Angrily, he picked it up.

"Yes?"

"We have found a couple of new locations. One is a part-built warehouse. We can finish the design ourselves if we want to. Half can be let out in a proper legal manner. We use the other half for our own businesses."

"Where and how much?" He asked. "Oxford and twenty-two thousand." "And the other one?"

"A warehouse in Eynsham. Near Oxford. Has been used before, has racking in place and apparently a couple of basement rooms. It could do, but the Oxford one sounds better in the longer term."

"Let's use both. The Eynsham one until the Oxford one is complete. I'll arrange for one of my lawyers to start on the paperwork. Fax me the details and the people to deal with. Have you emptied Marlow and the adjoining units yet?"

"Mostly. Unit 11 is secured by the police, but unit 10 is now just empty. What do you want done with the printer's equipment? Will they want it back?" Ivan smiled at this question.

"No, they will not be needing it. Leave it in the unit. We can sell it on as a business ready unit. I need to work on something else, call me in two days' time." He hung up and sat back in his chair and thought for a few minutes how things worked out.

A knock on his office door and Boris put his head around the door.

"Thought you should know that the only thing they really knew about was something called." - he looked at a piece of paper. "Amber. What do you want me to do with the bodies?"

"Dispose of them in the forest, along with the other two prisoners that we have downstairs. Find out about the Dacha. Then I need you to go over to Scotland for me."

+

Patrick sat back and listened to the policeman telling him that they would need to close the hotel for a few days. He nodded and went to inform his only guest upstairs. The letter he had been writing lay in its envelope addressed and stamped waiting to be posted. He made a mental note to get one of the staff to post it.

+

In Marlow, at the industrial estate, a woman was busy at the rear of the unit trying to get into unit 12. The police had sealed it and put a new padlock on it. The padlock was not really a problem, but the police seal was proving a bit harder to carefully remove. A sharp knife would have done the job, but she wanted to be able to enter and leave without leaving any trace that she had done so. She gritted her teeth and reached up again to try and remove the seal.

+

The two hitmen, last seen in Ireland, relaxed as their plane touched down at Inverness Airport. Both looked at one another, nodded and then as the plane rolled to a stop, got out of their seats and left the plane. Nobody bothered to stop the two of them from getting off first. With men that size you didn't stand in their way.

Once outside the airport, they made their way to the long stay car park. A bit of a walk, but after the long flight, that really didn't matter too much. Now they looked for the van that they had been assured would be parked here. A green van with no signage was what they had been told would be ready for them. One reached down and felt behind the rear wheel, smiling he stood up with a set of keys in his hand. Unlocking the van, both men got in and drove northwards to learn of their next assignment.

+

Ivan had arranged for his man to fly to Inverness by his private jet. It was landing as the two hitmen were driving out of the airport car park. Thirty minutes later, he was following their trail, first on a bus to collect a vehicle from Inverness. Then he headed northwards to the same east Sutherland villages.

# Chapter 21

Golspie Two days later.
Patrick left the hotel and headed towards Golspie police station. He had been asked to attend and wondered what they wanted. He pulled up in the carpark nearly opposite the large police station and got out. The sea was beating against the pier and coming over the pathway that ran along the seafront. He turned from looking out to sea and walked over to the police station.

"Good morning sir."

"I got a call to come and attend. I am Patrick O'Conner. I run the New East Sutherland." He produced a business card and placed it on the counter in front of the officer.

"Right sir, I think the officer you need to see is through the back, I'll go and tell him you have arrived." He left Patrick standing at the front desk. Shortly he returned with another policeman.

"Hello, I am DS Cooper. Do come through to my office." He led Patrick through to a back office and shut the door after them.

"Just to tie up a few loose ends. We are satisfied that the death was an accident. From the look of things, the person had been drinking heavily beforehand. Drink can make you do all sorts of things that you wouldn't do in the ordinary manner. We only have a couple of questions for you. It seems that the body had been lying there for around an hour before we were called. Any reason for the delay?" Cooper looked at Patrick and waited.

"I had only just opened that day, with staff and new customers coming in, I was probably in the kitchen or outside. You know how time flies."

"Quite so sir. Now as to the second question, it is a bit more problematic. You see the local postman found an envelope addressed to a Russian in the post box when it was emptied. The thing is sir, it didn't have enough postage on it. Normally it would go to Inverness, then have the appropriate action taken, and in due course, it would end up back at the sender. If there is no address of the sender on the outside of the envelope, then it gets sent to the central mail centre for them to open and see if there is a contact address inside."

"Now a cousin of the postman works for you. She was asked by you to post this for the hotel. She put it in the postbox as asked. Now why would you not ask her to take it in to the post office and get it weighed? I mean the box is right outside, set into the wall of the building so I ask again, why not get the correct postage? I am waiting." Cooper looked at Patrick and sat back in his chair.

"Probably a queue at the post office. I had put a stamp on it. Obviously not enough though. I do wonder why that is connected to the death of one of my guests." Patrick stared at Cooper who fiddled with a pen. Cooper looked up as he spoke.

"A guest you say. Yet when we looked in the hotel guest book, only two people had been listed. A lady and some Russian person. We couldn't quite make out the signature. Would that be the same person you were writing this letter to?" Cooper produced an envelope and slid it across to Patrick.

Patrick wondered if the policeman had seen the contents, for the top of the envelope had been slit open already. He knew that there was no address of the sender on the envelope, so he sat for a few minutes thinking furiously as to what to say.

"I thought you said it went to a central mail centre to be opened."

"I did, and you can see it has been there and back to us in two days. Quite an achievement, don't you think? I'll ask you again, is this the same person who was staying at the hotel that day?"

"Yes. He came for two nights and then went."

"Two nights you say. Yet the hotel, according to you, had only opened on the day the body was found. He wasn't in the hotel when we arrived. Now where would he be I wonder? It wouldn't be possible for him to stay there ahead of your opening, would it?"

"I'd need to check. Some of the staff were allowed to ask friends to stay in the week before we opened to give me feedback on things we could improve on and so on." said Patrick.

"You need to check. And yet you can write to a Russian, who may or may not have stayed at the hotel, but you can't confirm that it is the same person. I strongly recommend you go and look at the hotel guest book and bring it back here. You see, if he was staying there when the accident happened, we need to talk to him." Cooper stood up and Patrick did as well and they looked at each other, then Cooper opened the office door and led Patrick out to the front desk. "Tomorrow morning. First thing, I want that hotel guest book on the front desk. Understand?" Patrick nodded and left.

+

In the Rest and be thankful Hotel located on the southside of Golspie, the two hitmen had checked in for a week and now were walking along the main street towards the centre.

+

Boris pulled the hire car into the car park in the centre of the village. He got out, tired from travelling, and looked across at the small development of flats that were at the foot of the road. He locked the car and walked over to the large noticeboard that declared they were for sale and to rent. A show flat was at the top of the three-story block. He looked at his watch, the show flat was supposed to be open. He walked up the stairs and knocked on the door. A young lady opened it and looked surprised to see anybody there.

"Can I help at all?"

"This is the show flat? The one for the other five in the building?"

"Oh yes, it is just that we don't get that many walk-in customers, most tend to phone ahead or book through the solicitors. Do go through and look. Can I take your name, for the records you understand?"

"Boris."

"Boris." She wrote it in the book on the table. "And your second name?" He paused. "Yelsin." He said with a smile.

"No, really? I mean your real name."

"Lady it is Yelsin. I think you are thinking of Yeltsin our president."

"Sorry. Can you spell that for me?" "Y E L S I N"

"Thank you, Mr Yelsin."

"Call me Boris, everyone else does. How many rooms does it have?"

"Two bedrooms, both en-suite. A kitchen and a living room with views towards the sea and at the back of the flat, towards Ben Bhraggie." He stepped forward and followed her through to the rear of the flat. Boris thought that this might make a good base for his boss when he came to Scotland.

+

In Marlow, Justin had arrived in time to help get the rear door to unit 12 open. Both peered in and then walked through and down the stairs into the room set in the basement. Once inside, they switched on the lights, but nothing happened.

"Go next door and turn the power on. Here is the key to unit 11." She passed Justin a key and he went to do as she asked. In the meantime, she sat down on a chair that had been left and waited for the lights to come on.

Justin got into unit 11 and made his way to the electric board. There he found that the electric had been disconnected. Where before a meter and consumer unit had been, now just two long cables coming up from the ground were all that remained. He noticed the cable that had been used to run the basement next door had also been taken away. Angry, he left the unit, forgetting to lock it again and returned to unit 12.

"The electric has been disconnected. By that, I mean it has been removed. All that remains are the electric boards main cables."

"The consumer unit and the meter?"

"Everything. Go and look if you don't believe me." He tossed the keys over to her, and she caught them one handed.

"I believe you. Do you have a torch in your car?" "Don't think so. You?"

"In the boot. Under the bags of the drugs. I haven't had the chance to unload them yet. What is the unit at Eynsham really like? I mean does it need to be done up or is it ready for use?" They both walked back up to collect the torch.

"We can use it straight off. There are four rooms at the back, which were offices. One is big enough for the lab, the other three could be the staff room and initial storeroom for the finished product.

The racking in the warehouse is massive. A forklift would be helpful. We could buy the core ingredients in bulk and save money. Storing would not be a problem. The basement could be one though. There are wooden storage boxes of all different shapes and sizes down in one of them. I couldn't get into the other room in the basement, it was locked."

He felt in his pocket and produced the scrap of paper he had found on the floor of the unit. "I found this, just inside the warehouse on the floor. Can't read it though." He passed it over to her and she looked at it closely.

... часть двадцать шесть из ста двадцати шести посылок, составляют сторону ... ...

She laughed and then translated it for him.

" ...part twenty-six of one hundred and twenty-six parcels making up the side of the A......"

"Once you find the other one hundred and twenty-five parcels you will have a side of A, whatever A is. Probably some old instructions that were used as packing materials. Nothing that we need to know anything about." she said as she stuffed the bit of paper into her pocket. "Now can we find the safe that we put in here when we first moved in. The two of them went back down and started to search the walls carefully. After twenty minutes they had recovered the safe's contents and locked up the unit. The police seal was replaced, not that well, but from a distance it looked ok. Then they got in their cars and drove to the Marlow house where they would spend the next two hours scrubbing and clearing it of any trace of them having been there.

+

In the New East Sutherland Patrick was looking more and more worried. He had found the guest book and the spare one. He had first thought he could rewrite the spare one, but soon realised that not being able to write in Russian would be a problem. A knock on his office door made him look up. His only guest was standing in the doorway.

"What time do you serve dinner?"

"I regret to remind you that the police have closed the hotel, and while nobody minds you staying, I don't have the staff to serve meals at present. You could try the new hotel, half a mile before Golspie.'The Castle View Hotel' or there are a few places in Brora that serve good food." He looked hopefully at her, hoping that she would leave him in peace.

"Can you phone them and ask the Castle View Hotel to reserve a place at six tonight for two people? Thank you so much." Then she turned and left him speechless. He reached for the phone and dialled the number to do as she had asked.

+

Ivan reached over to his fax and removed the two pieces of paper that had just come through. He read both and then laughed out loud. He pressed the button for his secretary to come through, then remembered that he didn't have one at present. Boris, he recalled, was now in Scotland.

Boris had found out that two men, possibly from the Netherlands, had been seen at the Dacha shortly before it went up in flames. With his contacts in government, it had been an easy task to find them on the two flights in and out of Russia. Not that many passengers came from the Netherlands. He had arranged for a contact there to bring them back to his office for questioning. Ivan stood up and walked through to his secretary's office. He sat down and composed a fax to Patrick.

*Patrick, it is your friend from Russia. I need a small favour carried out. In Eynsham, at a warehouse I own, there are some very precious packets, I need you to go and bring them back to Golspie. I am sure you can store them somewhere safe for a few months. I think you wouldn't want your hotel to be an ex-hotel, would you?*

Then Ivan put it in the fax machine, typed the number and sent it off to Golspie. Not realising the chain of events that would be triggered in doing so.

+

Seumas sat at his table in his home in Belfast. He had a piece of paper in front of him and was frowning at the list he had made.

| | |
|---|---|
| Patrick O'Conner | Running hotel in Scotland |
| ~~Patrick Doyle~~ | ~~Found dead at his home.~~ |
| ~~Pat Reily~~ | ~~Found dead in his shop in Oxford~~ |
| Barry Ryan | Visiting the hotel in Scotland. Dead? |
| ~~Dutchman~~ | ~~Klass Van Miere Killed in London.~~ |
| Eva | Working in Golspie. Vanished. |
| Colleen | Last seen in Folkestone, working for? |
| Ivan? | Russian – fingers in too many pies? |
| Martin Fitzroy | LICD security officer for computers. |

Apart from Patrick, himself and Barry, the rest of the cell were all dead. He drummed his fingers on the table. Something was happening to ARI and had done so since the tunnel threat had gone bad.

Seumas knew that a small group were making a new drug, one that made you work faster and better. Hell, they had seen the effects on a team of workers in the Eurotunnel, productivity had shot through the roof. He had suggested they go legit and launch it on the public. But that had been turned down by the main leaders of ARI. He stood up and stretched his arms, then went and packed a small rucksack. He would take the ferry boat to Scotland and then make his way to see Patrick. They needed to find out who was behind the killing of their friends.

+

In LICD Martin Fitzroy had found a file that had not been on the LICD computer. It had made interesting reading. An attempt to blow up the channel tunnel. He sat at his desk and sent the file to the printer. He would read it later that night at home. Unknown to him, in doing so, an indication that the file had been opened was sent simultaneously to three other people, one within LICD, one in Russia and a retired policeman in Oxford.

+

Ivan had been about to leave his secretary's office when the computer lit up and a message appeared on the screen in front of him.

...ARI TUT FILE BEING PRINTED. ARI TUT FILE BEING PRINTED. ARI TUT FILE BEING PRINTED. ARI TUT FILE...

It continued rolling across the bottom of the screen. He knew from conversations with Patrick about the attempt to blow up the tunnel. But he hadn't been aware that he was linked to a file, apparently, on the attempt. He returned to the computer and hit the print button to see if anything happened. Sure enough, the printer started to print out reams of paper. Smiling, Ivan left the printer and the room and walked down to the lower interview room.

+

Ruth Sanders parked her car at the LICD car park. With her rank, she had a guaranteed space. Getting out she picked up her briefcase and walked the few short steps to the doors that connected to her floor of the offices.

Originally the offices were designed for BOTG (Boot out Terrorists of Great Britain), and had been designed for quick evacuation, with connections from each level of the building to the corresponding floors of the seven-story car park that was built alongside.

Since then, somebody had discovered it also made life a lot easier for unloading and loading equipment into vehicles. Only the ones that could get under the height restriction though. Passing through the double sets of heavy doors, she turned into the corridor that led to her office and was surprised not to see her secretary sitting at her usual desk. Ruth walked into her office and sat down. She had a lot of work to catch up on, but her main priority was to put Bill and Jane out of the current investigation and head them off in a different direction if only to try and save their lives. Ruth reached around the back of the computer and switched it on. Why do the firms that make computers put the switch in an inaccessible place she wondered to herself.

+

Patrick was on the phone trying to see if he could contact any of his old contacts in Oxford. He didn't plan on going all the way down to Oxford for some small packets that Ivan wanted him to store. At the same time, the thinly veiled threat to the hotel was not one to take as a joke, not when it concerned Ivan. Eventually he got through to the antique shop he had used in the past and spoke to the two Russians that had managed to get away from the clutches of Ivan.

"Hello, Patrick here, wonder if you and your friend would like to do a small pickup and deliver job for me." He waited for the answer, knowing that one had to translate for the other man to understand.

"We would if the pay is good enough. Where from and to?"

"Small warehouse in Eynsham. A few boxes in the basement apparently. Probably need to hire a van."

"We have a van; we can use that one. How many boxes?"

"Not too sure, not too many though. Then bring them to Golspie."

"Golspie, not really too keen to return to that part of the world to be quite honest. We didn't part on the best terms with Ivan. You understand that he can be quite ruthless."

"I know, but he is in Russia, He has no interest in the restaurant in Brora. Anyhow, the parcels would be dropped on here at the hotel. Once you have done that, you can return to Oxford. A nice round trip and cash in hand."

"How much exactly?"

"Five hundred?"

"Each and expenses for fuel and food."

"One thousand two hundred between you and you pay for the expenses out of that." Patrick could hear the two talking to each other.

"You have a deal. Fax us the place and the time and date and we'll do as you want."

"Doing that right now." He fed the paper into the fax machine and pressed send. "You should get that in a few minutes." He hung up and then picking up the fax, which had gone through, put it in the shredder. Best that nobody else saw the address and details, he thought to himself smugly.

+

In Golspie, Ivan's henchman had finished looking at the flats and were returning to the Rest and be Thankful Hotel. While not as refined as Patrick's, it had the advantage of being close to the centre of Golspie, a short walking distance at least and close to the railway station. He turned down the lane that led to the station and went and booked a couple of tickets, one for going to Inverness, the other for a return to Helmsdale and stopping at Brora. Smiling at the counter staff, he left whistling and continued his walk to his hotel. As he walked in the owner waved him towards the reception desk.

"A fax for you. I've put it in your pigeonhole." She reached back and passed it over to him. It was in a white envelope, which he tore open and then read the fax, while walking up to his room. Once inside he re-read it to take in what was being asked of him.

To: B Yelsin. c/o Rest and be Thankful Hotel Golspie
From:I. T. Russian Office.

Message:
Parcels being brought from a warehouse in Eynsham to New East Sutherland Hotel to be stored for safety. Once parcels have arrived, please find out if they have been opened.

If so, deal with them as you would expect for anybody, <u>ANYBODY</u> that now knows what they contain. Find suitable accommodation for four people. Money in your account to buy outright. Keep a low profile for now. Do not go near to the New East Sutherland for now.

Arranged for contact in London to sort out our insider. You may need to go and do this if he is not up to the job.

I. T.

Boris tore the fax into small pieces and stuffed them in his coat pocket. When he was next out, he would dispose of them in various wastebins throughout Golspie. He sat at a small table in the room and composed a reply that would be short and to the point.

+

Meantime, in the same hotel, two doors down were the two hitmen from Ireland. They had been there almost the same time as Boris, they didn't receive a fax but did know that they had to visit Patrick at some point. One of them was busy cleaning his gun, the other with a clean bandage around his knee where Seumas had shot him. A pair of walking sticks lay close by. They had decided, that for now at least, if they both had walking sticks it might be more difficult for anybody to identify them.

+

In a one-bedroom posh flat in London, overlooking the river a man sat reading a fax that had arrived from Ivan. He had already read it twice and poured himself a stiff drink.

Three years ago when he had got into money difficulties at the posh casino around the corner, he had been offered a way out. He just needed to keep an eye on documents that BOTG had on a project to build a tunnel under the English Channel. Copy them and pass them to the man who had bailed him out of debt. That had been easy until the man who had arranged this with him had died. Since he had not heard anything else, he had stopped looking for documents as the BOTG department had been closed down.

As a person who generally got overlooked to lead projects that might be in progress, he was ideally placed to keep his eyes and ears open for anything that might be useful. Something that the late

Chief Superintendent Rose had appreciated. Now, out of the blue came the fax that had stunned him. He looked down at the folded paper in his hands and read it for the third time since it had arrived.

To:
From: I. T. Russian Office.

Half of your debt has now been repaid, the rest could be wiped out if you can do this small task, or we can restart the interest and ask you for regular payments. Since your current pay is not enough to cover the flat and your outstanding debts (£20000+ interest), you probably would be wise to accept our generous offer.

In LICD is a person who has been reliable up to now. We need to arrange for them to cease being a bother to us. Having thought this through, the best solution would be to dispose of her and leave the remains as a sign for the department they run. Instructions and suitable devices to do this are in locker number 16TS at Waterloo Railway Station. Do confirm if you are happy to carry out this work for us. Tel:00710937689021

He picked up his coat and left the flat to walk in the direction of Waterloo Railway Station. As the fax had been at pains to point out, he didn't really have any choice.

+

Ruth Sanders looked up from her desk and smiled at the young officer in front of her. He was carrying a bundle of paperwork in his right hand.

"Something I can help you with?"

"Not really. I have my orders and while I don't like them, I have no option but to carry them out."

"What orders?" she asked, looking slightly alarmed as she didn't recognise him as being one of her staff.

"To kill you." He dropped the bundle of papers and revealed a sharp knife. Then he stepped forwards towards Ruth, the blade outstretched in his hand. Without thinking, she put her hands on the edge of the desk, intending to push it towards her attacker, but it didn't move. She stood up as he climbed onto the desk and made a lunge towards her neck. Ruth backed away, just in time, then he lunged again at her, this time towards her face. She moved along the wall, but he grabbed her by the arm and stopped her. Then he moved in closer, and she screamed loudly.

The phone rang on Ivan's desk. He picked it up, making a mental note to get a new secretary.

"Yes?"

"I've done as you asked, now write off the debt."

"Did you really do that? Take a photo and fax it to me first." "I can't do that; I have left the building. If I go back, I would be caught. Now do as you said you would."

"I like you; you have guts. I tell you what I'll do. I'll not add interest until it is paid. That is good, yes?"

"But you said if I did this, then the debt would be written off."

"Read it carefully, I said could, not would. And remember, I now know who really has killed her. You wouldn't want that revealed, would you? Thought not. Go back to your nice flat and wait for my next fax." Ivan hung up and laughed, then faxed Boris to instruct him to sort out the loose end.

# *Chapter 22*

London a day later.

Bill and Jane had decided early that morning to return to London and brief Ruth Sanders, their boss, about the files contents. They had stopped off at the flat to leave it in their safe. Now they stood outside Ruth's office both looking at the mess on the floor in front of them. Where her usual secretary had a neat and filed office, it was now wrecked. Files and their contents lay strewn across the floor. The door to the main office was slightly open and a light could be seen coming through the open door.

"Hello, anybody in there?" shouted Bill. A deafening silence was the reply. He nodded at Jane, and they both stepped forward, carefully avoiding the papers and files on the floor. Bill pushed the door open a bit further and looked into Ruth's office.

He stepped back forcing Jane to do the same and closed the door after him. Then did the same with the secretary's office door. Once in the corridor, they both looked at each other and sat down on two nearby chairs.

"Where is security? Where is everybody? Come to that why has nobody been in and reported this?" asked Jane in a frustrated manner.

"I don't know. But we need to find and report this." Bill stood up and walked towards his desk. On his chair was a note written in red in a rough hand.

'Leave your current case alone or you might end up the same way.' Jane reached out and touched it. The red came off on her finger and she raised it to her nose.

"That's blood. Not ink." The telephone light was flashing, indicating a missed call. He snapped the key down to listen to the message.

"Bill. It's Simon here, I hope you read the file I posted to you. As I said, don't try and find me. Whatever happens do keep investigating, there are bigger things than you can visualise going on here in England and Scotland. Don't let anybody put you off finding the real reasons for these killings. I'd suggest that you go to the…" A scream was heard and then the phone replaced. Bill looked at Jane and turned and started to walk back out of the office. Jane stood for a minute, then followed him.

He walked along to the stairs and went up to the floor where the evidence from Marlow had been stored. The door was wide open, and the lock had been smashed by whoever had got in. Jane peered around the door and gasped. The room was now totally empty.

"Looks like, whoever it was, has beaten us to it." she said. "Come on, let's go and look at the security' officers' room. Bet there is not much left there either. Bill replied with a shrug of his shoulders.

+

The phone rang in Ruth's office, but it went unanswered. In a house in Marlow, Justin replaced the receiver and looked across at the other two members of the group that had arrived earlier.

"She is not answering." "So, what do we do then?"

"Let's move the equipment to the new warehouse, she said that she would be getting the paperwork sorted. Most of the stuff is in the garage. Did either of you manage to get a van?"

"Yes, I hired one, false name and papers, and have put a new number plate on it. Doubt it will be traced somehow. I parked it down the lane. I'll go and back it up to the garage." She rose and left. Justin looked at the remaining member.

"Thought you were supposed to be in Oxford dealing with the students and the suppliers."

"Things were getting tense. Look Justin, there have been two deaths in the last three days. So far they have not been brought to the attention of the police, but it is only a matter of time before they do get involved. It is getting too risky. I want out." She stood looking at Justin.

"You want out? Fine, go ahead and leave the group. Doubt that you would live long."

"And just what do you mean by that?"

"You don't think that Ruth was in charge of this operation? That person is safely based in Russia. From what I hear, you wouldn't want to cross him in any way. But if you want to leave and take your chance then do so." Justin watched her as the realisation hit her that she couldn't leave, at least, not if she valued her life. Sighing, she walked towards the door.

"I'll go and help getting the equipment loaded then, shall I?" "Good idea, we'll both go." He stood up and joined her outside.

An hour later the van, followed by Justin in his car, could be seen driving in the direction of Eynsham.

Ivan looked at the paperwork that Ruth had posted to him. He wished she would use the fax but understood her reluctance to do so from the LICD offices. The figures looked ok on paper. He pulled a pad of paper and a fountain pen towards him and started to check the figures and the bottom line. It appeared to add up. He flicked through the rest of her report and picked up the documents to buy the unit. Then stopped and reached for his bottle of vodka.

It was his own unit. Moreover, it was the unit he had asked Patrick to get the packages from. If Patrick and the other team met up, they might put two and two together and make four. Patrick was no fool after all. Stuffing the papers together in the envelope, he reached out and took the large bunch of keys out of a shallow drawer in his desk. Then he put the bottle of vodka away and left the room, stopping only in the outer office to open and empty his small safe, where he kept the emergency cash in different currencies. He looked around the small office and shrugging his shoulders, walked out to his waiting car.

"Where to sir?"

"The Dacha, then the airport. My private jet will be waiting."

"That the one you have a share in sir?"

"The one that I now have a hundred percent share in, yes, that one." He sat back and the car drove off in the direction of the Dacha.


Half an hour later, he got out of the car and looked at the burnt remains. Ivan tapped the driver on the shoulder.

"Do you have a torch?"

"In the boot, I'll get it for you sir." Ivan started to walk towards the remains and the driver came up and passed him the torch.

"Do you need me with you sir?"

"Thanks, but I can manage. If I haven't come out in twenty minutes, you can come and find me. Stay alert around here. This fire was not an accident." Ivan made his way into the ruined remains and looked down at his feet, the trapdoor, while closed was clear of black soot and debris. Bending down, he pulled up the brass ring set into the floor and the trapdoor opened. Grunting with the effort, he switched on his torch and walked down the stone stairs. Flashing his torch around the basement, he could see that one of the sacks of XV3rd was missing. He crossed over to the remaining sacks and counted them just to make sure. Yes, one was missing. Now who would have taken that. Not the two men who had set it on fire, not that he could ask them now, with their remains buried in the forest along with the two women of his office. He turned around as he heard the squeak of the floorboards above him. At the top of the stairs his driver was peering down at him.

"You alright sir? Only twenty minutes have passed, and you did say…"

"…thanks, yes I am fine. Go back to the car, I am coming right up." Ivan returned and replaced the trapdoor. Then he moved some of the fallen beams to lay across it. He would know the next time if anybody had visited the cellar. Dusting his hands off on the grass, he got up and made his way to his waiting car.

+

Boris had got himself to Inverness airport and now was seated in the plane waiting to take him to London, from where he could sort out the loose end that his boss wanted taken care of. He knew that the gambler had been asked to sort out the insider of LICD, but somehow, he didn't think that whatever Ivan had been told, wasn't the truth. Sitting back, he closed his eyes as the plane taxied down the runway.

+

The two hitmen had seen the large Russian leave the hotel. On the way down to breakfast that morning they had heard him talking to the receptionist about the cost of telephone calls to Russia.

Putting this nugget of information in their heads, they decided to visit The New East Sutherland after breakfast. Finding the Russian had left for London had been a bonus.

One of them had searched his room, finding a pile of pieces of a fax in a coat pocket. Then he had taken photos of all the pieces, before returning them into the coat pocket. The only other thing of interest was a flight case, which was open and the moulded layout of where a gun should be was clearly to be seen.

The local taxi dropped them off outside the main entrance to the hotel and swung back up the drive to return to Golspie. The front door to the hotel was firmly closed and no lights shone from inside. The injured man sat down on the metal steps that led up to the front door.

"You go and check round the back. Maybe there is another entrance we don't know about." He watched his companion move off down the side of the hotel and took out his mobile phone. Something that his companion knew nothing about yet.

"Ok, we are at the hotel. No not ours, the New East Sutherland. Nobody about, place is locked up tighter than a prison. Do you want us to break in?"

"No, if there is no locked door, then go and park yourselves on the nearby broch."

"What is a broch?"

"The stone and grass mound near the hotel. It's in the grounds of the place. On your right looking down towards the main road." The man turned around and could make it out near the bottom of the drive.

"Got it. Why there?"

"I've left you a telescope, you will be able to see when Patrick arrives and can make your entrance after that." The phone was replaced, and he put his mobile phone away just as his fellow hitman appeared from behind him.

"I've been all the way around the place, there is a door at the side, but it is firmly closed. What should we do?

"Look there is a small hill over there, we could go and sit and wait. Come on." He stood up, grabbed his walking stick and started to walk in the direction of the broch.

+

The van pulled up at the warehouse in the early morning and the two Russians from the Oxford shop got out. One went over and looked at the door, a new padlock was in place. He smiled at the other man.

"Get the bolt cutters out, we need to be in and out fast." He looked up and down the industrial estate to check that nobody else had turned up or seen them. It was the work of a couple of minutes to cut the padlock and step in through the small door set into the roller door.

Once inside, he moved to a bank of switches and pulled the main one down. Lights came on in the warehouse. A motor started up and the roller door started to move up. The van was quickly reversed in and the door closed. The aisles between the racking were wide enough to reverse the van up through to the back rooms and the basement.

By the time the van had carefully reversed, the other man was already down in the basement and looking at both the red and blue doors. He pushed both doors and discovered the blue one opened, he stepped into the room and saw the small pile of packets. Going to the nearest one, he went to pick it up and found it was too heavy.

"Come and give me hand down here. These packets are big and heavy." His colleague came down and went to help.

An hour later the van was loaded and had just pulled out in front of the unit. Careful to make sure that their visit was not too apparent, they turned off the electric and got the doors closed again. A fresh padlock was put on the clasp and then they drove off, heading for the far north and Golspie.

Twenty minutes later, another van arrived. This one had come from Marlow, and it pulled up in front and Justin got out and went over to the padlock. He had been given a key, so put it in the padlock only to find it didn't fit. He tried again, but still it didn't fit.

Justin went to the back of van and lifted a heavy tool kit out. Taking out a large pair of bolt cutters, he cut the lock and it dropped to the ground. As he bent down to pick it up, his fingers touched the other one that had been cut and left. He reached into his pocket and took out the key he had been given and tried it, it fitted. Justin tossed the padlock and key into the tool kit and put it back in the van. Then he stepped inside and opened the warehouse door.

Leaving his van, he switched on the lights and walked to the back of the unit. It was big, but he wanted to check again the two rooms in the basement. He ran down the now familiar steps and found the door to the blue room open with a box holding it open. The red door was still locked. Smiling now, Justin returned to the van and turned it round and reversed it into the warehouse. He opened the back and started to remove the bags of ingredients that they needed for the drugs. The other two members of the group arrived in the car as he started.

"Took your time?"

"We stopped for some food and to bring some supplies. I doubt that you thought to do that, did you Justin?"

"Wrong, look in the room at the back, not the one with stairs going to the basement, but the one on the right of that. Now give me a hand with these bags first though." They went and did as he asked, and soon they had the bottom rack filled with the sacks. The large machine that was needed for the packaging was at the back of the van up by the bulkhead. All three looked at one another and groaned.

"Let's take a break first, we all know the weight of that piece of kit."

"True. Ok, we have a break and then come and move this." The three walked towards the back of the warehouse.

+

Ivan had told the pilot to fly to anywhere near to Eynsham. He could land on a public or private airfield. The plane banked and it approached Oxford airport. Ivan picked up the handset that connected him to the pilot.

"How far to Eynsham from the airport?"

"Six, seven miles. You can get a taxi or a hire car can come out from Oxford. Do you want me to arrange that?"

"Yes, a hire car. I need an estate one, year doesn't matter." Ivan put the handset down and sat back ready for the landing.

+

An hour later, longer than he had planned he was driving towards the warehouse. He hoped that he wasn't too late. Swinging the car into the industrial estate, he glanced at the paper on the seat beside him. The board at the entrance listed the number of the units and helpfully, a map as well. He gunned the engine and swept the car along the main road and took the fourth turning off it, to arrive at the unit. The roller door was up, and a van was parked just inside.

Ivan switched off the engine and got out. He went to the boot and opened his briefcase; the false bottom of the case revealed a small handgun and a small dagger. He took both, checked the gun was now loaded and put the dagger into a purpose-made small pocket in his jacket. Then he purposefully stepped into the warehouse and kept to the far side as he walked down towards the back.

He could hear voices, both female and male. Smiling he flattened himself against the rear wall and peered around into the room. The two women had their back to him. The man was busy pouring cups of tea, so he too had his back to Ivan.

Ivan reached into the room and quietly closed the door. Then fishing in his pocket, he produced the keys and locked the door. The sound of the lock being secured made all three look around, but the door was closed. Justin ran over and banged on the door. "Let us out. We have rented this warehouse." Silence was the only reply taken the key to the red door out and unlocked it and peered inside. The boxes and crates still were there. He stepped back and looked into the blue room. Apart from the one box holding the door open, the room was empty. Cursing, he made his way upstairs to the warehouse. Ivan walked back to the van; it was empty. He glanced at the racking. He saw the bags and smiled. The occupants in the room were not the thieves then. He turned and went back and unlocked the door. The three ran out and all started to speak at once.

"Who are you?"

"What did you think you were doing, locking us in there?" "What do you want?"

"Whoa! I own the warehouse; I had some very valuable items stored here. I needed to get them moved, and they have been. I'll let you get on. Tell her that she made a good choice." He turned and left the three of them looking at one another in silence.

+

Ruth Sanders had just managed to escape the man but had sustained a bad cut on her arm where he had slashed at her with his knife. She had moved towards the door at the same time he had leapt off her desk.

He had landed awkwardly and groaned. Taking advantage of that, Ruth had run from her office and headed upstairs. He hadn't seemed to chase after her, but not being sure, had decided to hide in the metal cupboard on the landing. It was a new one, that had paperwork attached to the door handles. In a few minutes she was in the dark cupboard and had pulled the two doors towards her.

Now she was listening to see if he was following her, but not hearing anything, she cautiously opened the door and peered around it. She saw Bill and Jane walking away from her and enter the security officers room. Ruth moved out and walked quietly away in the opposite direction. She had to get in touch with her team in Marlow. In the meantime though she would go home first.

+

Bill stormed out the office and looked up and down the corridor. Jane put her hand on his arm.

"What is it?"

"Probably nothing, but I thought I heard a noise." He looked both ways up and down the corridor, but only a door was swinging at the far end. "Come on, somebody is up there." Bill pointed towards the swinging door and ran towards it. Jane hesitated, then followed him, picking up his pace as she did so.

Up ahead, Ruth could hear the two of them pounding up the corridor after her. She reached the flight of stairs and started to run down them as fast as she could. When she was two floors down, she heard the door at the top open and the sound of footsteps coming down the stairwell. A fire door was on the landing, so Ruth pushed it open and then continued to run on down the stairs, in the hope that they might go out on to the fire escape.

Reaching the bottom of the stairs, she pushed open the door to the offices and walked in and ducked down behind a desk. The door was pushed back hard, and she watched Jane run through the office and down the corridor. If Jane had taken the trouble to look back, she would have seen Ruth, but she ran on towards the main entrance. Ruth waited there for a few minutes longer, as Bill followed Jane into the office and ran along the corridor to find Jane standing looking around the entrance.

"Where did they go Bill? We kept up with them for most of the time."

"The fire exit on the third floor, the door was open. I assumed it was a ruse, but it looks as though they did get out that way. Come on, let's go back to the car, we have this note." He held the written note in his hand and smiled at Jane. "This might be their first mistake. If we can analyse the handwriting, we will be a step in the right direction." He started to walk to their car, Jane followed, a bit more out of breath from her racing after him. From a window on the ground floor, Ruth peered out and watched them enter the car park. She smiled for the first time that day and went to collect her own car holding her arm to try and stop the bleeding.

+

As the van sped up the M6, the driver glanced at his companion. He had taken over driving at the last fuel stop and they had discussed if they should stop for the night or press on. The decision was to keep driving. At this rate, in about eight hours' time, they could hand over the boxes to Patrick and collect their money and be away. He carried on driving…

…Around five hours later he pulled into the service station at Perth North and refuelled. His companion had woken as the van had stopped. Now rubbing his eyes, he looked around to see where they had stopped.

"Where are we?"

"Perth North. From here on, we are on the road to Inverness. No fuel until we reach Inverness, hence the pit stop. You want anything from the shop?"

"Bottle of water, nothing else. I'll drive from here." He watched as the man stepped down and walked around to his side and opened his door to get access to the fuel cap. Soon they were back on the road and heading northwards. Now the other man was sleeping and snoring as they drove north past Pitlochry and on towards Inverness.

+

Ivan had driven back to Oxford airfield and had told his pilot to file a flight to Dornoch.

"I doubt I will be able to land there at night."

"Why not? You have lights, don't you?"

"Yes, but the people living nearby might not be too happy. You did say you wanted to keep a low profile. Inverness would be less obvious."

"Dornoch. I don't intend to have to drive the fifty plus miles from Inverness just because of a small thing like that." The pilot shrugged and set the plane on a course to land at Dornoch.

+

Patrick had returned to the Golspie police station and was handing over the book and a set of copies of the hotel guest book. He had decided not to do anything to it. Patrick had added a letter from a member of staff, which had been dictated by Patrick.

It said that Ivan had been a guest who had been invited a couple of days earlier to give feedback as to what it was like to be a guest in such a wonderful five-star hotel. He looked at DS Cooper who was reading the letter and had put the guest book on the desk in front of him.

"This appears to back up what you said last time you were here. You can keep the guest book and re-open. We think it was an accident brought on by too much to drink. That is what it is likely the Procurator Fiscal has indicated to us." Patrick stood up and went to leave.

"Mr O'Conner the police up here have a long memory; you would do well to concentrate on the hotel business and not allow anything else to distract you. Understand?"

"Yes, thank you." Patrick turned and left the office.

+

The van slowed as it went through the various bends in the road, then drove across the bridge and up towards Golspie.

"Nearly there." The driver said as he saw a sign saying four miles to Golspie.

"What was that?" said his passenger, half asleep. The driver reached out and shook the arm of his colleague. The distraction was enough. He was going nearly sixty miles an hour as it reached the bend in the road, and he failed to see the small amount of ice on the road surface. The van skidded and despite his efforts to stay upright, the van eventually came to stop on its side, teetering on the edge of a verge that sloped down to a nearby stream.

+

Half an hour later, at the police station, the phone rang and advised the duty officer that there had been an accident on the road into Golspie near the farm. The officer then phoned DS Cooper, who was on call that night. Cooper rose from his chair and made his way to the phone.

"Cooper."

"There has been an accident on the road near the farm, going out of Golspie. Two people in a van. I've phoned the breakdown firm in Golspie, but they say they will be another hour. On another job, near Rogart."

"Ambulance?"

"Yes, two bodies removed and taken to the morgue."

"So just need the van moved? Hardly worth my coming out tonight then, is it?"

"There are a number of parcels in the back of the van." "So?"

"The writing is in some foreign language."

"Then I will be there shortly." Cooper went and looked outside. It had started to freeze. In the moonlight patches of water looked as though they might be frozen. He went back and grabbed his heavy-duty warm jacket and picked up his torch and keys to his car and left his house.

+

A couple of guests had turned up at The New East Sutherland and Patrick had found them a room. It was in the bar an hour later that he heard one of the guests telling the others that there had been a traffic accident and the road was blocked south of Golspie. Patrick returned to his office and ran his finger down the list of numbers and people he had contacts for. Finding Golspie police, he dialled the number and confirmed what he had heard.

+

DS Cooper had arrived at the scene. Blue flashing lights threw their light amongst the trees and river. He took in the scene and walked around to the back of the van. One door was open and lying on the side of the road. He peered inside and reached in to try and grab one of the parcels. Tantalisingly, it was just out of his reach. He went and sat in his car, might as well stay warm, he thought to himself.

Around half an hour later, the yellow flashing lights of the recovery vehicle slowed and stopped. The driver, a local man, got out and made his way over to Cooper, who wound down his car window.

"Anybody still in the van?" he asked Cooper. "No, just a lot of parcels and packets."

408

"Ok, we can soon get this cleared for you." He walked over and stood and calculated the angle he needed to back the recovery truck up to, to enable the van to be swung upright.

An hour later the van was now upright and being attached to the recovery truck to tow into Golspie. Cooper looked at the traffic that was now stationary both going north and south. Funny how people just wait for things to happen up here, he thought to himself as the tow truck moved off in the direction of Golspie. The cars started to move and Cooper went and got back into his car to follow the tow truck. He bent down and picked up his car radio.

"Cooper here. I need two officers at the garage to move the packets and boxes into a safe place at the police station. They'll need some sort of van. Pick two of the strongest on duty tonight." He reached down and replaced the handset as the tow lorry swept into the garage forecourt on the other side of the railway bridge.

Golspie

As the last of the boxes were removed, one of the two officers picked up a large piece of paper off the floor of the van. He walked to the streetlight to see it better. It appeared to be a list of items and a contact telephone number. He stuffed it into his pocket and once back at the police Station handed it over to DS Cooper.

"Found this in the van." "That is a Golspie number."

"Any idea sir as to whose?"

"No, but I'll give it a phone and see who answers it." Cooper went into his office and sat down and dialled the number on the paper.

"New East Sutherland. O'Conner. How can I help you?"

"DS Cooper here. I need you to come down to the police station."

"What now?" exclaimed Patrick.

"Yes now. We have something of a mystery that concerns you." "How do you know it concerns me officer?"

"Because the number on the paper is the same one, I have just dialled, and you have just answered it. Now come on down and we can probably sort this out quite quickly." Cooper replaced the phone and went to see what was in the boxes.

+

Patrick stood and looked out from his office across to the broch. He thought he had seen somebody at the top earlier in the day. However, by the time he had remembered to ask somebody to go and look, the place was deserted as usual. Picking up the binoculars that he now kept near to him, he swept them north towards the layby. A few cars were parked up in it. Sweeping them down towards Golspie, he could see the traffic was just starting to move. Sighing, he put them down and walked out to his car.

+

Ruth struggled to drive her car; her arm was heavily bleeding every time she moved it. Not having an automatic car, she needed to move her arm each time she changed gear. Eventually she pulled up at her home and painfully got out and walked up to the front door. Once inside, she first went and ran the arm under a cold tap, then looked for a few plasters to stick over it. They would have to do until she got somebody to put a large bandage around it. As she passed her answer machine, she saw it was flashing to indicate a missed call, well three missed calls. Ruth poured a glass of gin, added a splash of tonic and sat down after pressing the play button.

*"Where are you? We have arrived at the warehouse. Unloaded and then some Russian guy locked us in. He said he owns the unit and to tell you that you choose well. He also mentioned some of his stuff being here, but it is gone now. What is going on? Call me on the new mobile you got me last week."*

*"Hello Ruth? It's Bill and Jane. Look we went to the office, yours and your secretary's office has been ransacked. Found some blood on a note that was left on Bill's desk. We are getting the handwriting checked tonight. Wonder where you are, and if you are alright?" We are heading towards Golspie again, we came back after we had read the file."*

*"Hello Ruth? Ivan here. Was at the unit today, see that nobody goes into the basement room with the red door. I'll get you some more of the XV3rd soon. Think we should up the price for the Oxford students? Get in touch."*

Ruth reached out and tried to touch the delete button. Really, she felt quite lightheaded. She took another mouthful of the gin and tonic and put her head back into the chair.

*410*

# *Chapter 23*

## LICD headquarters in London

Bill and Jane had dropped the note off at the LICD department who were best to deal with it. Now both were in the car driving towards Gatwick to catch a plane that would take them to Inverness. They had spent an hour or so arranging cars, plane tickets and, more importantly, a place to stay in Golspie. Jane had found a room at Rest and be Thankful and booked it for the week.

Golspie

DS Cooper sat back in his chair and looked at the man opposite him. Patrick had turned up as requested, not asked for legal representation and despite all the questions so far, had not really given Cooper anything he didn't already know. He leaned forward towards Patrick.

"Mr O'Conner, you have said nothing that explains why we have a van load of cartons and boxes and yet you say that it doesn't concern you." Cooper pushed a copy of the paper found in the van across the table. "Is that or is that not your telephone number?" Patrick picked up the paper and looked at it for the first time that night.

1408 6543210

Boxes 1 – 6

Boxes 12 – 13

Boxes 19 – 21

Missing? 7-11, 14-18, 22 onwards.

At BB?, IT? ,Aultbea? Warehouse Red door?


"I am sorry DS Cooper, but I don't have anything to do with it." "But the telephone number is that of the hotel, is it not?" "Yes, but as I am sure you are aware, there has been two other owners of the hotel before me, I just had the number reconnected." Patrick sat back in his chair and thought to himself that there was nothing that had linked him to the boxes. He had quickly realised that they were probably from the warehouse in Eynsham. The same boxes that Ivan had wanted him to look after. His problem now was how to get them into his hotel without the police knowing that he had anything to do with it.

Ivan would not be very pleased Patrick thought, and when Ivan wasn't pleased with somebody they usually disappeared without any trace.

"BB or IT? Would that be an IT Department?" asked Cooper breaking into Patrick's thoughts.

"I've already told you; I have nothing to do with this. What is in the boxes anyway?"

"We haven't opened them yet. We will do so in time. BB what do you think that would stand for?"

"Boys Brigade? Bored Boys? I've no idea. Look I have been here overnight and would appreciate that you either charge me or release me. There is nothing to link me to the boxes or cartons in the van. Why don't you ask the driver?" Patrick leaned back in his chair. Cooper stood up and wandered to the window set high up in the room, then turned back to Patrick.

"Didn't I say? The driver is dead. Killed in the accident."

"Sorry to hear that. No, you didn't say DS Cooper. So, are you going to charge me or release me?"

"You can go. But don't go too far and don't leave the country without telling me first." Patrick stood up and walked out of the room back to his car. He had a phone call to make, one that he didn't really look forward to.

+

Ivan put his seatbelt back on as the plane slowed and started its descent to Dornoch. The pilot had his full lights on and as it came to land, Ivan could see the golf course that ran along beside the sea. The plane touched down and taxied to a standstill. Already Ivan had undone his seatbelt and was standing up to make his way off the plane. He needed to see Patrick and soon.

About half an hour later, he stood gazing up at the dark flat that he knew belonged to Patrick. No matter, he had the means to get inside without anybody else knowing. Ivan pushed the gate open silently and walked up the path to the flat.

At the front door, he put his special tool to good use and was inside the flat in a few minutes. Ivan then swiftly checked all the rooms, before closing the curtains. Only then did he switch on the lights and smiled before making his way to the nearest bedroom, where he stretched out and went sound asleep.

+

In Russia a phone rang in the empty office, normally the answer phone or his secretary would have taken the call. However, with no secretary and Ivan forgetting to switch on the answer machine, it carried on ringing.

+

Patrick replaced the handset and tapped his finger thoughtfully against his chin. If Ivan wasn't in Russia, then where was he? Too tired to make the journey home to Dornoch, he left the assistant in charge and went to sleep in one of the few rooms that still were empty that night.

+

In Golspie police station, DS Cooper was looking at the box that had been placed on his desk. Inside, were shards of some yellow material. He reached in and took one of the pieces out and held it up to the light. It had some sort of sticky surface to one side. The other side had been polished to a high degree. Completely baffled, he put it back in the box and placed the box alongside the others that were piled along one wall of his office. He stood up, stretched and left the room, making sure to lock it after him and then returned to his home. It had been a long night.

+

In a house in Marlow, a body was lying curled up in a chair. Ruth had died and nobody knew it yet.

# *Chapter 24*

Golspie

At the Rest and be Thankful hotel, the two men had already eaten breakfast and now were walking towards the New East Sutherland Hotel.

"How much further is it?"

"I'll ask in the police station here." He went inside and shortly returned and smiled at his companion. "About another four miles. There is a car hire place at the garage just past the churchyard. Come on."

"He had better be there to pay us." "He will be. Now come on."

+

Patrick awoke, stretched and looked around the room, puzzled for a few minutes, until he remembered that he had stayed overnight in the hotel. He got up and after a quick freshen up, made his way down to the reception area. Seated in the chairs in the hall were two men. They looked up as Patrick walked down the stairs.

"May the road rise up before you." said one as Patrick reached the bottom of the stairs.

"Come into my office." He turned and nodded at the housekeeper. "I used one of the rooms on the first-floor last night, it will need changing." Then he led the two men towards his office. "Sit down. I assume you have come to be paid. Who have you finished with?" He pulled a pad of paper towards him.

"Doyle. Reily, Seumas, he fired at us."

"Too bad, you can add Barry to the list as well."

"That will be two thousand one hundred for the three then." "No! One thousand four hundred. Barry wasn't your killing was it?"The men looked at one another.

"No, but we have expenses, ferries, and so on."

"Sixteen hundred. Final amount. I do have another job for you up here."

"How much?"

"Clean kill and remove the body. Two and half thousand."

"Who is it?"

"I'll tell you once you agree. Think it over and phone me on this number tonight, one way or another please." Patrick moved to the safe and took out two packets. He handed one to each of them.

Then returned to the safe and removed some more money, which after counting, he split between them.

"We will be in touch." They rose and left the hotel. Patrick walked with them to the door and noted the car and its registration number, and then went back inside. In the car the two men looked at the money and the packets.

"We'll check it out at the hotel. Then we can talk about if want to accept this new job then. Come on."The car started and drove down the long drive.

+

In Dornoch, Ivan had awoken and having freshened up by using Patrick's shower, was now dressed and leaving him a little surprise. A note on the table and a large bundle of money beside it. He re-read the note again.

*Patrick, thanks for the use of the flat. I'll come and collect the boxes in a couple of days' time. We can store them here in your flat, nobody will notice them. I assume they are now at the hotel?*

*I. T.*

Smiling, Ivan left the flat and walked back across the green and on towards the airfield. As he did so, he passed a shop on the corner of the square that had a board in its window. To Let / May Sell. He made a note of the agents and carried on walking.

Just under half an hour later he was at the airfield. The problem was that his pilot and plane were not there. Puzzled, he scanned the horizon and sky in case they were up flying, but no sign of them. The only noise, in a very peaceful place, was the occasional 'Fore!' shouted by the golfers. Ivan stood and wondered where the plane had gone. Without it, he had no way of either getting back to Russia or more importantly, getting the parcels on to the plane to fly back as well.

+

Martin Fitzroy had spent the night reading the file he had printed at LICD. He had written a short note, which he intended to leave on Ruth Sanders' desk that morning, when he got in. As he entered the offices, he was struck by how quiet it seemed. He was usually the first to arrive and one of the last to leave, but the cleaners were usually present. He made his way up to Ruth's office and pushed open her secretary's door. The mess inside, made him stop in his tracks. He could see that Ruth's door was closed. Carefully making his way across the room, he tapped on it before pushing it open. The same mess was in her room as well. He placed his note on the desk and retraced his steps back out of the two rooms. Something was not right. He ran up the stairs to his own office and found it was as he had left it. He sat down and reached for the phone.

+

Bill swung the hired car into the large car park of Rest and be Thankful and switched off the engine. Jane was asleep beside him. He reached out and gently moved her arm. She awoke and looked at him.

"Where are we?" "Golspie. The hotel."

"Ok." They both got out and grabbed their two small cases from the boot and made their way over to reception to check in.

+

DS Cooper sat looking at the boxes and the piece of paper with the list. Having been thinking about this all night, he reached for his phone and dialled the number, a number that he hoped would connect him to Bill or Jane at LICD.

+

Having checked in and freshened up, Bill and Jane walked along to the police station. It had been Bill who had suggested that they should see DS Cooper to see if he could help them. Jane pressed the bell on the desk and waited. A short while later, DS Cooper walked through. He stood looking at them.

"That is amazing. I was just phoning you two. Come on through, I have a problem that you might be able to help with." He led them through to the back of the station. Jane looked around as they walked through.

"Refit?"

"And redecoration. The station has long needed it. Just waiting for the budget to do it. This year it was east Sutherland who got lucky." Cooper pushed open the office door and pulled out a couple of seats. "Sit down. Coffee or Tea?"

"Nothing for us. We hope you can help us as well."

"Suppose you tell us first what you want from us?" said Bill, smiling.

"Ok. A van overturned on some ice last night, nothing unusual, but the two men in the front died. No seatbelts on. In the back of the van were a number of packets and parcels."

"What you would expect, I'd have thought." said Jane smiling. "Well, yes. Thing is that there were no details on the parcels but there was a piece of paper on the floor of the van, under the parcels." He reached down into the drawer of his desk and took it out to show them.

1408 6543210
Boxes 1 – 6
Boxes 12 – 13
Boxes 19 – 21
Missing? 7-11, 14-18, 22 onwards. At BB? IT?,Aultbea?
Warehouse Red door?

"And the telephone number is?" asked Bill.

"The New East Sutherland. I phoned the number and got the hotel right away. Naturally I called in the owner and questioned him. Had to let him go eventually, as he said, the number for the hotel has been the same for years. Can't think what IT or BB are though," said Cooper, frowning.

"Ben Bhraggie?" suggested Jane.

"Ben Bhraggie?" said Cooper. "What made you think of that." "Last time we were up here." She turned to Bill. "Remember the body that was reported and then when the police went there it wasn't there?"

"Yes, I can, now you mention it." He turned to Cooper. "Didn't you call it something like," he paused to think. "No Body at Ben Bhraggie." They watched as Cooper rose and went to a four drawer filing cabinet and pulled out the relevant file.

"I'll look later, thanks for that. Now what can I do for you?" "It's complicated and long. How much time do you have?" asked Bill.

"Does east Sutherland figure in it? "It might."

"Then let me sort out a few things and I'll be yours for the rest of the day." Cooper got up and went to the front desk. After a few minutes he returned and sat down. "Do we need to order lunch and dinner?" He asked jokingly.

"Maybe lunch." said Jill with a grin. Bill looked at them both and started to speak.

"Both of us are being tried out for promotion, me for first six months, then Jane for the next six. I was called into our bosses office. Chief Superintendent Ruth Sanders. Got promotion herself. Anyhow, I had a day to think it over and we drove to Marlow. There we found and got involved in a murder and drug site. At some industrial units. They, whoever they are, appear to have taken over all the units in the block. Probably to keep anybody else from knowing what was going on. A basement had been made too, a real full setup. Stolen electric from one of the other units and CCTV, files you name it. We had most of it taken back to London. One of the firms in the other units were suppliers of industrial diamonds to firms, including the tunnel under the channel, when it was being dug."

"We got a file on that too." said Jane, interrupting Bill.

"As Jane says, we have a file on that. A group called the ARI, Armed and Ready for Insurrection. They planned to place a bomb or bombs in the tunnel and then threaten the UK Government they would explode them, unless they had a lot prisoners released. Naturally the Government didn't want that, so called in somebody to find and stop it. The ARI cell, most were caught, but a few got away. LICD, think, but cannot prove, that Mr O'Conner was involved. A drug that was introduced to some of the workforce seems to have made them work more efficiently. One of the ingredients for this drug is something called." Bill paused and looked at Jane.

"Sheepsbane." she offered helpfully.

"But that is deadly stuff to handle." said Cooper, "the farmers know what to look for and where it is most likely found. It's a real problem with farmers up here. It's biggest problem is that within a few hours the stuff is not visible in the blood of the creature."

"Then it wouldn't show up in any human either?" asked Jane. "No. But I have yet to hear of it being used with any humans.

I would think it would kill them outright and quickly too. You only need to touch it and goodbye." said Cooper with a shudder. "But this is supposed to be refined and blended with some other stuff. Apart from Mr O'Conner, has anybody else been up here that you wouldn't expect to be?"

"We had a couple of strangers in yesterday, asking how far it was to the hotel. We told them about four miles and said where to get a hire car from the garage beyond the churchyard."

"And the two in the van?"

"Not sure at the moment, but Eastern European for certain." "A lot of interest in Patrick's hotel or him then." said Bill. "More than you would expect at this time of the year." replied Cooper.

"Perhaps we need to take a meal there and see if we can find anything out for you?" suggested Jane looking at Bill and smiling. "It would be quite like old times."

"There is one thing. Somebody, according to Mr O'Conner, is trying to kill him. We told you that he had reported an attempt on his life, well we have kept an eye on his flat.

Last night, according to the Dornoch police, somebody was seen entering the flat. They must have stayed overnight and left in the morning. No break in was reported or from appearances, carried out. It may have been a friend of Mr O'Conner, but we haven't asked him yet. A plane was also reported as landing in Dornoch airfield after dark. The plane came in with all its lights on and landed. When the local police visited the site today, there was no sign of the plane. There were marks in the grass though where it had been parked."

"So, no idea yet as to who flew in and out?" asked Jane. "None whatsoever. There are not that many people who have their own aeroplane and one that can land at night as well." said Cooper with a wry smile. "Carry on Bill."

"It seems that Oxford may be seeing a resurgence in students taking drugs, some of whom seem able to work both at their studies and any employment they have, very fast and not need much sleep. We did drive across to Oxford but got side-tracked. We returned to LICD after we had received and read the file on the tunnel. There our boss's office was wrecked, as was her secretary's. Also, the evidence from Marlow was now gone. All of it. LICD was completely deserted. We have come on up here as was suggested to us some time back."The fax machine came to life behind Cooper, and he turned and picked the sheets up. He glanced at the top one and passed it over to Bill and Jane.

"Seems that your boss is missing from her desk," Cooper said. Bill looked down at the fax.

Chief Superintendent Ruth Sanders Missing from her London Office.

Anybody who might have information as to her whereabouts, please do get in touch with LICD London.

"Her office was really totally wrecked." said Bill. "It was as if there had been a fight in there. Look we'll go and see Mr O'Conner for old times' sake, have a meal and look around if that is ok with you Cooper? Come on Jane." They got up and Cooper nodded his agreement, then they left his office and made their way back to their hotel and car.

+

Ivan drove his hired car into the car park of the New East Sutherland Hotel and stopped at the foot of the stairs going up to the main entrance. The door was open. He got out and made his way up and into the hotel. Banging his fist on the bell, Patrick appeared from the office behind the desk and went pale when he saw who it was. Quickly recovering, he put out his hand towards Ivan.

"Long time no see. I was trying to get hold of you last night, and this morning as well. Where were you?"

419

"Travelling. Been down at Oxford, well Eynsham to be exact. It seems that you managed to get half of the stuff away. Not too surprised as the other room was locked. Still half is better than none. Eh?" He slapped Patrick on the back.

"Come on through Ivan, I've a lot to tell you." Patrick led the Russian through to his office and they both sat down.

"Well, what is it you need to tell me?" "The parcels and packets."

"Yes, where are they?" said Ivan looking round the office. "Safe in the police hands."

"What did you say?"

"Safe in the police hands. The two men who were bringing the parcels up here had an accident and the van tipped over. Both have been killed outright, no seatbelt it appears. Anyhow, the police took the van and the boxes into their safe storage. I spent the night talking to them as one of the two men had written down my phone number and a list of the boxes and the ones missing."

"What! Is my name on the list?"

"No. Just some initials, BB and I. T. Police are baffled as to what the parcels contain and what the initials mean. In the meantime, I can't get hold of them. Sorry and all that, but this sort of thing can happen to the best of us."

Ivan leaned close to Patrick.

"If you had done as I asked and got the parcels yourself, it would be very likely that I could collect them now. You know what the seasons can be like up here, those two didn't probably know the conditions they would be driving in. Now how are you going to get my items back?" He sat and looked at Patrick with a glare. "Don't disappoint me, for I don't like to be disappointed. I have a way of dealing with those sorts of people."

"Sheepsbane," he added, changing the subject completely. "I need a regular supply of it. About ten to fifteen large containers full once a month. Think you can manage to do that for me?"

"No! Of course, I can't do that. I am busy running a hotel and trying to get it established again. That is lethal stuff. The farmers get rid of it as soon as they see it growing in the fields. Why would you need that much of it anyway?"

"That is not your concern. Who would get that sort of quantity for me?"

"Ask the farmers, better yet, offer to take it off their farms. A regular collection each month, or they could drop it off somewhere."

Ivan looked at Patrick and nodded. "You might just have something there. I know that I can rely on you to arrange it for me.

Then I might just forget you messing up the delivery of the boxes. There is a place in Dornoch, on the edge of the square, that is to let or buy. Buy it and use that as the drop off point. Install some person who needs a job, simple task, take the sheepsbane, weigh it, pay the farmers. Yes, you have something there. It will be perfectly legal."

"Why were you in Dornoch and when were you there?" "Plane landed there last night. Now what are you to do about the boxes at the police station. If they open them, they will probably know what is inside."

"Just what is inside that is so important to you?"

"If I told you, then you would have to die. You wouldn't want that would you?" Ivan rose and reached into his inside pocket and produced a bundle of money, which he threw down onto the desk. "That will do for starters. Deposit on the shop, legal costs, wages etc." He turned and left the hotel and made his way down to the car. As he got into the car, his new mobile phone rang. He saw it was from Boris, his henchman.

"Hello Boris. Where are you?" "Golspie sir. And you?"

"Same. Where shall we meet and talk?"

"Nice flat in the centre of Golspie, a show flat. The other five are still empty. Could meet there perhaps?"

"Centre of Golspie you say? I'll see you there." Ivan replaced the phone in his pocket and gunned his car engine down the drive and south to Golspie.

A few minutes later, the lady in charge of the show flat had been told her options. Leave the flat for an hour or die. Sensibly she chose to leave them to it. The bundle of money had been a big factor in deciding as well as the fact that she rather liked being alive.

## Chapter 25

New East Sutherland Hotel.

Patrick stood for a few minutes after Ivan had left, then pressed a button under his desk. Within a few minutes all the staff, the few that he employed, gathered in the hall.

"I need you to urgently drop whatever you are doing and go outside and look for sheepsbane. I know it sounds odd, but the reason isn't your concern. Mark on a piece of paper the location and then later I'll arrange for it to be removed. I can't have the guests picking it and getting ill or worse, dying. Somebody had told me that there was some in the hotel grounds." He watched as they picked up the paper and pens that were lying on the desk and left to do as he asked.

Bill and Jane drove into the car park in front of the New East Sutherland Hotel and parked on the right-hand side. Once inside the hotel, they waited at reception for somebody, anybody, to come and see them. Despite pressing the bell two or three times, nobody appeared to serve them.

Bill walked down the hall, taking in the refurbished interior and made his way towards the bar at the back of the hallway. The double stairwell still was the focal point, though now it had been redecorated in white with gold leaf picking out the smaller curls of the ironwork. The stair treads had been replaced with light oak coated with a clear matt varnish. Jane followed him and they went into the bar and sat down at a table. They would wait to see if anybody appeared in the next half an hour or so.

+

Up on the broch, Patrick had been watching through binoculars Bill and Jane going into the hotel.

"Good luck trying to find anybody in there," he muttered under his breath. The staff were all outside searching for sheepsbane, when Ivan asked you to do something for him, you did it, if you wanted to continue to live that is.

+

Boris leaned back against the wall of the kitchen as Ivan took a quick tour of the flat. With the two views, one to the sea and one to the hill behind the village, it was a surprise that they had not been snapped up, thought Ivan. He walked over to the dining table and picked up one of the brochures on it. The prices for all six flats were less than what he had just given Patrick to start the other business. Ivan turned and looked at Boris.

"Good location, good price, get them all. We can move in to the top one and use the others as holiday lets or some other purpose." He walked out to the balcony at the rear and looked up at Ben Bhraggie. "I know that there is a connection with that place. I need to spend more time looking for it." He spun round and indicated to Boris to sit down and bring him up to speed.

Ivan leaned back in his chair to take in what Boris had just told him. Standing up, he wandered to the front of the flat and looked across to Embo and the horizon. For the time of year, the sun was blazing down on the golden sands that stretched out in the distance.

He turned back to Boris.

"So there are a few things for you to do." Ivan ticked them off on his fingers.

"One, sort out the purchase for all six. I think I might just move in here over the winter and autumn time, instead of Moscow it is not as cold."

"Two, buy furniture for the other flats. We'll use two for our purposes and the others, well they can be rented out during the summer, when we are not around."

"Three, get as much information about the history of this side of Scotland and Aultbea on the west coast."

"Four, research more of Patrick's background, I want to know his weak spot, so I can put pressure on him if needed." Ivan looked out at the rear of the flat towards the hills.

"Five. Get some locals from Oxford to keep an eye on the warehouse."

"Students with payment in the new drug perhaps?" asked Boris.

Ivan gave Boris a stern look, meaning get on with it. Then left the flats.

Once Ivan was in his car, he drove out and headed towards Dornoch. Patrick's idea of getting the farmers to offload sheepsbane to him had, he had to admit, been a brainwave. That small shop in Dornoch, that had been up for sale, would be perfect for doing the job.

+

In the warehouse, Justin and the two women had used all the material that they had brought from Marlow. The machine was busy bundling the tablets into packs of 10 with an official label being stuck onto each one. A small microwave oven had been adapted for cooking them before bagging, and Justin had just taken the last batch out. He placed them on the table and switched on the fan that was placed strategically to give maximum effect.

He left the small room and wandered down the stairs and gazed at the boxes that were still in the room behind the red door. He decided that whatever was in them, it was not worth knowing about.

Returning up to the warehouse, he walked to the front and saw the two women packing the bags of tablets into cardboard boxes.

Each box had an official label stuck on the top and one of the sides. The top had the address blank ready for whoever ordered it. The side simply said Tablets 10 x 100. Animal use only. Expiry date /. /. That would be filled in just before they left the warehouse, destined for whoever wanted them. Justin was aware that normally he would have been in Oxford distributing the boxes to the various people, but with Ruth not here, he had taken charge. Not for the first time he wondered where she had got to.

"Think I'll take a drive to Oxford, take a few boxes with me."

"Good thinking, we are needing some cash to buy more of the XV3rd and the other stuff from USA."

"True, but I have no idea where she sourced it from."

"Ask around in Oxford, see if anybody else is offering this drug."

"Ok, but I doubt they will know, but I will ask. Now let's load up the boot of the car and I'll get away."The three of them set to and soon he had a car boot full of the boxes. Slamming shut the lid, one of the ladies pressed a button to raise the door and Justin drove on out towards Oxford.

Twenty five minutes later, Justin drove over Magdalen bridge and turned right into Longwall Street. He negotiated the road's one way system and pulled the car to a stop in the front of Sutherland College. He got out and looked up and down the street, no policemen could be seen. A young student rolled his bike under the large arch of the entrance gate and looked at Justin. Then he rested the bike against the wall and turned to Justin.

"Can I help you at all?"

"Do you know a student called Mark Headover? He is supposed to be a student here."

"I don't, but the porter inside the lodge would point you in the right direction." He collected his bike and carried on into the college. Justin walked in under the wooden entrance gate and knocked at the porters window. The glass slid back and a head appeared.

"Can I help sir?"

"Yes, I need to speak to Mark Headover. Can you please point out his room or tell me how I can speak to him?" He watched as the Porter rubbed his chin thoughtfully.

"You some sort of relative to Mr Headover? Only you can't be too careful these days."

"No, he ordered some of our product and I am just here to hand it over to him. I was passing and said I'd drop it off. Safer that way, don't you think?"

"I am not paid to think sir. Now the best thing would be to leave it here with his name on it. I'll put a card in his pigeonhole, over there, saying there is a box to collect. How big is the carton sir?"

"Not that big. I'll go and get it and you can actually see it for yourself." Justin left the porter and went back to the car and took out a small box containing the drug. For anybody looking at it, it would have appeared as just a small parcel. Quickly he wrote the name Mr M Headover, adding, Sutherland College, Short Road, Oxford, OX1 21SCP Then he shut the car boot and walked back into the lodge and handed it over. Though concerned that he was just leaving it for Mark to collect, he felt that it would be safe. He had added a "still to be paid for" message on the underside of the parcel. Justin got into his car and drove towards his next contact in north Oxford at a large office on the outskirts of the city.

+

At the warehouse, work had stopped since they had now run out of all three of the essential ingredients needed to make the drug. Boxes of finished drugs were waiting on the shelves near the roller door. All was silent, except for the distant ticking of an electric clock in the staff room.

+

Patrick smiled as he read through the sheets of paper his staff had filled in. It looked as though there would be enough of the sheepsbane to keep Ivan happy for now. Putting on a heavy pair of gloves, he picked up a rubbish sack and, armed with the papers, went outside to start collecting it.

Three hours later, his back aching, he stood up and looked at the bag beside him. Full to within a few inches of the top. He reasoned that might be enough for now. He had been crossing off the points on the paper as he collected it and now knew where the remaining plants were to be found.

Patrick walked back to the car and put it in the boot. Then he drove home to his flat for the night. Once he was inside, he found Ivan's note lying on the table, along with the bundle of money.

*Patrick, thanks for the use of the flat. I'll come and collect the boxes in a couple of days. We can then store them here in your flat, nobody will notice them. I assume they are now at the hotel.*

Tossing the note back down onto the table, he quickly counted the money. More than enough to allow him to get out of Dornoch. If Ivan could get into his flat, without any signs of forced entry, what else could he do. Anyway, he told himself, he had the hotel to run, and it would be far easier to stay at the hotel.

In the morning, he would speak to a firm of estate agents and get the flat put up for sale. First thing in the morning, he would get the local locksmith to come and change the lock. He wedged a chair under the handle and went to his office and poured a glass of Golspie Scotch.

# Chapter 26

Marlow, the following day.

An officer from LICD pulled up outside Ruth Sanders house. Despite several telephone calls and a drive past three times, nobody had gained entry. It had been assumed at LICD that Ruth was away working on some case or other.

It had been herself who had asked if anybody had gone inside to see if Ruth was unable to get to a phone. A few quick calls between the heads of departments and here she was having to see if Ms Sanders was in the house.

Getting out of her car, she walked up the front path, noticing that the garage door was slightly ajar. She rang the front doorbell and could hear the sound in the house. While she waited, she peered through the letterbox, only to discover the inner part was the usual foam to reduce drafts, great at its job, but hopeless to see through. She pressed the bell once again, longer this time, then walked to the garage and prised the door open to look inside. It was empty of the usual car, but several empty bags, lying on the floor, were marked XV3-й Россия. It looked like some foreign language. Returning to the front door, she raised the brass knocker and rapped it several times. The only sound, it echoed through the hall. She retraced her steps and reached into her car to pick up her car phone and to update her superior.

"Hi, it's Lisa here. I am at Sanders' house, but despite ringing and knocking at front door there is no answer. The garage door was ajar and inside it was empty except for some empty bags with some foreign writing on the outside. Do you want me to break in?"

"No, don't do that. See if there is a way in through the garage first. If not, then call the local police, they can gain entry for you."

"Ok. I'll go and do that."

"Phone me back in twenty minutes if you have got in. Then tell me what you find." She hung up and Lisa replaced the handset and then purposefully walked back up to the garage.

This time she pulled the door right back and stepped inside as the sunlight streamed in. Dust could be seen on cardboard boxes that lined one of the two longest walls. But what made her feel better was the door that was set into the side of the garage that adjoined the house. Hanging beside it on a nail, was a yale key. She picked it off the nail and tried it in the door. It fitted, and she turned the key and entered the house.

+

Ivan had reached Dornoch in a speed that would have brought him to the attention of the police, had anybody been witnesses to his driving ability. Parking in front of the cathedral, he got out and walked across the green to the corner shop that was for sale. He paced out the side that was obviously part of the property and smiled, so it seemed that there would be a yard as well. He noted that the estate agents were based in Tain, so got back into the car and drove off towards it.

Had Ivan bothered to look in the direction of Patricks' flat, he would have seen a 'FOR SALE BY AUCTION' sign being hammered into the ground by the gate, by the same estate agents.

+

Ivan left the estate agents with less cash than he had when he entered. What he now did have was the shop. He had signed a paper to buy the property outright. With the large deposit that he left on their desk, they were more than happy to let him have a set of the keys. He turned left and walked down to where his car was parked.

Had he turned the other way, then he would have seen Patrick making his own his way into the estate agents to sign the paperwork to sell the flat complete with furniture by auction in ten days. He, Patrick, needed cash and quickly too.

+

Ivan stood in the yard at the back of the shop. Under a corrugated roof, lots of boxes were stacked up high. He reached up and took one down. Inside was an old bubble lamp, or lava lamp. Its base had been undone and left as two bits. Interestingly, the liquid was missing from it, though from the weight of the lamp, it would be heavy enough to kill somebody he thought to himself. He moved forward and took the keys out to see which one fitted the back door. As he did so, the door swung open and a man, wearing a black balaclava, pushed past him and out through the open yard gates. Ivan, shocked that anybody was in the shop, picked himself up of the ground and went into the shop. In front of him was a flight of stairs, leading up to a small flat. To the right, a door with a broken pane of glass by the handle, led to the shop. Ivan went into the shop, carefully avoiding the broken glass, and stepped up to the glass counter and peered over the top. More boxes, but this time full of books, one or two had been thrown to one side of the counter and Ivan bent down and picked one up.

Янтарная тайна.

С чего начать искать[8]

Why, Ivan wondered, would a small shop for sale in Dornoch stock a book written in Russian? He put the small book into his coat pocket and went upstairs to look at the flat.

Each of the rooms, living room/kitchen, bedroom and bathroom had nothing in them, well nothing, if you didn't count the painting of the cathedral, that is.

Ivan sighed and returned to the shop below. He would need to clear the yard, get it checked first though, in case there was anything of any value. Then arrange for the farmers to bring any sheepsbane to the yard. He could set up a counter that would weigh it and store it under the corrugated roof. As to the shop, that might be a good place to sell other, more difficult, items.

He returned to his car, having locked up and then found a local locksmith that would come and change the locks both at the shop and then drive to Golspie and change the six locks on the flats. Smiling he started the engine and pulled away from the square, leaving a trail of dust and grit in his wake.

+

"Hello, anybody there?" shouted Lisa as she pushed the side door from the garage into the house. A small corridor led into the utility room, and then on into the kitchen. A nice veranda was attached to the side and front of the house and led through to a large living room. Lisa wandered through the house, until she reached a study, where she found Ruth Sanders very much dead, a glass lying in pieces on the floor beside her right hand. A few flies buzzing around the room forced her open one of the windows and in doing so, noticed the red light on the answer machine flashing. Taking a pad and paper from the desk, she pressed the play button to listen to the messages.

*"Where are you? Justin here. We have arrived at the warehouse. Unloaded and then some Russian guy locked us in. He said he owns the unit and to tell you that you choose well. He also mentioned some of his stuff being here, but it is gone now. What is going on? Call me on the new mobile you got me last week."*

*"Hello Ruth? It's Bill and Jane. Look we went to the office yours and your secretary's offices have been ransacked. Found some blood on a note that was*

*left on Bill's desk. We are getting the handwriting checked tonight. Wonder where you are, and if you are alright? We are heading towards Golspie again, we came back after we had read the file."*

*"Hello Ruth? Ivan here. Was at the unit today see that nobody goes into the basement room with the red door. I'll get you some more of the XV3rd soon. Think we should up the price for the Oxford students? Get in touch."*

*"Hello Ruth. Ivan again. Do call me urgently. Have you made sure that nobody gets into the room with the red door yet? I have arranged for somebody to supply you with sheepsbane. I need to get some of the XV3rd. Have you got any of the USA component yet? We need to source a regular supply of that too. Phone me when you hear this message."*

Lisa played the messages back a few times, to check that she had written things down correctly, then dialled LICD and spoke to her boss.

"Ruth Sanders, she is dead. About four days ago by the look of things. There were a few messages on her answer machine. I've written them down. Two are from somebody called Ivan. One from somebody called Justin at a unit somewhere, and one call from Bill and Jane, sounds like they are under her. What do you want me to do? There was a key by the door to the house, off the garage."

"I'll contact Marlow," was the reply, "get somebody to deal with the body and you look around to see if you can see or find anything else. If you do, make a note of it, but don't remove or touch anything." The phone went dead, and Lisa replaced the handset and went to finish searching the rest of the house.

She made her way back to the hall, and up the stairs that led to the first floor and then, it appeared, a new additional set that led up to the attic. Deciding to start at the top of the house, she climbed the new flight of stairs and entered the attic. New floorboards lay out in front of her, the insides of the sloping roof had been also cladded with the same boards. At one end there was work in progress to make a window into the roof. Otherwise, nothing worth noting down.

Retracing her steps back to the first floor, Lisa walked into what was now obviously a spare room. Cardboard boxes lay stacked along one side, a table in the middle and small cartons piled on the opposite side of the room. A half-filled large box had the small cartons neatly stacked inside. Lisa reached in and took one of the smaller boxes out, then picked up one of the empty small boxes and held one in each hand. One was slightly heavier than the other. She put them both side by side on the table and went to the next room.

This was obviously the main bedroom, for a large queen size bed was in the centre, two small bedside tables with art deco style lamps on each one. Along one wall ran a floor to ceiling set of wardrobes, with drawers underneath. An archway led through to a dressing room and off that a large double headed bath with a walk-in shower beside it. The bedroom was bigger than her flat, Lisa thought to herself with just a hint of envy. She pulled open a few drawers and cupboards, but nothing unexpected was to be found.

Moving out onto the landing, she saw a door set into a small recess. Lisa moved over and turned the handle; the door didn't move. She looked around and lying on a small table, under the window on the landing, was a bunch of three keys. Picking them up, she tried all three and it was the last one that opened the door.

A flight of metal stairs winding downwards in a tight circle greeted her. She stepped into the cupboard and a light came on over the stairs. Making her way down, she eventually came into a large room with no windows. A very long counter ran the whole length of the room. A variety of machines and presses for making pills were on the top. Lisa ran her finger over the counter leaving a clear mark where her finger had been. On a wall were a bank of monitors, none working though. A number of cables ran from each one but were left unconnected to anything. Turning around, she saw a large safe set into the wall. She correctly guessed that she must be underground. Moving across to the safe, Lisa noted the make and number and then tried the handle. It was locked.

She returned the staircase and made her way back to the ground floor. A police car and police van were pulling up in the drive.

+

In Golspie Patrick picked up the mail on the small table beside his hotel office door. Then unlocking it, he went in and sat down to do the hundred and one things that running a good hotel are required of the owner. A shadow fell across his desk and he looked up, annoyed at the interruption.

"Seumas Kelly, what brings you to this neck of the woods?" "You Patrick. We need to talk, you and I. Are you aware that only you, me and Barry are the only ones still alive from the original ARI cell? Barry was supposed to be coming up to see you so has he been in touch with you recently?"

"You know Seumas, I said on the phone, that I don't have anything to do with the ARI anymore. I run a legit business, I keep my nose clean and earn my money the hard way. No, I have not seen Barry, not for a long time. Now if you want to look around the hotel, do so, but I must get on with my work." Patrick turned to his paperwork.

"Patrick, stop what you are doing and look at me when I am speaking. I think that you know more than you are letting on. This is a perfect place for our members to stay for a short while."

Seumas waved his hand around the room. "You would hate to lose it all, wouldn't you?"

"Is that a threat, Seumas? Because if it is, you ought to be careful. You are not in Ireland or Northern Ireland come to that, now."

"No Patrick, I wouldn't threaten you." Seumas leaned in close to Patrick's face. "It's a promise. Now I'll go and have a wander around this wonderful place you have here. Do the police know of your connections to the tunnel bombing attempt?" Patrick shook his head. "Thought not, best that you help us then, or they might just get a note telling them who was in charge of the cell that arranged it." He turned and left Patrick alone in his office thinking what he should do about Seumas. He knew that Seumas was a crack shot. The evidence of his two hitmen proved that. He had some nerve though, to come up here and threaten Patrick. He put his worry about the ARI and its few members to one side and returned to the bookwork.

Half an hour later, after a very heated call to his two hired killers had resulted in an agreed amount, more than he liked, but worth it. He replaced the phone and returned to the bookwork.

+

At the Rest and be Thankful, the two men were in deep discussion with one another.

"It is easy money - we set off the fire alarm, hotwire the van and drive it to where Patrick said we were to go."

"Sounds easy, right enough, but how do we get into the storage area where the police have the van. Who's to say that the boxes haven't been unloaded already? Right fools we would look if the van was empty. Doubt that Patrick would pay up then."

"True, maybe we need to have a recee of the police station first?"

"Now that sounds much more sensible. Now let's plan for that." The two men bent down over the desk and started to draw the outline of the police station.

+

Much later that evening, a phone call to the station informed them that there was a suspected bomb in the building. As per usual policy, the station was emptied, and the officers stood around waiting for the Army bomb disposal team to arrive. On being told it would be a few hours, lots of the officers went home, leaving instructions to call them.

The two men having made the call, worked their way around the back of the building and broke into the storage facility where they had learnt the van was being kept. One kept an eye open by the door, while the other opened the back door of the van to find it empty. His colleague waved his hand towards a stack of boxes that ran alongside one wall. Quickly the other man moved over to them and looked at the label on the front. Giving a thumbs up at his colleague, who left the door and helped move the boxes back into the van. Once loaded, they left the unit, planning to return next day.

# Chapter 27

Golspie, very early the next day.

Long before dawn had broken over the village of Golspie, the two hitmen, had made their way back to the unit. Being a small village, the doors to the unit were still ajar, so it was a matter of minutes to open them, hotwire the van and drive it out and onto the main road.

They drove north towards Brora, passing the hotel. Patrick had been insistent that the parcels were to be stored at the ice room on the harbour. He had already given them the key to the padlock. It was purely unfortunate that at the same time, Ivan was out on the opposite side of the river and taking a very keen interest in what were doing. He had learnt from Boris the previous day, that there may be an attempt to move some boxes from the police station.

Ivan admired the nerve of the two men and the speed with which they worked. In the space of just an hour the boxes were unloaded, the door relocked, and the van was being driven south to Golspie again. Smooth operators thought Ivan as he watched the van go south. He returned to the car park and got in and sat thinking before he drove around to the other side of the harbour and took a close look at the ice room. The padlock was a substantial one, one that would need a heavy pair of cutters to get inside. Grunting his annoyance, he went back to his car and drove towards the Rest and be Thankful. A word with Boris would be helpful Ivan thought, first though he would call at the flats. He now had the new key to the top flat.

Ivan turned his car into the car park and went up to the flat. He found Boris had left him a note on the front door of the top floor flat.

1   Purchase of flats to go through on Friday week.
2   Patrick doesn't appear to have much of a back ground that the UK security know of anyway.
3   Still looking into history of around here.
4   Why do you need to know about Aultbea?
5   Trying to get some students to watch warehouse in Eynsham.

Ivan tore the note off the door and screwed it up and put it in his jacket pocket. Then he unlocked the door and walked inside and picked up the phone. He needed to contact another businessman in Moscow.

+

In Ruth Sanders' house, a forensic team had been hard at work. The small boxes had been taken away to LICD to investigate more fully. A lot of excitement had been raised over the black sacks with the foreign writing as they had turned out to be Russian. London was now comparing them with some other sacks recovered from a unit in Marlow. A small bag of a compound that had been stored in the garage, had been found and identified as a substance that the USA used to keep their soldiers awake and full of energy. It had a downside that it was highly addictive if more than five tablets were taken each day. According to their connections in USA, the government over there had stopped using it after 1976. Too many deaths caused by overdosing.

A retired safe cracker had been phoned to come and open the safe door but hadn't yet arrived.

+

In Oxford, Justin had arrived at his last drop off point. This time the person was there to take delivery of the drugs.

"Here you are."

"About time too. The students are demanding them daily. Their grades are all going up and they seem to not need so much sleep."

"Please do tell them not to take more than four a day. If they start to take five or more, then they become to addictive and can lead to..." Justin paused, how was he supposed to say, too many and death follows as sure as night follows day. "...a real addiction that has very unpleasant consequences for everybody."

"I'll tell them, but not sure that they take it in. Here is the money." The young lady passed over a bundle of notes and Justin stuffed it in his coat pocket. He walked back to his car but as he went to get inside, he was stopped by the young lady. "It is safe, I mean it is for humans? It's just the box says for animal use."

"That is so nosy people don't go looking too closely. Does anybody else offer this sort of drug around here?"

"No, you have the market covered." Justin nodded his head and drove off back to Eynsham and the warehouse. Apart from the first one, which he had to leave, all the others had paid him their money. Now all they had to do was find a regular supply of the main three ingredients. Namely, sheepsbane, XV3rd and the USA one. Ironic that the two superpowers both supplied part of the ingredients needed for a drug that made the taker work much harder and needed less sleep. Greater efficiency all round.

+

Boris had dialled the number of the owner of the antique shop in Oxford. He waited for it to be answered.

"Oxford Antique Emporium. How can I help you?"

"Hello, my name is Boris, I have some bad news for you. Your two Russian helpers have had an accident while driving the van. Both are dead. I know that this is a terrible shock for you, but I need to find somebody who can undertake a bit of watching for me."

"Oh, my goodness, dead you say. Both?"

"Yes. Van skidded and overturned. They were not wearing seatbelts it appears. There may be some sort of financial settlement in compensation in due course." He let the sentence hang, then continued. "It is important I find somebody to watch a warehouse for me. It's at Eynsham." He waited patiently.

"Ring me again tonight. I may have somebody for you by then. Goodbye." She replaced the phone and so did Boris at his end.

+

In Moscow, a telephone rang, and the secretary picked it up. "Hello. Michael's office."

"Ivan here, put him on the line please."

"Ivan, long time since I heard from you. How are things going?" "I need some information. You have a contact on the west

coast of Scotland, don't you?"

"Well, I used to. Haven't been in touch for a while though. What do you want to know?"

"The Arctic convoys. Dates, times and where to and from. Also, as much as you can find out about the Germans and when they were at Konigsberg."

"Where?" "Kaliningrad today." "Why all the interest?"

"Something I am working on. What are you working on at present?"

"Would I tell you that?"

"Exactly, so why do you expect me to do the same, eh?" Ivan chuckled down the phone.

"How long do I have?"

"A fortnight, three weeks as most."

"You don't want much do you? I'll see what I can do and get back in touch. Where are you based these days?"

436

"Golspie. north Scotland, during the autumn and winter, the Moscow office the rest of the time. I'll look forward to hearing from you." Ivan hung up and went for a drive, a drive to Patrick's hotel.

+

Bill and Jane had made their way to DS Cooper's office and were now inside telling him what they had learnt.

"I tell you, the place was totally empty, wasn't it Jane." "Totally, we went upstairs, downstairs and in the bar and kitch-

en. It was as if everybody had just dropped everything and vanished. Didn't see a soul. Most odd really." DS Cooper leaned back in his chair and reached into his desk. He took out and tossed a black and white photo onto the desk. Bill picked it up and looked at it, a bit grainy, but clearly showed the hotel, the nearby Dunrobin Castle and more importantly a lot of white dots in the grounds around the hotel.

"What is this, I mean I know it is an aerial photo, but what are the white dots around the hotel?"

"Got it from the air force, they were trialling a new fast camera. They think the dots are people in the fields. If you look closely, you can see your car, at least I presume it is your car, parked by the entrance. If this was taken when you were there, then the staff were all outside in the field, looking for something or someone." He reached again into his drawer and produced a

folder, which he placed on his desk and opened it. Extracting a single piece of paper, he passed it over to Bill and Jane. "This is all I have been given on Mr Patrick O'Conner. Do you know anything else to add to this?"

Bill picked it up and ran his eyes over it, before passing it back to Cooper.

```
Patrick O'Conner. aka 'The Boss' Key Dates
1959 (Approx.) Born
1968  Saw father killed in revenge attack
1969  Joined 'The Young of Ireland' junior
      wing of ARI.
1980  We think he joined the main ARI 1980
      August Killed first person, no proof
      though.
1984  Promoted to run a branch of ARI
      following  death of its leader, (A
      Suspicious death)
1984  In Autumn, B̶e̶l̶i̶e̶v̶e̶d̶ ̶t̶o̶ ̶h̶a̶v̶e̶ Now known
      to have connections to Brighton Hotel
      Bombing.
```

1986  Wanted in connection with bombing of
      Europa Hotel.
1987  Leaves NI for Ireland and then we think
      to England.
1988  Vanishes off the radar. 1988-1990 ?
1990  Appears in Oxford in connection with
      drug  supplies to students.
1990-1992 ?


Born of a good family, kept his head down and
studied at school, then in 1968 saw his father
killed in front of him at his home. This made
him join the young ARI and he quickly made a
name for himself as potential leader material.
In 1980 following a brief training week in the
South, we think he joined the ARI and became
one of their fastest runners and in time a
killer. Careful always to clear up after any
killing, we and the Northern Irish police have
never had any evidence to hold him. The nearest
we got to anything tangible on him was that
he might have been seen with Ryan in Brighton
the night before the hotel blow up. In 1986
the Europa hotel was attacked; people spoke of
a man matching his description going into the
hotel ten minutes before the bomb went off and
five minutes before the radio warning was given.
He made an escape by crossing the border
to Ireland and then by boat to? He vanished
off the radar for a quite some time, but from
late 1989 the drug supply in Oxford seemed to
increase. It could be he diversified. At that
time a person called 'The Boss' kept coming
up in conversations with known dealers around
Oxford. The previous head of supply was found
dead. We think, but are not sure, he likes to
collect good antiques and paintings of renowned
quality.
No idea as to his actual base, has no record,
officially, in NI, England, Scotland or Wales.
European Connections:

It is thought he is known for connections to criminals In Europe.
A very clever and thoughtful man, who is highly dangerous.
Anybody knowing anything about his movements during the gaps in the above is asked to contact ~~DCI Harvey Parker~~ at LICD. ~~(Ruth Sanders)~~

"Not much more than you already suspected. We saw this earlier this year. We were surprised by how little LICD seem to have on him." said Bill with a shrug of shoulders.

"He seems to be made of Teflon; nothing sticks directly to him." added Jane.

"We may have found something that connects him to Northern Ireland." said Cooper, taking another piece of paper out of the file and sliding it over to Bill.

*1408 6543210*
*Boxes 1 – 6*
*Boxes 12 – 13*
*Boxes 19 – 21*
*Missing? 7-11, 14-18, 22 onwards.*
*At BB?, I T? , Aultbea? Warehouse Red door?*

"How on earth does this connect him to Northern Ireland?" asked Jane. Cooper, like a conjurer produced a third piece of paper and placed it alongside the others.

| | |
|---|---|
| Patrick O'Conner | Running Hotel in Scotland |
| ~~Patrick Doyle~~ | ~~Found dead at his home.~~ |
| ~~Pat Reily~~ | ~~Found dead in his shop in Oxford~~ |
| ~~Barry Ryan~~ | ~~Visiting the Hotel in Scotland. Dead?~~ |
| ~~Dutchman~~ | ~~Klass Van Miere Killed in London.~~ |
| Eva | Working in Golspie. Vanished. |
| Colleen | Last seen in Folkestone, working for ? |
| Ivan ? | Russian – Fingers in too many pies? Martin |
| Fitzroy | LICD Security Officer for computers. |

"This person, Eva, worked at The Grand East Sutherland Hotel. While that was before Patrick took it over, his name is at the top of this list. What is interesting is that we received this in the post, from the bank which Barry Ryan had lodged this paper at, with instructions to forward it to us if they didn't hear anything within ten days. They did as he asked, and we got it today. We have checked the ferry and airlines and Barry Ryan did come to Scotland. In checking the lists, we have also thrown up another member of the ARI, a Seumas Kelly. He crossed by ferry into southwest Scotland and then hired a car, in his own name, and drove to Golspie. But he has dropped of the radar, just like Barry Ryan. Interesting, isn't it?" Cooper leaned back and watched their faces.

"If, as you say, Barry and Seumas are both dead, then the only person who we know that is linked to the other names is Patrick. Nice, clean, hotel manager, Patrick."Bill looked at Jane. "Why does everything seem to come back to this part of the world? A man who may or may not be connected to ARI, comes to Scotland and sets up a hotel, alright, rebuilds a hotel and is Mr Nice Guy. Where did the money come from? That is usually the angle we tend to go for. Setting up and running a hotel is not the cheapest of ventures."

"Not too sure yet, but here is another nugget of information; he may have a connection to a warehouse in Oxford. The van that had the accident was hired in his name from a van hire business in Eynsham. A ANPR[9] spotted it going into an industrial park and leaving around three hours later. We have spoken to other owners of warehouses, but nobody was around that early in the morning. The next time we know anything about the van, it is on its side on the outskirts of Golspie."

"Did you ever find out what it was carrying?" asked Jane. "That is the question of the decade. The van was emptied of the boxes and stored. Last night, the boxes were all taken from here and now we have no idea as to who has them or where they are being stored."

"Bit of an embarrassment for you then, being stolen from the police station."

"It would have been, but the van was in a separate locked unit at the back. Seems it wasn't locked at the time. It is now, but that is too late." Cooper tapped the paper. "It says Aultbea, but that is on the west coast, miles from here." Bill took another look at the paper and then looked at Cooper.

"You say there is a link to a warehouse in Oxford? With the mention of a warehouse on this list, I'd go there first. At least give it a try."

# Chapter 28

Eynsham Industrial Estate. Evening same day.

Justin pulled the car into the parking space opposite the unit. He switched off the engine and walked over to the small door set into the larger roller door. Unlocking it, he stepped inside and switched the main lights on. He waited for them to flicker into life, then walked towards the back of the warehouse.

Outside two men, employed by Ivan, on the recommendation of Boris via the owner of the antique shop, were looking at one another and at the open door to the warehouse.

"We may not get another chance to get in there again, at least not without being caught."

"While that is true, what if he locks up and we are inside?" "True, how about you go in, and I'll wait out here." He smiled as his friend shook his head. "Thought not, now come on, two against one, what is the problem?"They made their way inside the warehouse and looked down the long avenues of racking that seemed to stretch into the far distance. A light was on in a room at the far end, so they both slowly walked towards it.

Justin had taken a heavy-duty torch with him, and planned to see what was behind the red door of the basement. A bunch of keys that he had found in one of the offices was in his hand. He intended to try each one and if by chance one fitted, then he could come back at his leisure. He had his back to the two men as he tried one key after another. The two men looked at Justin and then at one another and nodded in agreement.

He awoke with a headache and found himself bound to a chair with strong rope. Justin was seated on a pallet high up on the racking, near the edge. If he tried to move his chair, then he might go crashing to the ground. Sensibly, he closed his eyes and tried to think what had happened to him.

Down below in the basement, using the keys Justin had found, the two men had managed to get the red door unlocked. All that stood in the room were two small boxes and a very ornate padlock. It was the work of two minutes to remove the boxes and take them to their car. Boris had been explicit that the contents of the red door room must not be allowed to fall into anybody else's hands than that of Ivan, his boss.

The forklift truck that they had used,was left switched on,then they left the warehouse and locked up after them. Thoughtfully, they left the lights on. Now they just needed to find a phone and contact Boris.

+

A large ocean size boat slowly manoeuvred into Brora harbour that night. The Russian, Michael, who owned it had been using all of his contacts to see what Ivan was up to. The most recent tip off had led him here to this remote harbour in the north of Scotland.

Now all his men had to do, was to break in, remove the boxes onto his boat, replace the padlock and be away in an hour or less. At that time of night nobody was much about. More importantly, he may at last have some idea as to what Ivan was really searching for...

...Thirty-five minutes later, his men and the boxes on board, the ropes untied, the engine came back into life and pulled away from the jetty. Only a man out walking with two border terriers watched the boat leave the harbour. He made his way down to the icehouse and found it locked as usual, so didn't report it or say anything to anybody else about what he had seen.

+

Patrick stood at the bar in the hotel. He was listening to what the two men had to say.

"We have put all the boxes are in the ice house. Here is the key." He passed it to Patrick. "Now please give us the money and we'll get out of here."

"Let's go and check first, I have your money here." He led them out to his car, and they reluctantly got in and he drove them to Brora. Once at the harbour, he pulled in and turned off the engine. Then he walked down and switching on his torch, Patrick peered through the mesh that blocked the entrance. Nothing was to be seen. Angrily he ran back to the car and peered inside.

"Nothing there, where are they? I need them to give them to the owner. Now tell me." He slapped the roof of the car in anger.

"We did exactly as you wanted, try the key, it must be a trick of the light. We come and show you."The two of them got out of the car and made their way with Patrick down to the harbour. He led them round to the ice house and stepped back after giving them the key.

442

"Well, aren't you going to go in?" He watched as they unlocked the door and peered inside. It was as Patrick had said, totally empty. They looked at one another and stepped out again.

"We did put them in there, early today."

"Well, they clearly are not there now. Try and think, was anybody watching you as you unloaded the boxes?"

"Nobody was around, we were early, very early. There were four boats tied up alongside the quay."

"Take a look. Are there four there now?" The two men looked across at the harbour and saw only two boats tied up, one smaller one was pulling away from the harbour.

"No, the large one has gone."

"Large one? What sort of large one? Bigger than those there?" "Very big, almost large enough to go to sea. I mean across oceans and so on," replied one the two men. "Colour?" asked Patrick.

"Red. Red with a red white and blue striped flag on the rear. Horizontal," he added for good measure. Patrick looked at them both.

"Could be Russian. If so, then Ivan has the boxes already. As for you two, you can disappear and not get paid, just count yourself lucky to be still alive. Ivan wouldn't be so generous. Now get away from me." Patrick glared at them both, and they quickly made their way away from him across the road and towards the main road. Leaving Patrick standing alone on the harbour quay looking lonely.

+

In the boat, heading fast out to sea, Michael had the drinks open and was passing it around the crew.

"You did well. I'd like to see Ivan's face when he finds out that his precious boxes are missing," he said with a laugh.

"What is in them?" asked the new crew member. A silence fell across the room, Michael stepped up close to the crew member. "If you want to survive, you do not ask those sorts of questions. Understand?" He gripped the man and looked him in the eyes. "Do you understand me?"

"Yes. No questions." There was a collective sigh of relief and the high spirits and the drinks continued to be passed around the room.

+

Patrick returned to the hotel and looked up Ivan's number. He really wasn't looking forward to this call at all. Dialling the number he knew, he waited, hoping that Ivan would be out.

+

Jane groaned as Bill drove on through the night. His suggestion to Cooper that the warehouse link should be looked at, had resulted in them having to drive to Inverness to catch a plane to Gatwick. Unfortunately, fog at Inverness had meant they were now driving to Eynsham, through the night. She turned her head to the car door frame and tried to sleep.

+

That night, a team of cleaners had finished tiding up the office belonging to Ruth Sanders and had now moved to her secretary's office. There was a pile of faxes that had been placed on Ruth's desk for her successor, whoever they were, to deal with. Meanwhile they had to finish this before the morning staff appeared. The head cleaner urged them to work harder and took out a small packet of tablets.

"Try one of these. My son at Oxford university swears by them, you will feel great and work harder without really being aware of it." She passed the small packet around the team, and they carried on with their tasks.

+

Three floors up in the same building a team of scientists had been looking at a similar packet of tablets, those though came from Ruth's house. The team had identified the basic three ingredients were toxic, but not yet identified the names of them.

+

Mark Headover was at a student party. He had long ago run out of the tablets that they all wanted. Cross with his supplier, he made his excuses and went back to Sutherland College. As he walked in through the gate, the porter called him across.

"Parcel for you Mr Headover. Got it down here." He reached below the counter and passed it across. "Think there some post in your pigeon-hole too." he added as Mark walked away from the counter. Mark didn't recognise the writing on the top label, but a quick glance at the side, made him run quickly up to his room and open the box. Stuffing bags of the precious tablet in to his various pockets, he ran back down and jumped on his bike - with a bit of luck and a tail wind, he might just get back to the party and make some lovely money.

+

Ivan stood on the flat balcony looking out across the sea. A boat came into view. Struggling to see what nationality it was, he reached across to the small table and picked up the binoculars that already had been used twice that evening. He now could just make out a flag flying from the back of the boat. What would a Russian boat be doing this close to the coast, he wondered? Ivan looked back into the flat as the phone rang inside. Curious, as he thought the line hadn't yet been connected but he walked back inside and picked up the phone.

"Ivan. It's Boris here. Got a phone call from the two that are keeping an eye on the warehouse. They found a man down in the cellar trying a bunch of keys on the red door. He has been taken care of and they opened the door and removed the two cartons that were inside."

"Nothing else?"Asked Ivan in surprise.

"Only an ornate padlock. They left that though."

"Pity, that might have been more valuable in the long run. Where are the boxes now?"

"The two men have them. That was why I was phoning, what do you want them to do, keep an eye on the warehouse or take the boxes somewhere else?"

"Tell them to keep an eye on the warehouse for now. I'll sort something out as to what they need to do with the boxes." He hung up and turned his attention back to the boat, but it had already gone.

+

The two men heard the phone ring, and one rose and went and answered it.

"Keep an eye on the warehouse. Don't lose the boxes, and if you get the chance, get the padlock that was in the basement as well. The ornate one." He hung up and repeated the message to the other man. Groaning, they both rose, switched off the TV and went out to their car. It was just a ten minute drive to the warehouse.

+

In Ruth Sander's house, the team were finishing off their work, when the phone rang. The team looked at the phone and one of them started to move towards it.

"Leave it! If it's that important, they will leave a message." Sure enough, after a minute a voice was heard.

*"Ruth! We need to talk, there is no use in trying to avoid me. I'll phone your London office number in the morning, and we will discuss getting the USA part over to Eynsham. I have the sheepsbane side of things tied up. Also, will get the supply of XV3rd from the Russian embassy tomorrow if all goes to plan. We will be back in production next week. Marlow unit is now empty I presume?"*

The tape went silent and then the leader of the forensic team walked over to the answer machine, unplugged it and bagged it. "This needs to get to London ASP. Who is up for a drive tonight?" The team groaned; it had been a long day. The thought of a long fifty plus mile drive to London, didn't fill any of them with envy. Andrew, the newest member to join, raised his hand somewhat hesitantly.

"I'll do it, if you don't mind me being a bit late tomorrow morning?" The team leader nodded his approval and handed the package to him.

"Get that to LICD in London and take it to the head of LICD. Tell them it is a no delay job. Not a request, an order from me. They need to get arrangements in place to intercept this XV3rd and sheepsbane and the USA thing as well. Now go." He watched as the man took off his protective gear and tossed it in the disposal bin, before leaving the room.

+

On the boat, the party was in full swing, the captain and crew had been invited to join in. The captain set the boat on autopilot and went down to join the rest of them. Although the lights were all on, three large oil rig tugs were pulling the top section of an oil rig. With the momentum that the tow boats and their cargo had, the other boat stood no chance.

# Chapter 29

Eynsham Warehouse. Early next morning.

Jane pulled the car to a stop and nudged Bill awake. She had driven the last four hours and really needed a rest and freshen up. A pit stop at the privately run services on Junction 38A had nearly convinced both to stay the night at the nearby hotel. Bill had said no and carried on driving. It was early morning as they swung into Eynsham and now they were at the warehouse. Both got out and stood stretching their aching limbs.

"Well, we got here. Let's go inside and see what we can find." said Bill. He went to the boot of the car and removed a specialist tool kit, supplied by LICD. At the door it was the work of a few minutes to open the padlock and enter the warehouse. The first thing that struck both was that the lights were on. The second thing was a voice shouting at them.

"Hello? Anybody there? I am up here and can't get down." Jane looked up at the racking to see a man tied to a chair close to the edge of the racks.

"Hang on up there, we'll sort something out to get you down."
"What time is it?" Justin shouted back.

"Seven in the morning."

"Oh." Bill motioned to Jane to go with him to explore the warehouse, then shouted up to Justin.

"Locked in were you?"

"Yes. Two big blokes jumped me in the basement. When I awoke, I was up here." Bill nodded and led Jane up and down the warehouse. Eventually they found the basement and a forklift truck. The battery was totally flat. Bill picked up a set of charging leads and plugged them into the back of the forklift. Then walked back and shouted up at Justin.

"The forklift has a flat battery; it was left switched on. I've put it on charge, but once it is charged enough, I'll get you down."

"Have you driven a forklift then?" asked Justin nervously. "No, but it can't be that difficult, can it?" He nudged Jane and smiled. He knew that she could legitimately drive one.

"Naughty Bill." she said quietly. Then they went and found the basement. Once inside the room with the red door, Jane bent down and picked up the padlock.

"Bill, I've seen that design before somewhere. Any ideas?" He took it from her and looked at it closely.

"No. Keep it for now, maybe you will remember where you did see it. If that is all that is down here, it has been a long journey for that." he said as he pointed to the padlock. Jane ran back up the stairs and started to make her way to the front of the warehouse. As she did so, she passed a large plastic rectangular box on four wheels. Inside were piled black bags with writing on the outside. Jane reached in and took one out and moved to be under a lamp. Bill came up behind her.

"What have you found now?"

"Here you see if you can read it." She stroked her hand through her hair and passed the dusty bag to Bill. He rubbed his fingers across the dust to make out the wording on it.

ХV3-й Россия.

"As far as my limited Russian goes, I think it says something like XV3rd Russian. Didn't we see some bags like this one in Marlow?"

"The ones you moved? Yes, I think they did have this on them. Does this mean that they are linked, Marlow and here I mean?"

"Is anybody going to get me down?" shouted Justin. Bill looked at her and they walked back to the forklift. Jane glanced at her watch.

"Bill, it is nine o'clock in the morning." "So?"

"So where is everybody? This is a place of work after all." "Good point. We will ask our friend up there when you get him down." Bill smiled as Jane swung herself into the driving seat and Bill discontented the two leads charging the batteries.


Ten minutes later, Justin had been freed and having used the facilities, stood looking at them both.

"We work for LICD," Bill said.

"or London International Crime Department. To give it the full title." added Jane. "What we want to know is what is done here and where is everybody?"

"Drugs. Pure and simple. Manufacturer of drugs, we simply package them and distribute them to the buyers."

"And XV3rd from Russia?" pressed Bill.

"One of the products that they use I assume. Look, am I under arrest or what?"

"Or what. Well, to use that old phrase - you are simply helping us with the investigation."

"So, you take the drugs and package them into?" asked Bill. "We weigh them. Usually, packet of ten to a strip, and ten strips in the box. Ten boxes to the case. Simple. Sometimes a customer will want an odd number, say seven or nine."

"So they get the odd ones for free?" said Jane.

Justin laughed out loud. "Free? No chance. We cut the strip down to the right number. The odd ones are tossed into the box for returning."

"Costly, are they?"

"I'll say. A box is a thousand, so ten boxes are ten thousand. A single pallet contains a hundred boxes."

"Pound each? That is not too expensive." said Jane with a frown.

"Trade price. Retail is hundred times that."

"So let me get this right. You send out a box of a thousand tablets. They are bought by a dealer for a thousand pounds. Then they get sold at a hundred pounds a tablet. What do they do for that much money?" asked Bill.

"Focus the mind, make the body need less sleep, say only an hour at most, makes work go that much faster, efficiency is ramped up by about five hundred per cent. The USA worked on it first, in the Vietnam war for some reason. Now it has been refined by mixing it with two other ingredients. This XV3rd and something from Scotland. Sheepswood or something like it." Bill looked at Jane and then they turned back to Justin.

"Any known side effects?" asked Jane.

"If they take more than five a day, they become very addicted to them. If they take more than ten a day, death in a few hours."

"Do you tell them this?" asked Bill.

"We tell the dealers, and they are supposed to tell the customers."

"But they might not?" said Jane.

"Correct."

"You have a simple choice. One come with us, tell us all that you know, and we don't prosecute you, give you a safe house and go free. Or two, we arrest you now, and you spend about ten years in prison. Take your choice, but don't make us wait too long." said Bill.

Justin looked at both and shrugged his shoulders. "No choice really, is it?"

"Not really. So, who does own this place?"

"Somebody called Ivan. Russian, I think. Our immediate manager is a lady called Ruth, Ruth Sanders. Has been in charge for a few years now. It used to be somebody called Colleen,'Cats Eyes' Colleen. She stopped coming here for some reason or other."

"Come on out to the car, we can drive as you tell us." They marched the young man out to the car and put him in the back seat, Jane sat next to him, and Bill drove off towards London.

+

The two men came out from behind the metal container, which they had been peering round from and looked at one another.

"That looked like an arrest. They have left the place unlocked. We can go and grab the padlock and get away." The two did that but discovered the room was now empty. Leaving the warehouse, they returned to their car and drove home, Boris would need to learn about this and quickly too.

+

Two hours later, In the block of flats, Ivan had heard from Boris that the padlock must have been removed by a woman and a man. Also, a younger man had been marched out to their car. Ivan thought it sounded like it could be the police. How would they have got to connect the warehouse and the manufacturer of the drugs so quickly? He needed to try and somehow get the boxes up to Golspie. He remembered that he hadn't heard from Michael either. Picking up the phone he dialled his number and waited for Michaels secretary to answer.

"Michael's office. How can I help?"

"Ivan here, can you connect me to him please?"

"He isn't here. He is out on the boat he hires and is supposed to be back late tonight or early tomorrow morning. You could try again then." He hung up and went and looked at the Ben from the back of the flats.

+

Bill swung the car into the car park at LICD and turned round to speak to Justin.

"You need to keep close to us. Just do as we say and we will then take your statement down." Justin nodded and the three of them got out of the car and made their way across to their offices.

Upstairs in a department, the telephone answering machine was being analysed and arrangements made to get access to the USA and Russian embassies to get the XV3rd and the drug from the USA. Surprisingly, the Russians were easy to get to agree. They didn't want anything to do with trafficking drugs of any kind. The US would take a while to give their consent.

A group of LICD staff were standing around Ruth Sanders' desk. In the middle, connected to a range of electrical devices, was her answer machine. Ever since the message had been left the night before, the LICD team had been busy trying to decide where the caller was based. With the equipment on the desk, it was hoped that the caller may give away his location by talking too long. Her phone rang, and the answer message kicked in.

"*Ruth Sanders phone. I am away from my desk at present, please leave a message and I'll get back to you when I return to the office.*"

"*Ruth? Where are you? I haven't heard from you for days. Ivan here. We need to meet. I am now based in the far north, small village in east Sutherland. Now get in your car and drive to Inverness. Then phone me for directions from there.*"

The phone was replaced, and the tape instantly replayed two or three times. The team looked at one another and then left to return to their various departments. Bill and Jane, who had been called to the room, looked at one another.

"Golspie or somewhere near there, I bet." said Bill.

"Probably Dornoch or Brora. Golspie would be too much to hope for." replied Jane. "First though, we need to finish talking to Justin."

+

Waiting down in an interview room, Justin sat looking at the papers he had filled in since arriving. He was surprised to hear a knock on the door, then it opened to reveal a tall red-haired man.

"Thought you might like some tea?" He carefully placed a cup on the table in front of Justin and then produced from his back a packet of biscuits. "And a couple of biscuits wouldn't go amiss I dare say?" He opened the pack and shook out two or three onto a plate. Justin nodded his thanks and took a mouthful of tea and bit the biscuit in two. The man smiled and left the room. Once outside, he picked up a phone on a nearby desk and dialled the outside number he had been given.

"It's done. Now can my debt be written off?"

"No, but the interest remains stopped. Don't forget to remove the items and just leave the body, then go home and wait for my next task."

In the interview room Justin lay across the desk. His heart had stopped a few minutes after the poison had entered the bloodstream. A poison that was safe when in its two separate states, but once mixed was fatal.

Bill threw open the door.

"Justin, we need to…" He stopped dead at seeing the body slumped across the desk. Jane pushed past and felt for a pulse, then looked at Bill.

"He is dead. Must have been his heart."

"Mmn. Convenient though, don't you think? The minute we leave him, bang he dies." Bill reached under the body to try and retrieve the papers but found nothing there. "His written statement, it's gone. This was no heart attack Jane. This was murder. We need to secure the room."They stepped out and both placed a desk across the door after they had locked it and removed the key. Then they went up to their new, temporary boss waiting in his office.

+

In Oxford, at Kidlington Police station, the phone rang on DI Rogers' desk.

"DI Rogers."

"LICD here. We know that a firm have been manufacturing and distributing tablets to the students. They make them work faster, need less sleep and become much more alert."

"Sounds better than the usual drugs. So what is the problem?" "If they have five or more in a day, they can be addicted, once addicted, they will want to have more and more. Two days later, they die. What we want to know is, have you heard of any of the students dying like that?"

"I've not, but I'll phone around and get back to you."

"Good, thanks. My number is 0101345867023 extension 91." DI Rogers sat back in his chair and then looked up the number for the local hospital. Best to check there first.

+

Mark Headover was feeling a bit lightheaded. The party had gone on into the early morning. He had long since run out of the tablets. To start with, he had told the customers not to have more than three a day. As the party went on, he forgot to do that, and now with all of them sold out, and not having eaten for twelve hours, he didn't really feel that great. Popping a tablet in his mouth to keep him awake, he shook his head to try and clear it. A young man approached him.

"I need some more. Like now." "I don't have any more."

"Liar! Hand over some."

"I don't have any more. How many did you take?"

"Don't know, about six or seven. Why does it matter? I just need to get some more and soon." He turned away from Mark and made his way to a girl who was lying asleep on a couch. He opened her

452

handbag, but obviously found nothing, as he then reclosed it and moved towards another party goer.

Two hours later, a neighbour had called the police as a student had just left the house next door and then collapsed on his front path. He, the neighbour, had felt for a pulse, but the student was dead.

DI Rogers got the information about the death after the police had gone into the house where the party had been and found all, bar two, students dead in various rooms around the house. He had driven straight there only to find what he had been told could happen. Sighing, he found the phone in the house and dialled the number for LICD.

"LICD which extension do you require?" "Extension ninety-one."

"Putting you through to extension ninety-one." The phone rang on Bill's desk and Jane picked it up and passed it across to Bill.

"Bill Sutherland speaking."

"DI Rogers, Oxford CID, I need to speak to somebody urgently about a new drug that is now on the Oxford student scene. I was phoned earlier and talked about the effects of what overdosing could do."

"Hang on a minute DI Rogers, let's start again. You got a phone call earlier today from somebody in LICD informing you of the effect of a new drug?"

"Yes. If more than five are taken, then they become addictive and then after two days can result in death."

"Sounds like the department upstairs may have been in touch. Anyhow, how can I help?"

"I attended the remains of a student party, only two were alive. Do you know the source of the tablets? I think we need to stop the distribution as soon as possible."

"Agree, yes we do have some information on certain individuals that might be connected to the drug scene. Do you want us to attend?"

"Not right now but let's keep the lines of communication open."

"Will keep you in the loop if we find anything else." They hung up and Bill turned to Jane. "That was DI Rogers from Oxford CID. Somebody here has told him about the new drug. He has attended a student party that only has two survivors. The rest are dead."

"Must have taken more than ten then."

"The so-called cream of the brains of Britain. What a waste," Jane said, shaking her head in disgust. "Wonder who the killer of Justin was?"

"Forgot all about that. Let's go and report it. At least we have the keys to the interview room." Bill took them out of his pocket and walked over to his desk where he put them into one of the drawers before locking it.

+

Patrick stood outside his hotel and looked across towards Ben Bhraggie in the distance. The conversation with Ivan had been short to say the least. He, Patrick, had been told that he had to find the boxes and urgently. Patrick had tried to reason with Ivan, but he refused to listen to him. Ivan claimed it was Patrick who was responsible for the missing parcels. Ivan had asked him to collect and store them. Patrick had arranged for a third party to do that, fair enough, but it was still up to Patrick to sort it out. So, here he was standing outside the hotel gazing into the hills when he should be trying to find the boxes. He turned back into the hotel and picked up a copy of *The Northern Times*.

BOAT LOST AT SEA IN COLLISION WITH OIL RIG.
BOAT LAST SEEN IN BRORA HARBOUR.
Police appeal for anybody who saw a red painted boat - either arriving or leaving Brora harbour are to get in touch.

*An unknown red boat that collided with a tug pulling part of a new oil rig, is believed to have sunk with all hands. The captain of the tug reported seeing bits of boat, coloured red, in the water right after the two collided. "There was nothing I could do to stop it happening. With the platform on our tow, the distance we would have needed to stop was far too long. We stopped the tow, but by then we had gone about two miles further on past the point. I sent a small boat back to see if anybody had survived, but nothing was on the surface. It was a tragic accident, one of those things." Police are going to send down divers to see if there are any signs of the boat or bodies, but the exact position is not really known, making it difficult for the wreck to be located.*

Patrick thought back to the two men who had moved the boxes. One of them had said that he had seen a large red boat, with a possible Russian flag over the end. There couldn't be two such boats in this part of the woods. He picked up the phone and dialled the local police station.

"The red boat may be Russian. Seen yesterday leaving Brora harbour early in the morning." He replaced the phone and went to seek out Seumas. He needed to deal with him too.

+

DS Cooper replayed the tape and listened again to the message.

"*The red boat may be Russian. Seen yesterday leaving Brora harbour early in the morning.*" He scribbled a note on his pad, and phoned LICD. Cooper needed to speak to Bill or Jane. After a few minutes Bill answered.

"Bill Sutherland. How can I help you Cooper?"

"Is Jane there?"

"Yes, I am here. You are on speaker phone. What is the problem?"

"Russian boat, red in colour collided with a tug towing an oil rig platform. Went down fast, no survivors. How many Russians are there that have boats at their disposal? Do you have any ideas?"

"We have just heard a taped message left on an answering machine. Somebody called Ivan. The call came from your neck of the woods. They wanted to talk to one of our members of staff. Difficult as she died about five or six days ago. Have you ever heard of something called sheepsbane? It is an ingredient in a new drug that is supposed to make you work harder and need less sleep."

"Sounds ideal, send me some up here."

"No, it gets addictive if you have more than five in a day, ten and you die. A student party found that out the hard way."

"Sheepsbane, it is deadly stuff. The farmers hate it. Touch it with your skin and you die. Why use it in a drug? It is asking for trouble. No wonder your students died." said Cooper.

"Where can you get it, the sheepsbane, I mean." asked Jane. "Easy enough to find in east Sutherland. The farmers must use gloves to collect the plants, dig them up and then burn them. Like I said, deadly stuff. Grows like gorse does, everywhere you don't want it to."

"Ivan, that rings a bell, didn't someone called that, crop up in 'No Body at Ben Bhraggie'?" asked Bill. Cooper reached for the file of the same name and flicked through it.

"Yes, I have a number for somebody called that. Could be the same person?"

"Well, it is not Scottish, and probably stands out in a place like Golspie." said Jane, laughing.

"I'll get back to you both." Cooper hung up, ran his finger down the list of telephone numbers on the cover of the file and dialled the one next to "Ivan".

Patrick tapped Seumas on his shoulder, making him spin round.

"Don't do that, I nearly spilt my drink. Scottish is not bad, but Irish is better. What can I do for you Patrick? Have you seen sense?"

"Come outside for a minute. I want to show you something." He watched as Seumas eased himself down from his bar stool and walked with Patrick to the front of the hotel. Once outside, Patrick took Seumas's arm and pointed towards Ben Bhraggie.

"See that monument, to the first Duke of Sutherland? Up there on the hill."

"Yes. What about it?"

"Now run your eyes down the slope and along this way to the other monument."

"Got it. What about it?"

"Now get your halfway point between the two monuments." Said Patrick with patience.

"A small farm, at least it looks like that from here."

"A smallholding. In the grounds, there is supposed to be part of a great treasure."

"Why are you telling me this?" asked Seumas suspiciously.

"Look I don't want anything to do with ARI, but find the treasure and the money would be a good war chest, wouldn't it?"

"How much are we talking about here?"

"A lot, an awful lot of money."

"The owners aren't going to just let me go and dig their ground up though, are they?"

"No, but at the moment, it is empty." Patrick saw the gleam in Seumas's eyes and knew he had him hooked.

"So how come you are not up there yourself?" Seumas asked, looking suspiciously at Patrick.

"Look around you. I have a hotel to run. That is more than enough to keep me busy." smiled Patrick.

"I'll look. How far is it to walk?" asked Seumas with a frown. "Not too far, about two miles from here, say three maximum.

Take a shovel and fork. You never know what you might find." "Where would I find those?"

"Try Lindsay's & Co in Golspie. They are the nearest and the best stocked anyhow." He watched as Seumas weighed his options and then walked down the steps and turned back at the bottom.

"I'll give it a week."

"Fine." Patrick waved goodbye and walked quickly back in and phoned a contact he knew. He outlined the plan and replaced the phone. Patrick thought to himself now he is just a dead man walking. A week, well, we will see what develops.

# Chapter 30

Golspie two days later.

Ivan had received a copy of 'The Oxford Times' through the post, well the front page to be correct. The headline made him furious.

40 STUDENTS DIE IN PRIVATE PARTY.
Only two survive.
Synthetic drugs are being investigated.
New study drug found in student rooms across Oxford.
Police are now investigating warehouse in Eynsham.

Ivan threw down the paper and picked up the phone, he needed to speak to Patrick.

+

No sooner had Patrick sat down in his office, than the phone rang.

"Hello? New East Sutherland. How can I help you?"

"Patrick, Ivan here. We have a problem. The warehouse in Eynsham?"

"Yes?"

"The police know what it is used for. Get rid of the sheepsbane, I mean hide it. My contact in LICD has not replied in five days, despite me leaving messages for her at her home and office."

"You didn't leave messages at her office? You must be mad. They will trace you in an instant." said Patrick in a shocked voice. "This is nothing to do with me. You just asked me to go and collect some boxes. I had nothing to do with what was in either the boxes or the unit. What did go on anyhow?"

"Drugs, we were making a new refined version of something that the US Army first used in the Vietnam war. Designed to keep troops alert and needing less sleep. Their higher efficiency was measured by the Army. When they saw how good it was in the trials, then they developed it on an industrial scale."

"I hear a loud, BUT, coming."

"Correct, the effects dropped off after a day. If they gave the troops a further one the next day, they started to believe they were invincible. Run at machine guns and so on. When the war ended, it was quietly taken off the shelf and stayed that way for years. Then an old contact found that by adding a new ingredient, the effects would last twice as long."

"All of them?"

"No, just the efficiency and keeping sleep to a minimum. The other effects stayed the same. Three of the Ivy league universities trialled it for a year. Students who took a tablet, one every other day, were able to score much higher results on the days that they took a tablet. The other days, rest days if you will, they fell lower than before the trial had started." Ivan paused.

" I got involved, when it was smuggled into Russia and the military used another ingredient to replace the US one. Same results. It got shelved, I bought a company that had a warehouse in Russia. When I visited it, the contents of dozens of tins of this were stacked floor to ceiling. I didn't do anything for three or four months, then a friendly chemist helped to decipher the ingredients for me. Nice guy, pity he died. The one thing that improved it for marketing on a commercial scale was sheepsbane. A Scottish contact sent me some. Forgot to put instructions about opening the box, my staff did, and died. The chemist, managed to stabilise it before he died, touching the sheepsbane without gloves can do that to people."

"And you stored this in Eynsham? At the warehouse?" "Marlow to start with, near a firm making industrial diamond cutting heads. They got a contract to work on the tunnel boring machines that dug the Channel Tunnel. It was easy to convince the local man to give some to their gang on site. Their efficiency went through the roof. It was used from then on, unofficially, as the drug of the workers."

"So, what happened when that started to come to an end?" "We moved to selling it to students in Oxford to start with, then we are going to expand to Cambridge. Within a five-year period, we plan to be working and supplying all the universities in England and Scotland."

"So, what has sent you into a panic. The police?" asked Patrick.

"No, the deaths of around thirty to forty students. They must have taken too much of the drug. We tell the sellers to inform the buyers what the upper limit is. They obviously ignored it. Hence the deaths."

"What causes that then?" asked Patrick.

"Take more than five a day, you get really addicted, take ten or more, death follows pretty quickly."

"Ok. I'll go and hide the sheepsbane, I know just the place." Patrick hung up and returned to the front of the hotel and looked at where he had told Seumas to go and smiled. Patrick went and put the sacks of sheepsbane in the car and drove off towards the same place as Seumas had been told to go.

Twenty minutes later, Patrick pulled to a halt and got out. A small area to the right of the barn had signs of being recently dug over. Patrick pushed the door of the building open and looked inside. It didn't seem as though Seumas had been there yet. Quickly he returned and scattered the sheepsbane all over the floor of the barn. Once he had done so, he took the bags and put them back in the car and drove off down the track. Then stopped and went back to scuff the tyre tracks, before driving back to the hotel.

It would be another two weeks before a passing walker found the remains of Seumas in the barn. The police put it down to an accident that could not be explained. The procurator fiscal agreed with them.

+

In Eynsham, the police had raided the warehouse. Finding only empty bags with XV3rd in Russian and lots of empty cardboard boxes of varying sizes was not enough to help the investigation or stop the supply to the students they thought.

## Chapter 31

## London LICD headquarters four days later.

Bill rubbed his eyes and looked at the list of names in front of him. A team from LICD had been working through the TUT file to see if there were any connections to the current case.

What had shaken LICD though, were the high number of people working within both BOTG[10]and latterly, LICD who had been forced to help both ARI and other groups.

The connection of the supply of drugs to the workforce on the tunnel had now been proven. Arrest warrants were being raised for a lot of known criminals. Bill was trying to compose a list of those that had eluded capture or being on the radar of LICD or the police. He looked again at the list on the computer and added two more names to the paper.

Ivan.? Russian, warehouse owner, and runs businesses in Russia and England. Whereabouts, unknown.

Patrick O'Conner. Irish. Believed to be ARI supporter, no criminal record in Ireland, England or Scotland. Runs a 5 star Hotel in East Sutherland.

Simon Reed. Government Troubleshooter, worked for both BOTGB and LICD. Said to have contacts with Russian businessmen. Vanished without trace. Left note and file for Bill and Jane. Last heard on phone screaming.

Infiltrator at LICD. Known to cause death of Justin and possible attack on Ruth Sanders.

Russian Boat owner, disappeared in North Sea, accident? Killed? Ruth Sanders, Justin. Others?

Bill looked at Jane.

"A lot of the connections appear to be between LICD and ARI as well as the Russians. Why? What would they have to keep LICD staff on their side?"

"Money, blackmail, family, promise of promotion." replied Jane as she ticked them off on her fingers one by one.

"Point taken. So what you are saying then is that we need to investigate all the staff here, dig deeper into their backgrounds?"

"Yes. Also, get hold of Cooper, see if he has tracked down anybody called Ivan. I went through the computer files; do you know how many Ivans we have on the records?" Jane asked. "Common as Smith I am guessing."

"Correct. We don't even know if this name is his real one or an alias. Hence why we need to talk to Cooper. Did you get anywhere with the student side of things?"

"No, the death of the students at the party seems to have stopped the others taking it, if they can get it. DI Rogers said that their student liaison officer has it on good authority that it is not available. They think there may be a further couple of deaths that had been explained by another means. The party was the one that shook the students though. Thought they were considered the best brains, taking something so bad does make you wonder though," Bill replied.

+

In Ivan's office in Moscow, the phone rang. With no secretary to answer it, it went to the answer machine. A sophisticated one, that allowed Ivan to collect his messages from anywhere in the world.

+

In Golspie an hour later, Ivan collected his messages and was surprised to hear one from Golspie police.

"DS Cooper from Golspie police, I am looking for somebody called Ivan. Golspie police would like to speak to him to eliminate him from an ongoing enquiry. Please phone Golspie 6530100 and ask to speak to DS Cooper."

Ivan replaced the phone and picked up his coat and left the flat. He really didn't want to get the police involved. But he realised that if he went to them of his own accord, then it was probably likely they would not show any further interest in him. Twenty minutes later he was in DS Cooper's office seated across a desk from him.

"Thank you for coming in today. We just need to find a few details and then we know that you can be eliminated from the ongoing enquiry."

"Always pleased to help. I have bought the six flats in centre of the village."

"Do you intend to stay here then?" asked Cooper as he made some notes with his pen.

"Only for six months of the year. The autumn and winter most likely. It is better than back in Moscow. What can I help you with exactly?"

"We understand you own a warehouse in Eynsham, Oxfordshire. Is that correct?"

"DS Cooper, I own lots of properties all in different parts of the world. Now if you say I own a warehouse, then probably I do. I would need my secretary to check though." Ivan leaned back in his chair.

"This warehouse, it was used for making some drugs." "Nothing to do with me. If it is mine, which is what you say, what the tenants do inside it is their affair. If the rent is paid, I don't interfere. Why all the sudden interest in a warehouse in Eynsham?"

"It's not the warehouse as such, more the packaging that was found inside the warehouse."

"Packaging? But that could belong to anybody. I will look into the history of the tenants and let you have a list if that will be helpful."

"Very, thank you. You see there were some black bags with some foreign words on the side. Our London office had it translated." Cooper paused and looked straight at Ivan. "XV3rd. Written in Russian"He looked at Ivan, who was not saying anything. "- Maybe you could get that list and come back here tomorrow? Oh, and let me have your passport for safe keeping." Cooper held out his hand and Ivan gave him his passport without saying anything further. He got up and left Cooper looking at his notes.

+

To say that Ivan was shaken was an understatement. He quickly walked back to the flats and called Boris as he needed to discuss things and urgently too.

+

Cooper picked up his phone and dialled Bill's number. "Cooper here. Look I would appreciate it if either of you could get up here tomorrow. I started to interview Ivan today, mentioned the warehouse and think he is shaken that we knew about it."

"We have a few questions that need answering ourselves. We'll try and fly up today and see if you can get us a room at Rest and Be Thankful." Bill hung up and turned to Jane. "Cooper wants one of us to go and help interview Ivan. You heard what I said."

"Already arranging the flights. If we use the one from Gatwick to Inverness, we can be there late this afternoon. However, if LICD

463

charters a small private plane, we can land in Dornoch, but it will take longer. The private ones must avoid the commercial flights. Which do you want to do?"

"Go commercial. Get a car hired from Inverness Airport. It's only an hour or so to get to Golspie."

+

In a London flat, not too far away a man was looking at the phone on his sideboard. He hadn't heard from anybody for three days now and was scared to leave the flat. He jumped as the phone rang. He looked at it and made no attempt to answer it. It rang for a few minutes then stopped. He carried on looking at it. Sure, enough it rang again. This time he got up and walked over and picked it up.

"Where were you? When I phone you, I don't want to have to phone twice. Neither do you if you want the debt written off. I have a small job, nice and easy, half your debt written off on acceptance, the rest on completion."

"You said that before, why should I believe you now?"

"I mean it this time. Now do you want to hear what I want or not?"

"Can I refuse to do it?"

"Of course, you can. The interest starts again though and compounded daily, you might not want to do that."

"Go ahead then."

"Two people in LICD are getting close to finding out what some friends of mine have been up to. Understandably, they don't want LICD to do that. A small device fixed to the underside of their car with a remote-controlled switch would solve their problem. It was proposed that you follow their car out of London and when on one of the smaller side roads." he paused. "well, I am sure you don't need me to draw you a picture. If you accept, and I think you will, go for a walk and you will find the device and the control in your flat when you return. You have a day and night to fix it. Once done, keep your eye on when they leave. It is likely that they may have to drive to Golspie soon." The phone went dead and the man in the flat hung up his own phone. He would do as he was asked. He left the flat for a short walk around the streets, when he returned, inside was the device, instructions and the control. He sat down and started to read the instructions.

+

Meanwhile, across the street in an identical block of flats, "Cats Eyes" Colleen Kent stood with a pair of binoculars in her hands intensely studying the flat opposite. She picked up her mobile phone and pressed one of the buttons that connected her to her employer. She wasn't used to this sort of work, more breaking and stealing, but ever since both her Folkestone and Exeter homes had been discovered by the police and BOTOG later to become LICD, she had to resort to working for anybody that would use her talents.

This time she had been loaned a flat and told to keep an eye on the flat opposite. If he agreed to what was proposed, she was to leave the device in his flat and then go back and watch him. As soon as he picked up the device, she was to press the remote once to activate it, to allow him to use it for its intended victims. Who they were, she didn't want to know. For if the money was this good you didn't press questions.

She carried on watching him read the instruction manual. Then he put it down and moved towards the device. Jane was about to press the remote when he sat back down and started to re-read the instructions.

+

The retired safebreaker finished opening the safe in Ruth Sanders house and stepped back. She had been given instructions to unlock it, but not to open the door. First, she reset the lock and then she wrote the combination on a piece of paper. She stood up and stretched her body. As she had explained to LICD and the forensic team, the safe was a forty-eight hour one, meaning that it was not supposed to be able to open for forty-eight hours. She glanced at her watch. Forty-seven hours. Not too bad then. She made her way up the stairs to the team waiting in the house.

"Here is the code and instructions for opening it. It is unlocked at the moment; no I have not opened the door to the safe. It's all yours."

"Thank you. Your money is over in the envelope on the side." She picked it up as she left the house. The team leader looked at the group and they all descended to the safe in the basement. The leader swung open the door and looked inside.

Inside the safe, which was large enough to walk into, a model of the western part of Russia, north sea and north Scotland lay in front of him. Scale boats were placed at various points. On the edge of the model a small boat with the name 'Bragging Rights' was turned upside down and piece of paper stuck under it. 'Name Changed.' written on it. A dotted white painted line reached from a port in Russia to Aultbea on the west side of Scotland. Another dotted line ran from the same port to Brora and Golspie.

The detail was astonishing. A scale version of Ben Bhraggie and the two harbours were also constructed in the same fine detail.

At the far end of the safe under dust sheets, another model, made to the same high standard, sat on three trestles. Once close enough it became obvious that it was the model of the two ends of the channel tunnel and the south coast. Exeter, Oxford and Folkestone all clearly shown. Flags were dotted across the model in different colours.

"This needs to be taken to pieces carefully, removed from here and taken to a large room, big enough for people to get in and look closely at."

"LICD?" asked one of the team.

"No. Try and find a new unused office or warehouse, central to Oxford, Exeter and Folkestone. The police from those forces will want to see this as well. If central to them, it makes for easy relations, and nobody has to travel too far."

+

Boris knocked on the door of the flats. He had been told by Ivan to move out of the Rest and Be Thankful and take one of the flats now the ownership was all in Ivan's hands.

"Come in," called Ivan. Boris entered and put down his two cases. One for clothes and the other, well, customs would have had a field day if they had seen inside it.

"Something urgent you said."

"Very, the police and LICD know about the warehouse; also they found empty bags with XV3rd on them and other packaging materials. It sounds as though the team have been caught. I have handed one of my passports over to the local police. Now I need you to get down to Eynsham, use a plane if you need to, and see exactly what is in the warehouse. Destroy any evidence that might link it to me. Then fly out to Moscow and find where Michael has gone to. I think he wants to get his hands on what I have been looking for. I must return to the police tomorrow along with a list of tenants who have used the warehouse. Do you have the list?"

Boris walked to the suitcase and took out a large laptop and after a few minutes, wrote a list and handed it to Ivan.

"Don't lose it. Make a copy and give the copy, in your handwriting to them. There have only been three tenants anyway. Two of them will not cause you any bother. Do you want me to deal with the Marlow house? You may recall we stored the two models there for safe keeping." Boris waited for Ivan to decide.

"I had forgotten them. Yes, deal with it as you see fit, but Boris, remember you are in the UK, so nothing that would bring the police

466

to the house." He nodded to indicate that Boris could go. Ivan then went out and looked at the monument on the top of Ben Bhraggie. "You must know the answer," Ivan said out loud before going back inside.

+

Simon Reed sat outside the large railway station that overlooked part of the canals of Amsterdam. A large, paved area stretched out in front of him.

He had spent the last fortnight moving around Europe, trying to keep one step ahead of both LICD and the Russians. Today he had managed to rent a boat on the canal and now just needed for the banks to open to allow him to deposit his bag into a safe. Simon glanced at his watch for the fifth time, silly really, he thought to himself, time doesn't go any quicker.

An hour later, he stepped out of the bank and smiled. Nobody would get it from him now. Simon had left clear instructions that only three people could get access to it. Himself, and Bill and Jane Sutherland from LICD. He walked up the street and across to where his contact had agreed to meet him to show Simon where the boat was moored. It had been lucky in getting such a key mooring - the last owner had had the misfortune to be on the boat when it went up in flames.

# *Chapter 32*

## Golspie. The following day.

Ivan stepped into DS Coopers office and looked at the three people in surprise. Seated in front of him was Cooper, Bill and Jane.

"I thought that only you wanted to see me DS Cooper?" "Allow me to introduce Bill and Jane Sutherland. From LICD."

They flew up yesterday." "LICD?"

"London International Crime Department," added Jane helpfully.

"We work with police across the globe," added Bill, while watching Ivan's face.

"So can we get started then?" asked Cooper. Indicating for Ivan to sit down. "You did say you would produce a list of customers who have used the warehouse." Cooper turned to Bill and Jane. "He offered to bring in a list of the previous tenants as he had said the bags with XV3rd could belong to anybody." Ivan passed his written list across the table to Cooper.

"Only three tenants." Ivan ticked them off one at a time on his fingers. "A small supplier of electric gadgets to the UK. Items brought in from China and the far east. A firm that needed some space to store boxes of something or the other, I tend not to ask. And a firm that were making medicine for the third world, at least that is what they told me." Ivan sat back and looked at the three officers. Cooper looked at the paper and then at Ivan.

"Your Russian taxes will show this?"

"My UK taxes will. I am registered as a business in the UK. I tend to pay my taxes in the country where I do the business. I am sure you understand."

Bill leaned forward. "Do you know anybody called Simon, Simon Reed."

"Or Patrick O'Conner," added Jane. "Or Ruth Sanders," asked Cooper.

"Patrick, I did know a Patrick, don't think the last name was O'Conner though." replied Ivan.

"What exactly do you want in this part of Sutherland. Ok, it is nice to live here, but you are moving here. Buying up six flats. You have been here before, haven't you? A few years ago, perhaps?" said Cooper.

"Yes, I have been here before, you know that. I owned a restaurant in Brora. The Double Headed Eagle. Sold it. I own a warehouse in Eynsham. Rent it. So what?"

"Bags with XV3rd in Russian. Identical bags found in Marlow in an industrial estate and in a house in Marlow." said Jane.

"Now wait a minute. DS Cooper said nothing about a house or an industrial estate in Marlow having bags that are the same. Are you trying to frame me or what?" replied Ivan, clearly shaken.

"It may be of interest to you that the Russian embassy have confirmed that on several occasions bags of XV3rd were brought from Russia to the UK. They have been most helpful to LICD." added Bill with a smile.

+

In the LICD offices, a team had worked out the ingredients to the drugs. Knowing that Bill and Jane were in Golspie, they faxed up the details.

+

Cooper turned around as the fax came to life behind him. He got up and picked the fax off the tray and brought it back to show to Bill.

FROM: LICD

TO: Golspie Police. DS Cooper, Bill and Jane Sutherland. Identified three main ingredients in drug.

XV3rd Sourced from USSR Code Black Sourced from USA Sheepsbane.

(Only can be found in the far north of Scotland.)

Other smaller amounts of other drugs for stabilizing tablets. Any idea as to how much has been made?

"So, ingredients from Russia, US and Scotland. Is this the real reason you have set up your base here?" asked Bill.

"Are you the main outfit behind this or is there somebody else? Tell us and we can help you if there is anybody else that is." said Jane softly to Ivan.

"Look, I was asked to bring some XV3rd into the UK I knew an embassy member of staff. As to the other ingredients, I have no idea where or who would source them."

"Take a look at this photo." Cooper slid a colour photo across the desk. He also passed copies to Bill and Jane. "Taken by the US Air force. Special plane with a very special camera. Takes a photo high up, detail is amazing. This is of the hotel. The Grand East Sutherland Hotel or whatever it is called these days. Now those dots you see outside the hotel. In the field to the north of it."

469

"Those dots?" asked Ivan pointing at the photo.

"Yes. Now look at this close up." He passed a new photo across to Ivan. "In this close up, you can clearly see they are staff, wearing their hotel uniforms. They have paper and pens and if we look at this photo." He passed an even larger one across, on which were a list of crosses around the paper and at the top was written; SHEEPSBANE LOCATIONS.

"Now tell me you know nothing about this." smiled Cooper. "I don't. I wasn't even there."

"Not that time perhaps. Take a close look at this photo of the steps of the hotel. Taken a few days ago. The man on the left is the hotel owner. Patrick O'Conner. The man on the right, looks awfully like you. Don't you think. Yet you have told us that you don't know any Patrick O'Conner. That's right, isn't it?" said Cooper.

"You see, once we explained what was going on to our friends in the US, they have been so helpful. They put a new plane, top secret mind you, on a flight across this part of Scotland for a week. Photos as Cooper says, are just so amazing." added Bill. "Perhaps you should really tell us what is going on up here."

"Can I take a break. I need to think." asked Ivan.

"No! Start to give us some answers. Who is behind the new drug. Why do you show so much interest in east Sutherland and what do you know about LICD?" Said Jane. Cooper and Bill looked at her, mildly surprised at her outburst.

"If I tell you what happens to me?" asked Ivan.

"That largely depends on what you tell us." replied Bill. "What really made you come here?" asked Cooper.

"Drugs, we were making a new refined version of something that the US Army first used in the Vietnam war. Designed to keep troops alert and needing less sleep. Their higher efficiency was measured by the Army. When they saw how good it was in the trials, they developed it on an industrial scale." Ivan took a sip of water from the glass in front of him.

"Problems developed when the effects dropped off after a day. If they gave the troops a further one the next day, they started to believe they were invincible. Run at firing machine guns and so on. When the war ended, it was quietly taken off the shelf and stayed that way for years. Some of it was stored in a warehouse in the USA part of Berlin, when the USA eventually returned to America, it was left in the warehouse for the Russian army to find and retrieve. I got involved, when it was brought into Russia and the military used another ingredient to replace the US one. Same results. It got shelved, I bought a company that had a warehouse in Russia. When I visited it, the contents of dozens of tins of this were stacked floor to ceiling. I didn't do anything for three or four months, then a friendly chemist helped to decipher the ingredients for me. The one thing that improved it for marketing on a commercial scale was sheepsbane. Only problem was it could only be sourced in the north Highlands of Scotland. A contact sent some to my chemist but forgot to put instructions about handling it on the box,The chemist managed to stabilise it before he died. Touching the sheepsbane without gloves can do that to people." Ivan sat back.

"Then talk of the new Euro Tunnel started, somebody I know suggested we refine it and see if it made any difference. We found somebody inside the works, gave the tablets to a few of the workforce in the tunnel and their efficiency went through the roof. Result, at least that was what we thought." He took another sip of water and continued. "When the workings looked as though they would be finishing soon, we moved to supplying students, at Oxford and we hoped later, Cambridge. They loved it. Less sleep, more alert, exam and coursework results better than hoped.

What was the problem? It was very addictive if you took more than five a day. Take ten a day, you died. A student party in Oxford resulted in forty of the students dying. The lack of sheepsbane, meant production has stopped." Ivan looked at the three of them. "We did tell the dealers to inform their buyers to not exceed five tablets daily. If they did as they were told, then nothing bad would happen."

The fax machine came to life again and Bill this time went and fetched the fax. He glanced at it and passed it to Cooper.

"Ok. What can you tell us about a couple of scale models found in a safe in a house in Marlow?"

"Nothing at all."

"So for now, you stay in Golspie. Cooper holds your passport, and you may or may not be charged. Wait here."They rose and left the office. Outside Cooper looked at them both.

"What can we charge him with? The drug if the students had done as instructed would not have killed them. The ones that ignored the instructions are dead."

"We know he knew Patrick. The photo shows that most clearly. He was shaken when you produced it." said Jane.

"If we don't hold him, he may approach Patrick." said Cooper thoughtfully.

"He may do but isn't it better to bring Patrick in for questioning?" asked Jane.

"Probably. Lets see what Ivan does. Patrick has put his flat in Dornoch on the market. The sale is today, let's find out who buys it." said Cooper. They returned into the office and allowed Ivan to go back to his flat.

+

Patrick was in the church hall, the auction for his flat was about to start. It had only been the last ten minutes that people had started to fill the seats. Now, with every seat taken, the auctioneer stepped forwards and started to explain the bidding and the legal process in Scotland. Having done so, he accepted the first bid. Thirty minutes later it was all over. Patrick went and shook hands with a man who had been acting on behalf of a bidder. Then he turned and left the hall.

+

Cooper made his way to the front of the hall to speak to the auctioneer.

"DS Cooper. A quick question. Who bought the flat?"

"I am afraid to say it went to an anonymous bidder. The gentleman sent a person to bid for him. Quite a high amount for a three-bed flat in Dornoch. Fifty-six thousand pounds. Now I really must be going." He stepped down and Cooper looked back at the others in the chairs in the back row. They had been among the last to arrive.

+

Patrick pulled his car to a standstill outside the hotel and looked at the name. Rest and Be Thankful. He got out and walked inside as he had a proposal to put to the owner. The owner had already purchased two other businesses nearby and Patrick knew this.

+

Ivan was walking up and down inside his flat. On the table in front of him were three passports, all in his name. He was furious that the local police and LICD had found out so much in such a short space of time. The help from the two embassies had been a shock too. At least Boris would be relied on to do what he was told. The link between him and Ruth, well that was tenuous, at best. Though it was funny that she hadn't answered his calls lately.

+

In Michael's offices in Moscow they had learnt that the boat he had been on had sunk with no survivors. In line with his instructions, his secretary opened the envelope in the safe and took out the small envelope inside it. It was already addressed and stamped.

C10H160
PO Box 348
Rogart Post Office.
Sutherland
SCOTLAND
UNITED KINGDOM

She picked it up and put it in her bag to post on the way home.

+

Cooper sat alone at his desk and looked again at the two photos which showed Ivan and Patrick on the steps of the hotel. They both knew something, of that, he was sure. Bill and Jane had gone to their hotel.

+

As Patrick finished his conversation with the owner of Rest and Be Thankful, he stepped out of the office and saw Bill and Jane walk in. He ignored them and made his way out of the hotel. Jane looked after him as he left.

"Bill, did you see that was Patrick. Wonder what he wants in this hotel? I mean running one is a full-time job. You wouldn't think he had time to visit other ones."

"No, you're right. We need to tell Cooper this. Come on."

+

Ivan packed his small case and addressed the envelope as he had been told to do so. Then picked up his passport and dialled a number he knew from memory.

"Be at the harbour in Helmsdale in two hours. Use the fastest boat you have. I need to be outside the UK territorial waters as soon as I can. Oh, try and get hold of Michael as well. I have been trying for days without success." He replaced the phone and walked down to the road.

He could post the envelope at the post office, then catch the bus to Helmsdale. Once at the post office Ivan took one last look at the address to make sure it was correct.

C10H16O
PO Box 348
Rogart Post Office.
Sutherland
SCOTLAND
UNITED KINGDOM

He reached into his inside pocket and removed the smaller, but heavier one. It too was addressed and stamped already.

C10H16O
PO Box 121
Thurso Post Office.
Thurso
Caithness.
Scotland.

The recipient would know what to do next. Ivan got on the bus and headed towards Helmsdale.

An hour later, a large twin engine boat came into the small, protected harbour and Ivan got aboard. In a house overlooking the harbour, a woman had watched him leave. Smiling she picked up the phone and dialled a number she had been told. Outside her house her nice 2CV car was parked. She put her hand on the pile of five books beside her chair to steady herself, dislodging the top one. It fell to the floor the title upwards. *Pendent Keys and their locks in the USSR Book one.*

+

Cooper looked at his watch. Bill and Jane had explained to him that Patrick had been seen in their hotel. They had gone to see Patrick and ask what was going on. Cooper rose from his desk and went to see Ivan at his flat. Probably best to surprise him, he thought as he walked along the street.

+

In Marlow, Boris looked at the scene before him. A large removal van was taking the two models out of Ruth Sanders house and by the looks of things, had every intention of keeping them safe. He turned and made his way to the car, before driving towards Eynsham. At least the warehouse would be empty.

An hour later, he pulled his car to a standstill outside the warehouse. Being late at night, there was no signs of any activity on the industrial estate. He made his way towards the door and forced the lock. Then stepped inside.

The lights were off, so he flicked his torch over to the bank of switches. Pulling the master switch down, he watched as banks of lights, high up in the roof space came on. Then he switched the basement lights on and walked the length of the warehouse and down to the two rooms in the basement. Better to check first, he thought as he went down the stairwell. The blue door was wide open, a quick glance inside was enough to see that it was empty. The red door, that was closed. Boris pushed the door slowly to see if it was unlocked. It opened and he stepped inside. At the far end he could see a chair with a small, padded envelope on it. He started to make his way towards it and then the door swung shut behind him. Boris picked up the envelope and returned to the door. There was no handle on that side. He tried to put his fingers into the small gap but was unsuccessful. Boris sat down; he knew that it was just a matter of time. Air would be used up, the warehouse was deserted, it was late at night, nobody about. Even his phone had no signal down here. He looked at the address on the padded envelope.

$C_{10}H_{16}O$
PO Box 121
Marlow Post Office
Marlow.

He laughed bitterly and threw it across the room. Maybe the curse was right after all.

+

Cooper rang the doorbell and knocked on the door of the flat. But no reply came. He pushed the door, and much to his surprise it opened. He stepped inside.

"Hello DS Cooper here. Anybody here?" But a quick visit to the rooms made it clear that it was empty, Ivan had fled. Frustrated, Cooper returned to the police station and alerted the coastguard, airports, and railway stations as was normal in these cases.

+

Bill rang the bell on the reception desk and Patrick appeared in front of them.

"How can I help you?"

"Do you know Ivan? Don't say which one."

"Say I said yes, would that lead me into trouble?" Patrick asked. "No, just wondered what your connection was. We have a photo of you and your staff looking for sheepsbane. An item that is highly toxic. Now why would you do that?"

"As you say, it is highly toxic, and I wouldn't want my guests touching it. Bad for the hotel to have people dying on the premises."

"Ok, I get that. So, what do you do with it once you have found and gathered it in?" said Jane with a smile.

475

"The only thing you can do, burn it. If you look at the back of the hotel, you'll see a patch of the ground where we burn it." Knowing that was where the builders had burnt the last of the rubbish before clearing out of the hotel after it had been renovated.

"Oh, I am sure that we will find it exactly as you describe it to us. Thing is, Mr O'Conner, will forensics find any traces of sheepsbane." said Bill with a hint of a smile.

"Tell me, what do you know about the ARI, and particularly a group associated with a plot to attack the channel tunnel." asked Bill.

"Wow, bit of a change of subject there officer. Think I heard that there was a fire in the tunnel. Not a bomb though." He smiled at them.

"Who mentioned a bomb?" asked Jane quickly.

"I would assume that would have been the best means of causing disruption to the works. Wouldn't you?" replied Patrick. "What are you discussing with the hotel owner of the Rest and Be Thankful?" Bill asked him.

"They own a bit of land; I would like to buy it from them."

"Where is it situated, near this hotel?" Jane asked waving her hand in the northern direction.

"No, it is an old, disused quarry, near Rogart. The view from it is an ideal location for a small hotel."

"Did he sell it to you?" asked Jane. "Not yet."

"Perhaps you need to offer more money?" suggested Bill with a smile.

"Perhaps. Now if there is nothing else, I really must be getting on, running a hotel is hard work." He turned to leave them.

"Just one more thing. Have you ever seen a padlock like this one before, anywhere at all? Jane thinks she remembers seeing one but can't recall where." Bill produced a scruffy photo of the ornate padlock that had been found in the warehouse in Eynsham. He looked carefully at Patrick as he passed the photo across. Patrick tried to conceal his surprise but was not successful.

"Sorry, not seen one like that up here. Where did you find it?"

"An old warehouse, near Eynsham." Bill took the photo back and then they both left the hotel. Once in the car, Bill looked at Jane.

"He had seen one like that before. We need to research this. Come on, we'll go and tell Cooper what we have found out.

+

Ten minutes later, in Coopers' office the three met.

"Ivan has gone. I've put out an all points alert at the airports and so on. They have set up a roadblock on the A9. How did you two get on?" asked Cooper.

"We learnt that Patrick has seen one of these padlocks before somewhere but wouldn't say where. He denied it. Apparently, he wants to buy a disused mine near Rogart. The views from a small hotel would be wonderful, at least that is what he said. I'd have thought that was the last place any building should be built on." said Jane yawning.

"With Ivan on the run, and Patrick unable to help us, well, no crime that we can pin on him for now, the two of us had better return to LICD. We'll keep in touch." said Bill and they both rose and left the station to return to their hotel before returning to London.

+

In a solicitor's office in Folkestone the secretary put down the phone and went through to her boss.

"Ivan has left the country, Patrick has said nothing, the rest are dead. LICD seem to be winding the case up. What do want to do about Simon Reed?"The solicitor put his hands together and looked out of the window in the direction of the workings on the Eurotunnel.

"Is he still in London?" "No. He got away."

"And the gambler, in London?"

"Colleen is just waiting for him to finish reading the instructions. She has been told that it will activate the device once she presses the button."

"As it will, as it will." He looked again out of the window. "Such a pity that it didn't work. Still onwards and upwards. Bring me both the file marked 'Dounreay' will you, along with the one marked 'Rocks of Rogart'." She walked through to the outer office and found the two files he wanted.

+

In a flat in London, Colleen watched the man at last pick up the device and slowly she pressed the button to activate it.

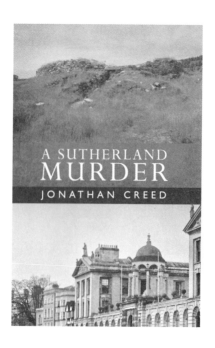

Any Sutherland Murder is very unusual. While staying at a hotel in East Sutherland, Bill and Jane are caught up in the investigation of a suspicious death.

While the police decide at first that it is easy to explain, it now appears things may not be quite as they first seemed.

Bill and Jane start to find out what might really be going on in East Sutherland. With their help, the investigation moves to a much higher level.

The action moves between East Sutherland and Oxford over three decades. The reader is transported from the bustle of the University City of Oxford into the small East Sutherland villages of Golspie, Brora, Helmsdale and Dornoch.

Early in the morning, two runners on Ben Bhraggie discover a body. They report this to the police, who then return and find no body there. A fortnight later, a body is discovered at the top of Fyrish. Is it the same body or is there a serial killer on the loose?

Bill and Jane Sutherland, from LICD, are asked to return to Golspie to assist for a second time in helping solve the case.

The Police now discover a lot more is going on in East Sutherland than they had first thought. A new restaurant owner and old adversaries appear.

Is it really all as it seems? What is the real reason why both Russian and Dutch criminals are so interested in the Far North of Scotland?

.